Survivor

The dog days of cancer

Jarred Lyons

DEDICATION

To Richard, the inspiration for putting my thoughts down on paper.

AKNOWLEDGMENTS

I thank G-d for giving me the drive, vision, and perseverance to accomplish this adventure.

I especially thank my beautiful wife Jennifer for her amazing proofreading skills, and supporting my dream of writing this book.

Thanks to my family for putting up with the late nights and early mornings it took to get it done.

Thank you, Randy Ladenheim-Gil for all of your help copyediting.

THE DOG DAYS OF THE PAST

PROLOGUE

EDDIE'S BEGINNING AND RICHARD'S END

I

JULIA
APRIL 1999

"We'll take him; he's perfect."

He had to have been the wrinkliest and cutest little puppy I had ever seen. He was about three months old with huge yellow paws, brown mischievous eyes, long dark brown ears, and looked to be a cross between a basset hound and a golden retriever. I wished we could've rescued the whole litter, but I knew that even one of them had been a stretch for David and me.

It was a somber time for me, having just confirmed two weeks earlier what David and I suspected after two years of unsuccessfully trying to get pregnant. I was never going to have children, and no amount of hormones, fertility specialists, or medical advances were going to change the fact that my body just wasn't built for it. I won't pretend I wasn't devastated, but those were the cards I had been dealt and I would live with them.

I had spent the last couple of weeks moping around the apartment only barely laughing at David's corny and stupid attempts to cheer me up, but I had needed out. And so David decided to whisk me away from my funk, suggesting we take a day trip up north to Venice beach and stroll the boardwalk. Being that Mother was out of town visiting her sister in Florida and Dad was left alone to fend for himself the week, I also thought it would be nice to rescue him, forcing him to leave his post at the hardware store for the day. He needed out too, and I loved spending time with him.

So after I convinced him to come with an argument only a Daddy's little girl could pull off, we all packed up and made the two-hour drive north to Venice beach. We started walking the boardwalk when I spotted what I thought was a homeless man, although he could've just been a beach bum who didn't care whether he showered or shaved. The guy's long, scraggly blond-and-gray hair was pulled back in an elastic band and reached past his shoulder blades, where it clung to the back of his tie-dyed shirt. He was standing on the side of the path playing an old, beat-up

1

acoustic guitar and looked to be in his midfifties although, judging by his getup, he was an obvious throwback to the seventies.

Directly in front of him were an open, coin-littered guitar case and a square, topless cardboard box filled with three of the cutest puppies I had ever laid eyes on. On the front of the box, scribbled in what looked to be a five-year-old's handwriting, was a sign that read, "Get your guard dog, fifty dollars apiece."

One look into that box and I knew my life was changed. Two of the puppies were sleeping, completely unaware of anything that was going on around them, too tired to deal with the world, but the third was staring directly at me, following me with pleading eyes. He was tilting his head ever so slightly so the bottom of his ear lay on the floor of the box, and he looked to be smiling at me. It was love at first sight.

Suffice it to say, fifty dollars later, with a chuckling father's approval and a husband caught completely unaware, I named my first dog ever Eddie.

II

JULIA
JUNE 10, 2008

It was 12:50 P.M. and I walked through the archway, forcing myself to take each individual step. I knew I needed to be here. I wanted to be here. I dreaded being here. The door had been left slightly ajar to let in fresh air, a conduit to the outside world. I opened it further, and the first thing I noticed was the light. More precisely, I observed the lack of light.

The hallway was dim, and I knew that all the shades must be drawn. The air had a familiar smell, the same with which I had grown up. But it was mixed up with something else, something indescribable. It pulled at some dark recess of my gut. There was tension and a supernatural staleness that froze everything in place.

I was numb.

"It's time. You need to get over here."

Had I really just received the phone call I was been expecting, the phone call I guiltily wanted to come for the last two days, the phone call I had feared and hoped would never become a reality?

I walked through the hallway toward the living room. The pictures on the walls were neatly organized: two baby photos, me at five years old, my college graduation portrait, and, finally, my wedding photo. They were arranged in chronological order and further testified to the fact that I belonged right here, right now.

The first thing I saw when I rounded the corner was his pale freckled back, his prominent shoulder blades, and his bony spine. I should have been shocked at how skinny he had become, but I felt nothing. The hospital gown was untied, but no one noticed, no one thought it was significant. He was sitting on the couch with his back toward me, leaning forward with his chest to his knees. His back was moving frantically up and down as he struggled to catch his breath. One light-blue–checkered blanket was draped over his legs, while another lay limp on the floor.

Lee was sitting to his left, gripping his hand, and Jiang was positioned to his right. They were holding him up with strong, supportive hands, helping him in his efforts to find oxygen. They were both dressed in white slacks and white smocks, the angels of Dignity Hospice.

Lee was the one who had called. Her shift was from eight to four.

"Richard. Take deep breaths, Richard. Is that more comfortable?" Lee practically shouted in his ear.

The unintelligible moan that emanated from his lips confirmed that moving to his current position had not helped. He tried to speak—at least that's what it had sounded like—but only a garble of monotone sounds had come from his mouth. It was drowned out by his frantic, shallow breaths.

I kept walking toward them as Lee and Jiang repositioned him so that he was lying flat on his back.

Mother was sitting on a foldout chair that was moved so its back rested against the wall facing him. She had her head buried in her hands and she was sobbing, hiding and trying to shield herself at the same time. She hadn't slept in two days. She hadn't stopped crying for the last two weeks.

He kept moaning, and Lee looked up.

"This would be the time to say something. He's very close."

What was I going to say to him? I wasn't just numb; it was much more than that. I felt like I wasn't part of this world, that this wasn't really happening. It wasn't real. I stared openmouthed, searching for my voice.

Should I be pouring my heart out to him? Should I be telling him that he'd been so good to us, that I loved him with all of my soul? That's what people did in this situation, right?

The back of my neck grew cold. The emptiness, the numbness that had overtaken my body and mind was replaced with a pulling, dragging sensation that threatened to swallow my being. I felt the start of panic setting in.

I questioned myself. Do I tell him it's okay to let go? No, that would make him lose hope. He'd know then that I'd given up on him. Given up what? This existence of pain and suffering that had no chance of improvement. I didn't believe in miracles.

Would he even understand me? Panic turned to doubt. Lee had said that he could understand, that his lack of lucidity was due to the pain medication.

Huh, the pain medications. He looked to be in so much pain.

I got down on my knees beside the couch and felt the hard, worn carpet pushing up and digging into my flesh. I took his left hand, his bony yellowing fingers, and sheltered them in both of mine and squeezed, willing him to hear me, to feel my heart pour through my touch. My fingers, my hands, my wrists, everything I was; I wanted him to feel that I was there. I was his daughter and I wanted him to hear me.

I finally opened my mouth. "Dad, I love you. It will be all right. Mom and I will be all right. Be strong, Dad. I love you."

I kept saying it over and over, "I love you so much, I love you, Dad. Please, please . . . I love you."

My father passed away at 1:20 P.M.

THE DOG DAYS OF THE PRESENT

1

EDDIE
APRIL 2009

The small white ringing box grew louder with its early light period howls. It was amazing that such a small, compact thing could be so darn loud and outright annoying if no one paid any attention to it.

I was upstairs in Mom and Dad's bedroom, a medium-sized, square-shaped cave with soft yellow walls, the same colors as most of the other rooms in our two-story territory. It was an old territory, but it had a comfortable, lived-in feel. I had spent most of my life in this territory, and I knew every smell in every nook and cranny of it. I knew where I could mark: anywhere out of sight of Mom and Dad, that is. Where not to jump—the sofas and Mom's side of their sleeping cushion—and where not to slide my paws in order to avoid splinters. The rough, worn wood floor had never fully recovered after my puppy marking days, and the floor had borne the brunt of the damage. I had woken up after the first howl, but it had been no surprise that Dad had still been fast asleep.

Dad was one of my best friends in the world, but like Mom and just about every other mom or dad I know, he was partly deaf. It pretty much took a slap in the face for him to wake up. He was also a large dad as far as dads go, and was about two and half times my height if I stood on my back paws. He had a dark, mud-colored head of fur, his cheeks had short roots of stubbly hair, and his teeth looked extra white when he smiled. And smile he did, being lucky enough to be blessed with a face that always made him look happy. It was mainly due to his sky-blue–colored eyes and the upward curved shape of his muzzle, and usually just one look from him was enough to send most moms looking dreamy eyed.

Dad finally blinked, gently lifted Mom's head from his shoulder, and sat up on their raised sleeping cushion. It had taken a grand total of three howls before his enormous pad had finally shut the thing up.

We were in the sleeping room upstairs, and the light period was just beginning. I was on my floor cushion next to Dad's side of the main sleeping cushion, while Paris was on hers next to Mom. It was just light enough to make out the yellow hue of the room, but not light enough to fully see the details.

Mom and Dad had both slept well through the dark period, although I couldn't say the same for Paris and me. What a night. They had managed to stay passed out through the meows and howls as the neighbor's clawed friend shrieked for his long-lost companion. His voice had been grating.

I wish he had just gotten over it, because she was never going to come back to him. Why couldn't he have just let it go and let the rest of the world sleep?

I was a little tired but overall felt well rested and awake. I always enjoyed this part of the light period. The quiet of the world and the calm in the air, and knowing that Dad and I were the only ones awake in the house. We shared this time together; it was our bond, our private time away from everything else and our little secret.

Paris refused to open her eyes. I wasn't too shocked, though. Paris was the other furry friend in the house and my best friend. She is a white curly furred poodle, was about the same size as me, which was about the height of Dad's midthigh, but given how bony she was, she looked taller.

Don't get me wrong, it's not like I'm fat or anything. I just had a little more skin than she did. That's because my mom was a champion golden retriever, while my dad was a champion coonhound in his own right. His champion status had nothing to do with any type of show or competition; his prize was that despite all obstacles, he still had managed to dig under the neighbor's fence to meet my mom.

I am a mostly yellow-coated furry friend, but with a whole lot of extra coonhound wrinkles and long, droopy, jet-black ears that hang down to my shoulders.

What a dark period it had been. After the please-take-me-back love song, I, at least, managed to get back to sleep, unlike Paris. That poodle had gone on to have one busy, busy dark period. Which was definitely surprising, because it was quite a change from her normal, true-to-Paris self. Number one: she hadn't gone right back to sleep, which was extremely strange for her, given that she spends most of her waking hours perfecting the art of snoozing. Number two, and untrue to her normal picky-eating behavior: she had spent a large chunk of time in chewing exercises on one of Mom's new hind-paw pad coverings. The same brand-new, red-jerky-treat–smelling pair of hind-paw pads Mom had just brought home yesterday.

They were the same shiny pair Mom trustingly had left right

beside Paris's sleeping cushion right after showing them off to Dad. They were the same pair that were now lying directly beside her floor cushion, as plain as poop on cement. If my predictions were right, it would also be the same chewed-up paw pad that would lead to a very angry Mom when she finally woke up.

Mom moved.

2

JULIA
APRIL 2009

I love him, he is a good man, but why the heck did I have to marry someone who goes to work so darn early? At forty years of age were the ripped biceps, six-pack you could bounce a quarter off of and sculpted face worth it? Maybe for the first year, during our honeymoon, but after twelve years of marriage, his sexiness had been outweighed these days by my need for sleep. I bet it wasn't even 6:00 A.M. yet.

All I needed were twenty more minutes and I promise I would be a sane and functional individual; just twenty compassionate and loving minutes.

I really hoped he had started the coffee brewing.

I needed to change that dreadful alarm clock. It was just plain obnoxious!

3

EDDIE
APRIL 2009

Dad swung his lower paws over the side of his sleeping cushion, stretched his shoulders and back, and started walking toward the territory room. It was only six short steps, and Dad made every effort to avoid the part of the wood floor that creaked. I followed him to keep him company and he waited until I was in the room before closing the door and putting the lights on. Like every early light period, he would do his best not to wake up Mom. She was happier that way.

I looked around at the baby-blue tiled room, took in the overriding smell of Mom's spiced smell, and watched for about the thousandth time as yet again he tried to claim the white stubby tree.

The oval, neck-high, furry-friend–length, wedged-against-the-wall, sour-tasting, white stubby tree. The same white stubby tree that fed an ownership marking battle between Mom and Dad, the same confusing piece of white cold stone that they insisted on trying to own. The thing smelled like overripe markings and served no greater purpose than being a continuous easy-access drinking source for Paris. I just didn't get Mom and Dad's crazy obsession with it.

Let me explain the craziness. Dad or Mom would mark it, but without fail, the white stubby tree would belt out its rejection whoosh with a monster belch that any well-mannered furry friend would be ashamed of. It would then without fail tease them with its cheeky gurgle while at the same time swallow the claim.

Yes, you heard me right . . . gulp down the claim that Mom and Dad had worked so hard to put together!

At least my territory battle with the spotted furry friend next door involved real outings and, better yet, real solid territory. Trees, bushes, yellow drinking spouts, all were in the running for claim. Neither of us had the dominant upper paw yet, although I think I was currently two territory decorations ahead.

Dad finished up in the territory room and killed the lights. He then tiptoed back out, careful to avoid the floor creak, and we headed to one of my favorite places in the world, the feeding room.

The room was white: white walls, white square tile floors, white cabinets, a white food warmer, a white feeding bowl washer, and the large white cold-food keeper. Dad started making breakfast, pouring this and mixing that. It was always so funny to me that he made such an effort to be so quiet upstairs but sounded so loud when he came down here.

I stared at him with my head cocked to the side. He was cutting up part of his breakfast with a narrow, pointed shiny silver claw and was getting ready to throw it onto the black flat bowl on the table fire. He was too deep in concentration to look at me.

As the sounds of Dad getting the light period started carried through our territory, Paris decided to join us. She looked terrible: tired, disheveled, her frizzy fur all out of place. Her eyes were dark red and she looked like she was still half-asleep. I had no pity for her, though. That's what you get when you party all night.

I joined her by our usual places near our food bowls. I couldn't wait to eat but sat patiently while Dad got ready to pour our meal. Paris also finally perked up and looked semifunctional when Dad grabbed our food bag from the tall orange cabinet across from the door.

Right before he brought his feeding bowl to the table, he opened the cabinet that hid the bury box and threw away the wrappings of one of his treats. I had just enough time to catch the slightest whiff of the heavenly smell of Dad and Mom's food from yesterday's leftovers. My thoughts returned to Dad's breakfast, and I watched closely while he ate his food. I knew I couldn't stay and scrounge for his stray food chunks for too long because it would only be a matter of time before Paris lost interest in her own food and tried to attack mine.

4

JULIA
APRIL 2009

The fresh vanilla fragrance was so powerful that it left me with no other choice but to get up and get the day going. How could any sane coffee addict resist that smell? I could practically taste the caffeine and, after soaking in the flavor and feeling it cling to the back of my palate, it would've been impossible to get back to sleep.

I slowly pushed the blue cotton duvet back, not entirely convinced I wanted to break my warm morning-blanket shell. It inevitably cracked as I bent my knees and felt the cool touch of the spring San Diego morning: not too cold, but not too hot either. The weather was just cold enough to keep the heater guessing. Mornings in the spring always started out cool, but I knew by 11 A.M. it would be an almost perfect seventy-two–degree beach day. With the duvet unceremoniously kicked down and curled at the foot of the bed, it became official. I was now getting up.

I got out of bed, slowly stood, and turned to face my dresser mirror. It was a nice garage-sale find, a gem that unintentionally had brought on a bonding project between Dad and David, who had spent one very interesting weekend restoring it to its original honey-colored glory. No one could tell it wasn't an original part of the rest of our bedroom furniture set; well, no person except my mother, that is. But seriously, who else would look that close, let alone make sure to point out its imperfections? I just loved that old country look, and I had done my best to decorate the house that way.

Every morning out of bed offered undeniable truth, and I couldn't help a quick once-over. Sure, I was pushing thirty-five, but I still looked pretty damn good. My butt wasn't as firm as it used to be, but I was still a size two. I had a couple of gray hairs—at least, that's if I let them grow long enough to be seen—and as I looked away, I caught a few small, barely perceptible lines forming around my eyes. This last year had definitely aged me, all right, but I still wasn't too shabby.

I looked away and began my morning routine, alone upstairs but comfortable knowing that David still hadn't left for the day. It was convenient that he was a man who showered at night, and as much as I hated to admit it, it made things easier that he also was an early riser. Marriage had cured that fight for shower time that came with roommates in college

We had a three-bedroom cottage with a bathroom connected to our room, and an additional one next to the other two rooms upstairs. We used one of the rooms as our dual office, while the other served well as a guest room. It wasn't a large house, and our bathroom only had one sink, which we shared. David had promised that we would remodel it two years ago, but life had thrown a wrench in that plan.

The hot water felt great, and I could feel myself becoming human again. The double massage showerhead was worth every penny, and I made sure to pay extra attention to the small of my back. I must have strained it running yesterday because I could feel the sour effects of lactic acid draining as the water worked its magic. I rinsed the thick coconut conditioner out of my hair, and now my day had officially begun.

What a week; I was so glad it was Friday. The dogs had been going stir crazy. I felt so bad, but I just hadn't had time to walk them in the last two days, let alone do anything else. Thank goodness for the yard. If there was one thing I had fallen in love with about the house when we bought it five years ago, it was the backyard. It was just as big as the house, layered in bright green grass and with three enormous oak trees scattered across. It served as a great substitute for the dogs to get some energy out if they missed their walk. Speaking of which, I just had to take them out this morning.

With the appropriate towel in place, I headed across the bedroom to the white paneled closet door to pick out an outfit. Maybe I should wear my gray dress because it would go really well with my new red shoes, which I was still on cloud nine about. I couldn't believe the deal I had gotten; it was like highway robbery, and I knew things like that only came around once. Now where had I left them?

I started walking and stepped over Eddie's doggy bed. As I passed my side of the bed, though, something went horribly wrong. Suddenly the ground under my right foot was replaced by a moist, soft, slippery thing that felt like a squeezed-out wet sponge as it momentarily bore the brunt of my full weight. I felt the thing only for a second, though, because in the next instant I experienced the roller-coaster sensation of being airborne as the sponge catapulted toward the closet. The laws of gravity were followed, but, luckily, momentum was on my side. Paris's semisoft doggy bed, thank goodness, absorbed the brunt of my fall.

What the hell was that?

With my right hip cushioned by Paris's bed and unconsciously massaging my left hip, I got my bearings. I could feel the hard, prickly wool of Paris's dog bed against my bare skin and instantly readjusted the towel. She was a clean dog overall, but I hadn't bought her a new bed in the last two years and couldn't remember the last time I had washed this one.

Realizing that no bones were broken, I looked to the source of the mishap. Up against the white baseboard of the wall, the slimy corpse of one of my now newly transformed red Jimmy Choo heels manifested itself as the chewed rawhide it had become.

I was going to kill her. "Paris!!!"

5

EDDIE
APRIL 2009

I knew that growl and feared it, and when I heard it, I usually did everything in my power to get the heck away from Mom. The good news was that Mom was finally awake, but the bad news was that she was definitely not happy. With my food finished and my belly full, I decided now would be a great time to seek shelter under Dad's chair before the source of the growl made an appearance and I got caught in the wide open. Dad was sitting in one of the same wicker chairs with which I had grown up, minus the one I had chewed a hole in when I was young. He was still sitting at the table, staring blankly at the water in the wall decoration, and I quickly ran toward him as he was taking the last bite of his food.

I could hear her paws pounding on the second floor as she made her way toward the stairs. Although our territory carried the smallest of sounds and magnified them ten times over, it still would have been impossible for even a deaf dad not to hear Mom as the roof moved with every heavy step. As she came into the feeding room, huffing and puffing with a face the color of a bright red tomato, I knew that whatever was going to happen wouldn't be good.

Dad's chair jerked up as my back hit one of its legs as I dove for cover, but before he had a chance to react, Mom stormed into the center of the feeding room wearing a large white blanket wrapped under her arms and a separate one wrapped around her head. There was no getting away; she was directly between me and the see-through flapping wall, and in her paw lay a red chewed-up corpse, the remnant of one of her new paw coverings.

She jerked the paw pad in the air as she looked at Dad and me and growled loudly. Mom may be a small mom by mom standards, but let me tell you, when she gets angry, what pours out of her muzzle is enough to scare a Doberman. Mom at that moment was ticked, and I knew that this would not be the time for me to try to make her feel better.

As she continued with her growling, the hair on the back of my neck stood up, and I sensed danger as soon as her stare focused on me. What did I do?

Dad, brave and daring Dad, took a chance and softly grunted back at her. He was still sitting down but had turned to her and was motioning soothingly with his paws, patting the air in an attempt to calm her. He managed to absorb the brunt of Mom's anger with just one soft grunt and five slow air pats. Mom wasn't done, though, not even close, and she kept growling and howling for what seemed like an eternity. Mom would growl, Dad would softly grunt, and throughout it all she planted herself to the center of the feeding room, blocking any attempt to get out. She was panting with anger but Dad was making progress and I could sense some of the anger leaving her.

After a small amount of time and air hand pats by Dad, Mom finally peeled her eyes away from me and instead was now searching the room for Paris.

Speaking of Paris, where was she?

She had been by her food bowl with me near the back territory door a second ago. Dad had taken the insert out of the see-through flapping wall to stop us from getting out in the dark period, but he had unlocked it while we were eating. She must have gotten out as soon she realized Mom was headed down.

She'd left me even though she was responsible for this whole mess, to take the blame. With no Paris in view, things took a turn for the worse as I felt Mom's eyes bearing down on me a second time.

I shuddered, my mouth went dry, and my throat felt like I had swallowed dirt. I shut my eyes as tight as they would go and covered my head with my paws, preparing for the worst.

But it never came. Luckily, and just in the nick of time, Dad found the secret soothing weapon and motioned with his paw for Mom to look over at the tar-smelling black liquid steaming on the countertop right behind her. A short, stout black contraption was gurgling and hissing, and while it spat out its foul black juice, a cloud of white tar went into the air all around it. It was dripping its water into a large, see-through round bowl.

Forgetting about me for the moment, Mom looked over at the tar-smelling liquid and then to Dad again.

Dad finished grunting, and I smelled some of Mom's anger fade. She folded her paws across her chest, tucking the chewed up paw covering under her armpit, and took a half step back to the countertop. She leaned against the counter, holding the black tar-smelling liquid, and I could see some of the red start to drain from her face.

Dad had that effect on her. He wasn't as good as a furry-friend, but he did do a pretty good job for a dad.

I waited and waited, and when Mom finally did turn to grab a cup to pour in some of the black liquid, I made my move. Dad's chair again jerked up as I sprang up and banged my head, misjudging its height entirely, and bolted past Mom through the see-through flapping clear wall and into our fenced outside territory.

It took just four steps outside for me to forget all about Mom and Paris given just how beautiful of a light period it was. I stopped in midstep to take in the scenery of our back territory. I loved it and had played there my entire life. The ground was covered from fence to fence with a thick, short layer of bright green ground covering minus the two straw-colored yellow spots used for marking. One was for me and one was for Paris; we both had our preferences as to location. There were two large trees scattered in two of the corners of the territory and one on the back wall that, besides being home to a couple of poop-throwing bushy-tailed nut-collecting furry friends, offered just the right amount of shade.

I was on the shiny black stone path that led to a large patch of dark gray square tiles in the rightmost corner of the territory, headed towards the rectangular silver-and-black smoke maker. It was where Dad usually spent hours stabbing meat while it smoked away. I knew that was where I would find Paris, who, being the lazy poodle she was, was most likely lounging in the early sun.

I was right. There she was, sprawled out on her snoring away with her stomach to the sun. I wanted to wake her up for a little company and I took a step forward.

As my right paw touched the ground, I was suddenly hit with a biting sensation directly beneath my right shoulder blade. I shifted my weight to my left front paw because if I had stood on something, I didn't want to wedge it in any deeper. It took a couple of moments to realize it wasn't my paw that was the problem but rather my shoulder, and I carefully put it back on the ground to see if it would happen again.

As my paw touched the tile, I waited for it to hit, better prepared now to figure what it was, but ..... everything felt normal.

Hmm.

Knowing that I had not imagined it, I flexed my right shoulder and lifted my right front paw and there it was again. It didn't actually hurt, like if you got bit by a not-so-friendly furry friend, it felt more like bumping your funny bone. It made its way through my shoulder muscles and tingled under my skin like bubbles in the water bowel. The more I moved, the more it tingled.

I was just about to sit down and try to scratch it when I heard the muffled sound of Dad grunting his good-bye howl. He was leaving for the light period.

So with my shoulder forgotten, I did a one-eighty and sprinted back to the inside territory.

6

EDDIE
APRIL 2009

What a strange feeling.

I had forgotten about it when Dad left, but now it caught my attention. I was still by the front territory door and I remembered that before Dad's departure howl, I had been readying for an investigatory scratch to my shoulder.

By this time, the sun was through the windows and the front room was getting warm. The floor, however, was still cold, and as I put my belly on it, it took my breath away. With a grunt, I lifted my back paw and reached, stretching it toward my shoulder while arching my back for added distance.

"Almost there, just a little farther, reach, reach . . ."

My paw was so close that I could smell the green covering and dirt I had just run through outside. It shook as I tried to stretch it past the limit. I just had to reach the tingle.

No luck. I was a claw too short and, worse yet, the tingle was still there. I thought that maybe if I angled my head just a little more it would help get me that extra stretch.

So I tried again, but it still wasn't good enough.

Now this was bad. I had never had an itch I couldn't get to, and the only thing I had managed to do was to cause the tingle to get stronger. I needed it scratched.

I turned my head and moved under the window to get some better light. The sun was just right, and out of the corner of my eye, I saw a small red bump. It was about the size of a small food chunk, and it glowed a delicious red.

Well, if I couldn't reach it with my hind paw, maybe some sliding on the floor would do the trick.

Now that hit the spot! There's something to be said about a very old wood floors, and my territory just happened have that very thing. The roughness was a beautiful thing for scratching!

As I lay there smelling the years of Dad and Mom's foot pads, the tingling came. I knew I couldn't keep dragging myself around all light period; but licking . . . now that was a different story. I could keep that up nonstop. So I turned my head, wet my tongue, and oh, it felt so good.

It hit the bump at just the right angle, and the tingle was put out. Not that I was too surprised, because a good lick usually made everything better. Unfortunately, the effects didn't last long, and as soon as I stopped licking, the tingling came back.

So why stop at all? As I said before, I could keep this up forever. I wiggled next to the couch, trying to bury my body into the floor fur like I used to as a puppy, and was just getting ready for another slurp when I heard a worried grunt.

7

JULIA
APRIL 2009

I was on my way to the garage to the washer and dryer because Friday was laundry day. It wasn't my favorite day in the week, and given the morning I'd had, it would've been the perfect day for something else to go wrong. The coffee was at least starting to take effect, which was getting rid of some of the pain of losing my dear, beloved Jimmy Choos.

I hoped the coffee would keep working its magic the rest of the day; vanilla roast had never failed me before. I said a silent prayer that today would not be the first time. Hell, I needed the energy and, more importantly, a new start to this day.

I was walking by our living room, lost in my thoughts, coffee in hand, when I heard Eddie licking something. Great, I thought, what the hell had he gotten hold of now? Wouldn't that just be the icing on the cake? I changed direction and headed toward the sound.

The house had gone to pieces over the last year; the throw rug was stained, the couches had become beaten and worn looking, and all our centerpieces were dusty. It gave the house more of a cabinlike feeling than we'd really planned, but the truth of the matter was that neither David nor I had the energy or desire to do anything about it.

There he was, wedged right between the faded brown love seat and the sofa, with his left ear practically covering both of his eyes. He was going to town licking his right shoulder.

"Eddie, what are you doing, boy? What have you gotten into now?"

That dog was forever a puppy. He'd barely changed since the day we got him; well, maybe he was a little calmer, but mostly he was the same old Eddie.

What was he licking?

Careful not to spill my caffeinated medication, I leaned down and put my hand on his shoulder, actually catching him by surprise because he jerked around to look at me. He had a guilty look, like he had been doing something he knew he shouldn't have. The morning hadn't started out that well, and this new development didn't bode well.

His shoulder was slimy, the fur around it red and wet. There was a little pimple right in the center of the red, and the whole region looked irritated. Despite the wetness and the now semimatted fur, I put my hand on it and started feeling around. The pimple part was just on the surface, but there was a hard marble underneath.

What was that? Had something bitten him? Paris?

Had he been chasing spiders again? By the look of it, it appeared to be really scratched up, and I wondered what the heck he had done to himself.

Great, that was all I needed today, but I should've known; I should've guessed something like this would happen after the way the day had started. I grabbed his leash and headed toward my red SUV.

"Come on, Eddie; come here, boy, we're going to the vet."

8

EDDIE
APRIL 2009

I had mostly been successful, and in my world, that means a job well done. I had kind of stopped the tingling.

As soon as Mom touched my tingly spot, her mood had changed. For the first time I could ever remember, the black sludge hadn't made her happy.

The change was obvious and the smell was a distinct scent. Even though it was being covered by the stink of the black sludge, I knew that if I let it go on it would take over the room.

I hated that smell. It was a sour smell and it made me want to do everything I could to stop it and cheer the mom or dad who was giving it off up.

So, burying my paws in the floor-covering fur, I stood up, faced Mom, and readied myself to make her happy again. I tilted my head and stretched my jaw to get a smile from her, waiting for a reaction. My tilted head move had always worked before.

Mom did snort for a couple of moments, and the air cleared; well, at least the sour stench went away, although I can't say the same about the stink of the black sludge.

The early light period passed by, and Mom did her regular light period routine. It was predictable, and I spent most of the rest of the early light period with Paris, who, of course, was trying to sleep, like usual. What changed all of that was where we headed next.

I have mixed feelings about the place. Let's start out with the name of the place, the Bee Territory. I've been there tons of times before; it seemed that I'd been going there ever since I was a puppy. One of my first memories of Mom and Dad involved the place.

There had been a whole lot of grunting and that same sour smell of worry from Mom when we had first gone inside. It had been a small brown and orange building that looked like it had been built about seven of my lifetimes ago. It didn't have a lot of windows, but it had an old scent, musky and wet.

It had been a interesting place to visit. Even back then, and still

24

to this light period, you got to catch up on all the neighborhood news and smell just about every furry friend who lived in the area, since it seemed they all found their way to this place. We all didn't get to be here at the same time, but just one whiff of the floor caught a friend up on all the neighborhood gossip.

Mom had been very nervous that first trip, and being a puppy, I could barely concentrate fully on any way of cheering her up. Back then I couldn't concentrate on any one thing.

I don't remember much else from that light period, but what I do remember was getting a bee sting. In fact, from then on and just about every other future trip to the Bee Territory, being there involved some sort of a bee sting or another.

That's how the place earned its name; it's because of the bees. They lived there and had the run of the place. They looked like outside-territory bees but they acted differently. Outside-territory bees are mostly things that mind their own business and leave you alone, unless, of course, you make the mistake of thinking they're a crunchy treat. If you do that, you can look forward to a huge tongue and no eating for a whole light period.

But the Bee Territory bees are different, meaner than any outside-territory bee I've ever seen, and the little thing's only job is to sting us furry friends. They are ugly with black-and-white heads and funny-looking necks that go in and out. I've never seen one with wings like outside-territory bees, but they do have a stinger, a long, silver, shiny spike that they like to dip into us at every moment they get.

Mom's large, black sniff box stopped its growling and came to a stop outside the Bee Territory. She opened the door and just in front of me stood the old brown-and-orange Bee Territory building. I could already catch the smell of some two-day-old news. So with my safety rope attached, I jumped out, careful to keep my balance, and headed in.

9

JULIA
APRIL 2009

I don't like hospitals. They reminded me of Dad, and what he went through. He put up such a long and arduous fight, and even up until the end he was so brave.

I started to feel my mind wander, but I knew I just couldn't go there now. I had to hold it together.

Jeez, Julia, this is your dog's veterinarian, not your dad's doctor, and what's in the past needs to stay in the past. Eddie will be fine.

Now focus!

The place was archaic, but since this was the only vet's office I had ever been to, since Eddie was my first dog, I didn't think they made vets' offices any other way. All the walls were plastered with old dog and cat breed club wallpaper that looked to be from the seventies. There were lost-and-found flyers, adoption flyers, and a mix of all sorts of thank-you cards stuck to a large pegboard behind the reception desk, and the overflow had been unevenly taped so that they hung over the table. Some of those flyers had to be at least six years old.

Guarding each side of the long, plastic blue bench that ran along the length of the wall of the small, narrow waiting room were two rectangular wood storage chests. Resting on their flat, distressed lids were a wide variety of old magazines, as well as a single brown vase filled with weathered polyester roses. I had always had a morbid curiosity about touching one of the roses to see just how much dust came off but had been too scared to find out.

We were led down a narrow, short hallway to a small room that served as the first exam room, given the number **1** nailed to the center of the door. It smelled of a mixture of bleach and old cat urine, with undertones of wet dog, and it reminded me of every other time I'd been there.

It wasn't the best smell in the world, but it was a familiar smell, entirely unique to this place. I had been coming to Dr. Smith's Veterinary Hospital ever since Eddie was a puppy, and just about everyone I knew in the neighborhood who had pets came here.

Besides being one of the only veterinarians within ten square miles, Sarah Smith was a fixture and had been practicing in this very office for the last thirty years and counting.

A woman who, by the looks of it, must've been in her late fifties, she had mostly gray hair that was streaked with the remnants of a youthful brown and, like always, wore it tied back in a tight ponytail. She wore a pink scrub top with a large picture of an overweight cat on it and a pair of dark blue slacks. Her lab coat gleamed a blinding white under the dull fluorescent lights, a stark contrast to the rest of the hospital.

She was a tall woman, and her round, full complexion was composed of perfectly smooth skin. She had a grandmotherly feel to her: warm, confident, and easy to talk to. I couldn't help but get the impression, whenever she gave me medical advice about Eddie, she was in reality lecturing me about the basics of life. That was probably just my subconscious grasping for what was missing in my own past, though.

She also had a soft but very intelligent voice.

"Well, Julia, Eddie's physical exam is normal except for this small bump. He's scratched the skin around it and it looks pretty irritated. It's hard to say exactly what it is, but it could be something as benign as a bug bite."

I scratched the back of my neck and looked down, feeling guilty, like somehow I had caused this.

I said, "I caught him licking it this morning. Oh, and one of them chewed up one of my heels last night. Do you think that was related? You know, I thought it was Paris, but maybe it was Eddie after all."

I suddenly had a flashback to the stocking incident and the fifteen- hundred dollars it had cost to remove it.

Dr. Smith smiled and shook her head, and I knew she had also been remembering his puppy days. I had, after all, been bringing both of my dogs here for a long time, and I depended on her to keep both of them healthy.

"Could this be an allergic reaction?"

She breathed out and wrinkled her forehead, and I could sense her mind working.

"I can't rule that out, but it's unlikely. Either way, the licking didn't help whatever caused it. As far as the bump is concerned, it's a little too small for me get a good needle sample. I'm going to be conservative and treat it like a bug bite with a possible infection for now. I'll give him a shot of Benadryl and put him on antibiotics.

"Let me see him in a week to make sure it's gone down, and in the meantime, I'll send in the tech to give him the shot. As far as the antibiotics are concerned, give him one pill every twelve hours by mouth for the next seven days, and try giving it at meal times to lessen any potential nausea. Do you have any questions, Julia?"

I smiled and shook my head. I was relieved, but still, an uneasy feeling persisted. Maybe I was overreacting.

She leaned back and put her arm on the dull silver exam table, and suddenly the vet had been replaced by an old acquaintance.

"Good. Now how are you getting along? How's David?"

10

EDDIE
APRIL 2009

The white-coated mom gave me a pat on the head and walked out of the room. She had been doing a whole lot of grunting, and Mom was definitely happier than when we had first arrived.

When the white-coated mom had first walked in, Mom had been very nervous, and her smell had been making my nose sting. Not exactly knowing what to expect and given Mom's state of being, I had readied myself for anything.

When the white-coated mom walked into the room though, and I realized who it was, I instantly settled down and knew that Mom was just in one of her nervous, stinky moods. I had known the white-coated mom for ages and had a sense that she would never hurt a living creature. She smelled harmless, except for that underlying odor of smoke to her. It was a deep-choke-if-you-breathed-too-much-of-it, give-you-a-pounding-headache smell. It was a common stench found on a whole variety of moms and dads, the same scent the coughing dad next door had. I did my best not to breathe in too deep.

She was wearing the standard white coat she always had, and she looked at me with large, gray eyes. After some initial grunting, Mom also managed to relax, and I watched both of them as their grunting continued. After the white-coated mom gave a short, reassuring grunt, finished what she had been saying, she turned her attention to me.

Here goes.

The smoky smell grew stronger as she started to give me the standard white-coated greeting. She was the only mom who ever said hello to me this way, but rather than fight it, I just let her do her thing.

She looked into my mouth, patted down my body, and shone an extremely bright light stick directly into both of my eyes which left me with little flickering bright spots. She then put into her ears two long, curved, black hollow tubes with tiny white bubbles on either end which connected to a long, single tube with a circular disc on the end against my chest.

With her greeting routine completed, she next had a long drawn-out conversation with Mom, and as quickly as she came in, the white-coated mom left the room. She was replaced by a tall, fat dad who was dressed in dark blue coverings. He had a serious expression on his pudgy face, and he stared at me with narrow, half-closed eyes.

He looked so unhappy because he had been given the job of having to control an angry, clear-bellied, liquid-filled bee, and judging by its extended neck, it was extremely angry.

The bee was headed my way despite the dark-blue dad's attempts to control it and the light shone off its sharp, silver little butt. Knowing what was going to come next, I looked for an escape route because getting stung was not my idea of a good time. I looked past the blue dad toward the door, which was halfway open, and I could see the long blue chairs against the front-room wall and the entrance door just next to it.

No one was in the front room and I had a clear path if I could just get past the blue dad. He was a pretty wide target, but I knew what I had to do. I tightened my leg muscles and took in a deep breath. I looked back up at him before my mad dash, but just at that moment, he lifted up his other pink paw. All thoughts of escape went away

Wrapped within his pudgy claws, I could see the partially exposed, rounded brown end of a thick and juicy-looking crunchy treat, and it stopped me in my tracks. He read my mind and raised his crunchy-treat paw in front of his round belly and opened his claws to show the full length of it.

Hmmm, what to do, what to do? Should I make a break for it and avoid a bee sting, or should I stay for the treat? I was so torn.

In reality, though, the decision wasn't mine; the next thing I knew, my hind end burned and I was crunching away at my beautiful prize. I turned my head to see a tired, satisfied bee making its way into the red beehive, the place where all the tired bees go when they're done.

I was still enjoying the aftertaste of the brown crunchy treat when the blue dad bent down, hugged my neck, and rubbed my head. I could feel the slight dampness of his underarm as it rubbed against the top of my neck, and I really hoped that none of the saltiness would rub off on me.

When he was done making himself feel better, Mom and I headed outside the room and into the front region of the Bee Territory. I kept my nose to the floor, looking for any crumbs or any interesting gossip along the way, and although I didn't learn of any new stuff about the neighborhood, I did manage to find a stray bit of something that tasted like a mixture of old cheese and dried fruit.

Mom grunted to the mom behind the front table, but before Mom could finish her sentence, the table mom had looked over at me and begun whining, completely ignoring Mom. She was a young mom, had shiny long wires connecting one side of her canines to the other, and a face decorated with pink dots. Most of them had white tops that threatened to burst at any moment. That mom kept switching between a high-pitched squeal and a low hum as she attempted to get my attention.

I then did what any furry friend would do faced with my situation, with an abnormal creature making all sorts of unidentifiable sounds. I sat down, and cocked my head to the side, and barked a questioning grunt.

She stopped yodeling, slapped her paw on the table, brushing some white-lined bark aside so it fell to the dotted floor, and went into a snorting fit. That only caused my head to angle more, which, in turn, led to more snorting, angling, snorting you get . . . the picture.

And so it went and on and on, but it stopped the moment I sensed Mom wanting to leave. It was just at about the time that my head was basically parallel to the ground, and I jerked my head back to normal as Mom gave a throat clear. After hearing Mom's quite obvious get-me-home-please comment, the table mom's snorting started to die down, but not before she let out some wet, clear-snot muzzle sniffs.

With a semiwet paw from a quick muzzle wipe, she then grabbed a large, white crunchy-treat–shaped container from behind the front table and in one smooth motion launched a red chewy treat my way. As the treat arced in midair toward my mouth, I quickly looked what I was about to eat.

I was focused on what was falling my way, but all of a sudden the hairs on the back of my neck twitched a warning signal. It was a change in the air, an electric charge that energized all the muscles in my body, a cold feeling at the base of my spine and snapped me into an ultra-awareness state of being.

Although my mouth was cranked wide open and there was a string of drool dripping from my front bottom teeth, out of the corner of my eye I saw a flash. It was barely perceptible and it was only for a moment, but it was enough. In that short moment of time I saw a blur of fluffy white, and it was running out of one of the back rooms and picking up speed.

11

EDDIE
APRIL 2009

Plainly put, I won.

No furry friend has ever beaten me, and no furry friend ever will. Especially one half my size and, by the looks of it, only a quarter my age.

I saw him bounding out of the hallway I had just come from, break loose from his dad's safety rope, and make a dash toward me. He was a fluffy little guy, and judging by the length of his legs, he was no more than the height of my knees. He had a short, pointed black nose and matching black almond-shaped eyes, and he was trying to get to my now airborne prize.

His dad, a very round dad with a belly that hung over his blue leg coverings, had been slow to react. That dad had a lot of black fur on his belly, and his stained chest covering was way too short to fully do the job. He tried to chase his fluff ball, but given his size, by the time his legs got the message, the furry friend was about four steps ahead of him. And, unlike his round dad, the fluff ball was a lightning-fast. He even managed to get two more steps toward me and all four paws off the ground before I reacted.

My muscles tensed and the next thing I knew, I was in the air too. I closed the distance between the crunchy treat and my mouth and caught it in midair while at the same time blocking his jump with the side of my neck.

I landed well but felt bad as I heard a thud, followed by a high-pitched whine as he hit the ground. Poor little guy, his landing didn't turn out to be as smooth as his takeoff. As soon as my paws made contact with the floor, I turned to face him, challenging him to try something else, but he still was flat on his side.

He was a young furry friend and when he righted himself enough to look up at me, I sensed a puppiness to him. It was that feeling of not being able to get hurt by anything and having no limit to your energy.

He was still on his side, staring at me, and I could see he was considering his next move. It was in his eyes, which were a deep black.

I faced him head on and stared back, both daring and judging him to see whether he would actually make a next move. He was all skin and bones under the puffed-out fur, and the only place missing a cotton covering was right under his pink belly, which was facing. There I saw a long, red, irritated scratch with multiple small ropes going from one side of it to the other, and I could catch the smell of injured wet iron coming from it.

With my full attention on him and just the tips of my teeth showing, he looked away. Either he'd thought better of further challenging me or, given his puppy age, he was already bored with the situation. He was winded and got up slowly, but not before he let out a loud, deep belch that would make even a mastiff jealous.

His rounded dad made it over to him—out of breath—and secured his safety collar while grunting sorry to Mom.

The air around me filled with the little guy's smell as the explosion of gas wafted my way.

I recognized that smell.

It was acidic with a touch of spice, and it was pouring out of the little guy's body. It brought back so many memories, things that I hadn't thought about in awhile, but they all came rushing back now.

Ropes on my belly, a deep scratch, the acidic stench; I had experienced the little guy's world. Now that I thought about it, I was about his age when it had happened.

It had been my second light period with Mom and Dad, the one directly after the great feast, when I'd managed to get at their bury box treats. The dizziness had started shortly after, while it was still dark out, and at first it hadn't been that bad. It felt like I had only done two or three circles chasing my tail, but as the sun began to brighten up the world outside, the room started spinning out of control.

I was really bad by the time Dad came downstairs. I had gotten free from the feeding room by making a hole in the thin wood backing of the chair they had put there to keep me in. I had squeezed through, but by that time, the dizziness had gotten worse. Not having the energy to make it upstairs, I had lay down in the front room. That's when the puking had started, and it had gone on and on and on. And when all the previous dark period's bury box treats were gone, I started dry heaving instead.

When Dad came downstairs, he had taken one look at me, the furry floor covering, the wall, the sofa, Mom's paw coverings that had been left out, and then he had taken action. After making it clear that I was never, ever, ever allowed near the bury box again, he yelled upstairs to wake up Mom. A short time later, he carried me to his short, shiny-silver sniff box, and loaded me in. He put me on Mom's lap and we rushed here, to this very place, to the Bee Territory.

Dad had given me a short head tap but had put his paw right back on the rawhide sniff-box ring. After that, I turned around and licked Mom's muzzle and lay down with my head resting on her thigh. The dizziness started to build up with every turn and jerk of the sniff box, and I felt an overriding need to sniff the outside smells. I had to have the smell of some green ground covering and tried to make it to the clear sniff-box wall.

As I lifted my swirling head, an orange, bone-fragmented stream of steaming vomit poured out and splattered the closed, clear sniff-box wall, bouncing droplets of spicy fluid in all directions. I had thought that I had nothing left in me, but I guess I had been wrong.

Mom had been pretty good about the whole thing, and being her sweet self, she stopped me from trying to lick her clean. I don't remember very much about our arrival at the Bee Territory, but I do remember waking up and feeling really tired and hearing a whole lot of grunting from the white-coated mom. I also remember the smell: that spicy, I-ate-something-I-shouldn't have, nose-hair–burning smell.

And that's what the little white fur ball stunk of. It was coming from every opening of his body, and I couldn't help but wonder what the little guy's feast had been.

"Eddie should be okay now, but we had to remove a stocking from his stomach. The surgery was a success, and he should recover just fine. Also, a little bit of advice, since both of you guys are brand-new parents: You should invest in trash cans with lids or, even better, hide the trash can in a closet. Eddie has the temperament of a golden retriever through and through; don't let the coonhound ears fool you. There are two undeniable facts about goldens; number one, they love to wag their tails. Number two is that they love food and can't get enough of it. They like to explore, and your trash cans are prime targets. David, Julia, just be careful."

THE DOG DAYS OF THE PAST

JULY 2007 RICHARD'S DIAGNOSIS
JULY 2007 RICHARD'S TREATMENT

-

-

-

-

-

* *FEBRUARY 2008* DAVID MEETS SOMEONE NEW *
MARCH 2008 RICHARD'S CANCER SPREADS
MARCH 2008 DAVID'S TEMPTATION
MARCH 2008 RICHARD'S FINAL DAYS

-

-

JUNE 2008 RICHARD PASSES
JULY 2008 DAVID'S LUNCH DATE

-

SEPTEMBER 2008 DAVID'S CHOICE

-

-

-

-

APRIL 2009 EDDIE'S CLINICAL SIGNS
APRIL 2009 EDDIE'S DIAGNOSIS
MAY 2009 EDDIE'S TREATMENT
JUNE 2009 EDDIE'S SIDE EFFECTS
JUNE 2009 EDDIE COMPLETES THERAPY
JULY 2009   EPILOGUE

12

DAVID
FEBRUARY 2008

I was bored, I was tired, and I was mad. There had been no loans or even leads in the last week, and as the economists had predicted, the industry was taking a break from the last three months of nonstop action.

I couldn't be too disappointed; the last eight years had been amazing for me. Even if things slowed down, I still had saved enough money to retire fifteen years ahead of schedule. Not bad for being forty without a master's degree. Suffice it to say, I wasn't too worried about one slow week. It wasn't like the market was crashing or anything.

I looked at my watch, the same Padres watch I had been wearing for the last nineteen years. Heidi, the girl I had dumped for Julia, had given it to me for my twenty-first birthday, and Julia, being an avid sports fan in her own right, had at least let me keep the watch when we had gotten together.

Heidi had been beautiful, with long, thick blond hair and bright, ocean-blue eyes. She had long, perfectly bronzed, silky-smooth legs and had all the right curves in all the right places. Unfortunately, though, once you got past the looks, there had been nothing else to offer, and inevitably my relationship with her became more of a chore than anything else. Sure, she looked great and the first six months were fun, but when I really got to know her, I realized that she was boring, superficial, and about as deep as a Frisbee. The relationship didn't work out, but, hey, the watch was a nice consolation prize.

It was 11:30 A.M. and the new applicant for the secretary position would be in soon.

I was alone in my office, killing time playing Tetris, and like most of the other mortgage agents in the building, I was bored stiff. It was a nice office; it had a beautifully polished mahogany desk, a black leather reclining chair I had picked myself, and Padres memorabilia lining all the walls. I had my 1998 signed Padres World Series ball, a reminder of just how amazing my wife was.

The moment I met Julia, there was no other woman in the

world who could exist for me. What that woman went through to get that ball I'll never know, but it was one of the nicest things anyone had ever gotten me.

I met Julia two and half years into my relationship with Heidi, and by that time I was looking for an excuse to end it. I was twenty-three years old, had finished college four months earlier, and had just gotten back from a post-graduation trip to Europe. I had gone with my friends, refusing to take Heidi with a lame excuse that I needed some space. I had run all the way across the ocean to take a break from her.

I got back to San Diego determined to embrace the world of responsibility. I was going to enter the work force, not just with a summer job but a real nine-to-five, year-round career. I wanted to succeed, I wanted to make money, and it was time I grew up and acted like a man. I had been on the beach, officially saying good-bye to my childhood, thinking about my future and my newly gained position at the mortgage firm. As the fates or angels would have it, there Julia was, ready to reshape my future.

She was a sight to behold: long, flowing, black hair that fell over her perfectly rounded shoulders, a knockout tan body models would fight for, and, best of all, a face that radiated quiet, soft-spoken intelligence. Only after we had been married did I realize just how far that intelligence extended. She was smarter than me by a long shot, even though I would never admit it, at least not to her.

I hadn't picked her up per se; we had just started talking. She had been one beach towel over, reading a freshman-year finance book I recognized from my time in college, and from there the conversation had just happened. I don't know who spoke first, but it felt like I was talking to someone I had known my entire life. It was familiar, natural, and my soul smiled because it knew I had found my other half. We spent hours speaking, neither of us accomplishing what we had originally come there for but paving the road to our future.

She was amazing. I got her number but didn't call her until I had officially broken it off with Heidi two months later. I wanted it to be perfect with Julia, starting the rest of my life with her with a clean slate that was pure, honest, and unfettered. I'm not a religious or superstitious man, but I knew that to deserve her, I needed to be free, single, and starting the relationship right, otherwise some cosmic force would determine that I didn't deserve her.

So how could the perfect woman, the angel I had called my wife all these years, who could be so caring and sweet, also have the ability to turn into a complete and raving lunatic? Yeah, the honeymoon had been over for a long time, but this morning was totally uncalled for. There had been no good reason, let alone a justification for her to blow up at me the way she did. So what if I had left the toilet seat up? It wasn't the end of the world, and I definitely didn't deserve to be shouted at like that. Would it have killed her to put it down herself? Hell, the thing didn't bite!

She had been edgy for the last three months and understandably so, but it was starting to wear on me. I knew she was going through a rough patch, with her dad and all, but I hated that she kept it all bottled up. He, thank goodness, was finally in remission, but the doctor hadn't given him a good prognosis. The guy had pancreatic cancer, after all, and everyone knew it was only a matter of time.

Everyone in the world but Julia, that is. She refused to talk about it, rejecting any hint of a discussion relating to any aspect of it. She was in complete denial, and I couldn't find a way to bring her out of it. Ever since he had told us about it three months ago, I had tried to get her to speak about it—a little hint here, a little nudge there—but she just wouldn't budge. I couldn't get her to open up, and the more I tried, the angrier she got.

It just wasn't healthy, and inevitably I knew it would have to come out one way or another. Unfortunately, as it turned out, she had begun to take it out on me.

I knew I needed to be there for her, but for the last three weeks I'd felt more like her doormat than her husband. I hated this feeling, but I despised being such a baby about it even more. What kind of a guy was I to even think about this stuff? So what if she wasn't happy all the time, so what if she was a misery; her father was dying, for Pete's sake. I knew I just needed to cowboy up and be a man about the whole thing; like my old high-school wrestling coach used to say, I just needed to "sack up." I had to be there for her, no matter what.

I had been so caught up in replaying the events of the morning that I had barely noticed that I was two lines away from losing the game. I looked at the computer screen, trying to find a place to put the red square, but there was just no room for it. I couldn't concentrate; my heart wasn't in it. I moved it left and then right, but before it had a proper place, it got trapped. The next piece, two small horizontal and three vertical blue boxes that together formed an L, instantly landed on top of the red square. And then, oh crap, game over.

I still couldn't stop turning it around in my mind, though, and the same thoughts kept nagging at me. Why wouldn't she talk about it? She needed to open up a little, bring just some of it out, let off some steam. It would make her feel so much better. Why did she have to be so stubborn about it?

But no, she thought she knew better, and I would have to deal with the repercussions. So here I was, all bent out of shape and bored as can be, playing a stupid game that came preloaded on my computer that I'd never liked as a teenager to begin with. I looked at my watch and saw it was 11:55 A.M. The interview was scheduled to start in five minutes, and I was in no mood for it. The applicant had better not be late. That would be an automatic ding against them. Who was I interviewing anyway?

I opened my appointment book and looked at the 12:00 P.M. slot. There was a big, empty blank square where *interview* should have been filled in. Hell, that was why I was getting a secretary in the first place: to fill in my schedule, to answer the phone, and stuff like that to free me up to do more loans. I had held out too long, but now it was time. Or was it? Not if every day was like today. No, today was a fluke, and at least the interview would eat up one hour of the day.

There was suddenly a soft knock on my office door, and I looked up from my computer.

"Excuse me, are you Mr. Freed?"

The knock had come from the well-manicured hand of a very attractive midtwenties blond-haired, green-eyed woman who was standing in my office doorway. Her teardrop-shaped face was perfectly proportioned, and it looked like she wasn't wearing a touch of makeup. Not that any was needed. She was wearing a pink blouse that hugged her upper body, accentuating her every round curve. She had on flawlessly pressed black slacks that were tight enough to outline her perfectly shaped hips and upper thighs, and her long legs stirred my imagination. She was carrying a small leather briefcase in one hand, and in the other hand, the one with which she had just knocked on the door, was a thin white sheet of paper that I assumed was her résumé. She was stunning.

With a soft, Jessica Rabbit–like voice, she lowered her chin ever so slightly and peered up at me with emerald-green eyes.

"I'm Allyson; I'm here for the job interview."

THE DOG DAYS OF THE PRESENT

JULY 2007 RICHARD'S DIAGNOSIS
JULY 2007 RICHARD'S TREATMENT
-
-
-
-
-

FEBRUARY 2008 DAVID MEETS SOMEONE NEW
MARCH 2008 RICHARD'S CANCER SPREADS
MARCH 2008 DAVID'S TEMPTATION
MARCH 2008 RICHARD'S FINAL DAYS
-
-

JUNE 2008 RICHARD PASSES
JULY 2008 DAVID'S LUNCH DATE
-

SEPTEMBER 2008 DAVID'S CHOICE
-
-
-

* *APRIL 2009* EDDIE'S CLINICAL SIGNS *
APRIL 2009 EDDIE'S DIAGNOSIS
MAY 2009 EDDIE'S TREATMENT
JUNE 2009 EDDIE'S SIDE EFFECTS
JUNE 2009 EDDIE COMPLETES THERAPY
JULY 2009   EPILOGUE

13

JULIA
APRIL 2009

I needed to take my mind off things; I couldn't bear to think about the *ifs* and *maybes* because at this point in time they would probably drive me crazy. It was just a bug bite; that's what we would go with. *Block it out, Julia; you know you're good at that.*

I kept repeating it to myself over and over as I loaded Eddie into the SUV, the black Ford Explorer Limited that had, surprisingly, lasted for the past six years without a scratch. It was the perfect car for the dogs, with enough room for them and any other junk I needed to fit comfortably in the back. Not that Eddie would ride anywhere without putting himself right next to me in the front seat; he was my Velcro dog, after all.

I had sworn to myself that I wouldn't look at it for one whole week, just so I would be able to really judge whether it grew or not. Otherwise, I knew I would be watching it minute by minute, and that wouldn't have done either of us any good.

The plan had gone without a hitch, and I had lived up to my self-imposed promise. I'll admit it had been hard that first day not to take just a quick peek at it, but the second day had been easier. I'm ashamed to say that by the third day I had stopped thinking about it, and by the time day six came, I had completely forgotten about it.

A full week had passed and today was meant to be a sweltering day, a preview of the Santa Anas to come in the summer. That was San Diego for you: a steady 72 degrees except when good old Saint Ann decided to heat the place and remind us all of how it would feel when we died and went to the place you wound up if you hadn't behaved. There wasn't a cloud in the sky, and even at ten in the morning, I could feel the humidity sticking my clothes to my skin. It was late April, and if San Diego had a groundhog, it would be sitting by the beach drinking a Corona. Summer was just dying to push spring away, and judging by today, spring had let down its guard.

Both the dogs and I had been going stir-crazy; I had been rearranging our home office and trying to get all the paperwork that had piled up over the last year filed these last seven days, but I needed some down time. And with a day like this, there was only one place to go. How could you live in Southern California and not go to the beach, especially on a day like today?

I hooked on their faded brown-and-orange Padres leashes, the same ones David had picked up four years ago, and marveled at how different the dogs were. Eddie was my middle-aged puppy. Nothing ever bothered him; he was your typical happy-go-lucky, wag-your-tail-at-all-times dog, and I had never met anyone who hadn't liked him. It was that wrinkly face, those long ears that looked like they didn't belong to a dog his size, and, of course, his temperament. He was happy all the time, and it was contagious.

And then there was Paris, the independent-minded, temperamental other half of the duo. By the way she acted, you would have thought she was a cat hiding in a poodle's body. She was the complete opposite of Eddie: nonsocial, only friendly to a select few, borderline prissy, and it had to be her to initiate any sort of contact. Everything had to be on her terms, but when she finally did decide to grace you with her presence and give you affection, you felt like the luckiest person on earth.

I stepped out of the car and felt the warmth of the sun as it beat down on my neck and shoulders. I inhaled a long, drawn-out crisp breath of salty air. This early in the year the beach was mostly deserted, so they wouldn't be enforcing the no-dogs-allowed rule they were such sticklers about in the summer.

The seasonal tourists had not yet invaded. They were probably still tied to their everyday lives and jobs, and that was fine by me. The place was pretty empty even for us locals, considering how hot it was, but the early morning does tend to siphon off the masses. I knew that would change in about an hour or two. People would trickle in, but at least it wouldn't be the June–September zoo of a summer crowd.

This was my favorite place in the world, all cares in life and stresses of the moment forgotten here. Ever since I was a kid, the beach had had that effect on me, and this particular beach held a special place in my heart. It was at this very beach that I had met David, a determined and intelligent man, almost fifteen years earlier, and it was here that he had proposed a year and a half later.

This was also my place of solace. I loved the feel of the soft, cushionlike sand as it gently massaged my feet. I had derived so much pleasure from that temporary sinking feeling as my toes touched the shifting surface of billions of individual grains of glass, only to be caught and supported by my full weight as it pushed down. I had spent lifetimes here watching the broken waves climb up the shore, marveling at their efforts to reach out to me, to comfort me, and then get dragged back into the abyss only to climb back up the shore again with arms open wide.

After my father's passing. It was here that I had escaped on those long, lonely days to heal. I had come to this place nearly every day, and it was here that I had come to terms with my feelings. They were my feelings, my emotions, and I had refused to share them with anyone else. I didn't want to let anyone in because this was between my father and me; it was private. Nobody could ever understand what I had been going through, and I didn't want to waste time or energy explaining it. How could anyone possibly know how Dad's passing had affected me, what it had made me feel? Nobody deserved to be in that part of my world with him; it was his and mine, and what was left of it was for me alone. They didn't know Dad like I did.

It was here that I had internalized the sorrow of watching him slowly shrivel away; here that I had escaped to come to terms with the pain of his sudden and unfair departure.

The dogs were having a ball. Eddie had just tackled Paris, who was now covered with dry sand. She had gotten up and was chasing him toward the shore with her tongue hanging out and her chest bobbing up and down. Her head stayed glued in place, and as she sprinted after him, she looked like a sleek, bony racehorse. This was one of the only places where she actually let loose and acted like a dog.

Eddie was pounding through the sand, leaving clouds of brown and white in his wake. His ears were flopping in the wind and whipping back and forth with every step. His run looked clumsy, overexaggerated, like a drunk trying to pass a sobriety test. The dogs were in heaven.

I took out the tennis ball; it was time to wear them out.

14

EDDIE
APRIL 2009

It was adventure day, and I loved every part of it, especially when it involved the place of sandy water. We had been coming here ever since I could remember, and it always meant that we got to run loose and go wild. There was white sand everywhere, and the water was a dark blue. The mixture made a smell that only this place could offer; there was no other smell like it in the world. It was fresh and salty, and it made you want to run, bark, and fetch just about anything that was lying around.

The best part of the place, though, was how Mom got when we came here, and it was the main reason why it was one of my favorites as well. It was that look Mom got, the moment right when her paws touched the white sand. No matter what type of mood she had started out in—tense, stressed, sad, or upset—it didn't matter, because as soon as we got here, that would change. Her face would un-crinkle, the lines around her eyes would straighten, and the end result was a relaxed Mom who smelled of peace and calm.

Let's also not forget that this place gave me the chance to show off one of my greatest skills in the world, yellow-rock hunting. Oh, yes, the wonderful furry-friend game of yellow-rock hunting, involving none other than the bouncy, hairy, and sometimes confusing yellow rock. The round, furry, collapse-when-bitten, squish-if-munched rock of fun that Mom or Dad would take out and start throwing pretty much every time we came to this place.

We all have different relationships with rock: Dad and his love/hate thing with it, Mom with her not caring one way or the other with it, and Paris and me with our worship of it.

Dad, well, he hated the yellow rock; he always tried to toss it as far as he could possibly get it to go away from him. But, he also loved it; he got so mad at it if it didn't make its way back after he chucked it.

Now, Mom was another story altogether. In the days of old, she was like Dad and his love of the yellow rock and, like him, got mad if it didn't find its way back. But for a while now though, she didn't care what the rock did after she threw it, and it seemed like it didn't matter to her if it came back or not anymore. She had been busy concentrating on other things, and she had usually been lost in her thoughts by the time either Paris or I brought it back. It took a good shove with the yellow rock to her thigh, one hard enough to leave a wet spot, to get her to notice that it was back.

Today had started out different, though, and by the way she was gearing up to toss the yellow rock, I saw some signs of the way she used to be. The water was rough today, and I could see plenty of white fuzzes pushing their way to the shore. After Mom had reached into her bag and her paw had come out with the furry yellow rock, she had grunted our names and waved it back and forth signaling the competition to come.

Now the title of grand yellow-rock getter paws down belongs to me, although, Paris was pushing a close second. The competition was only between the two of us, and as much as I appreciated her trying, it just didn't make up for my speed and skill. That was my advantage.

Oh, and there was one other thing: Paris was, and still is to this light period, afraid of the water, especially when it came to anything to do with the white fuzzes. It all started after that one time when a tiny, less-than-knee-height white fuzz caused her to lose her balance and be pushed underwater. She was under for not even a moment and nose planted into the wet sand as soon as she had tried to get up. It was so minor of a fall, but the sulking that went on after would have made you think a sniff box had hit her. She shivered and howled, and she refused to leave Mom's side the rest of that light period.

So when it came to any game or adventure involving the water I always won. Even if she had managed to beat me to the water if the rock flew that way, she'd lose because the oversized cotton puff never went in past her elbows.

Mom cranked out an amazing throw and the yellow rock soared high above our heads. It became a yellow dot in a blue sky as it made its way over the boundary between the sand and the water. It hit the water and was so far out that I barely saw the splash of its landing.

Paris and I had both started the moment Mom had wound up to throw. We chased after it with everything we had, digging in every step and spraying sand behind us as we ran. I could sense Paris right next to me, and I knew she was running a close race today. By the time we reached the wet sand just before the actual water, I knew we were muzzle to muzzle. I reached inside for that extra burst and felt myself pull slightly ahead of her.

As I felt the ground grow firmer, hardened by the mixture of water and sand, my lead widened. I'd like to think it was because I was faster than her, but I knew that the wet sand digging between her claws had made her hesitate.

I launched in the air right as I hit the water's edge, I made it over the white fuzz and kept running. Luckily, there were no other white fuzzes coming and so I made it a pretty far way out. I spotted the yellow rock as it bobbed up and down. It was moving ever so slightly, and I was close enough to see it spinning. Its fuzz was pasted to its back, and it was about twenty steps in front of me. I knew that Paris was still probably on the shore. I turned back around, and in just that short period of time another white fuzz had broken and was rolling toward me. It was barreling toward us, and I needed to get to the yellow rock fast.

The pain that cut deep into my shoulder and traveled down through my right front paw put an end to my speed, and I let out a loud, high-pitched yelp. It felt like a tree had poked straight through my shoulder, and despite how loud I had screamed; I was way too far out for anyone to hear. The shock of it, the heat that ran down my paw, had stopped me dead mid-paddle, but as suddenly as it appeared, the feeling went away. It was a good thing too, because my muzzle was just about to get dunked, and I didn't think anything in this world short of the pain going away could have avoided that.

I could run again, my shoulder still seemed to be attached, and I had no time to concentrate on what had just happened if I still had any chance of getting to the yellow rock. But it was too late already. The white fuzz swept it right past me.

I watched helplessly as it bobbed up and down as it was carried toward the wet sand to a smiling and bouncy Paris. Even from this far out, I could see her tail vibrating and as it made its way to land, she began leaping up in the air, launching off her bony hind legs and doing three-sixties.

I watched as she grabbed the yellow rock and the bragging rights for the day. She was careful to wait until it had been thoroughly dragged onto the sand so she wouldn't have to get her muzzle wet. She made a point of staring past the white fuzzes toward where I was and belted out a triumphant drawn-out howl and galloped back to Mom.

I kept up my pace, running back to the sand. The sharp pain had stopped but had been replaced by a very, very weird feeling. My leg felt heavy, like it was five times its normal weight, and although my mind was telling it to help pull me back toward the sand, it felt like it wasn't listening.

To top it off, the tingle I had felt earlier in the week had come back. It was in the same place as before, and it was the same tingle from a couple of light periods ago, although this time it was too strong to ignore. I kept running, though, pulling myself through the water. I needed to get back to Mom.

Three white fuzzes later and a nostril full of burning salt water, my paws finally touched the semisolid ground. It was then that there was no doubt or question that something was definitely wrong. Not only did my shoulder tingle but also my entire right paw didn't work like it should. It felt like dead weight, and it took a whole lot of extra effort to tell it what to do. I put one, two, three paws down, but when I went to use the right front one, the tingling in my shoulder became unbearable. I picked it up and just held it there while I tried to figure out what to make of the situation.

I started walking forward, hopping slowly, and making my way toward Paris and Mom. My three paws sank deeper than usual into the sand now that they were one-quarter less supported, and I could feel the wet sand digging between my claws. My other legs bore my weight just fine, and a little replacement hop for the right front was all I needed for balance.

After just a couple of steps, though, the tingling became less strong because I had been keeping my weight completely off that leg. It wasn't that bad if I just kept the leg in the air, and it only took a few steps to get the hang of the new walk. I had made it to the dry warm sand, and I looked up toward Mom.

What I saw froze me in my three-legged tracks. Mom's color had drained to white while her jaw was hanging wide open. She was staring right at me with eyes so wide that I could see the whites surrounding her pupils. Her head was angled to the side, her back was straight, and even from where I stood, I could feel her concern.

I reacted. Worry had been replaced by defensiveness, and the tingling shoulder was forgotten as I jumped forward toward her. I jerked my head left and right and then up and down, searching for any possible danger. I breathed a deep sniff of air and sorted out the various levels of smells, looking for any threats. I could see other moms and dads sleeping on their colored sand coverings, but they were too far away to be of any concern.

Paris had also snapped into action and I could tell her scanning also hadn't found anything. Her smiling had stopped the moment she had seen me do a three-legged-jump forward.

There were no signs of danger. I was caked in mud and, still not having had a good shake and was dripping water in my path. I wanted to get back to Mom as fast as possible because with a look like that, I knew she needed me around.

I reached Mom, and she started rubbing me down, slapping the sand off my wet fur in frantic slaps. Paris, completely unaware of anything but her own happy world again, was standing next to Mom, panting and smiling while the yellow furry rock lay indented in the sand. She kept looking at Mom and back at me, not understanding why she wasn't being paid attention to.

Mom stunk of worry but stopped batting the sand off my back and laid her paws lightly on my right shoulder. It was a gentle pressure, but it made the tingly sensation into an unbearable tickle.

Mom's anxiety level grew.

Before I had time to act, she grabbed Paris's and my safety collars and hooked us up. She turned around swiftly and we headed back to the parking lot to Mom's large black sniff box. Mom was walking slowly, but I could see by her jerky, tense steps that she would have run if she could, or if she thought I could have kept up. I wanted to, but with my shoulder the way it was, it would have been impossible.

Something had overrun the happy effects of the place of sandy water. Mom was squishing her eye muscles, and the creases in her forehead and under her eyes were showing. She reached into her dark red paw pouch, one of the many she carried around with her, and grabbed her small and rectangular ear scratcher.

These noisy little things have tiny buttons that glow green, and they beep and howl at the most random times. Whenever Mom— or Dad, for that matter— would hold their ear scratchers, the things would vibrate and buzz to soothe the ear itch, but they never worked. A claw is much easier and more effective in solving any issue with an ear. The ear scratcher woke up and its head suddenly glowed a bright white as Mom tapped a combination of the green, glowing buttons with her claws. She held it up to her head.

Could that be it? Was the reason for this freak-out and why we were leaving the place of sandy water so fast an ear itch?

15

JULIA
APRIL 2009

This was not good; the thing had doubled in size.

Watch it, monitor it; yeah, right!

Don't look at it for a week; what was I thinking?

I was so angry, but I forced myself to walk slowly so Eddie could keep up. I headed to my black SUV and thought, *to hell with rinsing the sand off the dogs*, because I'd get the car cleaned later. I dialed Dr. Smith's number and waited for two long, drawn-out rings before the receptionist answered.

It was Sarah, the girl who looked like she had dropped out of high school. I recognized her voice.

"Hello, this is Julia Freed," I said, and not giving her time to answer, continued, "I need to see Dr. Smith as soon as possible. When is the next appointment? This is very important!

"Uh-huh . . . great, you have an opening in thirty minutes. Wonderful, I'll be there in twenty. Thanks, 'bye."

16

EDDIE
APRIL 2009

With every step we took, Mom's worry increased. It came as no surprise that the ear scratcher had failed so miserably, so I decided to take action. I had let this go on long enough; something had to be done.

As the ground changed from soft, warm sand into a bluish-black, hard covering, I could see our sniff box straight ahead. The floor was so hot I could practically feel myself leaving melted sticky paw marks behind me. Paris was whining and hopping from one paw to the other in an effort to float to the car, but Mom was so busy thinking about something else I didn't think she noticed.

I had to snap Mom out of it, so I first used my happy bark and did a lap around her, of course slower and one leg less than usual.

No luck. Her eyes were fixed on the sniff box and nothing was going to stop her.

I then nudged her paw with my nose in midstep and cocked my head to the side, waiting for her to turn and look down at me.

There was still no response; she just kept walking. By this time, Paris had run ahead and was also pulling Mom in a panicked effort to get to cooler ground, and so we practically jogged to the sniff box.

The ground was cooler where the sniff box had thrown its shadow, and Paris was now in the process of lifting each paw in an attempt to lick them. Mom opened the back of the sniff box, and Paris took a break from her licking to jump in first. It was a pretty high jump, given the size of the sniff box, and by the time I made it to line up the leap in, I was huffing and puffing from the three-legged effort. I looked up, aware of only using three legs to make the jump, but before I had time to act, Mom wrapped her paws around me and launched me onto the seat.

Paris had left a sand trail as she had claimed the gray seat behind Mom's, and by the time I was in the sniff box, she had already lay down on her stomach and was eyeing her paw pads. I limped past her, adding my own pile of sand to the furry sniff-box floor, and made my way between the two front seats to be nearer to Mom. I sat down next to her just as she closed her door and settled behind the round rawhide ring.

Mom rolled down her see-through wall and grunted in frustration. Mom's face stayed unchanged throughout the ride. As the sniff box rolled to a stop, I finally took my eyes off of her and looked up. I recognized the place immediately.

Even from behind the water-streaked clear windows of the sniff box, I knew this place. Its orange-and-brown–paneled walls, its lack of windows, its tempting, green ground covering, I could practically smell the neighborhood gossip markings of the Bee Territory.

Wait a second, I needed to warn Paris; I needed to stop what I knew would happen next. I needed to . . .

I was too late; she had already lifted her head from her snooze, and I knew what would happen next. She looked out the window in a half-awake stare and saw her face change as her mind kicked into motion to realize where we were. Her eyes suddenly grew a very big, dark black, her ears pointed back, her muzzle fur started to tremble, and I knew all was lost. She began to suck in a long breath.

Here we go again!

And with that, so began the whining, the howling, and let's not leave out the uncontrollable shaking that was Paris at the Bee Territory.

I wasn't surprised about it; a little annoyed, but not surprised. Paris and I didn't see eye to eye about this place. Unlike me, who appreciated crunchy treats or even simply meeting new moms and dads—Paris was only interested in . . . well, Paris. All she cared about was sleep time, being patted when she felt the need for it, eating every meal out of my bowl, and, of course her newly developed love for Mom's paw pads.

She flattened on the seat in an attempt to blend into the sandy sniff-box floor, somehow hoping Mom would think she was no longer there. She forgot one minor detail, though: that in order not to be noticed, you have to take the simple step of being quiet.

But no, she was going on like her tail had gotten caught in the door, and I was amazed at the sounds that came out of her mouth.

Even Paris should have been bright enough to figure out that Mom wasn't right, and her going on like this wasn't helping to make things better. Mom started grunting soothingly to her as she attached our safety lines. I could still smell the place of sandy water on the lines, or it could have been my now almost-dried fur. As soon as my line was hooked up, I jumped out of the sniff box and almost made a perfect three-legged landing, but, luckily, my chin stopped my potential wipeout as it hit the soft green covering right beside where Mom had parked.

I was instantly overwhelmed by the variety of smells of the neighborhood. Toby had gotten a new furry-friend playmate and was complaining about how he did nothing but howl and go after his tail, Nipsy had the runs from a bad encounter with spoiled meat, Sierra was pregnant, Gertie got mange, and Otto had moved to the valley. And the smells went on and on.

Paris was still noisily complaining on the sniff-box floor, and by the look of it, she had no intention of moving. Mom pulled her safety line ever so slightly, but Paris howled like she had just been hit with a stick. Mom frowned and gave a second tug of the line, only this time harder, but Paris again let out a wail.

Mom got mad then and hissed loudly. Her face reddened, her voice dropped, and she barked at Paris while pulling her safety line so hard that Paris's howl was choked back as her collar tightened. Mom then dragged her to the edge of the sniff-box floor.

Paris made eye contact with Mom and even she wasn't stupid enough to mess with Mom when she was like this. The shock of the Bee Territory was beaten by the fear of what Mom would do to her next if she didn't fall into line.

She obeyed Mom then, hopping out onto the green covering and scampering in behind me. I kept sniffing the ground as we walked toward the Bee Territory, with Paris being towed five paces behind. Her tail pointed down and she was stretching the safety line to its limit. I led taking in the rest of the gossip and smells on the way.

We walked into the Bee Territory front room, and I smiled as I saw the red-dotted mom behind the counter. The place also looked the same as the last time.

Mom made it through the door and the red-dotted mom grunted warmly to her. She smiled at Mom, revealing her shiny silver thin-roped teeth, and then looked toward me. Mom turned around to finish reeling in a still being dragged Paris.

I took two hops toward the red-dotted mom's desk and watched as her thin, silver-roped smile vanished. Her forehead tensed, her mouth closed, and her happy-go-lucky face suddenly grew to a serious look of concern.

Mom, Paris, and I were led into the second room on the left side of the short hall. Mom and I watched as Paris scurried between us in a desperate attempt to put Mom and me between her and whatever lay waiting to come in after us. She wedged herself against the far wall and her eyes locked on the door, waiting for the unthinkable. After a couple of seconds, she realized there was more to the room to kill her than what could come through the door, and she jerked her head from left to right, scanning the yellow shelves and cabinets lining the three walls around us.

The walls were lined with the same white furry-and-clawed-friend wall coverings as out front, and Paris looked suspiciously at every single one of them. She made it to the far left corner, turned around to face us, gave one last nervous sigh, and lay down with her head on her paws in a pile of shivering poodle.

With the room fully examined, she slowly started to settle down. Her panting slowed, her eyes grew heavy, and in the next moment and in typical Paris behavior, she started to snore.

Yes, she started to snore; talk about being weird. When I get stressed or scared, I have an overriding drive to eat. It's not like I'm that picky to start with, but throw in some stress and I'll eat just about anything. But when Paris gets stressed, she'll usually scream at the top of her lungs for a good while and then she'll hit the floor like she hasn't slept in three dark periods. One minute she's whining and the next she's snoozing.

By the time the white-coated mom walked in, Paris was so far asleep that she didn't even budge.

17

JULIA
APRIL 2009

I just knew it. Everyone had told me to relax, but I had a feeling. Relax, don't worry, it's probably nothing. Well, I don't think so.

After waiting for what seemed to be an eternity, Dr. Smith finally walked in. Her graying hair wasn't in her usual ponytail but was pulled back in a neat bun held together by a series of black bobby pins. She had on her blue slacks, and today's blouse had a picture of two German shepherd puppies. Her white lab coat was immaculately pressed, like always, and it glowed a cheerful white. With just one look at me, her smile transformed and her face became all business. She was halfway through the door, but I just couldn't wait any longer.

My voice was panicked, hurried, as if I would forget what I had come here to say if it didn't come out in the next breath.

"Dr. Smith, I'm really worried and this is obviously not a bug bite. One minute he's running around without a care in the world, jumping over waves, and the next minute he's, well, just look at him."

I took a short breath, only filling my lungs halfway, while she finished crossing the room. She rested one of her hands on the aluminum exam table.

"He's in so much pain. And the shoulder, feel it . . . the bump is twice the size. The antibiotics obviously didn't work."

My mind was working faster than my mouth could keep up with, and I realized that I wasn't forming coherent sentences or putting together my strains of thought. I was speaking like I was winded, and knowing what I was doing only frustrated me more and made it even worse. She had been patiently listening, letting me expel my concerns. She had just stood there, half-leaning on the exam table on her one hand, while the other was slowly scratching her chin, internalizing what I said, filing it into sections of her brain and, hopefully, sorting out what was important and what was not. When I got to the part about Eddie not being able to walk properly, she nodded ever so slightly, and her eyebrows furrowed.

She barely responded with anything but a short, empathetic

"Uh-huh, uh-huh," and when it seemed that I had nothing more to say, she acknowledged me with an "Mmmm" and a big nod of her head. Without a word further, she bent down and examined Eddie, taking her time despite my prodding stare.

Paris, bless her heart, was still in the corner, not having moved since she had finally settled down. Her breathing was deep, and I could hear the steady, deep, rhythmic sounds of her breaths as she lay there in an overspent daze. I couldn't deal with her awake right now and thanked my lucky stars that she was out for the count.

I watched Dr. Smith's face, searching for a frown or a smile, looking for anything to prepare me for the news that something was terribly, awfully wrong. I tried to read into what she was really thinking because I hate doctor speak and hoped she knew better than to try to pull that crap with me. I had heard way too much of it in my time.

All of the doctors I've ever dealt with did it, dancing around the point and hiding behind their fancy terminology. If someone's going to die soon, his or her prognosis is *guarded*. It's a *terminal* cancer, not a *deadly* one. It's a *malignant* tumor and not an *eat-you-from-the-inside-out-and-spread-into-every-damn-bone-in-your-body* disease. Why didn't they just go ahead and spit it out?

My hands were shaking and I felt queasy. I had to get a grip.

So with every fiber of my being, I did my best to think about controlling my breathing. That's what they always said to do in all the movies, so why not try it this time out? It couldn't be any worse than where I was headed. It took about ten breaths to actually manage to choke down my fear and be functional again.

I decided I would let her finish Eddie's exam in peace and without interruption. I would use the extra time to concentrate on calming myself, and I would let her speak when she was good and ready. And so I waited, and waited, and after she had spent a full thirty seconds listening to his heart, I felt my impatience starting to get the better of me again.

I thought that this was getting a little ridiculous, and that she needed to at least say something, anything. I needed to hear that deep, reassuring voice, that "Oh, it's nothing, Julia; its harmless."

But she didn't say a word and instead began squeezing his belly.

I couldn't take it anymore, the silence and the suspense, and so, going against exactly what I had just told myself I wouldn't do, I asked, "What do you think is going on? I know it's not some kind of bite, that's for sure."

She didn't respond because we both knew I was speaking for the sake of speaking, filling the unbearable silence, and so, adding insult to injury, I let out a nervous laugh at the end of my sentence.

"Is this cancer? I mean, what else could it be? I'm really scared that it's cancer."

I was actually babbling now, and she still hadn't responded. What was I thinking?

I was embarrassed on top of being frightened, but again I resolved to just shut up, to stop talking and really just be quiet this time. She needed to finish Eddie's exam.

Had I really just said out loud that I was scared? It had just slipped out. How awkward. I snapped my attention back to Dr. Smith, because after keeping quiet and ignoring me for such a long time, I decided she had better have something very intelligent to say when she finally got around to doing it.

After an eternity of waiting, she did speak, but to my chagrin, her tone was not the relaxed, you're-overreacting, don't-be-such-a-hypochondriac kind of tone I had desperately hoped for.

Instead, she said, "Julia, let's not be too hasty here. I know you're worried, but we'll get to the bottom of it. Yes, cancer is one of the possibilities . . ."

I felt a sudden and overriding deathly silence hit the room despite the fact that she was still speaking. Time froze for me, and I felt something snap in my heart, a tearing, shredding feeling that was ripping open a scar that had been mended together and held tenuously by waxed paper. I gulped and forced myself to keep listening.

"But there are plenty of other things it could be. It could be a benign mass, an inflamed cyst, or a foreign body, like a foxtail."

There it was, doctor speak: *benign, cyst, foreign body. Come on, Dr. Smith* . . . now I knew it was cancer. She hadn't fooled me for a second.

"The first step, Julia, is to do an aspirate of it, especially since it's grown from last week. Eddie will barely feel it. We'll take a very small sample of the mass with a needle, put it on slides, and I'll send them to the lab. We'll have results in one or two days and I'll call you as soon as it comes in."

So that's the test that will doom him. A simple, sharp little needle will be the instrument, the fortune-teller, the messenger of his slow, painful, drawn-out death. I wouldn't let that happen; I'd put him down before I went down that road again.

"In the meantime, I'm sending him home with a nonsteroidal anti-inflammatory. It's like doggy Tylenol and will help with the inflammation and pain. It needs to be given every twelve hours. That should take the edge off until we get the results."

I was watching her lips moving but still in a semi-daze and thought, *So why are you standing there and wasting time? Just do it.*

56

Let's get on with it, I want to get this over with.

I resisted the temptation, suppressed the urge to tell her what was really on my mind, because she was a nice woman who was trying to be helpful, and I knew that my reaction wasn't her fault. I had no right to be rude to her because my feelings were tied to something deeper. There was no need to take it out on her.

With an almost sleeplike and frighteningly well-controlled tone, I answered in the sweetest voice I could muster, "Okay, Doc, let's do it. Can we put some sort of rush on it, though?"

18

EDDIE
APRIL 2009

Mom kept looking at me for support while she grunted. It stunk of worry and I wanted to do something, anything, to make it go away.

The white-coated mom was getting ready to grunt and had settled in her paw-half-supporting-her-weight pose with her elbow resting on the shiny table. She had just gotten through greeting me with her standard white-coated greeting, while all the while Mom had been chirping away like a nervous flying-winged friend. I sensed worry in the white-coated mom, but I also knew she wasn't going to grunt until she had finished her greeting properly.

She did finish, and afterward I sat between her and Mom so she could tickle me, which hopefully would make her feel better.

She grunted, and Mom nervously responded, and when Mom was finished gesturing with shaking paws toward me, the white-coated mom lifted her paw from the table and turned around. She walked to the far wall to the cabinet, reached up and grabbed the handle, and opened the door for all of us to see.

Nesting there and as relaxed as puppies after feeding were multiple swarms of sleeping clear-bellied bees. Their stingers were pointed right at me, and I dared not make a sudden move to wake one of the things up.

I turned my head slowly, looking first at the white-coated mom and then at Mom to see what they were doing. I had hoped that the sight of the bees hadn't freaked Mom out more, and that she remembered that they usually left the moms and dads alone; it was only the furry friends who made them angry.

I jerked my head toward Paris, but luckily she was still asleep, or was pretending to be asleep. One look at all of those bees would have driven her over the edge, and no amount of grunting would have talked her down.

I sensed movement behind me, and one of the bees must have stirred because suddenly the white-coated mom reached out and grabbed it. She had small paws, and her claws had on a clear coat of paint.

I had been watching the white-coated mom closely, but I suddenly caught a waft of the sour smell of worry moving past me. It had come from Mom who was reaching to put her paws around me and I prepared for what I thought would be a soft, gentle hug.

Well, she hugged me, all right, but wow, it was definitely not so gentle! I had seen Mom do some amazing things, like lift furniture and drag Paris halfway across the floor, but given how small and skinny she was for a mom, I had forgotten just how strong she could be.

Through the hug I managed to find the energy to look up and saw the white-coated mom walking toward us. Her paw was wrapped around the body of one of the see-through bees, but despite her efforts to hold it back, the escaped bee was making its way toward me.

Mom was scared; I felt the shaking of her biceps against my ribs, but to be quite fair, I wasn't completely sure if it was due to fear or her muscles growing sore from squeezing so tight.

Mom, as it turned out, wasn't the target, as I had already known, and I ended up getting pricked. It didn't get just one sting, mind you, but three stings in a row. And talk about aim; this one got me right in the tingly spot.

The white-coated mom backed away from me with an empty-bodied bee in paw, and Mom finally relaxed her grip. I smelled that Mom's fear had passed, but I still sensed concern.

I turned my head to have a look at the sting site. I smelled the salty red iron of injury and licked the small red droplets of liquid that had formed. I wasn't too crazy of the taste; it reminded me of the metallic taste of water that had been left sitting in a feeding bowl for more than three light periods.

Blaaachhh, it tasted terrible, and I kept licking the air around me in an attempt to wash my tongue of the aftertaste. Mom was still out of it and she seemed pretty down.

What could I do, what could I use?

Of course: my whining, bee-fearing crazy loud poodle; she would be perfect. Annoying, yes, but since she always liked to be the center of attention, I thought I would give her what she liked. So I decided to wake her up.

I doubted she was really and truly sleeping anyway, and so I *volunteered* her help. It had been a rough light period so far for Mom, and I needed all the help I could get. I put my muzzle about two inches from her ear, took in a deep breath, and belted out a long howl as loud as I could.

I saw the jerk in her body but, overall, the poodle didn't budge. I knew she had heard me; they'd probably heard me two territories away. She didn't open her eyes and was doing her best to pretend she was still asleep. I was getting ready to go again, but before I got a sound out, I felt something small and light rebound off of my lower back and hit the floor with a slap.

I saw a thin claw-tip length, bright-green meaty crunchy treat lying on the ground next to me. I forgot all about Paris, Mom, the Bee Territory, and just about everything else then, and inhaled the treat with only two chews.

What my bark hadn't done, the sound of my crunching did. I turned to face Paris, who was sitting with perfect posture just staring closemouthed at the white-coated mom. She was doing her best to look good, and even more amazingly, she was on her best behavior. No whining and no performing, it was truly amazing what the power of green-meat crunchy treats can do. And as it turned out, Paris had picked this very time to gain a liking for crunchy treats.

The white-coated mom tossed a green crunchy treat her way.

While Paris was sucking on the end of her treat, the white-coated mom grunted more to Mom, and then turned and left the room. Mom took her time getting up, moving slower than usual.

As we were walking out of the room and into hallway, the white-coated mom caught up with us and handed Mom a small round orange tube with a white round cap. It was filled with small, red-and-white nuggets that clicked with every step Mom took.

Hmm . . . now how do I get a taste of one of those?

THE DOG DAYS OF THE PAST

* *JULY 2007* RICHARD'S DIAGNOSIS *

JULY 2007 RICHARD'S TREATMENT

-

-

-

-

-

FEBRUARY 2008 DAVID MEETS SOMEONE NEW

MARCH 2008 RICHARD'S CANCER SPREADS

MARCH 2008 DAVID'S TEMPTATION

MARCH 2008 RICHARD'S FINAL DAYS

-

-

JUNE 2008 RICHARD PASSES

JULY 2008 DAVID'S LUNCH DATE

-

SEPTEMBER 2008 DAVID'S CHOICE

-

-

-

-

APRIL 2009 EDDIE'S CLINICAL SIGNS

APRIL 2009 EDDIE'S DIAGNOSIS

MAY 2009 EDDIE'S TREATMENT

JUNE 2009 EDDIE'S SIDE EFFECTS

JUNE 2009 EDDIE COMPLETES THERAPY

JULY 2009   EPILOGUE

19

JULIA
JULY 2007

Mom had said to be there at seven o clock sharp. I had asked her three times in a row what it was all about, why the mystery, but she had vehemently refused to tell me.

"Some things are better said in person, and I promised your father I wouldn't say a word. Now stop putting up such a fuss and be here at seven. Bring David."

It's truly ironic how life is sometimes. The call would have had to come on my way home from my session with Kirsten, my therapist for the past two years. We had made a lot of progress during that time, yet one of my goals—the source of my problems, as it turns out—still remained unresolved. I just had two words: my mother.

No matter how hard I had tried, no matter my intention when I had set out to do it, I couldn't bring myself to relive what I had so long tried to forget. And the thought of digging up that past, that sordid painful history with Mother, and, of course, the confrontation that would follow, had made me sick to my stomach. So what were the chances of her calling at that minute, as I literally walked out of Kirsten's office?

It was bad enough that I had spent the last thirty minutes making excuses to Kirsten about why it still hadn't been the right time yet to talk to Mother, and trying to justify my fear of the confrontation. To have Mother call right then had added insult to injury. But the call had been different from usual. There had been something off about her tone; it had been ominous.

The conversation had left me unsettled. Something about it hadn't felt right, and for some unknown reason it had given me a strong case of the butterflies. David had just shrugged when I told him about it, and he'd asked if my mother was at least making dinner. He had long ago quit trying to understand my parents, especially Mother. He knew our history, and wisely hadn't interfered.

Yet that ominous feeling had persisted for the rest of the day. By the time we sat down in their living room, I was a bundle of nerves.

I had racked my brain, trying to figure out what was going on, or how I had offended her yet again, but to no avail. My stubborn battle-ax of a mother had succeeded in unnerving me yet again. It was one of her talents, and boy, did that woman have skills.

What earth-shattering slight had I offended her with this time? Maybe it hadn't been me; could it have been David? Maybe Eddie? Maybe Paris? You never knew with that woman; she was completely unpredictable, except for the fact that you knew that whatever it was, it most likely had something to do with her and her alone. And offending her wasn't a hard thing to do.

Or was it something else? The economy was bad right now, but I assumed that Dad had put enough away for retirement a long time ago. He had kept working in the store because he wanted too, not because he had to. Right? He had sold his hardware store three years earlier on the condition that he could still work there as long as he pleased, and that's just what he had done.

My mother could be so frustrating, but in that call there had been something in her voice that had given me pause. It definitely wasn't out of character for Mother to blow something out of proportion, to make any situation revolve around her, but this had been different. It had been her tone of voice, which, surprisingly, had lacked the arrogant confidence of old.

"Come in, dear, have a seat in the living room. Your father's waiting in there for you."

It was obvious she had been upset but doing her best to hide it; heaven forbid I should know that she was a real person. Her eyes were red and puffy; she had been crying. She had put fresh makeup on in an attempt to hide it, but I could tell. What was going on here?

I had come prepared to have it out with her for making me so worried, for playing her old mind games, trying to control me. Finally, I had been going to resolve that thorn in our relationship that had left me so injured, so hurt, so damaged; it was time for me to get past it. I had been ready, and as we pulled into their driveway, I had let the frustration at her making me drive all the way out there for some more of her drama inspire me to do what had been long overdue.

But I didn't. One look at her and all my preparation had gone out of the window. I realized that this really hadn't been about her after all, and whatever this was about was very, very serious. I immediately shelved my anger and annoyance and stared questioningly as David had given her a kiss hello. She hadn't said another word but had just turned and led the way into the living room.

The lights were on, even the hallway light, which was abnormal because my dad liked to save energy. There was some Bach playing on the stereo, the same one Dad had bought thirty years earlier.

"No need to replace a perfectly good stereo," he had said when I'd suggested that he get with the times about seven years ago, during one of our father/daughter lunch dates. "Now, honey, why would I need a new one when this one works just fine? Haven't I always taught you to take care of your stuff and it will take care of you?"

Come to think of it, I didn't think a single tape had been played on the "new" cassette player that had been bought fifteen years ago, and I knew that Dad still kept his old records in a box in the garage, right next to the broken, forty-five-year-old record player. Dad was sitting on his worn La-Z-Boy recliner with a meticulously folded copy of the *Health and Fitness* section of the day's newspaper. When he had heard us come into the room, he'd draped the paper on the armrest of the recliner, careful not to crease the pages, and stood up to greet us. Like always, his face revealed no expression, at least not to anyone who didn't know him well. He had been born with the perfect poker face; a shame it had been wasted on a man who refused to gamble.

He looked pale, not his usual calm, healthy-looking self. He leaned in and put one of his large arms around my shoulders, and I felt his semidry lips against my cheek as he gave me a kiss hello. He let go of my shoulders and turned to David and with a slight nod of the chin gave him a firm handshake. I have always enjoyed watching David wince whenever Dad gripped his hand. I knew I shouldn't have, but I couldn't help it; Dad was still a strong man, even at his age.

We all sat down, David and me on the brown leather couch opposite Dad and Mom on the love seat to the right of Dad's recliner.

Dad sat back and crossed his legs, careful not to disturb the newspaper on the armrest or lean far enough back that the La-Z-Boy would recline. He started out in a low, measured voice, a tone that demanded attention without being loud or overpowering.

"Julia, I want you to listen to what I have to say without interruption. I know how you are, my sweet, so make me a promise before I begin, please."

His tender eyes bore into me.

"Umm, sure, Dad. What's going on?" I managed to drag out of my lips. With an opening like that, he had my full attention.

He continued without breaking eye contact. "About three weeks ago, I started getting this pain in my stomach. It started off feeling like a little heartburn, some indigestion, nothing I would ever have given a second thought to. I reasoned it would take care of itself after a couple of hours, like these things usually do, but it didn't, despite taking some Tums. Hours stretched into days. About a week and a half and two packs of Tums later, I thought I'd better tell your mother about it, but I still wouldn't listen to her and see the doctor."

He broke eye contact with me just long enough to shift his gaze to Mother, with a look that was ready to quell anything she would potentially have to say. I turned to Mother to see if she dared interrupt him, but she was staring at the floor.

He turned back to face me and went on. "I thought I did a good job ignoring it, but when my back started to act up as well, your mother insisted that I go to the doctor. Let's just say that I lost that fight. You know how I feel about doctors, but to make your mother happy, I went."

The fact that Mother hadn't butted in and stated her opinion by this point scared me. She hadn't said a word, hadn't interrupted to expound about how she had known more than most about these things because her Uncle Dean had been a doctor, never mind the fact that he was a psychiatrist and never dealt with anything other than mental problems. It's a pity he had never spent more time with Mother; maybe he could have given her a word or two of advice.

But no, Mother was seated quietly, with her legs neatly crossed and her arms folded, not taking her eyes off the ground.

Dad cleared his throat with a gruff, guttural cough before he went on in a voice lower than usual. "Julia, a lot happened after that, but I'll make a long story short because no person should have to get that many tests, let alone hear about them. One of the tests showed something. They saw a lump on my pancreas."

I couldn't help myself, forgetting all about his previous insistence on no interruptions, because at that moment the only thing reverberating in my head was the thing he had just said. "Dad, why didn't you call me to tell me . . ."

He uncrossed his legs and sat forward, jerked up his right index finger to stop me from going on, and in a choked-up but stern voice, he interrupted. "You promised, Jules, and I'm not finished."

It took every fiber of my being to stifle my next comment, but looking at Dad sitting there on the recliner, his face flushed with a seriousness I have seldom seen before, I sat back into the soft recess of the worn couch. The cushion had a faint smell of tobacco, a remnant of twenty years earlier, when Dad used to smoke, and I took a deep breath before nodding for him to go on. David reached for my hand, and I unconsciously grabbed it, probably crushing his fingers, I was so wound up.

Dad also took a deep breath and leaned back again. "Well, they did a biopsy of the mass."

He had made it sound so easy, like there had been nothing to it. I had a biopsy of a mole on my leg once, and they'd had to cut into me to get it. Heaven knows what they had needed to do to get to an internal organ, and although I hadn't been a science major, I knew enough to realize this biopsy had been a major medical procedure. Typical of my dad, he underplayed it.

The next words out of his mouth were spoken in the most sensitive and soft way my dad was capable of. He waited for me to make eye contact. "Now, honey, I need you to relax when I tell you what I have to say next."

The silence was deafening, and I could feel my heart pounding. My mouth was dry, my throat scratchy, and I said a silent prayer to please not have him say what I suspected was about to come out of his mouth. But he did say it, and even if I'd done everything in the world to prepare myself for it, it still wouldn't have made a difference. You can never fully be ready for something like that, especially from some you love. It's like preparing to take a bullet to the head.

And because it was my dad, a man who cut to the chase and never let emotion cloud any decision or discussion, he said it in a typical, matter-of-fact way. It was like stating a universal and undeniable truth: "The sky is blue, women have children, and it rains in winter."

But it hadn't been that; oh, how I wished with all my heart and soul that he had said something like that. If only it had been that straightforward and benign.

"Julia, I have pancreatic cancer."

20

JULIA
JULY 2007

I sat back stunned. The sudden, powerful monotone drone in my ears was overwhelming, and a white noise had heightened all of my senses. My mouth was dry and my palms were sweaty. I knew I could hear a pin drop across the room if need be. I was in shock and just stared at Dad as he searched my face for a reaction. Mother was in tears by this time, all her efforts of emotional concealment having obviously failed, and her newly applied mascara was streaming down her cheeks.

I was completely and utterly speechless. What do you say to that? How do you answer?

Gee, sorry to hear that, Dad. So what's on TV? Oh, that's horrible, I'm . . . sorry?

David responded first. "Richard, I'm so sorry to hear that. Is there anything we can do?"

Dad ignored David and continued to stare at me with a steady, expressionless look, his blue eyes burning two holes through my forehead that pierced into the depths of all I was, all I ever would be, the essence of who I am. He was searching, reaching, grasping to see how I would react and, in turn, seeing how he should behave with me after breaking such devastating news. At least, that's what I'd convinced myself of.

I had always believed I could read my father better than any other person in the world, and at that moment I truly believed that my reaction to what he had just said would drastically change the way he dealt with the journey he was about to undertake. He hadn't taken his eyes off of me, he hadn't even blinked, and so I forced myself to relax every muscle in my face, despite the panic and complete shock that was surging through every vein and sinew in my body.

I took a long, deep, measured breath, making sure to count to three on both inhalation and exhalation, concentrating on calming myself, my nerves, my voice, and any other outward expression of the fear that had just overcome my entire being. In that moment, those cleansing six seconds of life-changing reflection, I had made a decision, a choice, a resolution that would dictate exactly the kind of person I would be from that moment forward. I decided right then and there that I would be strong, positive, my father's daughter. There would be no giving up, no defeat, and no talk of losing. We would get through this, and he would beat it. There was just no other choice. I didn't know anything about pancreatic cancer, but I knew my Dad. He was tough as nails and I was his only child, a reflection of him, and he needed me right then. I wouldn't be a crutch for Dad; he would hear nothing of defeat from me. I would be there for him.

21

JULIA
JULY 2007

I could tell Dad was nervous. His face betrayed no emotion, but I could still feel the tension in his eyes. His deep, dark, chocolate-brown portals to his soul. Although he hadn't said anything, I still sensed the whirlwind of inner turmoil he had been going through. Ever since I had been a little girl, I had been able to gauge Dad and his moods, and Mother had always wondered how.

She had been married to him for forty-five years and still couldn't tell, but I had known. On some level, I thought that Mother and I hadn't had a close relationship because of it, due to some sick, childish resentment on her part. I knew that the problems in our relationship weren't solely due to this fact, but it still hadn't made things any easier.

David had gone back to work after apologizing profusely for not being able to continue to go through the painful wait with us. He had dropped us all off at ten o'clock in the morning but had had to rush to work to meet with one of his top clients. He had sworn that he would be back later to pick us up.

The waiting room in this part of the hospital was small, probably no bigger than twenty-by-ten feet, with two black fake leather couches. Four matching chairs faced a flat-screen TV. We were alone in the room, and I was doing my best to concentrate on the TV, on which a blonde reporter wearing way too much makeup was explaining how some prestigious economist was warning that the housing bubble was about to burst. Mother was reading an old edition of *Interior Design*. There we were, my Mother and I, a woman I hadn't been close to since I was a small girl, not saying a word to each other but holding hands for support.

That whole morning, Dad had showed no emotion, no fear; it was as if he had been completely unaware that he was about to have a major abdominal surgery in which part of his pancreas was going to be cut out. He had told us all not to worry, that this would be no big deal, and he'd even asked David on the car ride over how the loan business was going. I had played my part in the little charade, telling him that I wasn't worried about a thing, that he would be just fine, suppressing any internal doubt to the contrary. With his standard impeccable posture, he had headed into the surgical preparation room, turning around to wink at us before heading through the swinging double doors. I had winked back, feigning a confidence that wasn't entirely there.

I had to be strong because Mother was a mess and he didn't need any more stress. During the car ride and walking through the hospital to get to the surgical ward, she had been uncharacteristically quiet. She hadn't worn any makeup this morning, and the black rings under her red, bloodshot eyes told the story of her state of mind. Surprisingly, I actually felt some empathy for her and was taken aback when she responded, grabbing my hand after Dad left us. I hadn't said a word, but it was definitely unexpected, and I felt her trembling as she gripped my hand firmly with her cold, thin fingers.

I had led her to the surgical waiting room, just down the corridor from where Dad had gone in, and we continued to wait in silence, letting our minds torture us.

All of the tests had shown that the cancer had been confined to the pancreas. The doctor was fairly sure he had caught it before it had spread, or at least before he could see any overt evidence of its spread, and so he had recommended that it be cut out. My parents were told that at least the tumor had been in a good location for surgery, that if it had been somewhere else in the pancreas, the surgery would have been a lot more complicated, if even possible at all.

He told them a lot of things that day, including that the average survival was between three and six months after diagnosis, even with chemotherapy after surgery. Unfortunately, it was a lot shorter without. I had to do everything in my power to control my emotions when Mother told me those statistics. I had gone to their house that night, and Dad had gone to bed early because he wanted to get a good night's sleep. Mother and I were sitting at the dining room table, drinking cups of chamomile tea and discussing Dad's doctor's appointment.

She had been sobbing then, her usual controlled and uptight demeanor completely shed, no longer able or caring to hide her true feelings. Dad had less than a 5 percent chance of surviving for five years. That was yet another one of those thrilling statistics. After she had managed to get that sentence out, I had ended up cradling her in my arms like a baby until the storm of sorrow subsided.

I controlled my emotions because there was no need to cry; it was unnecessary. Damn the statistics; I knew Dad would beat this, he wasn't like everyone else. I would be strong for the entire family: for myself, for Mother, and, more importantly, for Dad. I knew that was what he wanted me to do. My response to Mother had been confident, even upbeat; I told her that the doctors didn't know what the hell they were talking about.

Dad hadn't let me go to the appointments with him, though; he had insisted that I not be involved in that part of things. I had been hurt by that, upset that he hadn't wanted to include me in those conversations, even though I desperately wanted to be part of them. I didn't let him see my disappointment, though, because I had imposed a no-negativity policy on myself and those around me. I would respect his request for privacy. Maybe it was because he hadn't wanted me to see any weakness in him when the doctor had given him the news, or maybe it was because he felt he needed to protect me; either way, I had missed that part of the process.

He also had refused to discuss the statistics with me, telling me that his life wasn't in the statistics' hands. Ironically, that was the same thought I had, but I asked him anyway, more interested in probing to see his reaction to the question. But just like with any question he deemed inappropriate when I was growing up, instead of disciplining me or making me feel like I had done something wrong, he just changed the subject and the discussion was closed. So I was forced to rely on Mother to tell me everything that had been said.

The surgery should have taken about an hour, but I remember it taking a lot longer than that. We had been sitting in the waiting room for two hours already, and I had been getting antsy. It had been so cold in that tiny, closed-in box of a lobby, and despite the low hum of the heater vent above the TV, I hadn't been able to get warm. I wished I had brought a jacket, but I'd been in such a hurry that morning, so terrified of getting to the house to pick them up late, that I had foregone the time to find extra layers, let alone grabbing something to eat. I wished I had at least put on a warmer sweater.

The wait had been excruciating, and I remember feeling like the peach-colored walls of the lobby were contracting. To say that I was becoming impatient would have been an understatement, and besides being cold and hungry, I was becoming nauseated by the smell. It was that damn hospital smell, comprised of antiseptic and nerves; no matter what doctor's office or hospital I had ever been in, the underlying smell had been the same. That smell was one of the reasons Dad gave my mother when he chose to skip regular checkups with his doctor all those years before.

No matter what he said, though, I knew the simple truth was that he hated going to see any doctor and despised hospitals even more, and now just look where he was. It was so depressing and so unfair.

Sitting there in those hard, fake leather chairs, battling the overriding impulse to get up and run away, I couldn't help but wonder how many other people had sat in these same chairs, scared out of their wits, pondering a loved one's fate. How much nervous energy had occupied this room, how many people had shed tears here? How many times had the words *it will be okay* been whispered? If only the walls could speak.

22

JULIA
JULY 2007

"You cannot go back to work, Richard, you just had surgery. Just the thought of it is preposterous."

Mother looked her age then, the lack of makeup revealing the gray sunspots on her forehead and cheeks and the bruised dark circles under her eyes. I almost felt sorry for her, seeing her look that worried and disheveled sitting on the worn, purple wool chair next to Dad's bed in the hospital room.

The hospital had done a decent job of attempting to make the room less depressing. It had decorated it with a framed print of a sunset on the white wall directly across from Dad's bed and two bouquets of plastic flowers adorning the windowsill that looked out into the parking lot. But the room still felt stuffy and depressing.

You couldn't escape the smell of sickness, and no amount of bleach or other cleaning products could cover up the fact that you were still in a hospital, a place we all knew was where people came when they were really sick or going to die. I hated being in this place and couldn't wait for Dad to recover so he could get the hell out of here. He didn't belong in someplace like this.

Let the man do what he wants, even if we both know there's no way he can do it right now anyway; just let him be, I thought after Mother's comment. Maybe not tomorrow or the next day, but I was sure Dad would be on his feet by next week.

"I'm fine, darling. I feel as good as new and as strong as a horse. It was just a little tune-up, nothing major. I'll take the rest of the week off, but on Monday I'm going back in."

And that was that, matter settled, according to Dad. Even in a plastic-railed hospital bed with an IV taped to his left wrist and just having had a portion of his pancreas removed, Dad was still a force to be reckoned with. Especially when he used that deep, no-nonsense, matter-of-fact tone of voice. He was a large man; not fat, but muscular, and even in his late sixties, he looked better than half the men I knew who were half his age. He had a low monotone voice that rang with self-confidence, and when he spoke, everyone in the room stopped what he or she was doing to listen. His presence commanded respect and was intimidating to anyone who didn't know him and his kindness, his warmth, his selfless regard for other people's feelings. Even to this day, David still isn't one hundred percent comfortable around him.

"Richard, you're meant to start chemotherapy in less than two weeks. You need to rest, to recover, to build up your strength. Don't you dare be a stubborn ass in this; don't be a ridiculous, absentminded fool. What on earth is going through your mind?"

I could almost have believed that Mother was genuinely worried, but I couldn't stay quiet and let the onslaught of criticism begin. The man had just had major abdominal surgery, for goodness' sake, and I couldn't hold back anymore, even if Mother was right in this. I didn't want anything more negative hurled toward Dad.

"Mother, he'll be fine. He's a strong man, and when was the last time you remember him missing a day of work?"

I stared directly at Mother with my eyebrows raised and my forehead wrinkled, trying my hardest to communicate to her without words to let the man think and say what he wanted. Let him believe he could do it, let him hold onto a goal, even if we all knew it would be too soon after his surgery for anyone to realistically be back to normal, even Dad. Why disagree and take that away from him? I stared at her, hoping she would understand what any rational being would find blatantly obvious, and that she would just drop the subject. It was a gamble, though, and I prayed that I hadn't inadvertently triggered one of her moods.

She turned her head away from Dad to look at me, then, and as much as I had wanted to be mad at her for starting to nag him after what he had just gone through, I couldn't be. She looks so worn, so beaten down, so tired, not anything like the picture-perfect-and-makeup-done-to-perfection woman she usually spent hours trying to portray.

Mother opened her mouth to say something but quickly closed it and let out a sigh of defeat. I know that it must've taken every ounce of strength and control to suppress the torrent of criticism and advice that was boiling inside of her, but to her credit, she didn't let it flow out. Rather, she took the high ground and, surprisingly, didn't bite my head off for offering her my advice. She must've been extremely tired.

I made a point of visiting Dad every day that week while he recovered in the hospital. We didn't speak much, and he passed most of the time watching TV, but I knew he was glad I was there. Whenever I came, Mother took the chance to go home to shower and eat. It served as a welcome break for her because she hadn't left his side during his entire recovery. Even the hospital couldn't escape my mother's wrath, though, and they had set up another bed in the room despite their policy of no visitors at night because she flat-out refused to leave. She made every threat of a lawsuit known to man against that policy. As predicted, Dad didn't return to work a week later; it took him a full ten days instead.

THE DOG DAYS OF THE PRESENT

JULY 2007 RICHARD'S DIAGNOSIS
JULY 2007 RICHARD'S TREATMENT
-
-
-
-
-

FEBRUARY 2008 DAVID MEETS SOMEONE NEW
MARCH 2008 RICHARD'S CANCER SPREADS
MARCH 2008 DAVID'S TEMPTATION
MARCH 2008 RICHARD'S FINAL DAYS
-
-

JUNE 2008 RICHARD PASSES
JULY 2008 DAVID'S LUNCH DATE
-

SEPTEMBER 2008 DAVID'S CHOICE
-
-
-

APRIL 2009 EDDIE'S CLINICAL SIGNS
*** APRIL 2009* EDDIE'S DIAGNOSIS ***
MAY 2009 EDDIE'S TREATMENT
JUNE 2009 EDDIE'S SIDE EFFECTS
JUNE 2009 EDDIE COMPLETES THERAPY
JULY 2009   EPILOGUE

23

EDDIE
APRIL 2009

No matter what I did, I just couldn't shake Mom's mood the rest of that light period. I tried muzzle-butting her, kissing her, rolling over so she could pat my belly, and even tilting my head at just the right angle to get a snort. It had never failed before, but this time nothing did the trick. I just couldn't get her out of it.

Paris, Mom, and I were in the front room and Mom was sitting on the brown fluffy couch staring blankly at the front wall. She had her head resting in her paws, and her claws were rubbing her temples in slow, circular motions. She hadn't moved; she was just staring and rubbing, staring and rubbing.

The tension in the room became so heavy that even Paris couldn't take it. Not usually one to care about anyone but herself, it even got to the point where she felt it necessary to try some halfhearted cheer-up maneuvers. She walked up to Mom, turned her back so that her rump was pointed at Mom's nose, and just stood there. In her mind, she was giving Mom the *pleasure* of giving her attention. She looked back over her shoulder, waiting for the back rub she expected to come, but when nothing happened, she instead tipped her muzzle and with a hmmph of defeat, lay at Mom's feet. She had about as much success as me, meaning none.

Mom finally stopped rubbing her temples, which now had two circular red marks from her work, and put her head on one side of the couch and her legs up on the other. As her mane sank into the wrinkles of the red pillow, she grabbed the blanket that was draped over its top. She covered her body, sighing as she threw it over her now bare feet and drifted off to sleep.

Paris looked at Mom and then back at me, and with a raised snout turned and scampered off toward the back territory. Mom was in a deep sleep before I left her alone.

As I pushed open the clear flapping wall with my nose, I realized just how worn out I was. Using three legs to get around was starting to take its toll, and it had been a hard day with Mom like she had been. She was sad and the worst part of it was that I had no idea why. I had tried everything to change it—even Paris had butted in—but even with our combined powers, nothing had worked.

I felt the warm air hit me as soon as my head broke through to the outside. As I took in a deep breath, I smelled the crisp, fresh-cut green-covering aroma. The high-pitched scream and pounding air vibrations beating against my chest could only mean that our neighboring dad had been gnawing away the ground with his mini sniff box. I walked over to the rotted wooden fence. I watched him as he sat on the ground-biter while it spat and launched the green grown covering into the air.

The smell always reminded me of rough wrestling games, rolling on the ground with Paris or Dad, crushing the green covering below and freeing that same earthy odor. It should have lifted my mood, but I still couldn't stop thinking about Mom

I ended up taking a snooze next to Paris.

I jerked awake because the noise was unmistakable. Dad's sniff box was getting closer and closer to our territory. Paris's head also perked up. She had sensed it too, and just like every other time his sniff box pulled up to our territory, I could feel the excitement building. Dad was coming!

I stood up, stretched, did a couple of hops to loosen up, and then started barking. Paris was also excited but she didn't yell. That didn't stop her, however, from running from one side of our back territory to the other like a furry friend who desperately needed to mark but couldn't figure out the way outside. After a couple of laps we both went inside, Paris still running while I slowly hopped behind.

The movable front door opened and in walked Dad with his rectangular, black-meat-smelling carrying box dangling from his shoulder. The black shoulder strap was barely hanging on, wrinkling his work shirt in its effort to avoid falling down.

He came into our territory and closed the front territory door, then walked across the room to the small white door under the stairs. His steps were slow and his paws dragged as he crossed the room. He slowly opened the white door that was barely taller than he was and put his carrying box on the floor below the hanging thick furry body coverings. Moms and dads don't have much body fur, and they depend on those kinds of furry coverings to keep them warm in the cold.

He closed the white door and I felt the wind tickle my whiskers as it blew by. He turned to us and clapped his paws.

That was our cue! From past experience, we knew not to crowd him until he had officially put his carrying case down; otherwise he could be one sour dad. He needed those couple of moments to get comfortable in the territory, to adjust, and to unload anything weighing him down.

We sprinted toward him, eager to begin the welcoming parade, and for the first time I could remember, Paris actually beat me to him. Amazingly, she managed to get the first sniff and head rub, and I saw that Dad was even more surprised than me.

He had the confused head tilt going and looked from her to me, and then back to her again. He smelled happy and relieved to be home, and he had a big smile on his muzzle as Paris and I bumped each other to get closer to him.

Not to be beaten so easily, I forced myself between her and Dad and managed to steal a hug and chest scratch. After a further greeting exchange, evenly balanced between Paris and me, he raised his head, opened his muzzle, and howled to let Mom know he was home.

Mom slowly walked into the room, and all the excitement of Dad being back was instantly sucked away. Seeing her like she was made my heart sink; her face still had a blank stare and her eyes were still red and damp. Her cheeks were shining with semi-moist streaks of just released drool, which I knew was never a good sign.

Dad looked up at her and I saw his face turn white. He was still on the floor with us, one paw on Paris's head and one on my belly. The tickling stopped as soon as their eyes met, and his paws stiffened.

He grunted to her softly, his tone one of caution, one of worry.

She didn't answer him straightaway but instead stood in the entryway staring at him in silence. At that moment nothing else existed for me; all I could focus on was Mom and Dad, hoping the stress in the air wouldn't cause anyone to gag. Dad continued to stare at Mom, but Mom, it seemed, was speechless. Her lips were shaking, her jaw was tensed, and it was taking forever for her to answer him.

Mom finally opened her mouth and started grunting rapidly to Dad.

It was then that his muzzle expression changed. I watched it all play out, wishing it would stop. But as painful as it was to look at, I couldn't pull my eyes away. I stared as his entire being completely changed. His happy smell, the one that had surrounded him when he had first walked in, was the first to go. His muzzle straightened, his eyebrows arched, and I breathed in the sour odor of sadness and stress. And the more Mom grunted, the worse the smell grew. Whatever Mom had caught earlier in the day was now in Dad and growing stronger with every grunt.

And then the grunting stopped and the air grew still. I could have heard a flea bounce off of the floor, it was so quiet. I didn't dare move.

Dad did, though. His movement was slow but confident, and he rose from his greeting place next to us and crossed the room to Mom. He took her in his arms and hugged her.

The silence was broken, but not violently. Together they continued to grunt softly, and even I had a hard time hearing them. Dad's grunts were smoother and more controlled than Mom's, but I could sense he was also worried. Whatever was eating away at her was affecting him twice as bad, and the smell coming from him was making my nose burn. He looked so serious.

Even Paris was affected, and I saw her twitching her nose as she lay staring at him with her eyes wide open and her head cocked to the side.

24

JULIA
APRIL 2009

My eyes were growing heavy. Talk about information overload. The Internet was a wonderful thing, but it also could be so frightening. Spindle cell sarcoma, Osteosarcoma, Carcinoma, what was *oma,* anyhow?

"Jules, I told you, I think we're getting ahead of ourselves. Why don't we wait to see what the results are?"

I just knew he'd say that, but it served me right for putting myself out there. Here I was, finally opening up and sharing, like I knew he had wanted all this time, and this was the response I got?

David got up.

He had been so supportive earlier tonight, so gentle, so loving, but I could see he was getting frustrated as the night wore on. I had cried when he walked in the door, attacked him with the storm of emotion that had been building throughout the day, and he had hugged me tight in his arms. I had felt safe then, and just for a moment had actually believed him when he'd said that it would all be all right.

We both were taken aback because me opening up like that, reaching out to him for support and comfort, hadn't been my usual way of dealing with things. But for that moment, just that moment, I had ventured out of my comfort zone, deviated from my now well-established reclusive routine, and had sought some solace through him.

It had taken both of us by surprise, and our embrace had given us enough time to absorb what had just happened. Something must have been wrong with me because the moment the gravity of what I had just done sank in, I felt myself instinctively pull back. I retreated to the safety of my internal protective wall.

He also felt it, sensed it, but knew better than to question it. It was a very awkward moment, and we stared at each other in silence, not quite knowing what to say. Christ, we had been married for twelve years and I felt like I had to force something out, say anything other than dealing with the uncomfortable silence that would only lead to a conversation I wasn't ready to have. That would mean acknowledging the problem, admitting a dysfunction in our marriage, and I didn't want to go there tonight.

So instead I broke free from the hug and felt his arms hesitantly slide past my shoulders as I backed away. I started pacing and ended the moment by telling him about the rest of the doctor's visit. The chance was gone; I had officially locked that door for now. I repeated what Dr. Smith had said, trying to remember every word, and he just stood there, listening intently

I knew I shouldn't have closed up like that, and that it wasn't normal. I wanted to tell him more, tell him about my fears, my hopes, but I couldn't. He would listen, would offer advice, and I knew he would do anything for me, but I just couldn't do it. Kirsten and I had been working on this, and she had said it would take time.

So instead of opening up, I enlisted his help in looking up some Internet information, averting any real chance at a heart-to-heart.

He had agreed to help, doing anything he could to be supportive, to be included in that part of my life. We used the old Dell in the living room; neither of us felt like going upstairs, even though it was where the new Apple was. We needed the light, the open space, and I was glad we had decided to keep the old computer down here. Sure, the screen was ugly, large and bulky and way outdated, but I couldn't throw it away. I was my Daddy's little girl through and through, and I wouldn't throw out anything that still worked, even if it was a five-year-old PC that was as slow as molasses and took at least fifteen minutes to boot up. It still got the Internet, and that was all I needed right then.

We had put it in the far corner of the room just before the stairs, and the garage-sale desk it rested on looked brand-new after it had been sterilized with a thick, clean coat of brown paint. It's amazing what people throw away these days, and after its facelift it perfectly matched the couches.

David had been so good and so understanding. For the first hour, he had even rubbed my back and shoulders while I read out aloud. But as the night wore on, even Mr. Perfect showed a kink in his armor, and I could tell he was starting to get impatient.

That's when he had made the mistake of asking me if I was getting ahead of myself, or being a little overly dramatic about something that we didn't know for certain. He should have known that that was a red button for me, an instant piss-me-off move. Sure, I was a little sensitive, but it had sounded like something my mother would say.

"Julia, stop that excited chattering, you sound like a blabbering monkey going on about how wonderful my vacation will be. I'm not looking forward to it, you must know. Life doesn't always go your way, and it's wrong to presume that I'll return from my trip in one piece. Who knows, maybe I'll like it there and not want to come back, or maybe I might die from a horrible accident while I'm traveling. Don't look so shocked, dear; would it have been better if I had said *pass away*? We could all go at any moment, die in a terrible car accident, a plane crash, or just walking down the street. It could happen to your father, to you, or even to me, for that matter. It could happen to anyone. You're only six years old, but it's better that you learn that early. Now, I've had a difficult day and I can't stand this noise. Julia, Julia . . . stop that. Why are you crying? There is absolutely no reason in the world for it; you're being overly dramatic. You need to toughen up, just like me."

And there had been "Julia, don't you think you're getting ahead of yourself. You're assuming you're actually talented enough to make the gymnastics team. When I was your age, I . . ."

There were countless other memories I preferred not to relive, and unfortunately, David had touched a Mother nerve, and the reaction that had followed wasn't directed at him. I knew I was wrong, but I couldn't control it. My shoulders had tensed and I could feel his grip relax.

The massage was definitely over.

I swung around, facing him, and before I had enough time or sense to gain any semblance of control, I had snapped back at him angrily. "David, you know I don't work that way!"

It had been unfair of me to raise my voice like that, to get so offended at his question. I wasn't thinking rationally and as lame an excuse as it was, I knew I was being ruled by misguided emotion. Besides, how could he have ever known what I felt if I had never allowed him access to that part of me?

His arms had dropped limply to his sides and he had taken a half step back. The dogs, which had been resting quietly near the couch, had jerked up their heads and questioningly stared straight at me, through me. The guilt had been enough to choke on.

David's face had been a mix between surprise and exasperation, like he couldn't decide whether to be hurt or bite back. Stunned, he had made his choice, softly replying, "Sorry," and shrugging his shoulders in dismay.

He hadn't given up, though, and as caring and gentle as he was, he wasn't a runner. I teased him when we were dating about his metrosexuality, but he was a man through and through. When it came to fight or flight, he charged toward fight, even if it meant getting hurt in the process. And I knew he would run into a burning building to save me. Unfortunately for him, over this last year he hadn't been able to find an entrance.

So despite my warning, my angry outburst, he had pushed on. He had taken a half step forward, gaining ground from his retreat, and, with his muscular palms up, gestured to emphasize his point.

"But I hate to see you like this when we still don't know. I just thought it was worth waiting for results before you stressed yourself out."

He couldn't help himself; he was so eager to be my hero, to save me, that he didn't realize he needed to slow down and not trip over me in the process. I could see he knew that he had crossed the line, though. I could feel myself starting to lose control of the anger, the suppressed grief that had just been dragged out from that deep, dark place. The guilt over my outburst was forgotten by that point, and all I could feel was hot, surging blood being pumped faster and faster to every inch of my body.

Hearing him trying to minimize the situation reminded me of how I had felt six months earlier, angry, helpless, and mad at the world for telling me how I should be acting and what could have been. Dad had only been sixty-five years old and it hadn't been fair. I thought I had suppressed those feelings, controlled them, moved past them, but they came back just as easily as breathing. I knew my reaction was entirely unrelated to David's statement, but the feelings and memories had boiled to the surface.

So much time had passed, yet they still festered, and this benign, well-intentioned statement had been about to unfasten the lock that I thought I had so skillfully forged to block away that part of my life.

I was about to respond, but thank goodness the doorbell rang.

25

EDDIE
APRIL 2009

Mom and Dad had been sitting in front of the paw exerciser, staring at the flashing wall screen. It was in the front room in the back corner, opposite the stairs, and Mom and Dad hardly ever used it. They mainly did their paw exercises upstairs, on the much quieter and shinier one. This one was bigger, louder, and had tons of paw dirt on its flat claw tapper.

The only movement up until this point had been the steady tap, tap, tap of the paw exerciser as Mom hammered away with her claws. The flashing wall screen had been changing colors rapidly, and I could smell Dad's impatience as Mom continued to tap away. He was standing behind her, tickling her shoulders, because he obviously wanted a turn at the flashing wall.

There was a point in their grunts, though, when she got real angry with him for trying to steal her turn, and it had almost gotten ugly. She had growled so loud that both Paris and I thought she was going to blow. Her face had grown red and her bark had developed a low I'm-going-to-chomp-you tone. I also smelled that spicy angry smell. It had started as soon as Dad had tried to steal her turn, and by the time he had grunted in objection at how much time she was taking, her angry smell had built.

Two long, musical howls in a row, one high and then one low, had saved Dad from her.

I had heard the sounds of a not-so-coordinated dad approaching the front-room door even before the howl announcement had gone off.

Hearing the territory announcement howl, I howled back in a greeting. It was a low howl that started in the bottom of my stomach and slowly worked its way up until the hound-dog roots in me always caused it to be a loud bark-moan.

Not to be left out, Paris chimed in about midway into my full welcome. My greetings have always been much louder and more controlled but Paris . . . well, hers sounded like a clawed furry friend moments after meeting its end against a sniff box. They always cracked halfway through.

We both jumped up and ran to the territory front door. I really hoped he had brought good smells from other furry friends, and I couldn't wait to find out.

Dad had started to back away from Mom before the greeting howl, realizing that she would not be bullied into giving up her turn. After a short pause and a semi-defeated grunt, though, he had started to move toward her again but was interrupted by the howl.

His back straightened, he swallowed down whatever grunt was just about to come out, and turned around. He walked across to the front territory door, stopped when he got there, and put his eye to the shiny silver hole that he and Mom looked through whenever the greeting went off. He opened the movable front door.

The checkered dad had a red head covering that looked like it was four sizes too big, and it hung on his head at a weird angle. It was tilted to the side, and his long, dirt-brown mane was poking out of a hole in the back. He was holding a large, square, thin box in one paw, and with the other was digging a waxy prize from his ear. The smell coming from that box was nothing short of amazing; it smelled like pure paradise.

It was driving me crazy!

Mom casually walked up, took the square box from the checkered-covering dad, and smiled at him as he nervously eyed Paris. Dad had grabbed Paris' necklace the moment the announcement howl had gone off and the scrapes of her claws as she desperately tried to get traction on the floor grew frantic.

Mom handed him some thin green tree bark and he grunted to Mom before turning to leave. He kept one eye on Paris as he made his way out.

Mom, with the square box in tow, walked toward the feeding room, leaving a trail of mouthwatering smells behind her. Dad let go of Paris's necklace, knowing she wasn't stupid enough to risk Mom's anger. There was no way she would try anything with her; even Paris realized that the results of messing with Mom would be beyond any possible prize that could be had. We all followed the sweet-smelling box and Mom into the feeding room.

They sat down to feed and after what seemed like forever, with Dad downing four triangles, and a large chunk of the yellow covering dripped off of Dad's slice midway to his muzzle. It hit the end of the table, dangling by a thread before finally falling so I could get a taste.

Mom and Dad stopped in midgrunt as my stomach let out a long, rumbling, multitoned growl. Paris, not willing to be left out of anything I did, also decided to have her tummy growl in response. Mom and Dad looked at me first, but then at Paris as her stomach chimed in. Then they turned to each other.

They broke out in violent snorting, and I knew that the food had helped pick up their not-so-long-ago bad moods. The air suddenly cleared of the stinky smell of anger.

THE DOG DAYS OF THE PAST

26

DAVID
MARCH 2008

"Allyson, can I see you in here for a minute, please?"

Allyson had been working for me for about one and a half months, and I was starting to feel like she was a little short in the brains department. The thing about it, though, was that what she lacked in organization and precision was made up for by her people skills.

She was extremely good with the clients, and without her, I wouldn't have closed three huge loans. She was very personable, extremely easy to talk to, and it didn't hurt that she was drop-dead gorgeous. Mix that all with a woman who had a skill, a gift for reassurance, especially with nervous clients who weren't quite sure whether they wanted to go through with the deal or not, and she turned out to be a fairly useful employee.

Heck, I even found myself wanting to spend time with her, talking about life, but I knew that would be inappropriate.

Wouldn't it?

THE DOG DAYS OF THE PRESENT

JULY 2007 RICHARD'S DIAGNOSIS
JULY 2007 RICHARD'S TREATMENT
-
-
-
-
-

FEBRUARY 2008 DAVID MEETS SOMEONE NEW
MARCH 2008 RICHARD'S CANCER SPREADS
MARCH 2008 DAVID'S TEMPTATION
MARCH 2008 RICHARD'S FINAL DAYS
-
-

JUNE 2008 RICHARD PASSES
JULY 2008 DAVID'S LUNCH DATE
-

SEPTEMBER 2008 DAVID'S CHOICE
-
-
-

APRIL 2009 EDDIE'S CLINICAL SIGNS
*** APRIL 2009 EDDIE'S DIAGNOSIS ***
MAY 2009 EDDIE'S TREATMENT
JUNE 2009 EDDIE'S SIDE EFFECTS
JUNE 2009 EDDIE COMPLETES THERAPY
JULY 2009   EPILOGUE

27

EDDIE
APRIL 2009

The next light period the tingling in my shoulder had grown so strong that it forced me to spend the time doing something I hardly did.

I did nothing.

I wasted the entire light period lying outside next to Paris in her favorite place next to the smoker. I was very limited due to my newfound shoulder problem.

The territory ear tickler howled, and I heard the thump, thump of Mom bounding from upstairs to downstairs to get to the sound. From all of her stomping, I figured that something important was going on, so I limped my way into the inside territory to see if Mom was okay.

I smelled the room and her worry before I even saw her: the bitter smell that screamed of stress. I could hear buzzing vibrations of the ear tickler that should have been taken off of its job of ear-itch relief ages ago. It should have been replaced with a simple, long itch-relieving claw.

Mom held it up to her ear and without warning, her eyes started to drool.

28

JULIA
APRIL 2009

"Are you sure, Dr. Smith? Oh my lord, oh my lord . . . Yes, I'm still here. You want me to go where? You faxed all the paperwork already? Okay, I'll call right now. Okay, thank you."

I struggled to get that last sentence out, hung up, and listened to the echo as the black receiver slammed down on the floor.

How was I sitting on the ground? I don't remember doing that. The silence that followed felt thick and heavy, and the only thing I was aware of was the violent thudding of my heart as it beat against my chest. I stared blankly at the wall for one, two, three heartbeats before I grew aware of my insides, and my stomach felt like it was on fire.

Reality snapped into focus then, and I realized I had indeed almost passed out and was now sitting on the floor next to Eddie. I was barely aware that I was crying, except that I could feel my shoulders were moist from where tears had fallen. I could hear sobbing in the background, a distant noise that I wanted desperately to block out, but some part of me realized it was coming from me. No matter how hard I tried, though, I couldn't make it go away. Is this what I had done when Dad passed? Did I have anymore left? I thought I had used them all up six months ago. How could this be happening again? It was too much too soon.

Eddie, my little Eddie, my poor lovely dog, how in the world did you get this? I didn't think I could go through this again. I didn't think I could handle it one more time; it was too soon.

No, that's selfish, Julia. You have to stay strong. You've done it before, and you can do it again.

I knew I had to pull it together, just for one more call.

"Hello, this is Mrs. Freed, for Eddie Freed. I think Dr. Smith just called your office. I need to confirm an appointment to see Dr. Lindy. Yes . . . oh good, I just wanted to make sure. What . . . oh, he ate at about seven this morning . . . No, I won't give him anything to eat until after the appointment. Great, 'bye."

29

EDDIE
APRIL 2009

The ear tickler just wasn't cutting it. Not by a long shot. Mom's eyes suddenly began to redden and fill with shiny water, finally spilling over as the drool poured down both cheeks. She then sat, no, fell to the floor, and the only good thing I could see was that she had almost broken the ear tickler.

I almost choked on the smell that came off Mom and that only took a moment to spread. I had to do something for Mom to cheer her up. She was really bad, and I knew that it was the ear tickler's fault.

So I lay down beside her, but she didn't move. Her being on the cold hard floor like this was strange because this place was usually for Paris, Dad, and me; Mom usually chose something cushioned. Something had to be terribly wrong for her to sit down here, and wrong it was, because the next moment she started whining softly. It was a quiet purr at first, but as the moments passed, it built up and grew to short bursts of uncontrollable howls. The louder she got, the closer I moved, and I ended up with my head on her lap.

It was terrible, horrible, and I've never felt so useless. She was completely destroyed, and the best I could do was just be next to her until it passed. So we had stayed like that, Mom sitting there whining and me with my head on her thighs until her whining finally died down, and after a while the only sound was the her breathing and her soft leftover whimpers.

She picked up the ear tickler again.

I wanted to scream, growl, run in circles, do anything other than just watch it play out again. Where was Dad? Where was Paris? No, forget Paris, she would probably have made this worse.

So instead of moving, I just lay there biting my cheeks as Mom picked up and scratched the ear tickler to wake it up again. She then scratched it harder and for a second time put it up to her ear.

The ear tickler didn't do anything to get Mom's ear itch, and the itch was so bad that Mom actually dropped the ear tickler, and as it hit the ground, I hoped it would break into a lots of pieces. But no, the thing was tough, but as it came to a stop, I promised myself that my next mission on any upcoming free dark period would be to put an end to that useless thing.

Mom fell completely apart again. Her eyes went from drooling to raining and not to be left out, her nose started dripping as her whining got worse. The room was still filled with the gross smell of sadness from before, and although I hadn't thought it could get any worse, I was wrong.

I began to feel sick and was doing my best not to gag. I lifted my head and nudged her thigh with my nose, trying to get her attention, trying to stop more of the stink from further fogging the room. The howling continued, but at least she touched my head with a light pat. I tapped her thigh with my nose again, and she shifted her position and got ready up to lie down next to me.

Instead of flattening out next to me, she wrapped her paws around my neck and squeezed me so tight that I felt one of my backbones click. As the hug grew tighter, her whining became louder. She had a hard time taking a proper breath through all the howling and whining, and if it weren't for the forced hiccups, she probably would've passed out.

My nose nuzzle had had the complete opposite effect of what I was going for, and as Mom howled away, I couldn't help being a little taken aback at what had happened. What had gone wrong? Never, ever, ever had I managed to make Mom or Dad sadder than when they had started. Me being around normally cheered them up.

It was a miracle, because finally all the noise had woken the poodle queen from her much-needed beauty sleep, and Paris decided to make her way to us to see what was going on. Even though my neck was being bent practically in half, I could still hear her pads as she made her way to the front room, obviously unsure of what was happening and too scared to find out. I couldn't blame her too much, given the stink pouring out of Mom.

Paris, like just about every other furry friend, hated sadness, and the smell and gut-twisting howling had forced her to see what was going on. She made it to the walkway and froze, and like a pointer who had just eyed a small flying friend, she stared right at us, not daring to interrupt Mom or get any closer. She sat down right under the arch of the walkway, knowing that at this point there was nothing to do but just be near. Even she sensed Mom's pain.

We would not be the first ones to move; we would just keep Mom company and hope that eventually she would cheer up.

It took a while, but Mom's whining finally did calm down, her hug loosened, and I could use my chest again and take a deep breath. She began sniffing to clear the water from her nose, and I nuzzled into her again. This time it actually seemed to make her feel a little better.

Maybe all the howling and whining had done something to her ear itch and she finally had gotten some relief?

I didn't get to finish the thought because Mom again reached for the ear tickler for another try.

30

JULIA
APRIL 2009

"Hello, David, it me . . . No, this is important . . . I'll be fine later, but now I'm just a little overwhelmed . . . Yes, the doctor called. David, it's cancer, just like I told you last night. I knew it. It's something called a fibrosarcoma.

"No, I'm not okay; in fact, I'm pretty far from okay, but I don't want to lose it again, so just let me talk. We have an appointment with a specialist.

"Yes, an oncologist . . . for dogs . . . yes, they exist now, just be quiet for a second. Dr. Smith made it for us, and we're able to get in this afternoon. It's at four today.

"Uh-huh, Dr. Smith thinks he's good . . .

"I'll be fine later, but forget about me for now. Just be here at three to pick me up and we'll go together. . . . Yes, I love you too, 'bye."

I was still on the floor with Eddie in the living room, one hand gripped around the phone and the other patting his neck. I was in a state of shock, dazed, but at least David knew now.

I had kept telling him it was cancer because I had that empty feeling in the pit of my stomach. He hadn't believed me, of course; he thought I was "getting ahead of myself." He could be so annoying sometimes.

I realized that I was not a stable being at that moment, and rather than direct this at David, I needed to focus my energy on Eddie. This wasn't David's fault, and I didn't need to take it out on him, despite his infuriating method of looking at challenging situations.

I loved him, but there's a limit to always being positive, a limit that borders on denial. I used to be like that, always reaching for the positive no matter what was staring you in the face, but oh, how I had learned the hard way. Life just doesn't go the way you want it to, and I didn't want to go down that road again. I wouldn't pretend that something just didn't exist, ignore the obvious, or think that not admitting to it would make it disappear. I wouldn't do that again. I had to be prepared for the worst.

I looked over at Eddie, who was laying down next to me, the constant guardian. He was such a good dog, always by my side when I felt bad. *Oh, Eddie, you poor, poor baby, why did this have to happen to you? Why now? You knew something was wrong, didn't you? You've been trying to tell us this whole time. Don't worry, my angel; we'll take care of you. You are family, boy, and it'll be all right. Don't be sad, we'll take care of you.*

He looked so miserable.

31

EDDIE
APRIL 2009

Well, it must have been a special light period because the ear tickler, that useless tickler, had actually worked this time. Mom's eye drooling had stopped.

She put the ear tickler back down on the floor and looked at me with eyes that sparkled like two shiny food bowls just recently licked and still moist from leftover drool. Her muzzle had a half smile, and I could feel her tender paws as she massaged my neck. I hadn't understood her grunts, but I knew what was in that stare.

She got up and went to the paw exerciser opposite the stairs and started scratching away. Between last dark period and today, she had been stuck to it, and yet again she was sitting in the black chair facing it, frozen in place and looking on the bright flashes of its shiny wall. The only sounds were the tapping of her claws and the steady rhythm of Paris's tongue as she licked her hind end.

Mom appeared to be busy for now, so both Paris and I quietly made our way to the outside territory. We both lay down near the smoker, enjoying the warmth of the sun as it beat down on us. After what I had just been through with Mom, I was tired, and I didn't have the energy to do anything else.

It seemed like I had just closed my eyes before I was being jerked awake to the sound of Dad's sniff-box barks. Today it let off two short, high-toned, sickly sounds, which usually meant he was in a rush to get somewhere because there was no time for long, drawn-out, howl-like barks. I looked up and realized that by now it was the mid to late light period, and I must have been snoozing for a while. It was pretty weird for Dad to be back so early in the light period, though.

Apparently, Mom also had heard the sniff-box barks, and shortly after their shouts, she howled my name. Not that it was necessary; I was already halfway to the back flapping door by the time she had opened her mouth.

Paris hadn't heard a thing, and if she had, she didn't let on. That is, not until my name was howled, and only then did her head jerk up. She looked at me limping toward the flapping door and decided to make a frantic dash inside. She passed me and, being the clumsy poodle she was, gave out a loud yelp as she bumped her head on the white solid strip at the top part of the flapping door.

Unfortunately, Paris wasn't the smartest wolf in the pack when it came to names. She still hadn't figured out my name versus her name and to this light period thought that any time either of our names were called it meant she was wanted.

We got to the front territory room and saw Mom with the territory keys in one paw and her shoulder bag draped over the same forearm. Her other paw was on the front territory door, wrapped around the shiny handle. Ignoring the crazy poodle and with an impatient grunt, she let go of the door and reached out and grabbed my blue necklace. With the keys between her claws, she took my safety rope off the hook that was its home and attached it to my necklace. Paris, who had now stopped panting and come to her senses, gave a questioning whine and pressed up against Mom, waiting for her safety rope to appear.

Paris was left behind and we hurried to Dad's white sniff box, which was purring like an overgrown clawed friend. Where were we going? Were we headed back to the place of sandy water? Was it the Hair Place.

I hoped not because I hated that place, that mom, that water; even the thought of it kept me up in the dark period. I really, really hoped we weren't going there. Getting wet, being rubbed down with bubbly liquid that smelled of land shrubbery, and having my fur cut in all the strangest and most embarrassing places; it wasn't my idea of a good time. Let's not forget the blow-air device; how embarrassing.

And worst of all was the hair mom. I didn't like her unlike Paris, of course, who absolutely adored her and anything she touched. How could she not? There were pictures of Paris-looking furry friends on her walls and her body coverings, and her ear decorations were even shaped like Paris. By the time Paris left the place, she looked more like a lion in leg warmers than a normal furry friend. I, on the other hand, usually was cold, wet, and lighter by a couple of pounds of cut fur.

No, we weren't headed there; otherwise Paris would have come with. She smelled just as good as I did at this point, and we were both one week fresh and counting.

As soon as Mom sat down, she started grunting to Dad. Her voice was higher than normal, and it was filled with worry. My nostrils twitched as they were invaded with the gross, burning odor only a stressed-out Mom or Dad could make. She continued grunting to Dad, and before long, her eyes began to sparkle with a thin layer of drool. It kept building and growing until it overcame her lower eyelids, and after one strong blink, it overflowed.

Just when I thought it couldn't get any worse, it did. She started whining, that heartbreaking, do-anything-to-make-it-stop whining that only Mom could do. I didn't think I could take anymore after earlier this light period, and luckily, I wasn't the only one.

Dad's face scrunched up as if he had just bitten into a crunchy creepy friend, the bitter ones with the juicy insides. He burst into action then, and started grunting softly back at her. I could see he was doing everything he could with his grunts, trying to take away the thing that had her so down. He put one paw on her shoulder and started massaging it with his claws, gently stroking it in an attempt to put her at ease. The sniff box lunged forward.

I lay on the seat with my head arched up so I could look out of the clear back wall but after a while, though, my neck started to feel the strain of having been held up for so long. I just lay there, enjoying the calm, but I knew it had to end.

It came sooner than I would have liked. I felt the sniff box slow and its purring wind down. With a sudden jerk, it came to a stop.

I lifted my head and got my first view of the new territory, one that was to become a regular place in my life. It was big, about the length of five of my home territories, and it was the shaped like a large rectangle. It was a long structure, and it appeared to be made from a million small red rectangular rocks. The red rocks were piled one on top of each other and shaped into long columns that stretched from its black roof to the ground. Between them, spaced every couple of yards, were large, clear, rectangular see-through walls, and I could make out the movement of Moms and Dads inside. I could also see the shapes of quite a few furry friends between them.

I squeezed myself through the two front seats of the sniff box and over Dad's seat, and he helped me down to the black flat ground.

I started walking toward the structure, Mom and Dad following closely behind. I led them through the green archway and its shade and felt the air cool. We kept walking as the archway ended and the red path was swallowed by the front part of the territory.

The building lay right in front of us and we headed toward the sliding territory door. My nose tingled as I caught wind of lots of furry friends who had visited this place. The gossip here beat by far my own neighborhood news. There were reports from furry friends I had never sniffed before, smells of neighborhoods as strange to me as this new structure was, and markings that I couldn't make either heads or tails of. There were tons of messages, and even if I spent the whole light period here, I wouldn't have had enough time to go through them all.

We walked through a clear sliding door and into in a very large and very brightly lit room, and between the clear walls and the rows of polelike hanging lights, the place looked like it had never experienced a single dark period. The walls were made of the same dark red stones as the outside, and there was long row of bright blue benches lining the wall. The benches were broken up by short, square tables lined with stacks of colorful bark-bound rectangles, very similar to the ones that lived next to the white stubby tree in Mom and Dad's marking room. This place could have been the Bee Territory, although newer and the size of two or three Bee Territories in one.

Facing the sliding territory door on the opposite side of the room was a large, wood-paneled semicircular desk with three older moms. They were all dressed in the same pink coverings, and two of them were buzzing about, looking very busy and carrying stacks of white bark. The other one was seated behind one of the paw exercisers and was tapping away.

32

KATHLEEN
APRIL 2009

They always arrived looking like this the first time. I could see it in their walk. They were nervous, overwhelmed, confused, and scared. The man was in his midforties, and I do declare, he was quite the looker. He was about six foot tall and had the beginnings of a blond receding hairline, and it was blatantly obvious by his firm and V-shaped torso that he worked out on a regular basis.

The woman was about five foot two and petite as petite could be. She had long, dark hair, and her eyes were as black as night, but my, oh my, was she skinny. The girl, in my opinion, needed to eat something, eat a lot of things, in fact. I just bet it would only take one delightful Southern weekend with Kathleen to get some meat on those bones. Some good old-fashioned fried cooking, that's all she needed.

Oh, I do declare, that little cherub was a breath of fresh air. He was just gorgeous. And those ears, those long, floppy ears, he looked just like my little Buckwheat. Poor, sweet Buckwheat, rest his gracious little soul, that coonhound was faithful to the last tick but as stupid as wood. Fancy trying to hunt down a grizzly bear; what in blazes had been going through his mind?

I gave my standard warm-as-apple-pie welcome.

"Hi y'all, and welcome to Paws Specialty Hospital. If you would be so kind as to just sign in here. Thank you."

I decided to see just how nervous they really were. Short, curt responses equaled petrified and overly talkative equaled denial on the Kathleen fear scale, and it never lied.

"What's his name . . ."

The lady, who looked like one of those typical Californians who lived on lettuce, whispered back, while her . . . well, what I assumed was her husband, just stared back. It also could have been her brother or boyfriend, you never knew these days, and I had learned long ago in this wonderful weathered state not to presume.

"Eddie," the woman said in a barely audible whisper.

"Eddie, oh, that's just perfect, and what a gorgeous creature he is. He's cuter than a speckled pup in a red wagon."

Nothing, no reaction, their faces were frozen like deer in headlights. They did both look down at the paperwork, though, and it was obvious they were not in the mood for chitchat. That was all right by me; I wouldn't hold it against them. I did, however, concentrate my love where I thought it was needed most.

"Hey, cutie pie, you little angel of a muffin, I could just eat you up for breakfast, lunch, and dinner. Sorry, sugar, no bones for you yet, but you hang in there and we'll see what Aunty Kathleen can round up later."

I looked up to two sets of very nervous eyes that belonged to two hopefully very sweet people. They were here for advice from a cancer pet specialist for their dog, after all; they must be good people.

They were just standing by the desk, waiting to be led to water, staring desperately at the paperwork like it was going to solve world peace. I wanted to tell them everything would be all right, to relax, that this would be as easy as water off a duck's back, but it wasn't my place. They would realize it in good time.

Instead, I said, "You'll be seeing Dr. Lindy, our radiation oncologist today. While you wait, can I get you folks a cup of coffee or a bottle of water?"

33

JULIA
APRIL 2009

I must admit, I couldn't help but be impressed. The place was huge. I had looked it up on the Internet as soon as I'd found out the news, and it had nothing but good reviews. They had two surgeons, two oncologists, a criticalist, an ophthalmologist, an internist, and a radiation oncologist. I had even taken a virtual tour, which hadn't done it justice.

It had red brick walls with tall windows to maximize its natural light. Its cement floors were spotless, while the front desk looked straight out of an interior design magazine. It was hard to believe that this was an animal hospital; it was almost surreal. To top it off, they kept the building cleaner than my own doctor's office.

We sat down on a long blue bench resting against the wall. It had a great view of the outside, and the landscaping was amazing. The receptionist was still staring at us and waiting for us to finish Eddie's paperwork. She was a large woman with big, rosy cheeks who looked to be at least in her sixties, and she reminded me of a Southern Mrs. Claus. Her white hair was pulled back in a bun, and she wore small, pink-rimmed reading glasses. She was nice enough, but a little overfriendly for my taste. What the hell was a speckled pup in a red wagon, anyway?

I turned to David, who was also looking around, and said, "I have a good feeling about this place."

"Yeah, it's pretty extraordinary but I can't stop thinking about how much they must charge to have a place this nice."

I felt my face grow warm and the anger start to build. David noticed it too.

"I'm just kidding, honey; I'm just trying to get a little smile out of you." He put his arm around my shoulders.

Really? How much of that was really a joke? I thought.

But before my temper got the better of me, I looked at him, searching for the sincerity in his face. His eyes were sparkling blue and he was half-grinning. I couldn't resist those eyes and that mischievous smile. The man did have a strange sense of humor, which was one of the things that had drawn me to him to start with. I relaxed somewhat, and realized that I was wound up tighter than a heart attack. But how couldn't I be?

I had been replaying this over and over in my mind ever since I had hung up with the receptionist earlier. What was the doctor going to say? Could Eddie be cured? Or was this the day I found out that I only had a couple of weeks left with him?

No, there had to be something that could be done.

I kept reminding myself that we were lucky we had caught this early. I was trying to do my best to stay positive, in my own way. The radiation oncologist was right around the corner from my house, after all. That had to mean something because today, as I was surfing the net, I discovered there were only sixty-five of them in the world. This guy was only ten minutes from us, which had to be some sort of sign.

I looked down at Eddie after I could have sworn I heard him let out a whine. Even though he was wagging his tail and panting, I knew I hadn't imagined it; he had truly just whined. I had heard it loud and clear, and it had been so heartbreaking.

"David, he's scared. Just listen to him, he's crying."

He shot me another of his sideways smiles. "No, honey, I think he's just hungry."

34

EDDIE
APRIL 2009

We turned away from the mom behind the semicircular desk and left her to her paw exercises. She was wearing thin pink eye decorations, and her silver mane was plastered against her head. She hadn't stopped smiling since we had arrived, and after only just a couple of grunts from her, I had sensed that this mom was very warm and caring.

The eye-decoration mom had handed Mom a small blue scratching stick and a couple of flat white pieces of bark. Getting no real reply from Mom other than a short, unfriendly grunt, she had stopped grunting at Mom and focused all of her attention on me. I liked this mom, strange pink eye decorations and all.

Her greeting was a standard high-then-low-toned greeting whine, but it was done with feeling.

Mom had pulled me away from the table and we joined Dad, who was already sitting up against one of the clear territory walls. He hardly noticed when we sat down because he was looking around the place. I pressed up against his inner thigh, and his paw started tickling my ears. Mom scratched the flat white bark with the scratching stick and when she was finally satisfied with all the scratches, she returned the bark and the scratching stick to the eye-decoration mom.

Dad was still checking out the place and Mom was at the eye-decoration mom's desk and so I took looked around. There were two other furry friends attached to safety ropes, one sitting with his dad farther down the bench from us, while the other was at the other end of the room with his mom. The furry friend closest to me, the one with his dad, had a tiny little black body and a rounded head twice the size it should have been. His head was enormous compared to his torso, and what made it look even bigger was the fact that there was a square bald patch directly above his eyes. It was perfectly square and painted in blue, thin, straight lines with an *x* in the middle. Poor little guy; he had obviously had a run-in with the hair mom.

The furry friend on the other side of the room was humongous, had a long, solid black coat of fur, and was sitting at the paws of his elder mom. To say that he was huge would have been an understatement; sitting down, he was almost as tall as the mom. He easily must have been twice my size, though his fur was so long, it was difficult to judge what was hair and what was muscle. He had big, droopy eyelids with dangly cheeks that hung down past his lower chin. There was so much skin to those cheeks that if he ran too fast, they probably would have poofed out with air. He also had two long, strings of drool hanging from either side of his mouth that swung to the left and the right as he was scanning the room for potential threats. His rounded ears were dangling against his large head, and as I looked him over, I realized that he too had a blue-painted square bald spot. His, however, was on his side, by his ribs.

A thought popped into my mind then. Maybe, just maybe, this was another one of the hair mom's places, after all; what were the chances of having two crazy fur jobs in just one building? Without thinking, a very soft, what I had thought was a silent whine came from my muzzle.

I hoped no one had heard it.

I wasn't that lucky; Mom had noticed it, and started to rub my belly vigorously. Not that I'm opposed to a good belly rub, but it had to be for the right reasons, and this one fell far from being that.

Her next eye-drool-causing whine to Dad was horrible, and what made it worse was that I knew she had been stressed out to start with. What had I been thinking with that whine? Now, because of me, she was even more out of it than before.

I love Dad for many, many reasons, but at that moment it was because of his sheer cheer-up talent. It only took one quick, upbeat grunt with a matching look, and he managed to repair most of my damage. Mom exhaled, smiled, and seemed better.

My body rub was stopped when the eye-decoration mom let out a loud growl and motioned for us to follow one of the other pink-covering moms who had been behind the desk. Like the eye-decoration mom, this one also had a silver mane, but hers was cut to shoulder length. She was about as tall as Mom, but must have been twice Mom's age.

From behind the desk, she opened up a waist-high door and stepped out into the front room. She then got us to follow her with a paw wave. She walked past the curved table to the end of the room, where she led us to a rectangular doorway. She pushed the door open, and we were suddenly in a long, narrow hallway.

The walls were all made of stacked red stones, and bright lights were hanging from ceiling poles to light the way. There were no wall decorations on the long hall, but I did see four identical wall openings. Two sets of doors were on the right and another two were on the left.

As we passed the first set of wall openings, I realized that these were entrances to other rooms and, unfortunately, the doors were closed, stopping me from seeing inside. The pink-covering mom kept walking until she reached the second set of wall openings. She stopped, and with a smile and a short grunt, motioned us to turn right and go inside. When we were all in, she closed the door.

It was a small room made from the same red rectangular stones as the rest of the territory. There was a picture of a clawed friend hanging on the back wall, while the side walls were bare. There were three blue chairs made from the same material as the benches outside, directly below the clawed-friend portrait.

There was a long, silver shiny table about the height of Mom's waist in the middle of the room, and it reminded me of one of the Bee Territory room tables.

The table was connected to the side wall, and on it sat a paw exerciser, a flashing screen, and a small red half-full beehive, the place that calmed bees went after stinging a furry friend.

Mom unhooked my safety rope, and I began to explore. It wasn't a big room, and I knew I could search it in no time. I started sniffing around, following the floor around the shiny table at first, and then moving on to the corners. I found plenty of traces of furry friends: little pieces of fur, a nail bit, and even evidence of a long-ago dried marking on one of the bases of the walls. Unfortunately though, there were no crunchy-treat fragments.

I was still in midsniff when the door to the room opened, and as his black paw covering came into view, I got the first glimpse of the dad I would be getting to know real well. As he walked in, I was almost blinded by the whiteness of his long bright coat; it actually made my eyes hurt.

The dad who wore it strolled in, and I was instantly overtaken by his relaxed and soothing smell. It brought to mind the feeling you got the moment you lay down on your sleeping cushion after a long day of running, that warm, tingly feeling you felt in that first instant, that moment of time when every muscle in your body relaxed. His smell was that feeling.

He wasn't a big dad, but his scent was strong. He was a short dad, taller than Mom but still shorter than Dad, and he had a medium build, but it was hard to tell under that blinding white coat. He had an interesting coat of thick black face fur, which extended from the top of his head, stretched around his muzzle, and then circled around his mouth.

Normally, if I was in a small room with Mom and a new dad walked in, the first thing I would have done would have been to stand in front of Mom, just in case of any funny stuff. But it was different this time around, especially because the smell that had come before his entrance; that calming smell that leaped from his body made it clear to even the Paris-level-of-intelligence furry friend that this dad was the furthest thing from being a threat.

He stared directly at me, smiled, and then turned to Mom and Dad. He walked right past me, grunted, and reached his paw toward them.

It was an average-sized paw, as far as dad paws go, but seeing him put it out like that announced that he too knew of the paw game. I waited for Mom or Dad to give him a crunchy treat for his paw touch, but it never happened. Instead, Dad grunted and then grabbed his paw and jiggled it. Mom also grunted and did the same.

I was still in a daze over his smell as he turned to me and grunted. I had thought that his smell was relaxing, but his voice proved to be sleep inducing, with its deep, smooth tone. I could tell he was trying to sound excited with his greeting to me, expecting me to get up and play a little, but between the voice and the smell, the only thing I wanted to do was lay there and have Mom finish my belly-rub massage.

35

JULIA
APRIL 2009

The guy looked professional enough, but, wow, he was young. How old could he be? Thirty-five, maybe thirty-eight at most; and what was with the facial hair? How did it go . . . you trusted guys with beards, or didn't you trust them?

Focus, Julia, focus.

He introduced himself and made sure to look me right in the eyes. His eyes were a deep brown and betrayed a wisdom far surpassing his youth. He was staring right at me, but I had the feeling that he was seeing through me, sizing me up with his semihypnotic stare. I was taken aback; for that brief second, I had the feeling that everything would work out just fine, and Eddie would be okay.

I was still a little startled as he introduced himself, and not wanting to be rude, I reached out and shook his hand. He had a firm handshake, which proved to be another point in his favor. I hated men with limp grips because it usually meant they were weak in other facets of their life. I liked a strong, firm handshake, and my dad always said they showed character.

Then the guy got right on the floor with Eddie and started hugging, patting, and speaking to him in baby talk. I'd never seen a vet do that before, and it was another instant point in his favor.

He was magical because Eddie, who normally would be trying to wrestle anyone who got down to his level, just rolled over and offered him his belly without so much as an effort to barrage the man with kisses. I had never seen Eddie so submissive with a stranger; normally, he was only that comfortable with either David or me, so this guy must have been something special. I guess you trusted guys with beards after all; that must be how the saying went.

First impressions are very important to me and, given the last couple of minutes, I knew I liked this man already. As with any man who had already won the difficult first battle in gaining the interest of a woman, the only thing he could do now was screw it up by talking.

He leaned down and gave Eddie a big hug, and when Eddie turned to lick his face, he closed his eyes and started laughing. "Okay, boy, okay, you keep that up and my wife's going to get jealous."

After a couple of more licks, he gave Eddie a big kiss on the top of the head, got up, and walked over to the computer.

"Wow, he's a licker, all right."

He grabbed the yellow, tubular lint-removing roller off of the counter behind the screen, unpeeled the nonsticky layer, and started rolling it over his coat. He was smiling and seemed a little out of breath, but he looked as happy as a clam.

"Eddie is a real sweet boy. I've already gotten all of his paperwork from Dr. Smith, and I spoke to her about half an hour ago, but I would love to go over a little bit of Eddie's history with you before we go on."

I decided now would be a great opportunity to just sit there and hear him out. There would be plenty of time for questions later. Both David and I nodded in acknowledgment

"I hope you don't mind if I type while we talk. We're paperless now; we finally made the switch, and between you and me, it cuts down on our trying to figure out each other's handwriting."

He smiled a little wider, and it was then that I realized that this guy's natural facial expression radiated joy. Some more of the tension in the room, mainly mine, lifted; just hearing the musical, upbeat tone of his voice made me feel more relaxed.

"So when did you notice a problem?"

David was quiet and was just staring down at Eddie, who was still sprawled out on the gray lacquered concrete floor, so I took control. I cleared my throat and started. "Well, I'm not exactly sure, but I think it was about ten days ago that Eddie started limping on his right leg. When we looked at it, I saw what I thought was a spider bite. It was about pea-sized and was red, so I was a little concerned. I really love this dog, he's like my child, so I took him to Dr. Smith straightaway, and she thought it was a bug bite as well. She told us that if it got any bigger, we should bring him back. She gave him a shot of . . . um . . . ."

"Benadryl, according to the record," he said.

"Yes, that's it. She also sent him home on antibiotics. The mass didn't change that much, and I kind of forgot about it."

"Then, yesterday, I took the dogs to the beach. I was running them—oh, we have a standard poodle mix named Paris, by the way—and that's when I thought Eddie had hurt himself. He ran to fetch a ball, and when he came out of the water, he was limping."

I was interrupted by a short, low "woof." I looked down and saw that Eddie, who had been lying down a second earlier, had perked up his head, was holding his chin to the side, and smiling and panting expectantly. His tail was in overdrive. I laughed and felt the cold air as it touched the newly forming tears in my eyes. I had just said the magic word: *ball*. It was one of the few words he recognized, along with *walk* and *no*.

I needed to concentrate and couldn't break down yet. That would be ridiculous, having just met this man, never mind completely embarrassing. This wasn't the time. I had to pull it together and, whatever happened, I needed not to cry.

"Sorry, boy, not right now. Sit . . . good boy, just lie down . . . good boy."

After hearing the change in my voice, David looked at me and put his arm around me. He knew I was on the verge of tears and, thank goodness, he took over.

To shift the attention away from me, David said, "You know, that's Eddie's favorite thing to do. He's been doing it since he was a puppy. He'll actually swim out past the breakers to get the . . . you know, B.A.L.L.; it's the most amazing thing to watch. One of these days I'm going to post it on YouTube."

I couldn't cry now; it would be so humiliating. I had to think about something else, and quickly. So I looked around, trying to find something to focus on. It was my standard defense. The wall? No, it was just plain, boring brick, nothing there. The table? No, it was an uninteresting silver vet table. The computer? Yes, the computer.

I focused on his fingers as they typed away. They were thick and stubby, and he had a bulky gold band on his ring finger. His fingers were moving a mile a minute, and I began mentally timing his finger strokes while attempting to work out how many words a minute he was actually doing.

Pull it together, Julia! This is ridiculous; you're a grown woman and should be perfectly capable of having a conversation without turning on the waterworks.

I took a couple of deep breaths and felt my sanity start to return.

"Which limb was he holding up?" Dr. Lindy interrupted David.

I had recovered enough to know that I could probably say something without breaking down. With a faked confidence, I responded. "It was the right front one. I checked to see if he'd stood on something, or if he had a cut, but when I touched his shoulder, I felt the bump. You know, I had forgotten all about it because it didn't seem to be bothering him, but now it feels like the size of a ping-pong ball. It had quadrupled in size in just a week. I feel so guilty and like such a bad owner. I'm usually very attentive to . . ."

I stopped myself then, because I wasn't there to throw a pity party; that role was already filled by another member of my family. I needed to keep on topic. This was about Eddie, not me. I didn't want to turn into my mother.

"I rushed him straight to Dr. Smith, and she did an aspirate of it. She just called me today with the news, and we got in here as soon as we could. Thank you, by the way, for squeezing us in. I know you're busy, but I really appreciate you seeing us on such short notice. It's a beautiful hospital, by the way."

Why did I say that? That's his job, after all, and who cares how the hospital looks? I must be nervous. Stop babbling, Julia.

He responded, "Thank you, and of course I was only too happy to see Eddie. The aspirate came back consistent with a fibrosarcoma, but before we get into that, how has Eddie's appetite been?"

I was a little flustered and didn't want him to get the wrong impression. I felt foolish because I had emphasized the "really appreciated" part of the sentence just a little too much. This guy must have thought I was a complete basket case. I decided to be quiet and let David answer this one.

"Great, Doc. He would eat a horse if we could fit one into his food bowl."

With a genuine chuckle, not one of your standard fill-in, polite responses, the vet said, "That's usually the case with these guys; their tails and appetites usually work without fail. What about his energy level?"

I could feel the lump in my throat coming back, but I forced myself to speak. "He's definitely slowed down over the last couple of days, and just today he spent the whole time sleeping with my other dog. That's very unusual for him."

"Has Eddie had any coughing, sneezing, vomiting, or diarrhea?"

"No," I said.

"What about his medical history? Any medical procedures or problems in the past?"

The air-conditioning in the building must have turned on; suddenly, I felt the room grow colder. I could hear the low hum of the fan and looked up to see a painted red vent right above my head. It blended in with the bricks, and I wished I had brought a sweater. I didn't need to start shivering right now; it would be the icing on the cake.

Ignoring the temperature, I said, "Nothing major, although there was the time Eddie got into the trash and swallowed a stocking. He had to have surgery to have it taken out. Other than that, he's been pretty healthy, except for the occasional ear infection."

David chimed in, "There was also the time he jumped the fence and cut his leg open. He hasn't been that adventurous since we had him castrated, though."

I looked over at David and smiled to myself; that one had been a battle I'd won. Huh; suddenly it wasn't so cold.

Dr. Lindy stopped typing and turned around to face Eddie. He put his stethoscope on the table, and a ruler-sized, thin yellow plastic object right next to it. It was long and circular at the end, with a round plastic head and, looking closer, I realized it was a pair of calipers. They were the same ones Dad used to carry in his hardware store. I wondered what they were for.

I looked down at Eddie, poor little guy; he didn't know what he was in for, and neither did I.

36

EDDIE
APRIL 2009

The white-coated dad stepped away from the table and headed my way. He was still giving off that friendship smell, and as he got closer, it grew so powerful, I couldn't help but smile. He reached me and then dropped to one knee in what could only be an invitation to wrestle, and I felt my tail start to swing and twitch in anticipation.

I had to answer back so I put my elbows on the floor, straightened my back paws so that my tail pointed to the ceiling, and prepared for his first move. But instead of wrestling, he grunted softly and instead reached slowly for my head. He had made no sudden movements or given any sign that we were about to go at it, and as it became clear that I had gotten the whole wrestling thing wrong,

This dad obviously wanted something else, though, and being of the white-coated breed, that something else involved going through the whole white-coated greeting.

And so began the greeting that every white-coated mom or dad I have ever been around has done. He gave me the white-coated paw and body rub, and then reached into his white-coated pocket and pulled out his own set of ear extensions. He then gave me the ear-extension chest pat, belly squeeze, and another round of a whole body rub-down. What was different about this dad's greeting, though, was that it took him about twice as long as I'm used to with this breed of dads and moms, and he really took his time, paying attention to every little detail of the greeting. He was really into it.

He wasn't that big of a dad, but his paws were definitely strong, and I felt that strength as they worked their way down my body. I won't deny it, it felt great, and between the massage and the cloud of happiness around him, I was more relaxed than a clawed furry friend locked in a room full of catnip.

His black-furred head was making its way toward my shoulder as his paws were moving toward my head, which I knew would be a great opportunity to give him a greeting of my own. And so, just as his paws started rubbing my neck and I could sense his breath on my ears, I turned my head and shot out my tongue in an attempt to lay on a quick, wet kiss of approval.

Instead of making contact with his cheek, though, the dad turned and I ended up with a waxy taste in my mouth as the tip of my tongue buried itself in his ear.

He jerked his head back like he had just been stung by a bee, but instead of the pain and anger, he snorted and rubbed his ear with his shoulder, and I felt his forearms wrap tightly around my neck as he attempted to give me a lick back. Like all moms and dads, though, he hadn't quite got the concept of kissing right, and instead of putting out his tongue for a nice juicy lick, he instead just bumped me with his muzzle and made a sharp, clicking sound with his lips.

He then reached onto the table and grabbed a thin, straight white stick with two small short claws at the end. The stick was about the length of one of my ears and had small, dotted marks along its side. The dad carried it toward my shoulder and adjusted it with one of his paws, and I noticed that he could make one of the claws slide up and down the length of the stick. He put it on my tingling shoulder bump, and I expected to feel the soothing sensation of a good scratch, given those two pointy claws.

Unfortunately, the thing was to be useless; the only thing I felt was my shoulder bump being gently pinched and squeezed between the two claws. I waited and waited, still hoping that the thing would be put to good use after it let go of its first pinch, but instead of a good, mark-leaving scratch, it changed direction and grabbed my shoulder bump from a different angle. Mom grunted questioningly at the dad.

37

JULIA
APRIL 2009

Holding up the calipers with a wide and warm smile, he said, "They're to measure his mass. Its three point five centimeters in length, four point two centimeters in width, and three centimeters in height. The rest of his physical exam is unremarkable except for a mass on the bottom of his chest. How long has that been there?"

Dr. Lindy was wrapping up his exam of Eddie, and I was mentally worn out from all his questions.

I answered, but the weariness was betrayed in my voice. "Oh, that thing. It's been there for years. Dr Smith aspirated it about two years ago, but she said it was fat."

"A lipoma?"

"Yes, I believe that's what she said."

His voice was soothing, calm, and borderline trance inducing. So far, I liked him, especially his bedside manner. His tone, his looks, his overall persona flowed with a contagious calm that was perfectly suited to his profession. By the expressionless look David was giving him, I could see he was still testing the waters. It usually took a while for him to warm up to anybody.

Dr. Lindy sat down on the floor next to Eddie and started tickling his belly. He looked like a man settling onto a sofa to watch a long movie, but I knew he was gearing up for a long conversation.

It had been such an overwhelming day already, but I knew everything had been building up to this conversation. It had been a roller-coaster ride of emotions for me, dredging up all the old memories I had so desperately tried to put behind me. And now we were approaching the climax, when whatever came out of this man's mouth would either leave me utterly destroyed or give me some hope that the world wasn't completely unfair.

I prayed that it wasn't somewhere in between; for me, that would have been the worst possible scenario, even worse than hearing that Eddie had only a couple of days to live. As crazy as it sounds, the thought of limbo was unfathomable. If it was bad news, at least I could prepare for it this time around. I hated feeling so helpless, so lost and at the mercy of some untenable force. I needed reality, facts, time lines, and this time I would do my best to believe them.

"Well, folks, I'm going to go over a lot of information, but before I get started, I want you to know that this isn't the only time you'll get to hear about it. I'll go over it as many times as you want, and I'm always available by phone."

My stomach had already begun to twist into knots, and I thought to myself, *Come on, get to it already, guy.*

I held my breath as he began.

"Eddie has been diagnosed with a fibrosarcoma, which is a cancer composed of fibrous tissue. Being a cancer, it has bypassed or lost the ability to stop dividing. Normal fibrous tissue is made up of cells that divide a certain number of times before they naturally die, but these cells continue dividing to a point where you can actually feel the mass growing. If left unchecked, the mass will continue to grow, and eventually its cells will invade into the bloodstream, at which time they can spread to other parts of the body. "

He had my full attention, and despite my nerves, I was able to take in every word.

"Fibrosarcomas fall into a broader category of tumors called soft tissue sarcomas. For canine tumors, there are a lot of different types of soft tissue sarcomas, but in general they all act similar. That's what we're mainly going to talk about today."

His voice was calming but articulate, and I couldn't help but realize that he was very well spoken. No ums, ahs, or repetitious fillers; his words just flowed.

"They tend to be locally invasive, which means they like to grow in a specific region and mainly only invade the surrounding tissues. In general, most have a low rate of systemic spread, or metastasis, but that depends on their grade. They come in three grades, a term we use to predict their behavior, although in reality we can divide them into two general classes: those that are locally invasive and don't like to spread, grade ones and twos, and those that are locally invasive and have up to a forty percent chance of systemic spread, the grade threes.

David beat me to it, "Which grade is Eddie's?"

"That's a great question, and I'll answer it in just a second."

He had avoided the question; why? What did that mean? Was it because it was bad?

"The first thing in this process is to determine whether there's any evidence of disease spread. We need to look for spread in places other than the shoulder. Metastasis occurs primarily through two routes: the bloodstream and the lymphatic system.

Given the location of the tumor, one of the most likely lymphatic routes would be to the draining lymph node, and in Eddie's case that would be the prescapular lymph node, the one that rests just under his shoulder. The most common vascular location would be to the lungs, given how many blood vessels drain there. To check out both of these places, I'd like to do an aspirate of the lymph node and an X-ray of the chest."

Did he feel that Eddie had a big lymph node? Is that what I had heard? "Is Eddie's lymph node big?" I asked, my voice higher than I had intended. I started panicking because I had read something about that on the Internet, and from what I remembered, that meant it was bad. "Does it mean that it's spread?"

Dr Lindy responded calmly. "That's a great question. Eddie's lymph node is normal-sized."

I exhaled a sigh of relief. I hadn't realized it, but I had been holding my breath, waiting for his answer.

"Even though it's not enlarged, there still can be cancer cells present in it. That's what we should check out."

I felt my stomach tighten a half turn more.

"The other thing I'd like to do is a full panel for blood work. Not because I think the tumor is in the bloodstream, but to test that all his organs are functioning correctly. The blood work also will help rule out any other concurrent disease processes. I'd hate to start treating this and find out that there was something else growing all along. By staging, or doing the tests that I just mentioned, we get an idea of his overall health status, and I can base my treatment recommendations on those results."

I hoped he was going to write all this down because my head was spinning.

"As far as what grade this tumor is, at this point we don't really know. Unfortunately, you can't grade a tumor based off of an aspirate; you actually need to submit a biopsy of the sample to get the grade. In Eddie's case, getting that sample will be part of his treatment, which I'll cover shortly. Any questions about what we've discussed so far?"

I looked over at David. He had a strange but familiar expression on his face that immediately jerked me out of any trance Dr. Lindy's voice had managed to induce. His eyebrows were tensed, he had his mouth half-closed, and he looked as if he was going to say something highly intelligent. Unfortunately, whenever he got that look, the exact opposite occurred, and something inappropriate trampled out.

If David was thinking what I thought he was thinking, I swore I would kill him if he opened that dumb mouth of his and verbalized his thoughts. I looked at him, knowing he was just about to ask the question, but luckily for him and any hopes of ever sharing my bed again, he looked at me before any permanent damage had been done.

38

DAVID
APRIL 2009

The guy sounded fairly smart, and I could see Julia really liked him. But hell, he mentioned a lot of tests he "would like" to do. I'm sure he'd like to do them; how else could these guys afford a place like this? The overhead must be insane.

And Julia . . . she'd do anything for Eddie, even mortgage the house. He's a great dog and all, but the guy hasn't even gotten into the treatment part yet and I feel like I'm in Vegas. Do this, *ching ching ching*, do that, *ching ching ching*. Poke this, *ching ching ching*, cut that and jackpot! I wonder how much we're talking about here: two grand, five grand, or is it sell-your-soul-to pay-for-it grand?

I looked over at Julia, who was hanging on his every word. Her eyes were fixated on him with such intensity that if there had been an earthquake and the building had fallen down, she wouldn't have noticed. Her face was an open book and I could see the storm raging within.

Damn it, did this have to happen now? She had just been starting to get right. She was too frigging attached to that dog, and it being so close to Richard's passing, how the hell can I say no to anything? Bye-bye, Hawaii vacation; it's only been two years in the planning. Eddie, you're going to owe me big time for this.

I didn't have a choice, not with Julia in this state. At the end of the day, it didn't matter how much it was; I knew there was no other way. It's a good thing this was a good year for loans; let's just hope business stayed good.

The vet finished his monologue and wanted to know if we had any questions. I was just about to ask the burning question: "So what's the bottom line, how much is all this going to cost?" But Julia cleared her throat right before I could get it out.

I glanced over at her, and her look of death sucked out any chance of my asking the obvious question I believed any rational person would. If pissed off could have taken a form, it would have manifested in Julia's expression. She was scary-looking, with a cold and piercing stare full of menace that communicated that she wasn't just going to kill me but rather rip me to shreds before tearing my heart out if I dared to say what I was thinking. How did she know?

Whether she knew or not wasn't important because after seeing her expression, I thought I'd better just be quiet. I turned back to the vet and shook my head.

39

JULIA
APRIL 2009

It's lucky for David that he was smart enough to keep his big mouth shut. After all these years of being with him, I knew what he would say before he even thought it. Call it intuition or a good guess, but I could swear I knew what he had been going to say next.

"So Doctor . . . what was it . . . Lindy, oh yes, Lindy. So between you and me, how much will this set me back?"

I would have decked him right there and then. Like this was even a choice, like money I knew we had was going to be the reason I gave up on Eddie? But he had had enough sense not to be a complete buffoon. The man was economically savvy, all right, but my biggest complaint about him had been that he sometimes bordered on being cheap.

David looked over at me. His cheeks were flushed, but he managed a little smile, and while the doctor was looking down at Eddie, he lifted his hands in surrender and mouthed to me *what?*

He was pretending innocence, but he looked like a kid who'd just been caught with his hand in the cookie jar. We both knew what had been on the tip of his tongue, and cute smile or not, he appeared to be as guilty as sin.

I didn't bother responding; he knew what he'd almost done, and there was no reason to get into it with him now that the threat of embarrassment had passed. Instead, I turned to Dr. Lindy and asked, "Does Eddie need to be put out for any of these tests?"

If he had seen David pantomiming, he gave no indication of it. He just stared straight at me and in a comforting voice said, "No, Mrs. Freed, it's literally a couple of pinpricks. He should be fine without sedation."

Before I had time to think of another question, he continued, "Now let's talk about what we can do about this mass. The most effective way to address a locally invasive cancer is to get rid of it surgically. Granted, that's if everything comes back negative and there's no spread. Ideally, we would remove the mass and a margin of normal tissue surrounding it in order to achieve surgical margins. When the pathologist looks at the excised tissue, he or she can quantify the margins and hopefully tell us that at least one centimeter of normal tissue surrounding the mass and one tissue plane deep to the mass had been achieved at surgery."

I was interested in what he was saying, but truth be told, I would have preferred just the bullet points. As comforting as he was, Dr. Lindy was very, very, descriptive. In fact, he was a little too descriptive for my taste; it was obvious he loved his job and discussing it.

"They do this because what you see isn't always what you get. Most tumors have little tendrils of cancer tissue extending out from them."

Eddie lifted his head as Dr. Lindy stopped patting him and got up. Without pausing in his description of how tumors like to extend microscopic blah blah blah, he walked over to the back countertop and returned with a pencil and a pad of white paper. The letterhead said PAWS SPECIALTY HOSPITAL, and there was the faint background of a paw in the center of the paper.

Eddie sat up, no doubt looking for someone to take over his head patting, so I reached over. I needed something to do, something to occupy my hands; I couldn't just sit still and keep listening. I was like a chain smoker, always having to keep my hands moving. I was getting antsy.

Eddie moved closer to me and maneuvered himself so I had access to both of his ears, "It's okay, boy, we're almost done. Hang in there."

Dr. Lindy patiently waited until I was quiet and then drew a circle with tiny squiggly lines extending in all directions. It looked like a six-year-old's rendition of a sun with rays of light coming out of it.

He continued, "This circle represents the tumor, and these lines around the circle represent the microscopic tendrils coming from it."

His hand moved slowly as he drew a large square around the circle and lines.

"This square represents the surgical site if we were to try to remove the mass with adequate surgical margins. Now in Eddie's case, the mass is directly over his shoulder blade, and even if the surgeon were to amputate the leg and the shoulder blade, he still wouldn't be able to get good surgical margins."

Hold on a second, what did he just say? Amputate what? I could feel the adrenaline surge as it was suddenly unleashed throughout my entire body. It felt like the temperature in the small orange room had suddenly increased by ten degrees and, like I always did in times of stress, I had an overwhelming urge to punch something; mainly Dr. Lindy, in this case. It was déjà vu all over again; the last time I'd felt like this was when I had first met Dad's oncologist in the hospital.

I couldn't think of that now, though.

I wasn't cutting off his leg; there was not a chance in hell! How would he walk normally? How would he get around? And the pain . . . I couldn't ever do that to him. No way, no how!

I felt my cheeks flush and knew I was going to lose it any second. My surge of energy was about to be overtaken by a surge of estrogen, and I could feel the tears ready to burst through. How embarrassing would that be, if I actually cried right now? I wouldn't do it. I needed to concentrate, to calm down, to breathe and focus. He said "even if," not "we have to."

I had to be calm.

During my hormonal tennis match, Eddie had managed to snuggle closer to me and was now resting his head on my lap. I looked down quickly and there he was, staring straight at me with the sweetest and cutest look he could muster. His ears were draped over my leg, his head was pointed toward my belly, and he was looking up with only his eyes. He sighed and rolled his head to the right, urging me to scratch behind his left ear.

I managed to control the floodwaters of emotion and focused all my energy on the weight of his head on my thigh. I could feel the contours of his ears as they pressed down and was relieved that the diversion had helped center me, focus my attention so I could regain control.

Don't worry, boy, I won't let them take your leg.

"The other option, and my primary recommendation, is to remove the mass without surgical margins and to treat the leftover disease with definitive radiation therapy."

I had forgotten all about David, who appeared to have recovered from his earlier foolishness, and seemed to be thinking the exact same thing I was.

"Let me get this straight. What you're saying is that we don't need to cut off his leg, right?" he asked as he leaned forward in his chair.

David's face was red, and the lines on his forehead were pronounced. He only got like that when he was angry or stressed, both of which happened rarely. He looked genuinely upset. I guess the whole amputation thing had gotten to him too.

"Yes, no amputation. Frankly, I don't think it will change what we do, given the location of the tumor."

David sighed and settled back into his chair, his forehead

wrinkles smoothing out.

"Definitive radiation therapy consists of giving high energy X-rays to the tumor site in order to treat what's left over after surgery." The doctor drew a second circle around the original circle that represented Eddie's tumor, drawing over the little lines representing the tentacles. "In Eddie's case, surgery would remove the macroscopic disease."

He pointed to the large square that had shown his definition of margins and said, "And radiation would treat the microscopic tendrils left over." He motioned the back part of his pen to everything within the square, pointing mainly to the tentacles part of the drawing.

"By treating with both modalities, we should be treating the tumor and all the tumor cells that would be left over post surgery. Definitive radiation consists of eighteen doses of radiation delivered on a Monday-through-Friday basis. We do three-dimensional radiation treatment planning when tumors are in this location, so the first step after surgery will be to do a CT scan. I use the CT scan to do a computerized, simulated radiation plan. I take the images from the CT scan and put them onto a special radiation treatment-planning computer, the same type of computer software used to treat human patients. Tissue is tissue.

"I outline or contour where we want to treat and what we want to minimize dose to. In Eddies' case, it will be his surgical scar plus three centimeters. Then I'll point the beams at this area and work out the best way to treat the abnormal structure—the tumor and its margins—without giving too high a dose to the normal structures around it. With the planning software, I'm able to see what to avoid, what to minimize dose to, and how much dose each structure is getting.

"This planning process takes about one to two days, and the first day of radiation takes about one hour or so. The time under the radiation beam is about two to three minutes and the rest of that time is the first day's setup. This is where we make sure that everything we did on the computer will match what we do on Eddie. We make sure Eddie is in exactly the same position, and to help us out, we set Eddie up in his own positioning device at the time of the CT scan. It's a bag filled with polystyrene beads. When we suck out the air, it keeps a mold of Eddie. That way, we can put him in the same position for all the other days of radiation. Since everything is set up, the other days only take about twenty minutes."

David nodded his head in approval at the positioning-device comment. He was paying close attention after all. He had looked bored most of the last twenty minutes, but one mention of a high-tech toy and he was all ears. How typical. You could be talking about the most boring and random thing out there, but as soon as you mentioned anything about high-tech gadgets, he was hanging on your every word. Seriously, boys and their toys.

I looked down at Eddie, who had closed his eyes and appeared to be half-asleep. He was still in a sitting position and still managing to balance his head on my lap.

"In human therapy, you can tell the patient to be still for one to two minutes, but obviously we can't do that with Eddie. So all patients need to be under a light plane of anesthesia for each radiation dose. We're dealing with exact measurements here, folks, and even a shift of one to two millimeters can make a huge difference. That's why they need to be under. As far as the anesthesia is concerned, it's roughly about eight minutes of anesthesia a day, and the anesthesia I use shouldn't make Eddie that lethargic or groggy after he wakes up."

Did I hear him right? He would need to go under every time? I couldn't have heard that right. I cut him off in midsentence. "Wait, sorry, Dr. Lindy, I think I heard you right, but just in case I didn't, let me ask you if what you said was that he needed to be anesthetized every time?"

He nodded, and like a seasoned pro waited for the follow-up question.

In a somewhat panicked voice, I managed to ask, "Isn't Eddie too old for anesthesia? I mean, he's ten, which is like about seventy in dog years. Isn't that right?"

With a calm and confident voice, he said, "Mrs. Freed, my average patient is ten to twelve years old, and the old adage that every one year equals seven dog years just isn't true. Eddie has a healthy-sounding heart, and if I guess right, he'll have pretty normal blood work. If that turns out to be the case, I would actually classify him as a fairly low risk for anesthesia. Granted, there's always a risk, just like with any other procedure, but in Eddie's case, it's probably going to be a low one."

40

EDDIE
APRIL 2009

I was jerked awake by a high-pitched yelp. Talk about a horrible way to wake up. I had been so relaxed before, and despite the tension from both Mom and Dad, the white-coated dad had managed to put me to sleep with his slow, steady grunts. On and on he had gone, just grunting and grunting; his voice was as soothing as a soft, warm sleeping pillow.

The loud, ear-piercing yelp changed all that, and we all turned to see where it had come from.

Walking—well, actually skipping—just outside of the room was a brown-coated furry friend about the height of my kneecap. He was a tiny little thing, with thin, twiglike legs that were moving a million miles an hour as he scampered past our doorway. He had a huge, round head with eyes that were ready to jump out of their sockets. It was as if someone had squeezed his body so hard that everything had emptied into his large noggin. He too had a bald spot in the center of his head, with a green square smack-dab in the middle. He was about the same size and color as the other mini furry friends I knew, which didn't sit well in the try-to-be-friends department.

I really don't like minis. I know it sounds bad, but in the past I've had some bad experiences. Their height is closely matched to their tempers: short. These guys are quick to bite and slow to make friends, and it's been my experience that the smaller they are, the more frigging vicious they are. They're out to prove to the world that they're the toughest things on four legs. Frankly, I think they are.

This one looked directly at me and wagged its tail, and a shiver ran down my spine.

No way, little guy, I ain't falling for that old routine!

Thank goodness he was attached to a safety rope, although I couldn't see if there was a mom or dad attached to the other end. I'm sure all the little guy was thinking about was the best way to get to me, and just how deep he could sink his teeth in before I could react. *Go ahead, keep smiling, little Mini, I'm not interested. Oh, and keep on wagging that rat tail, yeah right, you and I both know it's all just an act.*

I wanted no part of him or anything to do with the little thing, so I just looked past him and stared at the red stone wall behind him.

The white-coated dad grunted as the mini furry friend's mom slowly came into view. First there was the round white bulge of a belly in the doorway, then one of the thickest and fleshiest paws I had ever witnessed, followed by the rest of a round mom who now came into full view.

She was the largest mom I had ever seen, almost as round as she was tall. She had on a blanket-sized, one-piece tan body covering that miraculously reached from her shoulders to her knees, which swayed from side to side like an oversized body covering blowing in the wind as her body kept going forward. I only got to see her take two steps before she went out of view, but it was done with such an effort that I wondered how her paws continued to support her.

She had been in a midpant and breathing hard, and I had seen a thin film of wet over her red cheeks. She had turned her head to look into our room as she went by and although out of breath, this mom had still been smiling from ear to ear after the white-coated dad's greeting. The skin on her arm had flapped back and forth as she had lifted up one of her giant paws and waved at him. Before the white-coated dad had grunted anything else to her, though, she passed our doorway and moved out of sight.

41

JULIA
APRIL 2009

"Sorry for the interruption, folks, but I think he came by just at the right time. We're treating that Chihuahua for a brain tumor, and his radiation appointment finished twenty minutes ago. Like I said before, most patients are back to their normal selves a very short time after the mild anesthesia."

What a cute little dog that had been. He had been so petite, and those little legs; I could almost cry. I wondered how bad brain tumors were. They couldn't be that bad, by the looks of it, or maybe that owner also caught it early. Who knows, maybe Eddie was lucky compared to that dog. He was so cute, though; poor little puppy. He looked so helpless, awww.

Dr. Lindy continued. "Whenever I talk about radiation therapy, I always prepare owners for the fact that their companion will probably get radiation side effects. That way, if no side effects occur, you'll be pleasantly surprised instead of unpleasantly misinformed. What I'm mainly describing are reversible changes that will probably occur at week two or three of the treatment and will heal one to four weeks after we're done.

"They mainly get inflammation, but only in the region I radiate. At its worst, it will look very similar to rug burn or severe sunburn, what you'd expect if you scraped your elbow on a carpet, with a moist, weepy, oozing skin damage. Now we aren't burning anything, and there's no heat involved, but if I had to describe how it looked, that's my best example. In Eddie's tumor region, that's really the main side effect we see."

He would get a sunburn; I could deal with a sunburn. But for what, I needed survival numbers. I wish he would just get to how long Eddie would have. I didn't want to interrupt him because I knew this other stuff was obviously also important, but my mind kept coming back to the question of how long.

"I'm a big fan of pain medications, so if you or I think he's in any type of pain, I'm going to give him something for it. I would rather have a dog that's more sedate than usual and not feeling as much than one that's bouncing off the ceiling and feeling everything. The effects I just described are common, but the main thing to remember is that they'll heal. A common side effect that doesn't heal, though, is hair loss to the site I radiate. More precisely, hair loss to the site I shave on the first day of radiation. If it does grow back, be prepared for white fur. I'm losing my hair and my wife loves me, so I hope you'll be okay with a bald spot on Eddie's shoulder."

Did he just say what I thought he said? Did he . . . really? I laughed because at that point that was the only thing I could do not to cry. At least Dr. Lindy had a sense of humor.

"Other irreversible side effects are very rare and I tell you about them frankly because I have to. They include the muscle and bone turning rotten or necrotic. These effects are the entire reason we spread the radiation out over a month. If they were to occur, it would be most likely years after radiation, and I would probably write Eddie up as a case study because they're so rare. My outlook is that if a dog lives long enough to get a long-term side effect, that means they've been around for a very long time and we did a pretty gosh-darn good job. In all seriousness, though, it's extremely rare.

"As far as the statistics are concerned . . ."

David had been about to ask him more about the late-term side effects but stopped in his tracks after Dr. Lindy's last half sentence.

It was about time; the suspense had been killing me. This was what I'd been waiting for, the whole reason we were there. Why the heck didn't he start out with this? Why wasn't this one of the first things he'd discussed? I'm sure I would have paid more attention to all the other stuff if he'd just done that.

I held my breath, feeling my heart pounding, a painful hammering that beat on my chest so hard, it felt like it would push through at any second. My hands were clammy and there was also a pounding in my ears. I wiped my palms on my thighs and felt like I was going to pass out. Could I go through this again? Was I strong enough? Did I have anything left to deal with this?

He finally said it. "If we removed the mass and did radiation after, then the prognosis would be . . ."

The world decelerated and his lips moved in slow motion.

"Good."

Everything sped up again, and suddenly I could breath.

"At one and two years, eighty-six percent of dogs are tumor free, and at five years plus, seventy-six percent of dogs are tumor free. In the world of dog cancer, that's a great statistic."

My neck relaxed and I could feel my shoulders loosening. The pounding in my head stopped and my heart rate slowed. I looked at David, and judging by his expression, he was also visibly relieved. I knew how much he loved Eddie, even if he wouldn't ever fully admit to it. He had always referred to him as my dog, but I knew deep down he really loved the little guy.

Dr. Lindy had stopped talking, obviously seasoned enough to let that last part sink in. I enjoyed the sudden and well-timed silence in the room, but the anticlimax only spurred more questions. Now what? What do I feel now? Relief, hope, fear; what's next? I didn't want to be too positive because I feared disappointment, but I didn't want to be too negative because he had said Eddie's prognosis was good. I'm sure that's what I had heard.

Then why did I still have a lump in my throat, a feeling of impending doom, of disappointment, of failure?

Deep down, I knew the answer to that, though, and as much as I tried to avoid thinking about it, at that moment I felt the memories pushing through.

I had refused to believe Mother when the doctor had told them that with Dad's cancer, he probably had only months to live, and if he beat the odds, maybe a couple of years at most. It was terminal, but I wouldn't hear of it, refused to even consider that there was any truth to it, buried it deep within my mind and locked away any negativity from all conscious thought. I wouldn't listen to anything else, refused to even consider it, and attacked those who tried to convince me otherwise.

It had continued that way throughout his entire treatment, up until the very end. I only believed in being positive and continually insisted that he was going to beat it. I now realized just how extreme it had been, the way I'd been, how unrealistic my expectations were, and in retrospect, what I had thought had been being positive was really just being in a complete and utter state of denial.

I had blinded myself to the truth and it had kept me from honestly admitting what was really going on. It had hindered me from finding a rational balance between having hope and accepting the inevitable. I knew David would disagree, even though he had been one of the people who had unsuccessfully attempted to give me a balanced footing. He would tell me that of course I was right to have been positive, to have had hope. He would've said that there was nothing wrong with believing that Dad could get better, but I now know that the extreme to which I took it had been wrong.

I knew what David had been thinking during Dad's treatment, but even after all this time I still couldn't bring myself to discuss it with him. We still hadn't had a real conversation about the whole thing; I wasn't ready to deal with that yet. Besides, who needed to speak? It was over, and I could handle it myself.

Concentrate, Julia. That was different; that was Dad's cancer. The vet had just said over five years; they had said months for Dad. Come back to now. This was about Eddie. *Focus!*

I managed to push the memories back into the darkness and took a long, deep breath. He'd said greater than five years. It would be a miracle if Eddie made it to sixteen years old even without a tumor. The knot that had been in my throat loosened, and along with it went my last vestiges of control.

They weren't tears of pain but tears of relief that poured out. I could feel their heat as they slid down my cheeks and onto my shirt. I had been so strong in the office up until now, but I couldn't hold back any longer. It just happened, and it was totally beyond my control.

Eddie opened his eyes, looked up at me, and cocked his head to the side. He let out the cutest soft howl, and I couldn't help but let out a cough of laughter.

David put his arm around me and Dr. Lindy handed me a cardboard box of white tissues. It had pictures of flowers on it. I felt so embarrassed and so weak, and I knew I was being ridiculous.

"I'm sorry, guys, I can't help it."

"Mrs. Freed, please, it's perfectly natural. You love him and I can see that."

David joined in. "It's okay; it'll be okay, honey." He started rubbing my back with his palm and I could feel his soft but firm touch.

I needed to take the attention off of me. I hated being patronized.

"So from the sound of it, Eddie could be all right?"

The doctor took a second to answer. "Potentially, yes. But there are steps we have to take to find out more information before I can really tell. Do you have any other questions before we go on?"

David was still rubbing my back but asked, "I know you said he's a low risk, but tell me again about the anesthesia. Eighteen times under; are you sure that's safe? Oh, also, do you guys treat on the weekends?"

"Unfortunately, we only treat during the week. All the statistics I've mentioned take that into account. As far as the anesthesia, it's a very light plane, and it's short. I won't brush the risk under the carpet, but as I've said, these guys do really well. The hardest thing for them is getting used to a new routine, which usually takes about three days."

I felt tired suddenly and couldn't think of anything else to ask. The doctor had been pretty darn thorough, and I was emotionally and physically spent. I needed to process. I needed to get out of this small, stuffy room. I looked at David to see if there was any sign of hesitation on his face, and what I saw squeezed the last tear out.

He had that determined look, and I knew he would do anything to make me happy; it was in his eyes. There really was no decision here.

42

EDDIE
APRIL 2009

The bushy-tailed furry friend was within reach. I was one muzzle length away and gaining. I could feel the wind and small rocks as they were launched up from the ground as his back paws scampered inches in front of me. He was a light gray and spotted black little creature with a poofy tail one and a half times longer than his short little body. He was fast, but I was faster, and there were no safety trees in sight, no shelter to reach. That safety tree had offered protection for this little guy for way too long, and I had purposefully waited until he had moved past the tree safety zone before giving chase. I started sprinting as soon as he was just far enough away from the tree. Nowhere to hide today, you-long tailed, nut-collecting scavenger. Nothing to climb, nothing to throw at me today, huh! Just you, me, and two more steps . . .

I jerked awake, startled, as Dad moved all of a sudden. Oh, that had been such a nice dream. I had been so close, so near; just one more moment and he would have been mine. That nut-happy, poo-throwing, bushy-tailed furry friend had been teasing me for way too long, and he had been moments away from getting what he deserved.

We were still in the same room, and the white-coated dad had finally stopped grunting. The dad's voice had been so relaxing that without realizing it, I must have drifted off again. The blue chair creaked as Dad got up, I heard the cracking and popping of Dad's knees and ankles as they started to carry his full weight. I also got up slowly. I was a little stiff and still sleepy, but at least my body didn't make the funny noises Dad's did.

Dad handed my safety rope to the white-coated dad. As we walked into the large, open, next room, I looked around. The room was broken up into four sections, split up by three long, shiny silver tables similar to the room from which we had just come. Each of sections looked the same, mirror images of one another.

The place was buzzing with activity, and I counted at least seven other moms and dads busy with one thing or another. They were all doing different things. One dad was playing with a small, spotted, long-nosed furry friend, while another was pawing at a blue liquid-filled container. A mom was washing her paws at the most left-sided table, while there was another mom who appeared to be cleaning another one of the shiny tables. Even though they all were doing different activities, they did have one thing in common: they all looked like they were in a serious hurry.

43

BRANDON
APRIL 2009

It had been a busy day so far, but shoot, at least it was nearly over. The doc had overbooked, and there was just this last fit-in appointment to go before I had to jam.

Between giving the chemo and the staging, I was exhausted, and dude, that little Chihuahua punk had almost taken off a finger.

"He's real friendly and would never harm a fly," Mrs. Fernandez had said.

Yeah, right. And I've never inhaled. That little punk was a land shark and damn, if I weren't so quick, my guitar-playing days would have been toast. What was up with that? The lady could have given me some warning instead of trying to stare at my ass. Dude, I really hoped this last one was cool; I needed to get outta there.

Dr. Lindy walked through the swinging doors with a medium-sized Lab mix. He was pretty standard-looking, more Lab than mix, but he did have these crazy long basset-hound ears. His tail was at least wagging and he looked friendly, but he was limping bad.

Dr. Lindy was moving fast; looked like the guy wanted to get out of here early too.

"Come on, Eddie, good boy. Hey, Brandon, can you give me a hand? We need a lymph node aspirate, blood work, and a three-view chest."

He practically threw me the chart and then handed over the leash.

"Sure, doc, just give me a sec to get a good hold."

I grabbed the leash and the dog licked my arm. He was still wagging his tail, even having just been pulled double time with only three working legs and all.

The dog was panting and had a huge smile from cheek to cheek. He looked up at me and winked, and his tail started jamming even more. This guy was cool; we could do this.

"Hey, dude, how you doing? Good boy."

I gave him a pretty good rub-down while the doc got the slides from the cabinet. He also pulled out a twenty-two-gauge needle for the lymph node aspirate. I grabbed hold and made sure to tighten my grip; the last thing I needed was for the doc to get bit. That would score some points, not!

"All right, Doc, ready when you are."

44

EDDIE
APRIL 2009

A shiny-headed dad came over after some initial grunting by the white-coated dad, and started giving me a head rub. His paws were large, strong, and made their way backward, scratching and rubbing and he found my belly and then my ticklish spot. His aim was perfect, like a flea-finding blood, and instantly my back leg started moving a million miles an hour.

The white-coated dad had walked over to the counter and reached up to get something from one of the shelves. His white coat lifted as he stretched to put his paw on something, and I couldn't help but hope that he was getting something for me to eat. I'd take crunchy kibbles, soft kibbles, soft meat, or hard meat. Who was I kidding? I'd eat rocks at this point, I was so hungry. My stomach growled and I started drooling. I was starving.

From my angle, I had a clear view of the shelf the dad was so desperately trying to feel, and with a satisfied grunt, he closed his paw over something. They were small, clear, rectangular structures about the size of one of my toes, and from where I was, I couldn't pick up any scent to them.

The white-coated dad put two of the rectangular structures on the table, which made a sharp, snapping sound as they made contact. Then he turned around and reached toward the white counter, and the sliding, scraping sound that followed made me aware that he had pulled open a drawer. He grabbed something, but his back blocked my view.

It was at about that time that I quite paying attention because the shiny-headed dad began rubbing my ticklish spot even harder while putting his other paw around my muzzle. I couldn't move given my back leg reacting to the rub, but I became aware that the white-coated dad had put his paw right above my tingly spot. I felt the pressure of his paw as he began to massage it, and I could feel his claws kneading their way deep into my shoulder.

I felt a strange pressure, as if he was trying to grab something deep under my skin. It didn't hurt, but it sure felt funny. I tried to turn to the white-coated dad, but the shiny-headed dad was in the way with his paw around my muzzle.

And then the mystery of the place was solved. What happened next left no question as to what this building was for and who exactly called it home. The dads, the moms, the decorations, the smell, and the sharp prick in my shoulder right where the white-headed dad had been rubbing clued me into one simple fact. This was positively not the Hair Place, but this was yet another angry Bee Territory.

I hadn't had time to react; everything was happening so fast. There was a quick, sharp prick that surprised me more than it hurt. I hadn't been prepared; I had let down my guard.

The sting was over and the white-coated dad was rubbing the bee-sting spot. He had a guilty look on his face as he turned to me, and I could smell the iron liquid that had been pulled from my shoulder. Now that I had a good idea of what the place was really about, I just hoped they handed out treats like they did at the other Bee Territory.

The white-coated dad grunted, turned with the now-satisfied bee in paw, and grunted to a short, skinny mom who was standing at the next table over. She grunted back to the white-coated dad in a soft voice, and the mom started walking over to us. She made short little steps half-steps, and the front of her paws hit the ground just under where her body was.

Was she scared of me? I didn't think I looked that scary. It was the ears; it's always been the ears. Nothing in this world with ears like mine can ever look scary. Now if you took away the ears, it might be a different story.

Not one to be rude, I decided to introduce myself and ease some of her worry. I hated being feared; it upset my stomach. Just as she got close enough, I reached up and put my paws on her tummy. Well, actually, I mainly used my left paw, since my right was pretty much out of commission.

She just about went down from my weight and stumbled back in three of her half-steps. Right at the last minute, though, she found her footing and got her balance back. She snorted, and the shiny-headed dad joined in. She patted me then, and I sensed she was more relaxed than before.

We all started walking toward the left side of the room, passing the three shiny tables. We walked to a plain white door with a black frame, and just above it shone a red glowing and flashing square. It was a darker red, not too bright but not too dull.

CAUTION: X-RAY ROOM
USE APPROPRIATE LEAD PROTECTION.

It was a small room, about the same size as the room where Mom and Dad probably still were. It was hard to make out details because it was darker than any of the other rooms I had been in so far. I couldn't tell the color of the walls it was so dark, let alone see even a couple of feet in front of me, but I could make out a large shape up against the wall directly across from us. As my eyes adjusted, I realized that it was the only thing in the room.

I looked at the thing, focusing on its strange shape. It looked like it was a table, but there was a long pole with a paw hanging above it. The pole was about as thick as my neck, and it reached up from the table only three-quarters of the way to the ceiling. On the end was a thing that looked like a paw that had had its claws cut off. It was a big, big paw. It was square, and it had a see-through window where its pads should have been. I could see a light right in the middle of it, and it was probably the only light that was on in the room.

Without warning, the shiny-headed dad let go of my safety rope and started putting on thick, blue coverings on his chest and paws. Judging by his grunts and the slight bend in his knees when it draped over his shoulders, the coverings were heavy. The skinny mom did the same thing, but with a lot more effort, grunting, and knee bending.

It only took a few moments, but after they were done decorating themselves in their heavy coverings, the shiny-headed dad bent down and, out of nowhere, grabbed me, lifted me up onto the table, and lay me down on my side.

I froze in shock—okay, fear—as the shiny-headed dad grabbed my front paws while I could feel the soft grip of the skinny mom as she held onto my back paws. It's not like they needed to hold me there; I couldn't have moved even if I'd wanted to since I'm afraid of heights.

I was so scared that I barely noticed that the light-shining paw had moved directly above me and was shining its light right on my chest. What now? Was it going to burn a hole there? That would be just great, just perfect.

The paw moved to above my chest and made a clicking sound.

Ahhh! What the heck was that?

I didn't have time to be too scared because between the mom and the dad rolled me on my back and I heard the clicking sound again.

Ahhhhh! If I had marked by accident on these nice moms and dads, I couldn't be held responsible. Not now, not like this. A furry friend is a furry friend, after all, and right now I was pretty darn scared.

I was rolled over again, but this time to the other side, and I heard the clicking sound one more time.

I didn't think I could take anymore, and just as the table was about to get a wet, yellow reward, the shiny-headed dad lifted me off and back onto the ground.

45

BRANDON
APRIL 2009

Well, he wasn't light, but he'd been pretty cooperative so far. Hadn't moved a bit. I might actually make it to band practice if we kept up this pace. I just needed to take some blood and I was outtie.

"Hey, Suzie, will you hold him while I get some blood?"

She was cute, so it was a pity she was hooking up with that tool. Oh well, she was a little delicate for my taste, and besides, you don't mix business with pleasure, man. That's the oldest rule in the book. You don't shit where you sleep. Seriously, though, it would never have worked out anyway; she was too young for me, jailbait all the way, and besides, the chic hated the outdoors.

46

EDDIE
APRIL 2009

Sometimes it just doesn't pay to be right. After that first bee sting, I knew it was just a matter of time before there would be more. In any place where bees live, it's a general rule that the longer you stay, the more you get stung.

So I wasn't surprised when I saw another one of the bees wiggling its way into the shiny-headed dad's paws. At least I was on the ground, though, all three working paws planted firmly on spotted floor, and I was thankful for that much.

We were back in the large white room, with all the other blue-covering moms and dads, and I was finally getting over my experience with the clicking paw table.

I watched as the shiny-headed dad made his best effort at bee control, but it didn't do the job. He was a big dad, and he appeared to be really strong; I would have thought that would have counted for something, but no, even with all those muscles and his firm grip, he still couldn't stop the flying bee. Heck, he couldn't even slow it down. It just kept coming.

I must have flinched because the skinny mom, who didn't have the shiny-headed dad's grip, tightened her not-so-strong hold. Her hug was only about as hard as being licked by rain, but I could feel that the effort had been there.

Then, out of nowhere, that grip of hers became tighter and tighter. In fact, as her arms squeezed around my waist, I wondered where the strength was coming from. She had gone from being a weak Chihuahua into a Rottweiler in just a few short seconds, and all of a sudden, I was having a hard time taking in a deep breath. I didn't want to be rude, but if she squeezed any tighter, I was going to have to shake her off or pass out. I only got a break and managed to gulp in some short breaths when she let go of me with one of her paws and reached out to grab my muzzle.

I heard an unhappy and gruff grunt from the shiny-headed dad, and the skinny mom's grip relaxed, but she was still holding her paw around my muzzle and lifting my nose to point it into the air. His voice sounded a little annoyed. In a meek voice, she grunted back, and thank goodness, I could breathe normally again, but I was sitting there being made to point my nose to the sky.

I didn't get to think about it too long, though, because as the sharp prick jabbed into my neck, everything, including the timid mom, was painfully forgotten. It was a burning feeling, and being that I had the timid mom holding me, I couldn't back away or shake free. The feeling only lasted for a couple of seconds—it was over before I got too freaked out—but I got to see the little bee fly away. It was still in the shiny-headed dad's paw, but now it was filled with red fluid. The skinny mom let go of my muzzle and relaxed her grip, and I had the *pleasure* of smelling a full bee body's worth of my red fluid.

The shiny headed dad took out two huge what appeared to be both juicy and meaty crunchy treats. Suddenly being hoisted up on a table, almost suffocated by the timid mom, and being stung twice by a bee didn't seem all that bad.

The shiny-headed dad waited for me to swallow the last crumb before he led me out of the large room and back through the long hallway. It was the same way we had come, and I knew we were headed back to Mom and Dad.

I sensed them before I saw them, and when we rounded the corner into the small side room of the territory, I sprinted toward them as they popped into view. Mom had been in midstep, facing the red wall with one of her paws on her hips and the other one scratching her head, and by the look of it was still pretty stressed out. Judging by the way she was creasing her eyebrows and squinting her eyes, she'd probably been pacing in the room ever since I'd left. Dad was still sitting on one of the blue chairs that lined the wall and was watching Mom closely.

I felt the safety rope loosen as I broke free from the shiny-headed dad's grip and closed the distance between me and Mom and Dad in no time. With only a short, barked greeting to announce I was back, I launched up to greet Mom before she could fully turn around. And I managed to use all of my paws this time.

47

BRANDON
APRIL 2009

Dude, I have a half an hour. If I'm late again, the guys are going to crucify me. We've got to be perfect, it's got to be pristine, and it has to be as smooth as glass.

Now what are the chances that this goes without a hitch and they don't drill me with questions? Little to nothing, but a man can hope.

After Eddie almost took the chick down and she had professed her undying love for him, she started in with questions.

"Wow, what did you guys do to him? I haven't seen him so energetic this whole week."

Her voice cracked and she looked like she was about to break down again, but she managed to hold it together. The guy was looking up at her as well, and I could tell he didn't know what to say. He had that universal-guy stupid look on his face, the look all of us get when we see a chick cry. It's like you want to do something to make it stop, but you don't want to say something stupid and get burned. You just know as soon as you say anything, it's going to come out all wrong, make her mad at you, and suddenly instead of the hero you're the bad guy and instead of just being upset, she's pissed at you. So the best you can do is just shut up and look like an idiot. It's universal, man.

I answered, trying to sound as harmless as possible. "Nothing much; we just bribed him with a couple of bones. The doc said the surgeon is going to be coming in to speak to you in about five minutes, so just wait in here for now. The results of the tests should be back in the next day or so and the doc will give you a call then. In the meantime, he's instructed that you give Eddie two of these every twelve hours for pain."

I held up the orange bottle of pain meds for them to see.

"They might make him a little drowsy, but they will definitely take the edge off. The surgeon will be right in. . . . Nice meeting you folks."

I looked at them to see if they had anything to say, but the woman had gone back to practically frenching her dog while the dude was looking down again.

Could it be? No questions?

I waited another second to be sure.

Awesome; I ain't one to argue. Fifteen minutes left. I can make it.

48

DR. BERRY
APRIL 2009

He's really got to stop doing this to me. A freaking soft tissue sarcoma is not an emergency. Seriously, these people could have waited until tomorrow for this. I've been on my feet for the last twelve hours nonstop, and all I want to do is crawl into a nice hot bath with a bottle of Chardonnay.

He's got that way about him, though. He has that je ne sais quoi magic touch; it's all that time dealing with cancer and death. He's just so understanding and sweet; he's the perfect shoulder to cry on. I couldn't do what he does. It's too depressing, with way too much drama; hell, I wouldn't *want* to do it.

I knew that he'd been working me, but that smile, those eyes, and that smooth honeyed voice, how could I have said no? Who could have resisted?

These guys had better be nice or he'll owe me double for this . . . Showtime.

"Hi, I'm Dr. Berry. I'm one of the surgeons in the group. Nice to meet you. I just touched base with Dr. Lindy, and he told me all about Eddie. He was right; he is a handsome boy. Come here, let's have a look at you. This should keep you busy."

The man and woman looked shell-shocked, like they'd been in here sniffing the cancer vibes way too long. The room was stuffy and hot, recycled, and the air smelled like it had been breathed one too many times. It had a faint odor of sweat and nerves, and I could feel the life had been sucked bone dry. The woman looked like she'd been crying, and the guy looked like he was about ready to fall asleep in the corner. The only real energy in the place was the dog, a golden mix that had the damn near longest ears I had ever seen. He was smiling and panting, and there were white drool bubbles on the right side of his mouth. He was planted right between the woman and me; Mrs. Freed, according to the chart.

I handed Eddie a small Milk-Bone before I started my physical exam. I made sure to let it go right before he got close to my hands, just in case. One could never be too careful, and since my hands were my livelihood, there was no point in taking risks.

I proceeded with my exam, which proved to be pretty boring

except for some dental disease. Then I started in on his orthopedic exam. He had good joint motion, no pain, and had some minor thickening of the joint on his right stifle. It was otherwise boring for a dog his size and age. I moved on to the shoulder.

The right front limb was sensitive to the touch. The shoulder mass felt hard, almost tennis ball-sized, and was resting on the lateral aspect of his shoulder blade. It didn't feel like it extended beneath it, but there was a portion that reached past the shoulder and toward the direction of the spine. Unfortunately for him, that disqualified getting adequate surgical margins even if I took the leg off, but at least I wouldn't have a problem closing with all that skin.

Mrs. Freed was staring intently at me, eagerly waiting for the moment when I would give her my take on things. Mr. Freed was looking at his wife, and I could tell she was his primary concern.

"Well, I definitely agree with Dr. Lindy, folks. This is going to take a multimodality approach. Given its size and the fact that it's extending beyond the shoulder blade toward the central aspect of his body, I'm not going to achieve adequate surgical margins even with an amputation. So if the tests today don't show any disease spread, I would recommend taking out as much of it as possible and radiating after."

Mrs. Freed was slowly nodding her head, while Eddie lay flat at her feet. I decided to sit down because my feet were throbbing, and positioned myself on the floor right next to Eddie. It had been a long day: two gastrointestinal obstructions and a torn cranial cruciate repair. Not to mention there was a ruptured spleen en route, which, despite being utterly exhausted, I had to stay for. And I thought my residency days were over; yeah, right!

I needed to get this consult over as quickly as possible.

"It's called debulking it. Like Dr. Lindy said, we'd follow with radiation therapy to clean up what's left over."

She continued to look at me, or through me, I couldn't decide which. Her husband finally looked away from her, and I could feel the weight of his eyes. Both of their expressions were nothing short of intense, and I couldn't gauge whether what I was saying was getting through or not. I waited for a question, but one never came, so I went on. Time was short.

"The surgery should take less than an hour, but Eddie will need to stay the night. Depending on how well he's doing, he'll either go home the next day or the day after that. Generally, these guys are walking around after one day and can be discharged then, but it really depends on the dog. He'll need an Elizabethan collar for about fourteen days afterward so he doesn't lick his stitches. It will need to be on at all times; otherwise, he could chew the surgery site, and that wouldn't be good."

Still their faces were the same, neither registering understanding or communicating confusion, just intense and nonreadable stares.

"Generally, the stitches are ready to come out about fourteen days after surgery. After the results from today come back, we'll call you to schedule a surgery date. My guess is that it will probably be in two days, but Dr. Lindy will call you tomorrow with the results.

"Any questions?"

Here is where I knew things could change. Every blue moon, there's a client who understands everything the first time around, sees no reason to repeat what I said just for the sake of speaking, and truly, truly internalizes what I said.

This was probably not going to be one of those times, especially this being a Dr. Lindy patient. They needed the extra hand-holding nine times out of ten, and that's where the guy excelled. Me, on the other hand, I'd rather be cutting than hand-holding.

So of course there were questions. And just as I had predicted, I ended up repeating what I had just gone over. You had to go through the motions, though. It made them feel better to talk it out, to get it all out of their systems so they felt "comfortable." There was no trying to get out of it; frankly, even if you did manage to get out unscathed, there would always be those two or five phone calls afterward, asking the same questions because you didn't take the time to let them feel satisfied. I'd rather nip it in the bud to start with; it was way more efficient that way. Of course, there were those people who didn't get it no matter how many times they heard it, and they just liked to hear the sound of your voice. It soothed them, but it drove me up the wall.

How will he feel after surgery? How bad is the anesthesia? Is he going to be in a lot of pain? Is he too old for this? Do animals really recover faster than we do, or is that your way of forcing me to do this? Would you do this to your own dog?

Blah blah blah.

So on and on it went, and just like with every other client I see, I played the game to its conclusion. After they had asked everything to their hearts' desire, left no rock unturned, and asked what color the sun was twenty times over, they finally just stood there staring at me, racking their brains to think of anything else they might have missed. I could practically see them gasping for air, holding their sides after just crossing the finish line.

No, just head shakes. Good. The woman looked calmer, at least, and I could see her husband just wanted to get out of here as well.

Job accomplished!

I told them I'd probably see them later in the week, and then I walked out.

I looked at my watch and clocked a half an hour consult. That wasn't too bad, and as many questions as they had had, they were nice enough people. I guess Lindy only owes me one after all. Now where's that spleen dog? They'd better be here by now!

49

EDDIE
APRIL 2009

Wow, talk about a presence. The new white-coated mom looked like she could have led a pack of the worst behaved furry friends out there; she was definitely a leader. She had a forceful voice and was slightly shorter than Mom, but a full head shorter than Dad. She had a wide and chubby torso, and her white coat seemed tight-fitting to her shape but still could easily have fit around two Moms. She had short black hair, chocolate brown eyes and a plump, semicircle of a face that reminded me of an oversized kibble. She had on blue leg and torso coverings under her white coat, and there was a pair of ear extensions dangling around her shoulders.

She had marched into the room and had started grunting in midstride. Her grunting had been fast, tense, and had a sense of purpose that I couldn't quite make out. I wondered if she was being friendly or if her tone was serving some other purpose that I couldn't make heads or tails of. Had her quick and jerky paw motions meant that she was a threat and I needed to be on guard, or had it meant that she was just excited? Had she been planning to hurt Mom or Dad, or had she just been overly happy and expressive at being around them?

As soon as she had stepped into the room, I had positioned myself in front of Mom, just in case the round white-coated mom hadn't been the friendly type. I had watched her carefully for her next move.

She had kept grunting, looking down at me while she had gone on babbling to Mom and Dad. Her paws had been moving a million miles an hour, and I had seen the skin under her arms jiggle as her arms had flapped from left to right. She had walked to the center of the room and leaned against the silver table, which had caused it to shift slightly and let out a squeak.

As if she had read my mind and noticed that I had gone into threat control, she had casually reached into her white coat and wrapped her claws around something long, narrow, and paw-sized. When she took her paw out of her pocket, there was a small, crunchy treat in it, which pretty much settled any doubts I had about her and her intentions.

It was a small, white crunchy treat, and from where I sat, I could make out the smoky smell that clued me into the fact that it was the kind that crumbled after the first bite. It had been nowhere near as tasty as the one the shiny-headed dad had given me earlier, but it had hit the spot nonetheless.

With that, I stopped being confused about whether I could trust her or needed to protect Mom and Dad from her. She could flail her wiggly paws as much as she liked, as long as she kept the crunchy treats coming.

After I had inhaled the majority of it in just two bites, I checked the floor in front of her for any splattered leftovers. Only after I had licked the ground near her paw coverings and under the table did I feel ready to look up, because I would have hated to let any treats go to waste. I stared up at her while she continued to grunt to Mom and Dad.

She must have felt my eyes on her because at that moment she had stopped grunting and had looked down at me with a smile that split her face in half. The skin below her eyes had wrinkled and her chin had stretched, and she had looked like a mixture between a bulldog and a pug. Her grunting had suddenly stopped and been replaced with what obviously had been an attempt at a cooing sound, although it had come out sounding more like an over excited Paris burp.

Despite its scary sounds, I still felt the full force of her intentions. My tail had gone into overdrive, my ears had stood up to full attention—well, at least the base of them had—and I had planted myself right next to her so she could give me some more attention.

She had been no different from any of the white-coated breed I've met in the past, and after she had given me a few good rubs, she had started on the standard white-coated greeting. There had been a little bit of patting, a whole lot of rubbing, and a touch of looking in places where most other moms and dads wouldn't ever have bothered to go.

There had been a difference, however, between her greeting and the other two white-coated greetings I had already been through that light period. This mom really, really had concentrated on my tingly shoulder, way more than any of the other white-coated breed. I had felt her pull my fur up and down, this direction and that, and then stretch it one way while pulling it the other. She had yanked on my leg, lifting it up, forward, backward, and then to the side. She had made it go in circles, and then stretched it to its limit both outward and away from my body and then to the opposite, so I had felt my biceps digging into my chest. All the while, she had been staring fixedly at my face with those deep brown eyes. It was as if she had been trying to see what I would do with such a strange greeting.

Once she had finished playing with my shoulder, a whole lot of grunting had gone on. First with the round white-coated mom, then Mom, then Dad, and then the white-coated mom again. Around and around the grunting had gone, with Mom grunting a little and then the white-coated mom dominating the majority of the conversation. I tried to follow Mom's tone during the grunting, and it went from being scared at first to nervous but accepting by the time we were done.

It felt like we had been in this place for light periods already, and I had sensed that it was getting late. I felt worn out.

As if they read my mind, the grunting wound down. Mom and Dad had looked back and forth between each other and then shrugged at the round white-coated mom. Mom had looked liked she was searching for something more to grunt, but she had used up all her grunting for now. Dad had just looked tired, like he was ready for his sleeping cushion, and what followed was a silence.

After realizing that there was no more to say, the white-coated mom had looked at me, and her face had filled with that puglike expression again. She had slowly reached into her pocket and pulled out another paw-sized crumbly treat. She had turned and left the room while I was still in midchew.

Before we left the building for the day, Dad stopped by the large desk right in front of where the eye-covering mom was sitting. There had been no other moms, dads, or furry friends left in the bright, red-stoned room by then. Looking through the clear window, I saw that the sky had taken on dark purple and red hues, and it would only be a matter of time before it was the full-dark period.

THE DOG DAYS OF THE PAST

50

JULIA
JULY 2007

"How's he doing, Mother? Did it go okay? Let me speak to him."

"No, Julia, this is definitely not a good time. He is . . . well, unavailable, dear."

Mother's voice had turned shaky, and the usual arrogant confidence in her tone had dissipated. Something was obviously very wrong, and my suspicions were confirmed as I heard coughing, followed by the sinister, unmistakable noise of vomiting in the background. The sound was quickly muted as the phone's speaker was covered, and then I heard Dad, obviously out of breath, mumbling.

My heart started racing and I couldn't control the volume of my voice as I half-whispered, "Is Dad okay? Speak to me, Mother . . . hello?"

There was no reply, and I heard static as a hand covered the speaker again. There was the muffled sound of my mother voice as she asked my dad a question. I couldn't make out what she said, but I could hear the concern in her voice, a very uncharacteristic thing from the person I called my mother.

I waited for a couple of seconds and then heard more static, mixed with what seemed to be a heated conversation between my mother and father. I raised my voice in the hopes of miraculously peeling away Mother's hand from the speaker and said impatiently, "Mother . . . hello . . . Mom, can you hear me?"

The cloud of muffled static lifted, and a second later, my mother's frazzled voice came on. "Today is not a good day. Come by in a couple of days, dear. . . Julia, I have to go now. We'll see you on Sunday, and try not to be late."

I was flabbergasted; she had actually hung up on me. I had called to see how Dad had been doing, and from what I'd just heard, the chemotherapy was obviously taking its toll and making him sick. His first treatment had gone well enough, and for the first four days he'd had no side effects, but this was day five and obviously things had changed.

I had been calling the house every night to see how he'd been holding up, and like always, our brief conversations had been shy on words but had delivered volumes in their unspoken messages. It didn't take a bunch of shallow words to communicate how we felt, and a couple of sentences had been enough. My mother had sucked the life out of both of my father and me for years with her rants and self-aggrandizing tangents, and after dealing with her so long, to be able to communicate like this had been a relief that both Dad and I naturally had gravitated toward.

"How's it going, Dad?"

"I'm fine, sweetie; how are you doing? Is David treating you well?"

Yes, Dad, of course he is. I'm doing fine."

Then came the usual brief silence before one of us asked another quick question, followed by promises to call again the next day. According to Mother, Dad had never been one for long conversations with anyone, which was ironic, given the fact that he'd married her. Or maybe he'd been more talkative when they'd first gotten married, and being with that woman all these years had changed that. Hell, I barely had any energy to speak growing up with her in that house.

With my Dad and me, the fact that I called and we heard each other's voices was what truly mattered, and the couple of minutes of talking over those last four nights had assured me that everything had been going fine.

Today had been different, though, and I hadn't gotten to speak with him. So this was the start. Was it all downhill from here?

No, I refused to think like that. This was just one bad night, a fluke, something that could happen to anyone. It was just a one-time thing; it wouldn't be like this every time. Maybe he'd eaten something bad, and his vomiting had nothing to do with the chemotherapy.

But the panic in Mother's voice? Why wasn't the antinausea medication they had given him working?

I felt so powerless sitting on the couch with the phone in my hand, knowing that my dad was bent over a toilet, going through lord knew what. I heard the bland voice of the recording: "If you would like to make a call, please hang up and try again."

Still in a haze, I hung up and set the phone down on the cushions, not caring if it wedged itself between the pillows. My strong, tough, caring, loving Dad, a man I knew nothing could keep down, a man who had always stayed positive no matter what the situation, would beat this. He had always been a fighter, and he would win this round, too. And I would be right there next to him, fighting with him. I would be strong with him.

51

JULIA
AUGUST 2007

"Do you realize what a toll this is taking on me, Julia? I haven't slept for more than three hours in a row since your father began therapy. It's been such a challenge for me, and I don't know how I've been managing to cope so far. Did you know, dear, that the man is up nearly all hours of the night, pacing around the house, wandering aimlessly, making every floorboard creak, with no regard to how I'm meant to get to sleep or stay functional?"

I gripped the white portable phone so tightly that I thought I was going to break it. Here I was at home, worried sick about my father, and this is what I had to go through to get an answer? Was I being punished by the powers above? What had I done in my previous life to deserve this? Why couldn't the woman just give me a straight answer?

Her statement shouldn't have surprised me; no matter how much I had prepared myself, she'd still managed to get under my skin again. All I'd wanted to do was to hear how Dad was doing, how he was handling the therapy. It should have been a simple thing to ask, right? A daughter simply calling her mom to find out how her father, who had just started chemotherapy, was getting along. It should have been a very easy thing to answer for any normal person, right?

But *normal* was the keyword here, and definitely not in my family, not with my mother. To get an update about him, I knew I'd have to trench through the minefields of Mother's self-absorption to get to my father. And only after hearing about her—how her day was going, how her week seemed never to end, how she had brushed her teeth too hard and made her gums bleed, how the weather was affecting her hot flashes, how everything was affecting her, yada yada yada—would the subject of my father finally come up.

I had to jump over the hurdles of a long-winded, detail-by-detail, play-by-play recitation of every occurrence involved in every aspect of her life that had transpired since last I'd spoken to her to get to him. It came with the territory, and I knew that. It was unfortunate and completely unnecessary, but that was the way it worked in my family. I knew it was part of the deal, and if I wanted to find out about Dad, we would have to cover her first.

"Oh, it's just terrible, Julia"—there was a slight pause, and with it came some hope; only a record three minutes into our conversation, her voice had changed tenor as it crackled through the phone—she continued, "for the both of us."

I tensed my jaw to clear my ears, like you do when you equilibrate on a plane trip; amazingly, I had just heard the words *both of us*, which meant that there was a chance the conversation was turning toward Dad. This had to be a record, if it proved to be true.

"The poor man, your dear father. He gets so tired from being up all night that finally he just collapses from exhaustion during the most random hours of the day. Your father, the man who never believed in resting during work hours, no matter what day of the week it was, the man who could function on four hours of sleep . . . well, dear, he is only human, after all."

I felt the weight of my heart as it sank down in my chest like a ten-pound weight. In all the time I had spent growing up in that angst- filled household, the poster child for a dysfunctional environment, I had never known my father to take a nap during the day. I had never seen the man so much as even lie down on the couch on a Saturday, let alone sleep in past seven A.M. It was Dad, the man who had put in fifty hours of work every week, every year since I could remember. Of all the men in the world, it must have hit him really hard; he never minced words about how unmanly and weak he found it that grown men felt the need to rest during daylight hours. Unless, of course, you put in a decent overnight shift, of course. He made an exception for them.

I had actually started to pay attention to what Mother was saying before she shifted the conversation back to the status quo, her. It was such a tease; it had been within my grasp: real, solid, meaningful information about Dad. That was all I had asked for, but with only that small tidbit of real information, the conversation had turned back to being focused on the person whom she was most comfortable with, herself.

"You know, dear, he's making me so worried. Even when he does manage to finally get to sleep, I find myself just staring at him, watching him to make sure he's still breathing. It's mental torture, and it's draining me physically as well. It's taking such a toll on me. Julia dear, can you believe that I haven't eaten a good meal since he got sick? It's just utterly unfathomable; I can't even bear the thought of food.

"I'm a nervous wreck, not to mention that I'm sleep deprived as well. Seriously, dear, I must have lost at least five pounds since all of this craziness started, and my ability to think about anything other than your father has gone out of the window. Being a caring woman, while he's in this condition, he's dominated every one of my thoughts, and I can't seem to focus on anything other than your father, which is troubling, given the fact that I'm responsible for taking care of the household."

As I listened to her ramble on about herself, I felt the steady haze of boredom wash over me, my mind starting to zone out.

"Julia darling, I actually had to order takeout for the last five days in a row. What a travesty! Restaurant food during the middle of the week, could I be any more embarrassed? Of course, you know that any decent wife finds time to cook for her husband, and I have always had a meal on the table ready for your father when he walked through the door. But Julia, with everything that's going on in my life right now, I just can't find the time. Can you believe that? Me, your dear mother, not having time to cook for your father. Me, the mother all the other children and wives in the neighborhood have always been jealous of. Can you imagine how hard it is on me?"

I didn't bother to answer; she wasn't expecting a comment from me.

She continued to ramble. "It's not like it would have mattered; your beloved father cannot keep anything down right now anyway. I won't go into the sordid details, but the poor man is practically starving because of the effects of the chemotherapy. It's made him so nauseated that even the smell of food sets him off, except for boiled chicken and plain rice. It took a couple of days, but at least we found that out. He can tolerate it only in small quantities, though, and that's the sole thing he's been living off of for the past week, the poor man.

"And with all your father's nausea and vomiting, with everything I've had to go through since he started treatment, one thought keeps coming to mind: what happens if he can't tolerate the therapy? What am I going to do without him? Heaven knows he has his faults, but deep down, I really do love the man. How am I going to manage without him?"

I was listening to Mother, but truth be told, it was very hard to actually hear what she was saying. Not the part about her, that is— I mainly blocked that part out—it had to do with what she had been saying about him. It was difficult to believe that my strong father, the iron dad, the toughest man I had ever known, could be so troubled by the drugs. I knew they could cause side effects to the average person, you heard stories about it all the time, but to Dad?

I felt beads of moisture start to form on my lower back and the beginnings of an acid stomach starting to form. It was a burning sensation deep down in the pit of my belly that felt very much like indigestion but was really just a reaction to stress. It had been like this ever since I was a kid, another gift that had developed during my childhood from my mother's drama. I took three long, deep, slow breaths in, knowing that my silence wouldn't be noted.

My poor father; it must be very difficult for him. I felt so sorry for him, and sad that he had to go through this. It hurt me to think that such a wonderful teddy bear of a man had to suffer through sleepless nights and nausea, and have his main support system be such a self-absorbed wife.

But then there was the other part of me, the part that couldn't accept that things were going wrong. The part of me that was convinced that this was just part of the road to recovery. I believed that this was a temporary setback, and that because he was such a tough man, he would get through it. He would get better, regardless of the fact that the woman who was meant to be taking care of him only cared about herself. He just needed to get through this part and then he would beat this thing.

My deep breaths appeared to have helped; thank goodness, my stomach stayed under control. My mini yoga exercise had allowed me to relax enough to temporarily tune my mother out and get my thoughts under control, but as my breathing returned to normal, so too did my hearing. My mother, of course, was still speaking.

Any other person listening to her mother relating what a hard time she was having dealing with her husband's cancer would definitely have had a strong empathetic reaction to her plight. I'm confident of that. But what I've come to realize, and what my therapist has so thoroughly and repeatedly explained, is plainly due to past circumstances, I am not *any other person*." And, more importantly, my mother is not your average mother. Unfortunately, given our family history, I have grown somewhat shall we say immune to her and, as bad as it sounds, to her feelings.

Listening to her go on like this, I knew that I should've felt sorry for her, felt pity, should have at least comforted her more. From a logical perspective, what she was saying was perfectly normal for a woman going through what she was experiencing with Dad. It would have been the natural thing to do. But with our history, the years of being forced to listen to hours upon hours of monologues about her and her life, and all the crap she had put me through in between, I was completely and utterly burned out. I was unaffected by her and her feelings, I was numb, and even if I wanted to change and feel empathy for her, it was impossible. As bad as it sounds, I just didn't care.

I heard a pause in the conversation and knew that usually when this happened, she expected some kind of response or acknowledgment from me. It usually involved telling her how bad I felt for her, or how sorry I was for her, or how I couldn't believe that so-and-so wronged her in some way, and if I didn't say something, she would instantly become pissed because I wasn't paying enough attention to her.

I attempted to find from deep within some emotion I knew should have been there in order to sound as genuine as I could, despite the fact that Mother sounded as if Dad had already lost the battle. I had to be the strong one here; without someone filling that role, how would Dad continue to have the support he needed? Someone had to do it, and it sure as hell wasn't going to be Mother.

In one of the sweetest voices I could muster, I said, "Mother, I'm so sorry you haven't slept. This must be really hard for you, but rest assured that Dad will get through it, and you will, too. You can't give up hope. It's normal for people to get sick from the chemotherapy, but it doesn't mean Dad won't get better. Mother, Dad will definitely get through this; I just know it."

There was a brief moment of silence, something almost unheard of in any conversation with her, and I could feel the heat of the phone radiating against my ear. This couldn't be good; silence was never a good sign in any conversation that involved her. Unless she was blowing her nose or she had dropped the phone, my performance somehow had failed miserably. How long had I been on the phone with her already?

After five long, drawn-out seconds, she replied in a curt and holier-than-thou tone, "I wish I could believe it, dear, but frankly, I'm trying to be realistic. Julia, you are, as always, being utterly naïve. Just like when you chose that creative writing major in college, which was a complete and utter fantasy. But Julia, this is serious; my feelings are of primary importance here, and you aren't a little girl anymore. You're a grown woman, and it's time you stopped living in your imaginary world. Julia, I would have hoped that you'd have matured by now. Now, what was I saying?"

Wow . . . it never ceased to amaze me how the woman could completely transform herself. One minute she was going on about how hard life was, about what a difficult time she was having with this or that situation, doing everything she could to be the center of attention, and the next she was firing off a nuclear bomb of an insult, attacking my career path and me.

You could call it a talent, you could call it a skill, you could pretty much call it anything you liked, but you couldn't deny that she was the master. It came so naturally to her to belittle me that I truly believed she put no conscious thought into doing it. It was just a reflex for her. To be able to beg for sympathy and seriously offend someone in one breath; now that was something you couldn't teach. It was remarkable, if you could call it that.

And like the countless other times when I had been the target on the firing range that is called my mother, I ignored it. For me, at that moment in time, it wasn't worth it to justify a response. My therapist would have cringed; this was one of those prime opportunities she said would come up to have me set some relationship boundaries. An opportunity to let her know that some things were just not going to be tolerated anymore, and that if she wanted a relationship with me, she would have to afford me some respect. A large part of the problem of my relationship with my mother, according to my therapist, was that I had let her get away with statements like that for way too long. She wanted me to let me Mother know that they were unacceptable.

But I hesitated because, as much as I wanted to stand up for myself, I didn't think this would be a good time for it. I didn't want to be selfish, and the last thing I needed was to get into a fight with Mother that could go on for months. Dad didn't need that right now. As my mother started to talk again, I felt the gnawing anger of a missed opportunity and knew I would replay that moment over and over in the next couple of days and wish I had said something. But it wasn't the right time, right?

I could answer my own question, which made me even more frustrated because I knew that there was always something going on that I'd use as an excuse. It seemed there was never a good time to call her out on her inappropriate remarks.

And as I stewed over my cowardice, yet another transformation came over my mother. Completely oblivious to having deeply insulted me, Mother shifted from her holier-than-thou tone to an Oscar-worthy performance in her woe-is-me voice.

"Oh, Julia, I am so tired of this, all this stress, and your father being sick all the time. I spend every waking moment thinking about it. You know, when my mother was dying it was the same, of course. It was a different era, though, because as the oldest child, I had to move back into the house to take care of her. Heaven knows I couldn't leave that burden on my father to do by himself; what kind of a daughter would I have been then?

"It didn't make a difference that I was married and had been out of their house for at least five years; I was their daughter, and it was the right thing to do. Your father completely understood and never said a word to contradict my decision. In fact, he insisted that I move back into my parents' house to help out because that's what was done back then . . ."

The only thing that occurred to me was that either my dad had wanted a break from her for a while or that there had been something more to the story that she was conveniently leaving out. Either way, I really didn't care, nor would I ever put forth the effort to find out.

And, as the monologue officially launched into overdrive, I realized this was going to be at least another one-hour marathon. Luckily for me, though, I had a dentist appointment at two o'clock, which would give me the excuse I needed to hang up. I put the phone on speaker so my hand wouldn't fall asleep and kicked myself for not being brave enough to end the conversation by going through with the whole boundary thing.

Oh, well, another opportunity lost. I would live through the torture of the coming hour and look at it as punishment for being such a wimp. Time to pay the piper.

52

JULIA
AUGUST 2007

There were a total of only three ducks there now. On the far side of the pond, the side where the loose moss and leaves would gather as the wind gently herded all the debris steadily throughout the day, were two of the most beautiful snow-white ducks I had ever seen. Their feathers glistened in the mild winter sun. They were near the far bank of the pond, smoothly gliding in tiny circles around one another, oblivious to any pain the world had to offer.

In the middle of the pond, near the worn, circular water fountain, which was turned on only during the summer, was a brown duck with speckled black spots. He was about the same size as the other two pristine white ducks, but unlike them, his movements were not as graceful. They were awkward, ill timed, and a stark contrast to his cherubic counterparts. He was paddling briskly and clumsily around the stone fountain and appeared to be looking for something, squawking loudly in his quest. He had either separated himself from the other ducks, or the other ducks had separated themselves from him. Whatever the reason, he was isolated, alone, and looked to be searching for something he'd lost. Maybe he was looking for the countless other birds I had remembered being at this pond, but given we had only visited this place during tourist season, in the summer, maybe he, too, was lamenting their absence.

Like all childhood memories, the Duck Pond seemed so much smaller than I remembered it. The stagnant pond water still possessed a dull, dark green hue, and a faint smell of ammonia permeated the air. The white, knee-high picket fence continued to guard the water's edge, encircling the entire periphery of the pond. Judging by its color, it had recently been repainted. It was a mere five feet away from the actual pond, a feeble attempt at keeping overzealous five-year-olds from chasing the birds. The surrounding grass continued to be unnaturally green even at this time of year, only sparsely littered with dead leaves but still inviting, with its call to spread out a picnic blanket.

And picnic here my family had done over the years. Ever since I had been a little girl, we had come to the pond at least once a month. It was our family activity, our time to bond, and an opportunity to catch up with one another's lives. The memories were still so fresh in my mind, like the afternoon that Dad had tried to teach me to play football here, finally coming to terms with the fact that his only daughter couldn't and would never be able to throw a good spiral. Or all the countless hours he had spent with me, feeding our stale, leftover bread to the ducks, or the pride he had in demonstrating the proper way to throw a pebble so it would skip at least four bounces before finally sinking to the bottom.

We had spent a lot of time here, the last time I recalled being the summer before I left for college. Mother had been taking a nap in the sun, sprawled out on a red, oversized blanket that had cost double what it should have. Dad and I had spent the afternoon walking the perimeter of the pond together, something we had always done when he wanted to talk.

It had been an afternoon I will never forget, and it stands out in my mind because it's one of the only times I had ever seen him choked up. I don't remember exactly what we had been talking about; maybe it was how to stay safe from ill-intentioned boys, or how I needed to stay on top of my studies, but what I mostly remembered about our walk that afternoon was the feeling of how much he was going to miss me. He could've been talking about his new stock of hammers or basket weaving, for all I knew, but what I most recalled was the look in his eyes and the pull at my heart. I could see the loss, the emotion, and the pure, unadulterated love pouring out of him. Seeing him choked up like that, and how sad it made him to see me leave; it's forever burned into my mind.

So here we were again today, one surgery passed and three weeks of chemotherapy under his belt. We had decided to come to the pond for lunch, just for old time's sake. It was to be a father-daughter lunch, some much-needed alone time for Dad and me. Without a word and as natural as breathing, Dad had driven us here. David had conveniently stayed at the house to do some yard work, and Mother had gone shopping.

We had found a spot in the brisk winter sun about twenty feet away from the water, and we were sitting on the same red blanket Mother had bought all those years ago. There was a mild chill to the air, and even with my warm blue wool sweater, I still felt cold.

It was a good lunch. Mother had insisted on packing a picnic for us, and Dad wouldn't insult her by refusing. I wasn't going to get into it with her by saying no either. Mother had made me a pastrami sandwich on rye bread, completely ignoring my request for something vegetarian. Not that I was a vegetarian; it was just that I didn't feel like anything heavy today. She had packed Dad a plain chicken breast with a small amount of white rice, which lay untouched on the paper plate in front of him. I had learned from Mother that he was still getting sick from the chemotherapy, although now at least they had managed to keep his nausea to a minimum. He could only keep down bland foods, something I pretended to ignore as he eyed my sandwich.

He looked thinner to me now, and there were thick black rings under his eyes. He looked like he hadn't slept in days, and his skin had a pale, blanched pallor to it. As much as he had wanted to continue working after the surgery, circumstances had dictated otherwise. He had only truly managed to go back to work for two days after he had recovered from surgery and started chemotherapy before he finally had accepted, in his words, "a well-deserved, open-ended vacation."

I knew that it had been a blow to him, a concession in his fight. Cancer one, Dad zero. I was convinced that it was a minor setback, though, a loss of a small battle in a war that had to be won. By this point, he had already had three doses of chemotherapy over the last three weeks, and he had four more weeks to go before he'd have a one week break before beginning the cycle all over again. I kept telling myself that he would be more normal after, and I'd convinced myself that he would be able to go back to work then.

We sat there, enjoying the beautiful and serene view, me eating the pastrami sandwich while Dad used his plastic fork to move around the rice on his plate. I could tell that he wanted to eat but probably felt too queasy to take a bite. So we sat there in silence for a good twenty minutes, just enjoying each other's company. When I was done and had finished the Coke Mother had also packed, Dad suggested that we do some laps around the pond. His plate was still full, but I didn't dare say anything that would embarrass him.

We spoke about everything that day, and I talked to him more in those couple of hours than in the last couple of years combined. We talked about sports, David, Mother, work, and just about anything else that came to mind, all topics except the one I was thinking about the most. I mentally forced myself to stay away from it because I knew that this day was a chance for him to escape. He didn't want to be reminded of his cancer, he just wanted to be, and after a short time, even I got lost enough in old times to forget about the elephant in the room we were pretending not to notice. We spent hours there and must've done at least three laps around the small pond, but in retrospect, it felt like minutes. It was too short, there hadn't been enough time, and I wished the day could have gone on longer. It was amazing, and I will always cherish that day. It was pure Dad.

After about the third lap and a good two hours of walking, I noticed that his pace was slowing. I could hear he was breathing harder, and when I looked at him, his face seemed a shade paler. He looked visibly winded.

I must've looked concerned because the next thing I knew, he said with a smile, "We should probably get back now; your mother will start to get worried about me. You know how she gets, and nobody wants to deal with that."

He was obviously tired, and for a man who had worked the majority of his life with his hands, it must've been very hard for him to accept that he had gotten winded from such a small activity. This was Dad's way of telling me that he had had enough for the day, a way to keep his pride, and I wasn't about to question him any further.

Besides, he would never admit to it anyway. So instead of asking him if he was all right or if I could do anything for him, I forced a smile and pretended that nothing was wrong.

I answered him, doing my best to ignore the obvious, "All right, Dad, you're right. You know how she gets."

53

JULIA
FEBRUARY 2008

I knew it, I just knew it. For the life of me, I couldn't imagine why Mother had ever thought otherwise. Of course he was in remission; why wouldn't he be? He was Dad, old tough-as-nails, nothing-was-going-to-get-him-down Dad. He was going to beat this thing.

I was taking Paris and Eddie for a walk around the block, and Eddie had just stopped in front of the Carsons' lawn to pee on one of their rose bushes. I didn't feel too guilty, given that they'd refused to trim the things and there was usually at least one thorny branch sticking out onto the sidewalk. I had lost my favorite red sweater to those darn rosebushes.

Eddie, like usual, was being typical Eddie and watering everything in sight. That dog couldn't go twenty steps without trying to claim his territory, and it was one of the seven wonders of the world how he stored so much pee. Paris was about five steps in front of him with her nose in the air and her tail pointing straight up. She usually never stopped for anything or anybody, preferring to walk in straight lines. The dogs had such different personalities, it was a miracle they got along so well.

We were moving at a slow, relaxed pace, and I was holding both of their leashes in my left hand. Eddie was an incredibly strong dog, and if he wanted to, he could have broken free at any point. Hiding under those rolls of skin was the strength of a retriever. He was well past that phase, though, too well trained and old to pull a stunt with me and, more importantly, he knew where his next meal would or would not come from if he stepped out of line. Paris was tenacious when she wanted to be, especially when the doorbell rang, but she didn't have the mass Eddie did. I had no problem controlling her.

I had trained them well though, so they didn't dare pull. It left me with one free had to talk on the phone if I needed to, which served me well because Mother had just called.

"Julia dear, I have some positive news. I just finished chatting with the doctor, a pleasant-enough man but very rushed, I must say, and he told me that your father's six months of chemotherapy are now officially over. I'm pleased to say that as far as they can tell, your father has no evidence of cancer spread. He is in, as the doctor said, 'remission.'"

Before I had a chance to respond, to even take a relieved breath, Mother had changed the subject, proceeding to tell me about how her friend Maurine had just bought a new multimillion-dollar vacation home in Florida. She had been complaining to Mother because she would now have to spend time furnishing it.

"And can you believe that she actually had the nerve to say that to me? To me, Julia, who has been her shoulder to cry on, her sounding board for all these years. Like I need to hear her troubles with what's going on in my life. How trivial; she should have real problems like me. Julia, are you aware that my fiftieth high-school reunion is approaching and I haven't done a thing to prepare for it. I still have to . . ."

I had blanked out then because I really didn't care about anything but the fact that Dad was in remission. No cancer seen anywhere, that's what I had heard, right? But as much as I wanted to ask her to repeat it, the only thing I wanted was to get off of the phone. It was such amazing news, and as much as I had known that Dad would beat this thing, it still was nice to hear confirmation.

I was too happy to get annoyed at her, too relieved to have to subject myself to the usual frustration that came with having to speak to her. I didn't want to ruin this moment by getting angry. And about the last thing I cared about was one of her childhood friends and the pissing contest that had gone on between them for all these years. Maurine's husband was not only an inheritor, he was also a plastic surgeon; suffice it to say, they were loaded. And as much as Mother pretended she could keep up with them and their lifestyle financially, could afford to spend their hard-earned cash on things like a twenty-four-thousand-dollar time-share they had used a total of once, she never had had a chance against Maurine and her husband Neville

Much to my chagrin, Maurine also had one daughter who was my age who had ended up following in her father's footsteps and was currently practicing medicine in Los Angeles. She had proven to be the ultimate example to Mother of the path I should have chosen, and she had taken every opportunity to point that out to me.

I had given up counting how many times Maurine's golden child had been used as fodder for Mother. "Katherine has a perfect 4.0, dear, why can't you apply yourself like her?" "Katherine finished her biology degree in only three years, Julia; you should take a page from her book." "Katherine just got accepted to medical school; why are you wasting your time with this writing nonsense?"

I never had told Mother that the golden child had also been the high-school slut who had slept with half of the football team and had had an abortion at sixteen. Or that she had a raging coke habit that lasted all through college and helped her stay up at night to finish that oh-so-desired premed biology degree. No, that one I kept to myself to shield me from being more screwed up from Mother's advice than I already was.

I was rounding the corner to our street, and Eddie was taking the opportunity to pee on the silver pole holding up the stop sign. I was so incredibly happy; the news was the most amazing thing I could have heard, even if it had come from Mother. Dad still insisted that I not go with him and Mother to the doctor, in an attempt to shield me from his cancer. So, much to my annoyance, I still depended on Mother for the updates.

It had been two weeks since his last and final chemo dose, and obviously all of the tests had shown no disease was left. Mother had told me that it would be the determining factor as to whether he needed to keep going with the chemo or if he could stop. The two weeks off had helped Dad regain most of his energy. He was even going to start working again, according to Mother; at least that's what I had heard between her hour-long explanations of how the manicurist had messed up her cuticles. Dad had mostly been home for these last six months, and he must have been going stir crazy by now. There were only so many crossword puzzles one could do, or TV shows to watch, and frankly, being around Mother twenty-four hours a day was enough to motivate anyone to get healthy.

THE DOG DAYS OF THE PRESENT

54

EDDIE
MAY 2009

My usual reaction to happy howling is to join in, even if I don't know the reason for it. Today though, I just wasn't in the mood. I had been feeling like this over the last couple of light periods, ever since we came back from the Crunchy Territory. I can't quite explain it, but the best word that comes to mind is *woozy*. I just didn't have the energy. I felt strange.

It all started the dark period after the visit, that same dark period during which Mom began giving me those new pink treats. They were small pink ovals with a bitter-tasting sand inside that stuck to the sides of my throat as they went down. I'm not quite sure what was in those little pink treats, but let me tell you, after taking one of those little puppies, I started seeing the world in a completely different way.

Something really strange happened to everything around me. It was as if someone had made everything go in motion. Mom and Dad were acting like sloths, sniff boxes that usually raced at Greyhound pace suddenly were crawling around like old, overweight Shih Tzus, and no matter how fast I tried to move, I just couldn't get any speed. My body felt as heavy as a bunch of rocks.

Things also changed when I launched into the pink-treat haze. Take for example Paris. I'd grown up with her, seen her every day of my life, and knew just about every inch of her body, but as soon as I popped one of those crazy little things, the poodle looked like a completely different furry friend.

She looked scary. She was ten times furrier than usual, which wouldn't have been all that bad, but instead of her usual cream-colored semidreadlocked hair, which only slightly poofed away from her body, she changed into a puffy, white cotton-ball monster that shot out giant fur balls all around her. I actually couldn't stand to be around her too long because I thought I wouldn't be able to breath in all her loose poodle fur.

I guessed that it had to be the pink treats and not me flipping out, just like the furry friend two territories down. He had spent a full two light and dark periods yelling at the sky, and I actually grew worried that they would get rid of me just like they had done with him. We never did see him again after that, and I've always wondered where they took him.

On a positive note, though, the tingling feeling in my shoulder had grown less annoying. I was aware that the tingling was still there, but somehow it didn't bother me. Actually, pretty much nothing bothered me while on the pink treats.

Even though I was tired and probably not knowing what was real, at least I could walk on all four paws if I wanted to. I could even put weight on all of my legs again without the constant tingling that had only been getting worse up until that point.

Mom started howling right after she put the ear tickler down. Apparently, this time the thing had worked, and after all those tries, it had finally come through. She slammed it down on the kitchen table with a loud thud, smiled, and got ready to let out a loud grunt of happiness. She took a big breath and let out a high-pitched howl that carried throughout the entire house, and probably down the block as well.

As I said before, normally I would be there right next to her, but I had barely managed to drag myself downstairs this early light period to eat, and to join in with a howl party now would be pushing it even for me.

I spent a lot of time switching between lying on the eating-room floor and my sleeping cushion, and before I knew it, two light periods had passed. It was on the third light period that my woozy resting routine was interrupted. It had been pretty early in the light period, as Mom and I made our way to her black sniff box for our second trip to the Crunchy Territory.

By the time we arrived there, I had been very hungry, and I also a little angry. Mom and Dad had forgotten to feed me again, but by the time we walked into Crunchy Territory, I had lightened up a little. The smells of the sniff-box ride had done wonders for my mood, and I had forgotten about my grumbling tummy. We were greeted by the eye-covering mom, who obviously hadn't moved from her place behind the large, semicircular table, and a blue-covering mom with a blond mane had rushed toward us and started grunting to Mom.

I had seen her as she had burst out of the door that led to the back of the Crunchy Territory, and had watched her walk quickly across the room. She was a young mom and was about the same height as Mom. She had Dalmatianlike brown-and-black– pinpoint dots all over her face and arms and practically out of breath, she had grunted to Mom and held out her paw.

Instead of answering her, Mom had suddenly bent down,

wrapped her arms around me, and almost squeezed the life out of me. She gave me a wannabe lick on the head, and before I knew it, she had handed my safety rope to the Dalmatian mom and we were walking toward the back-territory door.

I struggled to keep up as we came into the large, four-tabled room. It was buzzing with activity, just like last time, with moms and dads in blue coverings everywhere. I grew excited because maybe I would get to see the shiny-headed dad and the timid mom again, and maybe, just maybe, they would give me another one of those chewy treats. I looked to the far right side of the room, the place where they were last time, but they were nowhere in sight. Dalmatian mom led me left instead, to the other side of the room, and to the left-most shiny table.

55

DR. BERRY
MAY 2009

This shouldn't take long; I figure about thirty minutes or so, and then on to the ligament repair.

I looked at Stephanie, my freckle-faced head technician, who, with a bead of sweat on her right temple, looked visibly out of breath. Being the little busy worker bee she is, she had made sure to get to work early today to look out for the Freed dog Eddie. The day was going to be jam-packed, and I had made it crystal clear that the moment the dog walked through the door, it was go time. There was no room for wasted time today, no messing around, no dilly-dallying, and everything needed to be perfect. Stephanie knew the drill. Get the dog, make sure paperwork is signed, try to keep their questions to a minimum because they would talk your ear off if they were nervous, and get back here as soon as humanly possible. She had done well, had remembered to ask all of the important questions, and we were even five minutes ahead of schedule.

"Hey, you asked the Freeds if he was fasted?" I said, because the one time I didn't ask would be the one time Stephanie forgot.

"Yes, he's all set, Dr. Berry. The last food he had was at six last night, although they did give him his pain meds this morning."

Stephanie had earned her way to becoming my head technician, and she had been with me for five years now. She was fast, efficient, and, most importantly, had thick skin. She had been in the army before she had come to work for me, and she was the most disciplined and well-mannered technician I've ever had. I knew I wasn't the easiest person to work for, had even been accused of being . . . well, let's just say *curt* at times, but it hadn't fazed her. I liked her; she knew how to cowboy up and get the job done and was worth every penny of the raise we had just given her.

"Good, let's get an IV catheter in him and prep him for surgery. Let's go, let's go!"

I saw her grab one of the animal helpers; what was his name, Brad, Greg? Oh hell, I couldn't keep track anymore. I turned to Eddie's chart and absently started writing up his record. I wondered what John Lindy was doing right now. Hopefully, sending more surgeries my way. But knowing him, he was probably in a room making someone cry. I didn't know how those oncologists did it. I sure as hell couldn't. Give me a scalpel, a bone saw, some sutures, and a beer after; that's all I needed in life.

I finished the chart and looked down at my limited edition Mickey Mouse watch. No one dared laugh at it; they weren't brave enough to deal with my response. It had been a gift from my late mother, right after I got into Washington State, and it only left my wrist for bed, a shower, or surgery. Some of my fondest memories of her were when she took me to Disneyland all those years ago. She had tried so hard to get me on "It's a Small World," but I had insisted we go on Space Mountain instead. That watch was the embodiment of my mother, and it kept perfect time. It was eight thirty-five.

It had been ten minutes already and my technicians still weren't done yet. What was taking so long? How long did it take to put in a catheter, for crap's sake? I should have been scrubbing in by now.

I could feel beads of sweat forming between my shoulder blades and knew I was starting to get pissed. This was taking way longer than it should have, and I sure as hell didn't want to be behind after my first surgery of the day. Given that I had another four surgeries to do after this, one of them being a hip replacement, I could feel my blood starting to boil. It was a darn IV catheter; it should have taken three minutes, max.

In a barely controlled tone, I asked, as sweetly as I could, "Steph, how are you guys doing? What's the holdup?"

She looked up and wiped her forehead. "Sorry, Doc, it's in now. For a big dog, he's got small basset veins, but I've already pulled up the drugs, so we're ready to go when you are."

Good girl. That's just what I wanted to hear. I started to relax; it was showtime.

The familiar presurgical excitement grew, and I could feel the high coming on. Just like before every surgery I had ever done, I felt the anticipation building. No matter how many times I've cut, it had always been and hopefully will always continue to be the same. I love my job.

"Good, go ahead and induce; let's get going, people."

56

EDDIE
MAY 2009

I was excited to be here, but my heart just wasn't in it. I was exhausted and moving a lot slower than usual, thanks to Mom's new pink treats. I was led to the shiny table on the far left side of the big room, and before I knew it, the Dalmatian mom had hoisted me up with a strength that was out of this world. She might have been small, but she was she strong.

Another blue-coated dad had run over in an attempt to help her, but I was already up by then. He was a tall dad, and he had a short, spiky black mane that glimmered with a sheen of what looked to be a wet coating that was holding it all in place. He had black whiskers that covered his entire lower jaw, and he reeked of rotting flowers. He had started rubbing my back, and I had started breathing out of my mouth to not get a deeper whiff of him.

He grabbed my left elbow and stretched my arm so it was pointing to the door we had just come through. The Dalmatian mom rubbed a now wide-awake buzzer over the top of my forearm in four long, quick strokes, and the thing tickled worse than fleas in summer. I tried to pull my arm back, but unfortunately, the black-whiskered dad had my elbow locked forward, and just like that, the thing licked away a small square of fur.

As I watched my yellow arm fur float off the buzzer, I felt the black-whiskered dad readjusting his hug. I felt his head being pressed against my tingly shoulder and he started grunting in my ear. Now, if the dad was trying to get me to relax any more than I already was, his efforts were wasted; between the hugs, the belly rubs, and, especially, Mom's new pink treats, if I relaxed any more than I was, I'd be asleep..

The only things keeping me awake at that point were my needs for some fresh air and the hunger that was tearing my stomach apart. I couldn't think about anything else, didn't care what happened to me, and would do anything for just one breath of non rotten smelling air and a small bowl of kibble. I kept as still as possible because to move or try to get away would have meant I would have had to breathe more, so when the bee flew from the Dalmatian mom's paw and stung me, it didn't affect me in the slightest.

The bee landed right where the buzzer had just licked me. When it was over, the Dalmatian mom wrapped a long orange decoration over the sting site. I continued watching as the Dalmatian mom wrapped layer upon layer of decoration around my paw; and around and around she went. She must have wrapped about ten layers over it before she was finally done, and I remember thinking to myself, *Now how am I going to chew through all that orange?*

57

JULIA
MAY 2009

"Calm down, Julia, he'll be fine," David said as he stroked the air between us.

Calm down, calm down! Was he serious? Had he really been married to me all these years? Calm down? Yeah right!

I felt like telling him what he could do with his calm down and his little hand motions. He was motioning in the air, like that was going to relax me. I knew he was just trying to help, though, and I knew that I was wound up so tight that anything would set me off. He was just being sweet David, the hero trying to tame the stress that burned deep inside me. So rather than bite his head off and regret it later, I ignored him and started pacing again.

I had dropped Eddie off earlier, and they had told me the surgery would be at ten A.M. sharp. It was already eleven, and one long, drawn-out hour had passed. It had been one of the longest hours I could remember, and I must have looked at my watch about fifty or so times. They had told me that there was no use in waiting at the hospital because I wouldn't be able to see him until tonight anyway. He needed to be monitored closely after the surgery, and I could visit later. So I had headed home and been a nervous wreck ever since.

The surgeon should be done by now. The technician had said that she would be surprised if the operation took longer than forty-five minutes when I had dropped him off, so what was taking so damn long?

I was worried sick. What if something had gone wrong? What if Eddie had reacted badly to the anesthesia and they were doing CPR at that very moment? What if they were too scared to call me to tell me the bad news? Wasn't this doctor supposed to be the best? She had been so confident when I had first met her, but maybe that was all a front. Maybe she didn't know what she was doing. Or maybe she was that good but despite having the best, something still hadn't gone according to plan. There's always a chance of a complication; they always tell you that. But whoever really thought it would be them?

I was so nervous and had no more nails to bite. I had ripped them all to painful stubs, and the small crevices of red, burning cuts on the margins of my fingertips were a reminder of where intact cuticles had been. I was doing my best to resist the urge to bite more, and I could feel the small drops of sweat on the small of my back as the air sent a chill down my spine.

Poor, sweet David had taken the morning off and, being the wonderful, unappreciated husband he was, was attempting to make me feel better. But hell, nothing but having my Eddie back to normal would make me feel better, and his calm-down routine just wasn't working. In fact, it was doing the opposite; every time he opened his mouth, I grew more annoyed. It would have been better if he had stayed at work.

What a nightmare this was. How nerve-racking. I felt so powerless, so out of control.

I told myself to relax and reminded myself that it wasn't up to me at this point. I needed to sit back and pull myself together. I had been through worse.

The shrill, high-toned ring of the phone pierced the silence like a bullhorn.

58

EDDIE
MAY 2009

All right, this is where the world turned upside down. Reality blurred, and what appeared to be real became unreal. One minute I was staring at my orange arm decoration, and then, well, haze. . . .

Black and white faded in and out, and then some gray, followed by a horde of angry winged furry friends carrying me in some sort of pouch hundreds of feet above the ground. Then there was a high-pitched droning sound, then black again. I felt woozy, head-spinning sensations, saw flying crunchy treats of all colors, shapes, and sizes, saw Paris grunting to the hair mom, Mom and Dad throwing shoe coverings, and then everything faded to black again before another wave of craziness began.

And on and on it went. Nothing seemed real, I couldn't feel my body, and I had absolutely no idea where I was. I felt like I was floating in midair one moment and then sinking to the bottom of a deep, never-ending water bowl the next. Every inch of my body burned like it was on fire one second, while I felt completely disconnected the next, a thing entirely separated from any form. I felt like I was just a furry friend in the middle of nothingness, reaching out my paw to tap something solid.

I don't know how long it went on like that, nor will I ever fully understand what had happened. I could have been that way for only a couple of moments, or maybe I had been that way for a countless number of light periods—a lifetime maybe—but one thing was pretty obvious: I had lost awakeness by either falling asleep or drifting off for a snooze, and snapping out of my dream did not come easy.

I didn't feel that good kind of feeling you usually get after a nap. As I started to wake up, I felt like my body weighed a thousand rocks, my paws felt like tree stumps, my head felt like a giant rock, and the rest of my body felt like it was molded to the floor. I had a real hard time thinking straight, and it took every ounce of energy I had to try to open one of my eyes. They, too, felt heavy, like they were tied shut. I did manage to force open my right eye just enough to have a quick peek.

I was staring straight at a red-and-black–flannel sleeping cushion, and resting on it was the best-looking furry friend I had ever seen. He was lying flat on his side, was of medium size, muscular, and probably middle- to late-aged. He was well shaped, except for the fact that he had one of the longest ears I had ever seen. I couldn't see the other one because it was tucked beneath him, but the one I could see ear was behind his head and reached to about the end of his back. His fur was shiny, although the shoulder that was up looked like it had gotten into a fight with the hair mom. It was as bald as a puppy's rump, and right in the center of the bald spot were bunches of tiny, pointy black strings. They were spaced about a claw length apart and ran in a line from his biceps to between his shoulder blades.

He was breathing slowly, like he was concentrating on not puking, and looked like Dad the morning after he drank too much of his bubbly burpy water. He looked barely awake, and if it weren't for his one half-open eye, I would have thought he was fast asleep. He was staring straight at me, and as I blinked, he blinked as well. As I sniffed to get a whiff of him, I saw that he also sniffed, copying everything I did.

I didn't have the energy to say hello, let alone move, and against my will my eye snapped shut again. I took a long, deep sniff and decided to forget about the long-eared furry friend for now; I was too out of it to be friendly. I focused on the smells around me instead, and hoped he wouldn't think I had been too rude. Taking a deep breath in and still not entirely sure where I was, I realized that I wasn't in my own territory, although I can't say the smell was altogether unfamiliar. It was a clean and non earthy smell, a smell I couldn't quite wrap my nose around. I knew I had smelled it before, but given my current state, I couldn't put my claw on it.

It wasn't long before I think I passed out again.

The next time around was the same as the last, and I still didn't know how long I was out. What I do know is that waking up this time was completely different from the last one because now I actually felt more like myself, not like my head was filled with water. Granted, my head was still woozy, and there was a pounding feeling above my ears, but at least my body didn't feel like it was being pulled into the ground. It didn't take much to open my eyes now.

I was still lying on my side on the red-and-black–flannel sleeping cushion, but the long-eared furry friend that had been in front of me was gone. I was in a different room from the one in which I had seen him, but given that I had been half asleep the last time I had attempted to open an eye, that furry friend could have been a dream. I took a moment to look around.

Now I was in a small, silver-walled den. It was about three furry friends' distance in length, about one furry friend's distance in width, and the shiny silver walls stretched up to the white, square-paneled ceiling. Light reflected off the silver walls, revealing the hundreds of tiny scratches, and it appeared that there were more scratches toward the front of the den. Directly in front of me was the door to the den, or at least that's what I thought it was, made of a bunch of small, thin, round, shiny, silver beams. They were spaced just close enough that you couldn't fit a whole paw through them but far enough that you could see through them.

There was a silver bowl on the floor of the den, in front of me, and I could just make out the reflection of the roof on the surface of the water inside.

I pulled up my head to have a better look around, and even though I was much better than before, my head wasn't completely right yet. I still felt woozy and light-headed, but I'd hoped getting up would improve that. Boy, was I wrong!

As I lifted my head, the world around me turned into a bunch of bursting white spots, and I could've sworn I had just been hit in the face with powerful, breath-sucking white foam at the place of sandy water. Except instead of feeling the sensation of the cold water as it hit my face and forced its way into my muzzle, I instead felt sweaty, sticky feeling of dizziness. I froze in place, not daring to move because I couldn't tell between up or down. I took a good ten deep breaths, slowly enjoying the air as it hit my lungs.

The breaths helped, and my dizziness started to fade. I looked through the see-through silver beams and into the room beyond.

It was a medium-sized room with a row of silver dens lining both sides of the walls. Every den looked to be about the same size as where I was, and each had its own see-through beamed door. I looked from one den to the next and saw that every den had room enough for a furry friend, and from my angle, I could make out furry friends in the two dens across from me.

One of them was a small, brown, flat-nosed furry friend. He was lying down on a flannel sleeping cushion much like the one in my den, and he had a small curl of a tail with spiky, thin fur and big, bulging black eyes. He had a large, bulky blue wrapping extending down the entire left length of his front leg and was just lying there relaxing, completely unaware that I was staring at him.

I looked at the other den, which housed a medium-sized, pointed-nosed furry friend who had a thick coat of short, black fur. Unlike the flat-nosed furry friend, this guy was bouncing up and down, yelling at the top of his lungs. He was jumping so high that his muzzle touched the topmost portions of the shiny beams, and I was sure that if he kept that up he would get it caught on something in midflight.

There were also two blue-coated moms in the room. One was a middle-aged, tall and skinny mom with a straggly brown-and-gray, ungroomed mane, while the other was an ancient short and fat mom whose face shone with wetness. The short one moved at a slow pace, making sure to spend way more time outside each of the dens than the taller one. After looking at each individual den, she would scratch into her piece of rectangular white bark with her scratching stick, and then look up to see what the tall mom was doing. The tall mom was moving much faster, taking way less time between dens, but, like the short mom, she, too, would stop outside each den, stare through the see-through beamed door, scratch her bark, and then move on.

They kept grunting to each other as they moved, every now and then snorting in approval. They went from den to den, scratching and snorting, snorting and staring, and it didn't take me long to lose interest in their game.

I still had no idea where I was, or what was going on. I tried to sit up more but realized that I was still feeling really strange, my head still feeling like it was too large for my body. I felt weak, like I hadn't eaten for a long while. My mouth was dry, my stomach was grumbling, and I was definitely giving off hungry breath.

I was also aware of a distant, barely noticeable throb in my right shoulder. It was a light pulling sensation, one that hadn't jumped out at me since I had been awake. Between the white spots and the checking out of the blue-coated moms, I hadn't really cared about anything else, and the shoulder throb had been in the background

But after the newness of watching the blue-coated moms had worn off, I needed something else to do and focused all of my attention on my shoulder. I tried to feel exactly where the pulling feeling was coming from, and more importantly, how I was going to get to it and lick it better. I tensed my right shoulder and relaxed it again, making sure that was where the pulling was coming from. Just to be sure, I tensed again and felt the same thing. Right as I was going to tense a third time, I realized something new.

It felt . . . well . . . almost normal, and I had, in fact, been using all four legs to stand up. The tingly feeling was gone, and although I knew I was not back to normal, I was so excited to be using all four legs again. I'd take the dull throb over the tingle any day.

I took a first happy step forward and felt a wave of dizziness hit. Just before my legs gave out though, I saw a blur appear out of the corner of my eye and heard a loud, scraping sound. It was the same sound our back territory door made when it was scraped open in the cold, and my den wall opened. I smelled who it was long before I could see him.

I felt two strong paws catch me just as my legs lost all control. He had reached me in the nick of time, and let me tell you, his smell caught me just as much as his paws did. Before I knew it, I was on the sleeping cushion, flat on my chest.

He was sitting right next to me on the cushion at a safe enough distance to be out of a direct whiff of him, and he was gently patting my head. He was grunting softly, and despite his smell, I actually found myself getting sleepy again. I didn't want a repeat of my almost passing-out experience, so I decided that I would just stay there and let the smelly dad give me love.

"Dr. Berry, he's almost recovered from the anesthesia. Do you want me to wait on putting on the Elizabethan collar until he's totally awake or do it now?"

"Do it now Rick... the last thing I need is a call because the knucklehead chewed out his sutures."

59

EDDIE
MAY 2009

When I awoke the next time, my head had cleared. The air was cold, and given that my nose hairs weren't burning, I knew the smelly dad was nowhere around. I felt like I had slept like a puppy, and besides the dull throb in my shoulder, I felt like I was back to myself.

But all was not normal.

Besides being a bit cold, the air around me also felt stuffy, second hand, like it had been snorted way too many times. I could feel a pressure and a something hanging out around my head, and something was muffling the sound all sound. Whatever it was, it was pushing my ears forward because I felt them tickling the lower part of my jaw.

I got up slowly and without any dizziness, but I knew that something was still out of place. I could see just fine in front of me, but everything to my left and right was blurred. Even up and down was hazy, and it was only in front of me that things looked normal.

I took my first step forward and realized something pressing down on my neck. It wasn't pushing hard; it was just resting on my shoulders and the top of my back. It felt like a really awkward and large necklace.

While keeping my head still, I looked up and then to my side, making sure only to move my eyes. That's when I saw it, and I felt like such a goof for not noticing it before. It was huge and circular, and it wrapped around my entire head. It jutted forward like a white, big cone, with the narrow part sitting on my shoulders and the widest part stretching forward past the tip of my nose

It was probably the reason why everything sounded so soft. Heck, between not being able to move my ears and this thing in the way, it was no wonder I couldn't hear properly.

The thing also had a strange smell to it, a not-from-the-ground, new-food-bowl smell, and being that the thing pretty much covered my entire head, it was the only thing I could sniff. I tried to get rid of the smell by turning my body to the left and then the right and even backed up three steps until my butt hit the silver den wall, but still the scent followed me.

I wondered what this thing was, why it was on my head, and, more importantly, how I could get it off.

I hadn't been up for that long, but my shoulder had started to throb again. The throb wasn't as bad as the tingly sensation; it felt more like a regular pain, like one of the hundreds of times I had scraped myself on our territory fence. It was still obvious enough to deserve some much-needed lick therapy.

How the heck I was going to get to it with the clear thing around my neck? It was ginormous, and it couldn't have been in a worse place, totally in the way.

The clear necklace . . . that thing needed to go, and as soon as possible. I needed to get it off because as much as some furry friends like their ears in their faces, the smell of fresh food bowls, bumping into things when they turn, or not being able to lick certain parts of their body, I would never be one of them. It needed to come off and it needed to happen two light periods ago.

So I put my butt on the cold floor, arched my head back, and pushed up against the outside of the thing with my hind paws. I kicked and kicked, and on the third kick, the clear necklace bent so that the cone turned into a long funnel and my unfortunate paws slipped right past it. The thing instantly bounced back into its shape with a *thump*. It hadn't budged; the only thing that had changed had been me, because now I was a little out of breath from the effort. I tried again, but no matter how hard I pushed, no matter how hard or how many times I kicked, the thing didn't give an inch.

With one final effort, I bent my neck back and then threw it forward and stepped smack dab into the center of my water bowl. I only felt the wet sensation of the paw dunk for a moment because the bowl slipped out from under me, and, with a sand-scraping crunch, it launched forward into the den wall with a bang as I belly-flopped onto the cold floor

Things had definitely not gone as planned, and two thoughts crossed my mind. Number one, all the shaking and bobbing had left me with a big urge to mark some territory; I really, really had to go. Number two, I had just spent the last couple of moments jumping up and down, using my right shoulder and mostly pain free of the tingles that a couple of light periods earlier would've been impossible. Beside the fact that I was flat on my belly in a puddle of water with a crazy need to mark, things seemed to be pretty good.

I needed to get someone's attention, anyone's, anything's attention, otherwise it wouldn't just be water on the floor. I had never had an urge this bad and if I didn't get outside real soon, I knew that this *pressing* feeling would take care of itself. I felt like I was going to pop.

So I did what any reasonable furry friend would do in need of a tree. I howled like I have never howled before and stopped only when I was sure pawsteps were approaching.

THE DOG DAYS OF THE PAST

60

DAVID
JULY 2008

I took Allyson to lunch after we closed the Hutchinson loan. It had been a huge deal and she'd had a big part in helping to close it. We deserved to celebrate, and I wanted to do it with style, so I decided to take her to Vito's. It was by far one of the best Italian restaurants in town, the kind of restaurant where wine is a must.

Given the last two months of misery I'd been going through at home, this was the first happy thing I'd done in a while. Richard had passed, Julia was a mess, and our relationship was at an all-time low. We were barely speaking.

She was a closed book, and she didn't want to talk to anyone, even me. After her father had passed, she'd spent a lot of time crying, as expected, and I'd done my best to be there for her. The crying had become less and less, but she'd grown even more distant and silent. We'd been married for a long time, but neither of us had gone through the death of a parent.

Her reaction was strange, a new phenomenon in our relationship, and what had started six months ago was still in full force. I was used to a talkative wife, a woman who usually could find something to say in even the most boring situations. I missed the old Julia, and I too was having a hard time dealing with this new twist in our lives, this new her.

It seemed that we had nothing to say to each other now, or more like she had nothing to say to me. She was so damn quiet. I tried to talk to her, tried to get her to discuss even the most harmless and nonthreatening subject, but she just wanted to be left alone. I knew that eventually she would open up and I sure as heck didn't want to push the issue, but I couldn't help feeling the strain on our relationship. So I had decided to back off and give her space and, more importantly, time.

It wasn't a happy time in our household, and I missed our long conversations and the bond we had. As selfish as it was, I missed my wife and hated that she was like this. I wished she would just snap out of it, but that was the spoiled kid in me speaking.

Allyson had been great, though; real easy to talk to, and she couldn't stop telling me how sad she was for me. She had told me that if I needed to talk about anything I could always come to her, or even call her if I wanted, and truth be told, she had made a great sounding board. I don't know how it happened exactly, but I ended up having long conversations with her that led to all sorts of topics: my life, my likes, my dislikes, even my marriage. The girl was quite pleasant to be around, had a great sense of humor, and I enjoyed being able to speak with someone. I missed that, and Allyson had been so nice to me. It didn't hurt that she was drop-dead gorgeous, as well.

It was a pity, though, that her office skills weren't that great. She couldn't take messages down properly, was terrible at filing, and couldn't handle juggling more than two phone lines at once. I hoped she'd absorbed some of the advice I'd given her three weeks ago, when she forgot to give me the message that Julia had called. Jules had been having a real hard day and had given Allyson a message to have me call her back ASAP to discuss when we were going to go to Richard's house to visit, but Allyson had denied that Julia had even called.

There was also a pile of files that had been building up on her desk that needed to be sorted and put away. She'd been making an effort since, and I wish I could say she'd improved, but that would be an overstatement. I couldn't be too hard on her today, though, because she had done so well with the Hutchinson loan, after all.

We had a great lunch. I had the fettuccine Alfredo and she had a grilled chicken salad. The fettuccine was amazing, like always, with just the right amount of Parmesan. We also managed to polish off a bottle of very smooth Chardonnay, and by the end of lunch we were both giggling like schoolchildren. After an hour and a half, much longer than I had intended, we planned to head back to the office, but Allyson insisted that we have one more drink.

Why not? How could I resist her mischievous little smile? We deserved to live a little.

THE DOG DAYS OF THE PRESENT

61

JULIA
MAY 2009

I was a complete nervous wreck. Was his shoulder going to be bloody? Would it ooze? Would he even be able to walk, or would I have to carry him everywhere? It was going to probably look awful, red and swollen, and he was going to hate me for doing this to him. He would never forgive me for putting him through it, and I couldn't stand the thought of that. How would he know it had been for his own good?

Would I be able to handle seeing him injured like that? Would I pass out at the sight of blood? That had happened when I was five, after I cut my finger on a piece of glass, and ever since I haven't even looked down when they give me a shot. I would never forgive myself if I passed out.

Besides the embarrassment and probable paramedic call to this place, I would never live it down personally.

I was in the lobby of Paws Specialty Hospital and was staring at the semicircular front desk. I had arrived at nine A.M. sharp, the time they'd told me he would be ready to go.

Dr. Berry had called me after the surgery was over the day before to let me know that Eddie had recovered well, and she'd assured me that he had been resting comfortably. She said she'd kept him on some strong pain medications for the night but that he should be back to normal today. I had been mildly relieved to hear that, but I still hated the fact that he hadn't been at home last night. I knew he had probably been lonely here, and I'm sure he had been pining for us.

I called at ten last night, just to make sure he was still doing all right. The assistant had been kind and had informed me that he was fast asleep in his run, but I had still felt terrible. I had missed him so much, and I had had a hard time sleeping without feeling him in the room.

I had been up since six this morning, just lying in bed and staring at the clock. Time couldn't have crept by any slower, and every second had seemed like an eternity. David had to be at work for an early meeting, so it had been up to me to get Eddie by myself. At eight forty-five, after three cups of coffee and a leftover piece of vegetarian pizza, I had headed over to get him. At least the gods had decided not to burden me with traffic today, because with all the caffeine in my system, I probably would have had an accident because I was so wound up and jittery. My nerves were frayed, and I had a hard time keeping the steering wheel steady, my hands were trembling so much.

The drive had been a series of faceless buildings and unmemorable houses, and I had been doing everything I could to avoid speeding. Even though the car thermometer had read a comfortable seventy-two degrees outside, I'd felt cold and couldn't quell my shaking. It was ironic, because there I was on a beautiful sunny, cloudless California day, the sky a perfect ocean blue, and I had the heater cranked up the whole way and still wasn't warm.

When I had finally gotten to the hospital, the receptionist, Kathleen—I think that's her name—had been generous enough to offer me another cup of coffee. Unfortunately, instead of just saying "thank you, but no" I had been such a strung-out mess that I had snapped back at her with misplaced nervous energy. She had just nodded, but I had seen the surprise and hurt in her expression. I would be sure to apologize to her at a later date, and although I knew it was no excuse, I'd been so nervous about how Eddie would be. I hadn't intended to be rude.

The waiting room had also felt cold, so I couldn't help but shiver. It was two minutes past nine, and Kathleen had told me that they would be bringing Eddie right up two minutes earlier. There had only been one other person in the lobby, and she had been sitting by the window reading *Newsweek*. She had looked to be in her thirties and had dirty blond hair and a pair of round, thick, black-framed glasses that hugged her face. The lenses were so bulky that they looked more like mini-binoculars then glasses; that poor girl. If I had vision that bad and required a prescription so powerful, being that young, I would have considered getting Lasik or contact lenses.

There was a photograph of some war scene on the front of her *Newsweek*, but I couldn't make heads or tails of it. Nor did I care, for that matter. I looked at the double doors again, and then at my watch. It was four minutes past nine.

Where was he?

Just as I was readying myself to ask Kathleen if they had forgotten to bring him up, I heard him barking. I would have recognized that bark anywhere, that happy, never-hurt-a-fly, always-in-a-good-mood bark. I had been listening to it for the last eleven years, and I knew it had to be Eddie.

He was getting closer; now I could hear his whining, his cute, energetic panting, his low-pitched bursts of coonhound barks, and, of course, the jingle of his leash hook jerking against the metal loop of his collar. I smiled to myself and kept staring at the white double doors in anticipation.

I heard the desperate scraping of his claws waterskiing on the smooth, slippery floor behind the door as he desperately tried to get a grip. Whoever was trying to control Eddie was in for it; I knew just how hard that dog could pull. He could practically take my arm off if he saw a squirrel on a walk.

I watched as the double doors burst open and practically fly off their hinges, and felt the wind as it blew across the room and passed me.

And there he was. It was pure Eddie, unadulterated, long-eared, happy, beautiful Eddie, except . . . well, he looked absolutely ridiculous and undeniably hysterical. Just about the last thing I had expected at that moment would be that I would laugh to the point that I thought I would wet my pants. I had been up all night worried sick to death about him, about how he was going to handle the surgery, about how frightened beyond belief I was at my reaction to seeing him. How I would handle him all cut up, with a large gash across his shoulder, watching him having to deal with the pain of the procedure, and taking care of him while he recovered. And now I was laughing?

I just couldn't help it, though, because he looked so comical. It must have been the buildup, or the coffee, or even my spent nerves, but with the giant clear cone encircling his entire head, he looked utterly ridiculous. It was huge, about three sizes too big for him, and practically touching the ground it was so wide. And his ears, oh his ears, that's what made the scene so funny. They were pressed up against the collar and pushed forward because that's the only place they had room to go. They were sandwiched flat down against his face and met under his jaw, where they bunched together. He looked like he was wearing a shawl. Eddie could have been one of the daughters in *Fiddler on the Roof.*

He was bounding straight for me, dragging the poor technician, who was desperately trying to hold onto his leash. Poor girl, she was a small and didn't stand a chance against my overgrown, sunflower of a dog, who managed to break free from her grip and went into a full sprint, his tongue hanging out and smiling all the way.

I was too happy to be scared or even care that he stood a good chance of doing me some real damage if his collar hit me, but luckily, he didn't try to jump. He braked at the last second, so instead of knocking me over, he swung his waist around and pushed his butt into me. He did manage to push me a good two steps back while he continued to whine and bark, but at least I was still standing and he was making happy sounds. I could tell that he had really missed me. I bent down and gave him a giant hug, not realizing that my forearm had brushed against his surgery site until I felt the bare skin of his shoulder and the prickling sensation of about fifteen pointy suture ends digging into my arm.

The realization of what was digging into my skin sunk in, and I instantly jerked my arm away from him. I stood up with my hand over my mouth in shock and prayed that he wouldn't scream. I hadn't meant to touch it. What had I done? Had I hurt him? I waited for the cry of pain that any normal person who had just undergone a major surgery would make.

But it never came. Instead, he started running around me in tight circles, barking and smiling and letting the whole hospital know just how happy he was to see me. He hadn't even winced or shown any indication of pain. Hell, I think those prickly little sutures had hurt me more than him.

I couldn't believe it; he was actually running and using all four of his legs without any sign of a limp. Had he really just had surgery? Was this the same dog who hadn't even been able to put his leg down two days ago, who had spent the last week on his doggie cushion, only getting up to go to the bathroom?

To say I was flabbergasted would be an understatement, but having the time to internalize what I was seeing didn't prove to be an option. All of a sudden, I was in pain.

I felt the shock of a sharp, semicircular, knifelike object digging into my stomach, and suddenly the air was violently knocked out of me. I probably would have ended up bent over to catch my breath if it hadn't been for the two large, yellow paws pushing on my shoulders, forcing me backward, and the wet, slobbery tongue scraping the entire left side of my face.

"Eddie!" I managed to get out in a wheeze.

I had regained my balance and managed to fill my lungs with a deep, much-needed breath. He continued to lick me, and even though that was usually a big no-no in our house, I didn't have the heart to discipline him. His cone had almost decapitated me after it had knocked the wind out of me, but at least I had reflexively turned my head as he had popped up and, luckily, avoided a doggy tongue in the mouth.

I ever-so-gingerly grabbed both of his paws and slowly put him back on the ground. I was obviously more afraid of hurting him than he was of being hurt, by the way he was acting. I bent down to look at the surgery site, preparing myself for something straight out of a horror movie.

The entire right half of his shoulder and back were shaved, and the skin beneath had a soft, muted pink sheen. In the center of the shaved region was a long incision line that stretched from the top of his back to the bottom of his shoulder blade. There were about fifteen neat, parallel crisscross stitches running the length of it, and the edges of the skin where it was sewn together looked red and somewhat puffy. There was no blood, no pus, or anything else, for that matter, leaking out of it, and it appeared to be perfectly aligned.

Surprisingly, the first word that came to my mind was *clean*. It looked clean and neat, and Eddie didn't seem any worse off for it. I had been expecting the worst, but looking at his shoulder, seeing the perfectly sewn skin, I felt a wave of relief wash over me. Was this what I had been so worried about, why I hadn't slept all night, had pigged out on pizza and soda, and had spent hours crying?

I felt the warmth rush to my face and knew I was flushed. I probably looked like an overripe tomato; anytime I got embarrassed or felt foolish, my face reddened. For anyone who knew me and had seen me in any of these situations, my face had proved to be an open book, and at that moment I could feel the heat radiating from my cheeks.

The poor technician who had been attempting to bring Eddie over had finally made it to where I was standing. She had short, black shoulder-length hair and the greenest eyes I had ever seen. She must have been in her late twenties and was only a little shorter than I was but looked to be at least ten pounds lighter. Her wrists were so skinny that I could have probably fit one of them between my thumb and forefinger; she was mainly skin and bones. I'm surprised they had trusted her with big dogs and that he hadn't broken free earlier.

She had been out of breath by the time she had reached me, and I could tell she was a little flustered. I did my best to stop smiling because I didn't want her to feel worse than she probably already did at having her charge escape, but it proved to be very difficult. I had my boy back and he was in one piece.

"I'm sorry I kept you waiting, Mrs. Freed," she began, "but Eddie had a little accident on the way out and I needed to clean him off. There are a couple of things we need to go over."

It was difficult to concentrate on what she was saying because Eddie was still panting and whining up a storm, and despite the technician's efforts, she was speaking quietly. Her voice was high-pitched and naturally soft, and I could tell she was attempting to speak up, but given the background noise, I was having a hard time hearing her. I nodded my head in acknowledgment because I caught most of what she said.

"First, he's real hungry. He hasn't eaten since yesterday because he was too sedated for us to feed him earlier. He was scheduled to be fed half an hour from now, so go ahead and give him food when he gets home."

She handed me a piece of paper titled DISCHARGE INSTRUCTIONS.

"Eddie needs to stay out of the water until his stitches come out. He shouldn't go on long walks and should avoid roughhousing with your other dog. Even though it's obvious he's not the kind of dog to stay sedentary, we recommend that he stay pretty calm over the next week to give the site time to heal."

We both looked down at Eddie, who was looking at the door, clearly anxious to get out. He was wagging his tail and tilting his head to the side with the same look he got when he was gearing up to run after something. His saliva was making a small puddle on the ground under where his tongue was hanging out, and whatever was out there had caused a temporary lull in his whining, though he kept panting.

The technician and I looked back at each other, and she smiled at me.

"Just do your best, Mrs. Freed, to keep him calm."

She added, "We're also sending him home with an Elizabethan collar to prevent him from licking the surgical site. It needs to stay on at all times so he doesn't traumatize the region. Don't take it off for any reason or he'll probably chew out the sutures. If he does that, it means another surgery, and we'd like to avoid that."

She paused for effect, allowing that to sink in.

Before I could ask, she said, "It's fine for him to sleep in it, and he'll get used to eating with it on. Actually, he'll probably forget it's there in a couple of hours. We're also sending him home with an anti-inflammatory in addition to the pain medication he's already taking."

I looked down at the paper she'd just given me and followed along line by line as she read it verbatim. After about the fourth sentence, I stopped following along and looked down at Eddie. He had stopped panting and was really fixated on the entryway. He still had his head tilted to the side, but now he was sniffing the air. I knew that look and tightened my hand around his leash because I knew that in another couple of seconds he would want to take off after whatever was hiding outside.

"He'll be due back here in fourteen days for suture removal, and at the same appointment we'll do his CAT scan for radiation planning. Please don't feed him that morning; he needs to be fasted for at least eight hours before anesthesia. The doc has written this all down on these instructions, and if you have any questions, please call. We're open twenty-four hours a day. He's a real sweet dog and he did great. Do you have any questions?"

I gave Eddie's leash a short and firm tug to remind him that I was next to him. We had taken him to an obedience class when he was a puppy, and about the only thing he'd retained was how to walk on a lead, but it only worked with me. With anyone else, including David, he would ultimately try to pull him wherever he wanted to go.

"Any questions, Mrs. Freed?"

I looked up and saw that the technician had been staring at me with a forced smile on her face. She must have realized I hadn't been fully listening and obviously wasn't happy about it. She couldn't be outright rude, though I sensed the annoyance in her tone.

"Does this thing really need to stay on? Are you sure he'll be able to sleep with it?"

In a high, soft, and borderline impatient voice, she answered, "Mrs. Freed, if there is one thing that is probably the most important of all during healing, it's the E collar. There's no need for two surgeries, and that's exactly what will happen if it comes off."

62

EDDIE
MAY 2009

By the time we returned to the Crunchy Territory, I had mastered and even grown used to the clear necklace. I had discovered so many cool uses for it, bugging Paris and the like, and for the life of me, I couldn't remember why I had been so upset about it in the first place.

Yeah, sure, I couldn't get to my shoulder to lick it, but the small ropes in my skin were doing the job of making it better just fine.

So when we finally returned to the Crunchy Territory what seemed ages later, I was sad when they took my clear necklace off.

63

BRANDON
MAY 2009

I remembered this guy; he was a trip. The dog has the coolest ears I've seen, and he wags his tail at everything. He still had his E collar on, and by the looks of it, he'd worked the thing over. And if I remembered right, the dog was pretty quick with his tongue as well.

Dude, that was perfect! Quick Tongue, that's what I was going to rename our band. Forget Thunder, I always thought it sucked. But Quick Tongue, that was awesome!

The lady looked freaked out already and it was only ten in the morning. It was a little too early to be spazzing. She had on tight blue jeans that outlined some solid, tight legs, and she had on an oversized, baggy gray wool sweater. I could see she had a kicking body under it, so it was a pity she was hiding it. She was thin and looked to be in good shape, and I'd guess she was probably in her early forties. She could pass for midthirties, though, if it wasn't for the lines in her face that gave her away. She was pretty hot, though, for an older chic, and must have been a real babe when she was younger. I wouldn't have said no to her!

But the chick was ultra-emotional, way more than the average client. I could tell she was bugging out already, and we were only going to do the CAT today. Just wait until we actually got to radiation time. I could just tell this one was going to be high maintenance, though I hoped I was wrong.

Kathleen had called me up to get him after the lady had filled out all the paperwork and pretty much signed her life away. Just looking at her, I could tell she was wired, unlike me this morning. Hell, I was definitely out of it today. My two Red Bulls still hadn't kicked in, and I was wiped from our gig last night. We tore it up, even if it was for some lame, small-time afterhours party. Three hours of sleep and two Red Bulls hadn't done the job yet, and I couldn't help yawning as the white double doors to the front lobby closed behind me.

I rubbed my eyes, felt the scratch of an eye booger nick my lower left eyelid, and did my best to avoid squinting at the glare coming from the windows. Whose bright idea was it to build this place facing east and put so many damn windows in? Yeah, sure, it lit the place up, but even with the tinting the glare sucked. Genius, pure genius.

I desperately wished I had my sunglasses as I walked toward the lady and her funny-eared dog. I felt my head throb and a wave of nausea wash over me. Man, I'm not as young as I used be.

I continued walking across the obnoxiously bright lobby toward them, and with each step I did my best to get back into work mode. It was time to get professional. I cleared my throat, cleared the residual cigarette phlegm, and in the best work voice I could pull off, I said, "Hello again, Mrs. Freed; glad to see Eddie is doing well."

She nodded, and I felt a shooting pain in my left temple. It took everything I had to keep smiling, and I pulled out every stop not to squint. Man, I was suffering this morning! I looked down at Eddie and took the opportunity to shy away from the light.

I said, "Mrs. Freed, I'm going to give you Eddie's E collar to hang onto for now, just so it doesn't get lost back there. Don't trash it, though, because he may need it during radiation."

The lobby was pretty quiet; it seemed like a lull between appointments. Normally, there would have been at least a couple of other people hanging out, but at the moment it was dead.

She answered in an unsure and semi-on-the-verge-of-flipping-out voice, "Um, sure."

She was staring at me all confused as I undid the silver buckle to his orange-and-brown Padres collar. It was threaded through the circular loops of the base of the clear E collar, and I pulled off his collar as Eddie turned toward us. He gave a short, playful bark, and then stuck his wet, cold nose straight into the hand holding the collar. The little dude was trying to get back into the thing! What a trip.

All of the tension suddenly lifted, and I actually saw Mrs. Freed break into a smile. There were little laugh lines at the corners of her mouth, but otherwise she had smooth, tanned skin. Her teeth were white and straight, and she had sky blue eyes. I gotta say, she was a pretty lady, especially now that she was smiling and not so strung out.

With Eddie still jamming his nose and now his tongue into my hands, I followed her lead and also started to chuckle. Funny thing, laughter; it cures everything. Even my headache started to chill.

I tried to keep her smiling by saying, "Calm down, boy, you'll get it back. Man, Mrs. Freed, Eddie's quite a character." I know it was corny, but it was early and I was hung over; give a guy a break.

She nodded while I freed the Padres collar from the final loop of his E collar. I lifted my hands high enough so Eddie couldn't get to them, and unintentionally looked straight into the glare. Instead of feeling a laser burning through my skull, my head actually felt somewhat human. My Red Bulls must have finally been kicking in.

I handed her both the Padres and the E collar, and as her small, delicate hand brushed against mine, I saw her smile bail. She took the collars from me just a little too fast.

Oh, damn, I hadn't meant to touch her; our hands had barely made contact. She overreached, man! Again she had the freaked-out look, and judging by her face, I could swear she was going to cry. Dude, I wasn't hitting on her or anything, and I sure as hell hadn't meant to brush up against her. I hope she wasn't freaking because of me!

It was like night and day, first unhappy, then laughing, then bummed out again; the lady was a mess, and I hoped it was just because of her dog and all. I looked down and knew my face must have been red as a cherry Slurpee. That always happens to me whenever I get embarrassed. My dad always said I wouldn't last five minutes in a poker game. Aw, hell, it was too damn early for this, and I did my best to keep in work mode.

I forced myself to keep going because I knew I was probably just imagining it. This lady was a wreck from the start, and I'm sure she hadn't even thought twice about the hand touch.

Forcing on my most professional work-mode face, I went on, "Mrs. Freed, I'm going to take him back for his CAT scan now, and he'll be ready to go in about two hours. In the meantime, you can schedule his first day of radiation for two days' time, on Wednesday, with Kathleen over there. I know you spoke to Dr. Lindy yesterday, but are there any other questions I can answer or pass on?"

I had to say it, but I really, really hoped the doc had gone over it so many times that he had burned her out. He was the master, after all, and his usual Jedi mind tricks soothed even the craziest stress cases. Granted, most of these folks were decent, loving people, but you have to understand, once in a while we got some that could get pretty nuts. I've had to deal with some of them, and they are just plain over the deep end. But somehow, some way, they all love the doc. He's got some mad skills.

I like the job, and even on days like this, being hungover, sleep deprived, and getting my hand licked like a Popsicle and all, I was happy to be working here. I had never thought that I'd feel like this about any job, especially working in a cancer specialty hospital for dogs and cats. You'd think that would be bummer, right, doing chemotherapy and radiation on dying pets, huh?

But that wasn't the case. We helped out a lot of the dogs and cats, and that makes you pretty happy and everything, but it isn't just about the animals. I knew I was a good technician and all, and I helped treat plenty of cancer, but half of the job was actually for the people. I got to personally help some folks going through some pretty rough times, and that was one of the coolest things about the gig. Like how many people can say that?

Dude, when I first started out and all, I'll admit that it took me some time and getting used to. But after two years of doing this, I think I've gotten the hang of it. The truth of the matter is, I really dig doing this stuff, adding my ying to the yang, being there for the animals and the people. I look at it as my way of doing good, doing right by the world, doing my part and all.

Mrs. Freed said in a nervous voice, "No, I think I understand the schedule; Dr. Lindy was pretty thorough yesterday. Take care of my boy, please. He's been so brave so far."

The corners of her mouth fluttered, and I could see her eyes start to cloud up. Poor lady, it was only a matter of seconds before I knew she was going to blow.

Maybe . . . yup . . . wait for it . . . wait for it . . .

And . . . there we go.

64

EDDIE
MAY 2009

It happened without any chance of stopping it. I felt it hit even before I looked up. When I did get a chance to see the damage, I saw Mom with her lips trembling, her forehead creased, and drool pouring from her eyes like water spilled from a water bowl. She was taking small, short, whistling breaths, sucking in air with tensed lips and letting out a whining groan after each one

It was sudden and it had taken me by surprise. Sure, she had been nervous this morning, shaky, and she hadn't been able to keep still, but I hadn't expected this. But now, wow, the drool was just flowing from her eyes and it was really upsetting me.

The room was still empty and quiet, aside from the eye-decoration mom behind the desk, tapping on her paw exerciser, and the shiny-headed dad standing in front of Mom. The eye-decoration mom was still hammering away, staring at her hypno box and unaware of Mom's downpour. The shiny-headed dad wasn't fazed either, but at least he was looking at Mom with a sad face; he had even taken a half step toward her, preparing to try to cheer her up. The fold in his forehead, the way he pulled his mouth straight, the sudden change to slow breathing; it was as if he knew the downpour had been coming. Once it hit, he had started grunting to Mom, and his tone had been soothing, caring, and soft, like he had been around eye-drooling moms hundreds of times before.

Mom pulled the sleeve of her gray body covering back and wiped the drool from her eyes with the back of her paw. She reached into her paw bag and took out a white, thin, bendy piece of bark. With a loud blast, she held it up to her muzzle and blew into it as hard as she could, and I could see little particles of white bark floating in the air.

She kept snorting at the shiny-headed dad, who had taken a half step back. I guess he hadn't wanted to get hit with the white bark pieces. He took a step forward again, closing the gap that had opened between them.

I was still confused about what was going on, but as it turns out, there was no time to figure it out. Mom reached out and handed the shiny-headed dad my orange safety rope, and before I knew it, he had taken off my clear necklace and had started pulling me to the swinging wall.

Again I was greeted by the white-coated dad with the standard white-coated greeting, again my arm was licked clean of its fur by the timid mom playing with a shiny silver-and-black buzzer, and again a bee tail ended up burying itself in my arm. This time, though, instead of orange wrapping to hide it, they used purple layers on me.

With all the greetings and stingings out of the way, I was then taken to a different room, one that I'd never seen before and was probably the closest thing to furry friend bliss that I will ever experience. Not that you could tell it was paradise the moment you walked in, but when my eyes finally adjusted, I realized it was just a lick away from the best place you could ever imagine.

When we first walked in, the first thing I noticed was that the place was freezing. The second thing I noticed was that it was dark. I could only make out general shapes without details. So, between the dark and the not completely knowing where I was, I froze in place while my eyes adjusted and my fur poofed up trying to get warm.

As things started to come into focus, though, I saw that I was standing in a room that was about a quarter of the size of the large, four-sectioned one we had just come from. It was divided in two by what looked to be a gray wall that extended about three quarters of the way across, although with the lack of light I couldn't be completely sure. I was standing just behind and to the left of where the wall ended, and I could only make out the details of the smaller section of the divided room to my right. I managed to see a head-high, desklike structure, with tons of blinking lights on it.

CAT SCANNER CONSOLE: DO NOT ATTEMPT TO OPERATE WITHOUT PROPER TRAINING.

Right ahead of me was the larger of the sections of the room, and I could make out the outline of something really big. I squinted more to try to get a better look but was distracted by the shiny-headed dad behind me. He was trying to scratch something on the wall, and I could hear him fumbling and grunting in frustration.

The rectangular door next to the shiny-headed dad squeaked as it swung open, and I could make out the shape of the timid mom as she shuffled in. I could smell the salty odor that usually came with moms and dads when they had been running around, and the timid mom's scent was strong. As the door started to swing closed, I heard a grunt of satisfaction burst out of the shiny-headed dad.

There was then a quick and short click, and then paradise shone its beautiful light period on us.

The thing that I had been struggling to see in the dark turned out to be nothing less than amazing. Right smack in the middle of the room stood the largest crunchy treat I had ever seen in my life. It was humongous and pure white , and the first thing that caught my eye was the large, circular, shank bonelike circle. It was sitting upright and reached toward the ceiling like a furry friend on two legs dancing for a treat. It must have been at least six times the width of any furry friend I'd ever seen, and at least four large furry friends in height. It had round hollow center and through it was a long, narrow rectangular bench. It was the most beautiful thing I'd ever seen.

I took a deep sniff in, expecting a strong meaty smell but the only thing I could pick up was a salty, metallic odor laced with a hint of sniff box.

I had to get closer to the thing because I was having a hard time accepting that this had no crunchy treat smell. It was impossible that something so big could be so empty of meat, and I had to believe that it had something, anything left over.

Now, while my nose was trying to sort through all of this, my stomach had decided that smell or no smell, this thing was too crazy for me to stay calm about. Let's not forget that Mom had skipped feeding me—again, I might add—and I could feel my belly starting to rumble.

I just had to get closer, had to sort it out, had to taste it to believe it. I just had to . . .

Without a thought, without even actually deciding what to do, I felt my necklace start to tighten as my paws attempted to carry me forward. I had started pulling on my safety rope, and I couldn't have controlled myself even if I had wanted to because something that big, that close, and so incredibly tempting was too much even for the most disciplined furry friend to handle.

I heard the shiny-headed dad snorting, and I felt the pull around my neck as he held my safety rope. Even though I knew I wasn't going anywhere with a grip like that, I still couldn't keep my paws from trying to dig into the floor to try to get traction.

The shiny-headed dad grunted to the timid mom then, but still I kicked to move forward. The timid mom grunted back, and I even sensed her bending down and trying to shake my recently licked paw. I was still looking at the world's largest crunchy treat, and no amount of paw touching could move me. I felt some of the pressure loosen around the paw on which they had decorated me with purple wrappings, but still I kept my eyes on the treat. I ignored her; I ignored everything.

All I could think about was the serious, muzzle-watering licking ahead of me when I got a piece of that white . . .

And that was the last thing I remembered before the world went black.

Dude, you ok? Who would of ever thought he would have put on such a fight? But seriously though, that had to be the funniest thing I have ever seen. He was full on trying to get to the CT like it was lunch. Friggin hysterical man...ok party's over, lets get this scan running.

65

KATHLEEN
MAY 2009

Bless her heart; she looked so worried, the poor gal. She'd been sitting there for the last thirty minutes and I didn't think she had a nail left on one hand. The poor lady was going to chew off a finger if she kept it up.

Mrs. Freed was sitting on one of the chairs directly in front of me with her back resting on one of the windows, and she looked about as nervous as a pet turkey a week before Thanksgiving. That pretty little neck of hers was going to get whiplash if she kept that up, looking up from her magazine to the door every couple of seconds, like that would speed up time. She had picked up the latest copy of *Good Housekeeping*, the one with "Recipes on the Run," but I didn't think the gal had gotten past the first page.

Judging by her waist size and that pretty face of hers, she probably hadn't spent much time in the kitchen either. She looked to be more of a takeout or salad type, like most of the young people in this city. Folks these days have lost the art of fine cooking, and the love, care, and precision it takes to get a dish just right. "If you poured your heart into it, it would love you back." That's what my mother used to say, bless her heart, and ain't that the truth?

I felt sorry her, she was so petite and fragile-looking, like a little ceramic doll. I hated seeing the clients looking as nervous as that, and this one looked worse than most. She looked scared, uncertain, and was probably thinking about just about anything that could go wrong. I knew the look, and I desperately wanted to let her know that it would be all right, sooth her, make her realize her baby was going to be just fine. I had seen it a hundred times over, and with a procedure like a CAT scan, they all made it through without a hitch.

I called out to her. "Don't worry too much, darling; he'll be just fine and righter than rain before you know it. He'll be okay back there, and you'll see, he'll come out any minute. Can I get you something, a new magazine, maybe a new cup of tea?"

She lifted her head, but instead of looking at me to answer, she glanced at the treatment-room door.

In a distant voice, a voice that was obviously too preoccupied to pay any attention to what she was saying, she answered, "No thanks; I don't think I could drink anything even if I wanted to."

She peeled her eyes away from the door, and our eyes met for an instant. "But thanks, though ... umm ..."

She quickly looked back down at her open magazine, and I finished her stammering for her. No need to make her struggle more.

"Kathleen. But hon, most everyone calls me Kat. My grandkids, though, they call me Kleen. Frankly, they can call me what they want, as long as they call me. You know how it goes."

I waited for her to respond, and after a three-second delay, I heard a forced, "Uh-huh."

She looked up again, and I could see it in her face. She was being polite enough, but her expression was the poster child for please leave me be. Her eyes had a semibegging quality, and this sweet child was too polite to tell me outright to mind my own business and leave her the heck alone.

In a strained voice, forced and filled with an effort to remain soft, she said, "Umm, it's nice to meet you, Kathleen."

She jerked her head back down into her magazine, and if I could read minds, I knew hers would be praying that I wouldn't say anything more to her. She wanted to be left alone, and I could take a hint. I didn't want to be that annoying old lady who sits next to you on a plane and rambles on for hours about much to do about nothing. At least not yet; there would be plenty of time later for small talk. I knew she'd come around once she got the hang of this place. They always did.

It wasn't long after that that they brought out her dog, and as soon as that door opened, I watched her face brighten as the whirlwind of ears and brown hair bounded her way. Once she saw him coming toward her, his tongue hanging out and leaving a spit trail as he ran, her face completely changed. I saw her eyes open wide as she sucked in a deep, relieved breath, and her shoulders rolled forward as she exhaled the world of tension that had been fermenting like old moonshine. She smiled from ear to ear, and I could see a perfect set of pearly whites as her fears melted away like butter on a biscuit.

After a whole lot of hugging on her part and a whole lot of licking on his, they walked on over to me. This was a different gal from only five minutes ago, and I could see her face was still flushed with relief. She couldn't stop smiling, even after I handed her the bill. She was happier than a pig in mud.

Her dog was also quite the charmer, and before I knew it, there were two large, brown paws on the desk. His tongue was still hanging out, and I could see a wet spot where some of his spit had dripped. He was staring at me with those big, brown eyes of his, and I could feel his hot breath as he panted my way.

"Well, aren't you handsome, sugar. I'm sure you're hungry as well? Don't you worry about a thing; Aunty Kathleen will make it right as rain. I've got just the thing."

66

EDDIE
MAY 2009

Two light periods passed before we went back to the Crunchy Territory. Again Mom forgot to feed me, again the white-coated greeting, again with the buzzer licking my arm fur away, and, unfortunately, again another burrowing bee sting, with green arm wrappings this time around.

The shiny-headed dad was as friendly as ever, grunting up a storm to a dad I had never seen before. He was a tall, skinny dad, and judging by the uneven thin, black fur over his lips and near his ears, he was only old enough to just start to get face fur. He was much taller than the shiny-headed dad, but given his slouchy standing and rapid eye movements, he was definitely not a pack leader.

The tall dad was wearing the same upper blue coverings as the shiny-headed dad, but unlike the shiny-headed dad, his lower blue coverings ended at midshin, showing his white ankle warmers and worn pad coverings. He was walking real close to the shiny-headed dad and seemed to be glued to every grunt he made. He had a thin, black scratching stick and white, crunchy, rectangular bark in his paws, and he scratched the bark every time the shiny-headed dad grunted. His smell and actions reminded of Paris as a puppy, when she had first been brought into our territory. She had followed my every move and copied everything I did.

There were two things, though, that hadn't sunken in, no matter how hard I tried and no matter how many times I attempted to drill them through her thick, curly-furred poodle head. Number one, sleeping all day isn't the best way to enjoy life. I don't care how tired you are or how much beauty sleep you *require*, no amount of sleep is going to make you any less ugly. Number two—and this one was just plain gross—no matter how thirsty you are, no matter how lazy you feel, even if there's no water in the water bowl, there's no excuse in the world to use the white, stubby tree as your own personal water bowel.

We were walking down a white hallway and reached a long white door. This one had a white border and a red, rectangular decoration hanging above it. The shiny-headed dad smiled mischievously at the tall dad, reached with his thick paw to get the door opener, and that's when the grunting got interesting.

THE DOG DAYS OF THE PAST

67

JULIA
MARCH 2008

I realized that the lady must have been in her seventies, and that was probably the only thing that held me back from saying something. I knew that the supermarket would be crowded today, like all Mondays, but it had been the only day I could get there this week. It had only taken me five minutes to get some eggs and milk, push past the multitude of people wandering down the aisles, and make it to the express lane, ready to fly through.

I knew I was in trouble the moment I stepped behind her in line. She was old—very, very old—in her eighties or nineties, by the looks of her. Her back was arched and she was wearing a knitted blue sweater with large, plastic buttons running down the front. Her ankle-length red-and-white–checkered skirt looked almost as old as she was, and her outfit was topped off with a faded khaki gardening hat and large, square sunglasses that had the kind of lenses you get after having your pupils dilated. She was hunched over, her bony, blue-veined forearms barely supported by the red plastic handle of her shopping cart. She looked to be resting all of her weight on it, and its true purpose as a walker revealed. She slowly shuffled forward into the check out aisle.

There was only one other person ahead of us, and he was paying the cashier for the single long-stemmed red rose he had just bought. He had on a black suit and looked like he was late for whatever meeting or lunch date he was headed to. The old lady let go of the handle of the cart and proceeded to unload its contents. That's when I realized this wasn't going to be an express line.

The sign clearly said ten items or less, but by the looks of it she either couldn't count or had ignored it completely. I eyed the toilet paper, the three bottles of ranch salad dressing, the two cartons of eggs, a dozen cans of cat food, one box of cat litter, mayonnaise, two frozen boxes of microwave vegetables, and at least ten other things.

I could feel my anger surfacing; this was just plain rude of her. I realized all of the lines were long today, but that was no excuse to use the express lane when you have dozens of purchases. Just because she had made it past eighty didn't automatically give her the right to damn the rest of the world and its rules of supermarket etiquette. The express lane was made for people in a hurry, people who had places to be, people who didn't have the time to stand around waiting while people like her futzed around unloading their denture cleansers. This behavior was a real pet peeve of mine, and it took every ounce of my self-control not to say anything to her.

And then it got even worse and I remember thinking to myself that she had to be kidding me. With her curled, shaky decrepit fingers, she reached into her oversized denim bag and brought out what could only be either a checkbook or a museum piece belonging to a Roaring Twenties exhibition.

The sign had said CASH ONLY, as clear as day. It couldn't have been more visible with its bright red flashing light right next to where it had said EXPRESS LANE. Oh, for heaven's sake; I thought I might kill something.

The brown leather-bound case was worn and cracked, and as she slowly opened it, I saw a pink clown with balloons decorating the face of the check. I took a long, deep breath and tried to force a smile as her unsteady fingers searched for a pen in the binding of the case. It was one thing to hold everyone up with a cart full of groceries on the express lane, but it was just plain obnoxious to take your merry old time fumbling around on a cash-only lane. I swore to myself that when I got to be that age, if I reached that age, I sure as hell wouldn't be like that.

Unsuccessful in her search, she asked the cashier in a raspy, chronic-smoker's voice for a pen. For some reason, that was the straw that broke the camel's back for me; despite her age and frailty, I was going to speak my mind.

My lips opened a fraction of an inch, but before I got a word out, my cell phone rang. It saved the little old lady from the fury of the pent-up frustration that had been aching to rear its ugly head. The phone was ringing with the *Jaws* theme song tone, and the low, impending doom of the bass riff could only mean it was Mother calling. Forgetting about the old lady in front of me, I picked up the phone and simultaneously felt my stomach tighten in anticipation.

"Hello?"

There was a pause and some static, and I didn't hear a voice answer back. I repeated myself, but between the static and the background supermarket noise, I could barely hear anything. As I battled to hear an intelligible sound, I watched as the old lady finally waved good-bye to the cashier and started shuffling forward.

"Hello . . . Mother . . . hello," I repeated but still only heard static.

The cashier had already scanned both my eggs and my milk and was staring at me, waiting for some kind of response. He was a mostly bald man, and the top of his head reflected the light of the EXPRESS aisle sign. He had black, thick-rimmed glasses and a speckled gray mustache and was eyeing me impatiently.

"That will be five fifty," he said with a southern drawl, and I could hear the contempt in his voice.

It must have been the fact that I was on the phone, or that I wasn't eighty, because he had been as sweet as honey with the old lady. I put the phone between my shoulder and ear and reached into my purse for cash.

I took a half step back while trying to get a good hold on my wallet and got nudged on my left thigh as a short, acne-decorated teenage kid behind me lifted his basket onto the checkout counter.

I heard his prepubescent voice crack as he said, "Yo, lady, do you mind? Like, this is the express lane; could you like get a move on?"

I was concentrating too hard on listening for Mother's voice, so I didn't even turn around to offer a response. I saw his Snickers bar on the conveyer belt as it stopped before the scanner.

I still hadn't heard my mother's voice because the reception in the place was obviously horrible. As much as I dreaded speaking to Mother, I did want to hear what she had to say; with everything that was going on with Dad, I knew this might be important.

I didn't want her to hang up, so I said, "Hold on, I can't hear you, give me a second to get a better signal. Just hold on," practically screaming it into the phone.

I didn't care how annoyed Mother got, couldn't give a damn about the cashier, and as far as I was concerned, the prepubescent punk could take a long walk off a short cliff. I handed the glaring cashier exact change, grabbed the plastic bag, and headed for the door.

"Hello . . . Mother, is that you?" I said impatiently as I made a beeline for the door.

There was a pause, which was followed by a curt, measured response. It was, indeed, Mother, and I braced myself for her being either upset about something or another or, more likely, just being offended at having to wait. There were no introductions, no "hello," no "how are you doing?" She just fired away.

"They found a spot on his lung, Julia."

There was still some static in the background, and I hadn't quite made it out of the market, so I thought I might have misheard what she had just said. Still gripping the phone with my shoulder, I asked, "What did you say, Mother?"

I was walking fast now, doing my best to get outside, where the reception would be better and it was quieter. I really hoped I hadn't heard her right. I slung my black leather bag over my right forearm and grabbed the phone from my shoulder with my left hand. Now at least I would be able to hear better.

I felt the hot air of the summer day as I stepped through the sliding electric door of the supermarket and into the parking lot. I headed toward my car while with obvious annoyance, Mother repeated herself in the berating tone she was famous for.

"I said, Julia," she paused, and then spoke the next sentence emphasizing every word, "that they found a spot on his lungs. Your father, Julia."

That sentence was like a gunshot, and it stopped me in my tracks. Instantly, I felt a pounding numbness engulf my entire being. Everything froze and my body went limp. My annoyance at having to speak to Mother, the desire to deck an acne-faced teenage boy, and the reasons I had come to the supermarket in the first place all of a sudden seemed to be distant memories, superfluous and unimportant. I was aware that I had started walking to the car again, but I couldn't feel my legs consciously moving; I couldn't feel anything, for that matter. I felt like I was dreaming or, more accurately, having a nightmare, and I hoped that I would soon awaken.

In a zombielike trance, my legs led me to my car. I put my grocery bag down on the asphalt, by some miracle carefully enough not to let any of the eggs break. Still numb, I turned around and leaned against the car door. Normally, I would have cared that my perfectly white jeans were brushed up against a surface that hadn't been washed for over two months, but at this point I was incapable of thought.

I hadn't realized it, but I hadn't responded to Mother. I had just been holding the phone to my ear, and there must have been a long silence after she'd spoken. In a voice that would make smelling salts tickle, her voice jerked me out of my fugue state.

"I don't have time for this . . . Hello . . . Julia, are you there? Did you hear me, or are you just being daft?"

I managed to find my voice, and with a short grunt to clear my throat, I answered, "Um . . . yes, Mother, I heard you."

I had to get my control back, and no matter what she had just said, I couldn't be weak, I couldn't show emotion yet; that would be for later, when I was by myself. I had to be strong for my family, for my dad, even for Mother, for despite her tough exterior, her pretend strength, I knew that when times were tough, she would only look after herself. She would also probably fall apart and go into a self-pity mode. I needed to be a rock now; I needed to be my father's daughter.

I hated having to ask her the next question because despite setting myself up for a probable insult, it would more importantly mean yet another defeat. It would mean a step back, a step closer to losing a battle we had to win.

I realized it was a stupid question as soon as I asked it. "Is it the pancreatic cancer? I thought he was in remission... Did it spread so fast?"

There was no hesitation in her response, and as expected, she answered me in a tone that might have left a red handprint on my face. "Yes, Julia, what else do you think it is?"

It seemed like she was the strong one in this conversation, but hell, she had had some time to internalize it before calling me. I didn't have the energy to answer her, and right now the last thing I wanted to do was let this conversation be about her. Dad's cancer had spread, and that's what I needed to be thinking about. Unfortunately, my mind reeled from that last remark.

No "hello, Julia, how are you doing?"

No "are you sitting down? I have something to say that's important. Prepare yourself, dear."

Not my mother; it was just "your father's cancer has spread and it's really bad news. Now be fine with it and speak to me. Don't be such a moron."

How typical of her.

I grew aware of the car door as its heat made its way through my jeans. I could feel my heart racing as adrenaline kicked it. My mind had cleared and I had managed to regain my composure.

I shook my head, banishing any demons of negative thought, shrugging off any animosity I felt. I would not respond to Mother; this was about Dad. I needed to focus.

Ignoring her comment, I leaned forward, pushing myself off of the car and starting to pace. "So what's the next step, Mother? Are they going to remove it? Will there be another surgery?"

My mother's voice softened, then, and she actually sounded somewhat motherly. "Julia, why don't you drive over; your father wants to speak to you. I know it's a little short notice, but he could really use you here right now. Were you in the middle of something?"

I put the phone back between my ear and shoulder while I reached into my bag for my keys. I responded as I fumbled for my car door, almost completely forgetting the grocery bag by my feet.

"I'm headed over right now." I hung up so I could call David.

68

JULIA
MARCH 2008

"The scan showed that there was a spot in my lungs and one on my spine. They're one hundred percent sure its cancer spread."

We were in my parents' living room, and I was sitting cross-legged and barefoot on the white couch with my feet folded under me. I was watching my dad in complete and utter shock while I sat there, in the very same spot I had been in during our last serious conversation. He was standing and pacing in front of me as he spoke, and Mother was slumped in a chair at the dining room table, a cup of tea in her hand. Dad had on a pair of dark green slacks and a white, collared golf shirt with a picture of Arnold Palmer taking a swing on it, both of the top buttons undone. I could see the blanched white skin of his chest and the wisps of gray chest hair as they peeked sheepishly through his shirt.

My dad's monotonous voice betrayed no feeling, just the facts. Its baritone quality carried through the entire house. It seemed solid, steady, and full of strength, just like the dad with whom I had grown up. His eyes, posture, and walk, however, betrayed a different truth. This was the first time in six months that I'd sensed a shift, and just looking at him, watching him pace, watching the effort it required for him to take each individual step, seeing the dull, worn-out sheen of his eyes gave me cause for concern. It didn't faze me outright, though; sure, he had been tired physically, but throughout those past six months, mentally he had been a rock.

But now . . . now there was an obvious change. His normally proud, sparkling brown eyes, eyes that usually carried a glow so bright it lit up any room he happened to be in, now were dull, sullen, and worn out. It was as if all of his vitality had somehow been siphoned away. Maybe it was from all the past chemo, or maybe it was just because he was extra tired today, but at the moment I definitely saw the change.

I also noticed that his usually impeccable posture had shifted, and he now walked with a slight hunch in his back. That wasn't like Dad. The ever-rigid soldier, the athlete, the man who had always seemed three inches taller than his actual six-foot build, he had always carried himself well. But not today; unlike any day I could ever remember, Dad was slouching as he spoke. The effect was dramatic; for the first time he looked frail. So frail, in fact, that it seemed his spine wouldn't support the full weight of his beautiful strong head for a second longer.

For the first and only time during my dad's cancer, I took a realistic look at him, and for an instant, just an instant, what I saw brushed aside the veil of denial I had put up so artfully. He had lost a lot of weight especially over the last couple of months, and I could see the outline of his collarbones as his shirt hung loose on him. The bones of his face were jumping out, giving him a skeletonlike appearance, and the rings under his eyes were a dark, bruised black.

His pants were sagging on him, no longer held up by a size thirty-six muscular waist. I knew he had been vomiting all through his six months of chemotherapy; the only thing Mother said he could eat without being sick was rice and chicken. He looked frail, feeble, and just outright old to me then, a defeated man who had accepted his fate. I wanted to stop it; I wanted to reach out and make him stand straight, scream at him not to let up for even a moment. He couldn't give up, he couldn't give the cancer even an inch; I wouldn't let him. Why was he slouching? *Stop that!*

What I saw only lasted an instant because I refused to accept that reality, refused to see what was so obvious to everyone else. I couldn't and wouldn't do it.

He continued as he turned to pace but made an extra-long walk to the window. "The doctor said that the chemotherapy they tried didn't work."

He paused just long enough for that statement to sink in, and then went on. "I have a couple of choices left."

I looked over at Mother, who was staring down at her white porcelain teacup. The light above her from the cheap crystal-and-gold–based chandelier reflected off of the brown hard wood table and outlined her entire form. The proper, reserved, battle-ax of a lady who normally ruled this house with irrational inflexibility was not present today. Instead, I saw a scared, sad shell of a woman contemplating the unfairness of life, who refused to look up and meet my eyes.

"Jules, one of the choices the doctor gave me was to try a new chemotherapy drug."

Dad paused and stared at me with an intensity that turned my blood cold. I had to look away.

"Now, you know how I feel about medications. It's no secret that I hate doctors, almost as much as I hate taking the poison they give you. So I asked the doctor to be blunt with me, to tell it to me straight, so I could be the one who made the decision of what to do next. I asked him if the new chemo he wanted to give me had a better chance of getting rid of this thing than the regimen I had already been on."

I could feel Dad glaring at me, but just like Mother, I didn't want to look up. I was afraid of what I would see, and I couldn't bear to look at him while he said what I thought he would say next.

"Jules, the doctor said no. In fact, he said that this one had even less of a chance at fighting it than the other ones did."

I didn't like where this was going. The new drug had little to no chance of working, Dad was telling me he hated doctors and medications, and that there had been only two choices with which to fight this thing.

So, in a state of pure denial, suspecting but not daring to admit what Dad was going to say next, I remember actually asking myself, *What other choice could there possibly be?*

I could feel that Dad had finally stopped looking at me, and instead of the weight of his stare, I felt the heaviness of dread and fear. I could hear the dragging of his loafers as they started to shuffle across the hardwood floor. He was pacing again, and I looked up to meet him as he walked past. He seemed upset now, irritated, as if he was gearing up to say something he knew wouldn't be received well.

"The other choice, Jules, sweetheart, is not to do anything else, to just live the best way I can for the time I have left."

He had said it in a calm but resolute tone, despite his body language. And with that I knew he had already made up his mind. This had not been a question or discussion of what he should do next; he had already come to his conclusion, and there was no trying to convince him otherwise. It wouldn't have been like arguing with him because he had grounded me for a week for stealing his car in high school, or attempting to convince him to buy a foreign car when every *Consumer Reports* article said that despite being made in America, his car choice was a bad buy. No, this was different. This was Dad telling me that he was giving up fighting; he was stopping, accepting defeat. This was Dad signing off on his death warrant.

Unconsciously and obviously a little too quickly, I jerked my head to the left to face him. Before I even had the opportunity to move my lips, Dad put up his finger to silence me, heading off any possible objection. He wasn't finished, and he knew me well enough to catch me before I could protest.

He was wrong, though. I hadn't been going to say a word this time. I couldn't. I was too upset to speak, and if I had opened my mouth, I wouldn't have been able to get three words out without crying uncontrollably. I couldn't break down; I refused. I had to be strong for him.

I continued staring at him, willing my facial expression not to betray what I was feeling.

"Your Mom and I have been discussing this possibility for months now, Julia. What if the treatment didn't work, despite the drugs, despite the poison that, frankly, I didn't want in the first place? It's no secret, Jules, that I hate hospitals, and it's no surprise that I like medicine even less."

His voice softened, and I was suddenly reminded of the time he had held me for hours while I cried myself to sleep in his arms. It was the night that he had had to explain to me that Grandma had died, that she wouldn't be there for my birthday party the next day. I had been only five years old, but I remember the smell of his Old Spice, the warmth of his arms as he held me, and his tone of voice. It was the same tone he was using now.

"I had to try, though; I had to try for you. For both you and your mother, I did it; I need you to know that, Julia. I need you to understand that."

His eyes were glossy as he looked at me, and through the deep, dark brown windows to his soul, I could see his desperation, his longing for me to understand. He wanted me to recognize that he had done what he had so far for us, and, more importantly, he wanted me to forgive him, to support him in his decision not to do any more. I knew the meaning behind that look, and I saw all the pain and sickness that lay behind it. I looked deep into my dad then, and I got an overwhelming glimpse of the pain and anguish he had endured thus far. He had hated the last couple of months, hated going to the doctors, hated having to take medicine, and more than anything else, hated having to be taken care of by us.

He looked away this time around, and turned to continue his pacing.

"I know this is going to be hard for you to hear, but Jules, honey, I have decided that I'm not going to do any more treatment."

69

JULIA
MARCH 2008

In retrospect, I shouldn't have gone over there half an hour early. If I'd been a superstitious woman, I would have paid attention to the full moon the night before and the black cat that had darted across my path as I'd walked to my car. It just happened that Dad had still been out with Daniel, his old work buddy, and I had been forced to be alone in the house with Mother.

We had been seated in the living room and, like usual, everything was immaculately clean and well organized. There wasn't a speck of dust to be seen—even floating particles had been banished—and the white carpet looked like it had just been professionally washed. The light yellow throw pillows were flawlessly aligned on the white couch and matching white love seats, mirror images of each other down to the precise distance from the elbow rests. The love seats were perpendicular to the couch on each side, and together they formed a perfect U. In the center of the U sat a rectangular, silver-legged, glass-topped coffee table with a fresh bouquet of bright yellow daisies centered between two stacks of circular cork coasters. Ever since she had bought those yellow pillows, Mother had insisted on replacing the daisies every four days, refusing fake flowers as "gaudy." The glass was exceptionally clean, with no hint of a smudge or a scratch, and I could smell the faint odor of Windex in the air.

There were porcelain cups of steaming mint tea laid out on two of the coasters, and a matching white teapot was centered on the silver serving tray. Mother had insisted on using her formal wear, right down to the silver teaspoons and saucers.

So there we were, sitting across from each other. I was staring at the wisps of steam as they rose from my cup, dreading what would inevitably come next. Mother had just sat down, and I could see she was looking me over, scanning up and down for something she disapproved of. She was wearing a gray business suit, and her hair was up in a bun. I was prepared for what she would probably say about the outfit I had worn: my old gray sweats, a Padres T-shirt, and flip-flops.

"Julia, dear, you're a grown woman, do you really want to dress like a twelve year old?" Or, "Darling, was today a bad day to get out of your pajamas?" Or maybe this would be my lucky day, and she wouldn't say a thing about me. Hell, the only thing she liked better than criticizing me was talking about herself, so maybe today would be just another personal monologue.

Why had I come early today of all days? This was the last thing I needed, and it was probably the worst day ever for me to get stuck alone in a room with her. I just couldn't deal with it. My defenses were down, my patience was practically nonexistent, and I would rather have had one of my fingernails ripped out than have to listen to her pass judgment on me or give another play-by-play action report on her "this," or her "that," or on her "whatever,"

I had been in a horrible mood ever since Dad's revelation three days earlier that he was going to stop chemotherapy despite hard evidence that the cancer had spread. I had been sad, withdrawn, depressed. I was also angry. How could he just stop? Why just give up? It was so unlike him. Was it Mother who had convinced him? No, with all her faults I knew the woman loved him and wanted him around as long as possible; otherwise who would be left for her to torment? It sure wasn't going to be me.

Even though I knew that this had impacted her, I didn't have enough room left to care. Sure, she was hurting; I could only imagine that she also needed to unload, but did it have to be on me? Why couldn't she have had another kid? At least then we could have shared the burden. With my luck and the upbringing I had had that kid would also be in therapy by now, or a drug dealer, or a murderer, or maybe he would have been smart enough to disown his family a long time ago.

I just couldn't take it today, though; I didn't have it in me to listen to anything that came out of the woman's mouth. Right now I didn't care how she felt, I didn't care what she thought, and if she told me one more time about how all of this was going to affect her, I think I'd have to shoot myself.

Her, her, her, that's all it was ever about with my mother. Ever since I was a kid, the only thing she talked about was herself, unless, of course, the subject involved how bad or what a failure I was.

Today was not the day for that; today, just today, I only wanted to think of Dad and my feelings. I was entitled to it. I only had enough room for how I felt, how he felt, how he was handling things, and how he was holding up. That was the only thing I wanted to think about, so why couldn't I have been late today?

It was so quiet, I could hear the seconds ticking away on the clock in the kitchen, an imitation antique decorated with bulky silver hands, gold-plated Roman numerals, and a shiny, veneered-wood background. It was the only sound in the house. I had made myself comfortable and was sitting back on the large white couch. Mom and Dad had paid a lot of money for their living room set, and their couch was one of the best-looking and most comfortable pieces of furniture I had ever sat on. If it hadn't been for Mother sitting across from me, I would have curled up and slept until Dad got back. Instead, I had to make do with his brown TV blanket, the same one Mother had insisted he keep in the closet so as not to ruin her décor.

While Mother was getting the tea ready, I had grabbed it out of the closet and held it to my face, inhaling a deep breath and catching a hint of Dad's aftershave. I had still been resting it against my cheek, lost in disappointment and heartache, when Mother had walked in, and I followed her eyes as she glared at the blanket in disapproval.

Surprisingly, she didn't say anything regarding the blanket, but it didn't stop her from starting our conversation. She had kept it harmless in the beginning, mainly concentrating on the details of Dad's last visit with the doctor, which had, according to her, gone well. She had actually been speaking about something I was interested in, Dad and his oncologist, and I had actually paid attention to what she had to say for a change. I didn't have to just pretend to listen with a blank stare and the appropriate nods.

"Dr. Stillwater says that the disease will probably progress at some point in the near future. Your father seems the same to me, though; in fact, I would argue that he doesn't act like he's even sick. They're going to repeat his chest X-rays in a couple of days and compare them to the last ones, but your father refused to have another CT scan. He can be so pigheaded sometimes, but at least Dr. Stillwater convinced him to repeat the X-rays."

Just as I had started to think to myself how normal the conversation had been going, she started in and became typical Mother. I felt the hairs on the back of my neck stand up like a canary in a mine passing out from asphyxiation as soon as she started the next sentence, and I knew I wouldn't like what came next.

"Your father appears to be well, even though you and I know differently, dear."

I knew it was coming, but I had clung to a shard of hope that she wouldn't dare tell me bad news. I braced myself.

"It's only a matter of time before the cancer in the lung starts to grow, or he feels pain from the spread to his spine. It could grow somewhere else . . . Don't look so upset, dear, you asked me what the doctor said, and that's what he particularly called to tell me. He didn't want to say it while your father was in the office, but he deemed it important enough for a private call."

Mother was right; I wasn't happy about hearing that. And judging by her tone, I remember thinking that the whole conversation was also about to turn south. I dreaded that possibility because I knew how little it would take to set me off.

Like a shark attracted to blood, she picked up on my reaction and started circling. She took my disappointment as an invitation for her to give me some gem of motherly wisdom, which ultimately meant she would have to impart something that directly involved or affected her.

Undaunted and completely oblivious, she went on. "You know, I remember when my father passed away . . ."

With that, I decided it was time for me to only pretend to listen. It sounds callous, but to survive in our household, it had been a necessary part of life to mentally check out. Unfortunately for me, I hadn't learned that trick early enough in life, and I was still trying to recover from the scars my childhood had left on me.

Pretending to listen and not getting caught up in what was said was an art form I had picked up in college in order not to have to deal with her. It was a way to be more productive with my time and avoid getting caught in hours upon hours of being forced to sit on the phone listening while she went on and on. I just let her speak, let her talk tirelessly, until she got it all out of her system, not even attempting to get a word in because once she started up, there was no stopping her. It was like the giant stone ball in the first *Indiana Jones* movie, where once it started rolling and destroying everything in its path, there was just no stopping it.

I leaned back against the couch and felt myself sink into its white embrace. I had learned that if I was on the phone with her, I could literally put down the phone on the counter and come back five minutes later; she'd still be talking. She wouldn't even know that only the dresser had been her captive audience because she didn't expect an answer from me when she spoke; she just wanted to speak. Heck, how could someone take part in a one-sided conversation anyway?

After exactly five minutes—and I made sure to time it—I would check in, lifting up the phone and giving an "uh-huh," and then I would have another five minutes free. And with the advent of the speakerphone, life had gotten even easier. I'd also learned that there was no point in trying to interrupt or shorten the conversation; instead of making life easier, it would only lead to a fight and a bout of sulking on her part. Trust me, that took much more effort than just letting the lady speak; the monologue that would follow would be five times as painful as just letting her get out what she wanted to say. She insisted on being heard, even if you didn't want to listen.

"No one listens to me; you should have more respect for your mother, blah blah blah."

So I usually let her speak to her heart's content; it took less time in the long term. Except for today . . . I just wasn't in the mood.

As Mother started in about how Dad was going to lose his battle, I found myself struggling to tune her out. In my current state of mind, I was having a really difficult time not listening to what she was saying. The thing was, I didn't want to hear her negativity; in fact, I couldn't give a rat's ass about what she or anyone else, for that matter, thought. Dad was going to get through this; he would beat all the odds, he would survive. He was Dad, after all.

As much as I tried to block out her words, they managed to penetrate, and despite my best efforts, I couldn't help but hear what was being said. And so the fires of anger had started to burn.

"My father had treatment until the very end, and my mother .... well, when she died, it all happened so quickly."

Why the hell was she telling me this? Her timing was horrendous. I needed encouragement and support, not doom and gloom. Should I have been surprised, though? She was, after all, the same lady who'd repeatedly told us the story of how her nephew had survived a horrific plane crash whenever we'd boarded any type of a plane when I was younger, at the top of her lungs, no less. The lady had never learned the definition of the word *whisper*.

Was this a motherly thing to do? Did she really think I needed to hear this? Right now? How could she be so insensitive? Yes, she was talking about her husband, but damn it, it was my father as well.

"I was only twenty-six when my mother passed, and I remember every detail of that day."

She proceeded to describe every demise she had ever witnessed, and as much as I had tried to ignore it, I knew it wasn't going to work. If I was going to have to be stuck there for another twenty minutes, she'd just better stop.

Risking the inevitable confrontation with her but not caring enough to keep my mouth shut, I asked, in the nicest, sweetest voice I could muster, "Mother, can we please talk about something else? This is really depressing me. It's not that I'm not interested in Grandma or Grandpa, Great-Uncle Paul, Cousin Rick, and the rest of our family; it's just that I'm really not in the right state of mind to listen to it right now."

Her head jerked up and like a snake coiled and ready to strike, she responded, "Really, Julia, that's the most ridiculous thing I've ever heard. There is never a right time to discuss these things."

Even though I had made sure to let her know it wasn't about her, had done everything I could to walk on eggshells, and desperately had tried to communicate that I wasn't attacking her, her tone shifted to the defensive nonetheless. Her next question clued me into the fact that she had only heard what she'd wanted to hear.

"Aren't you interested in learning about your family, Julia?"

I needed to stay calm; *no fights, no fights*. I needed to stay relaxed. It wasn't too late . . . yet.

I did my best to answer in the least threatening or defensive tone I could muster. "No, it's not that; I just . . . well, Mother, can we just talk about something else? I'm not feeling that well and I really don't want to talk about death right now."

That hadn't sat well with her, and I actually saw her upper lip curl inward, and the same expression appeared on her face that she got whenever she felt she'd been wronged.

"You know, dear, it's perfectly apropos to talk about it. You have to talk about these things. When your grandmother passed, I spent nearly every day discussing it with my sister. Before that, I would speak to your grandmother about things such as sickness, death, loss, and just about anything. I was so sad when she passed. As you are well aware, your grandmother and I had an extremely close relationship. We would speak every day, rain or shine. It didn't matter how busy I was, what was going on in my life, or what I was doing; I always made the effort. I knew how important family was. We even spoke after I married your father. She was my mother, and that's what daughters did back then, unlike today."

She clearly articulated that last sentence, making sure to venomously emphasize the word *daughters* as she raised her eyebrows and stared straight at me.

All right, a girl could only take so much, and in my state, *so much* had been ten sentences ago. Hadn't I made it clear that I didn't want to talk about death? Hadn't I specifically said I didn't want to talk about Grandma? And that last comment . . . well, that had been just plain uncalled for. I had never been a fan of the passive aggressive, and as fate would have it, I was born to the passive-aggressive queen. To top it off, the irony of her statement was just too overwhelming for me. "That's what daughters did back then" as opposed to what? Me... now.

If she had wanted to say just how bad a daughter I was, she needed to just spit it out and get on with it, not hide behind generalizations.

I knew the consequences of what would happen next, and if I had been a perfect person, I would have just ignored her and gone on with my day without comment. But I wasn't perfect; in fact, I was beyond irritable and my patience was nonexistent. Hell, I was in therapy for heaven's sake.

So I did something that was very uncharacteristic of me, something my therapist had been urging me to do since I had first started seeing her. I sat up on the couch, put the brown blanket on the cushion next to me, and called my mother out on her comment.

"What do you mean by that, Mother? Daughters did what exactly back then?"

My tone was inviting, caustic, and my filter was gone.

She replied with a tone of haughty surprise and a faked innocence only she would attempt to pull off. "Excuse me, dear, I'm not quite sure to what you're referring. If it's the talking-with-mothers part of the sentence I so clearly said, then I don't know how else to explain it. It's pretty obvious, I imagine, and you have a degree in English, no less. Not that you're using it, of course, but let's not get nitpicky."

I was so angry and my emotions so unstable, I couldn't help myself.

"Mother, don't play innocent with me, not now. I'm sure you and your mother had a better relationship than we do, but I'm also sure you guys didn't have the history we do. And I'm also positive your childhood didn't involve a fraction of the things you put me through either."

I stared directly at her; I wouldn't be the first to look away. I saw her lip tuck in even more as she turned to fully face me. I had just passed into the unmentionable zone and there was no turning back. I knew she would try to change the subject now; any time I had even come close to this zone, the conversation had quickly and forcefully been shifted by her or me. It had been an unspoken pact between us, one that we had lived by all these years. But, as I said earlier, it just wasn't the day to upset me.

Predictably, Mother attempted to shift the course of the argument. She looked away and, with a visible effort, relaxed her face and proceeded to play dumb. I knew her next move would be to try to turn everything against me.

"Julia, I don't like your tone of voice, and frankly, you're being exceptionally disrespectful. You never did learn how to respect me, and I am partly to blame for that, but that will never change the fact that I will not accept such insolence from you. Your father and I never disciplined you enough, but you were my only child. I gave up my job to take care of you. I . . . "

Before she got on a roll about giving up finishing college, slitting her wrists, and crucifying herself for me, I did the unthinkable. I raised my voice and overpowered her diatribe, interrupting the beginning of her rant. I shouted over her, and it seemed I could be pretty darn loud when I wanted to be.

"Respect? Are you kidding, Mother? You don't just wake up one day and demand respect. You aren't just born with it, no matter who you are. In my book, you have to earn it, and after what you did, after the way you acted with me, you lost all right to respect. You should be happy I'm willing to even be in the same room with you."

Looking like a cat that had just been dunked into a tub of water, she said, "Julia Grace Freed, you had better stop this right now! How dare you raise your voice to me? The nerve . . . well, I never! I am your mother and you will show respect for me. I will not listen to your irrational outburst any further."

She started to get up to walk away, but I wasn't finished. Her face was bright red and I could see the whites of her eyes. She was so taken aback, but I didn't care.

"Mother, don't you dare walk away from me. You will let me talk and you will damn well listen to me, no matter how much you don't want to hear it."

I was beyond angry, visibly unstable, and with what Dad had chosen to do, to say that I was frustrated would have been the understatement of the century. Unfortunately for her, all my frustration had been swirling around in my head during the past couple of days, and like a sniper, I focused everything I had on the moment, on her.

"I will not be spoken to like that, not by you, not by . . ."

She had been standing up from the couch, and I didn't care if she was standing or sitting; if she started to walk away, I would follow her. I needed to be heard.

I lowered my voice to a whisper, a rough, penetrating hiss. "Yes, you will. You demand respect? After what you did? After all those years and everything you put me through? After the life you forced me to live?"

She froze in her tracks and stared questioningly at me, and despite the offense that I had just committed, she seemed morbidly curious as to what I would say next. I waited, though; I wanted to see if she was going to try to walk away again. Surprisingly, she just kept looking at me, frozen like a deer in the headlights. I had opened the deep, festering wound of the past, and despite her shock, I could see she was wanted to know what was coming next.

The room felt eerily still, the silence overwhelming. It was as if the world had paused and then stopped turning on its axis. I lost track of time. We could have been frozen like that for one second or for an eternity, and I was only briefly conscious of the sudden and complete stillness blanketing the room. If I didn't have her full attention before, I had it now.

"Did it ever cross your mind just how incredibly wrong it was for you to do what you did?"

She flinched as I raised my voice again, shattering the disconcerting quiet.

I jerked up my thumb and yelled, "Not one," then proceeded to raise my index finger, "not two, Mother," my middle finger "not three," my ring finger, "not four," and finally my pinkie, "but five miserable years of it."

I clenched my fingers into a tight fist and slammed it into the top of the backrest of the perfectly white couch.

"It's unfathomable. Respect? Are you kidding me?"

She was still frozen in place, but I could see her face go from a bright red to a blanched white as she slowly looked down at the now receding fist mark in her couch.

She snapped out of her trance and recovered enough to look back up at me. In a quiet and distant voice, she said, "I don't know what you're referring to, Julia."

I paused for an instant. Oh, she knew, and judging by her expression, there might actually have been a part of her that was ashamed of it all. Or, Mother being Mother, maybe she was just shocked that I had decked her couch and now was worried that I had left a permanent mark. If I said what was on the tip of my tongue, I knew there would definitely be no turning back. I would be officially bringing up the past, a past that all of us had so artfully buried. I would be crossing the threshold of no return, and I knew the consequences would be dire.

I couldn't stop myself, and by this point I really didn't care. My emotions were boiling lava, making their way from the previously dormant volcano of my childhood. So I kept going.

"Yes, yes, you do. How could you use me like that? How could you put me through that? Five years, Mother, five long, drawn-out years of it. Of course you know what I'm talking about; hell, you even took me to Olive Garden that first time. Of all the places in the world to go, Mother, we went to Olive Garden, You might as well have picked McDonald's, got your hourly motel room, and called it a night. At least McDonald's would have had some video games to keep me busy, keep me away from having to listen to you and that fat little imp of a man. What was his name, Jack . . . no, Roger, oh, who gives a damn! Their names weren't what was important.

"But no, you forced me to sit through your date, and the countless others after that one, because you thought babysitters weren't safe. What kind of a screwed-up rationale was that? When I think back now just how crazy it was that you actually preferred to bring me with you, to expose me to that craziness, that infidelity, rather than hire a babysitter, it utterly blows my mind. Forget the fact that you were a married woman to start with, you were a mother as well. What did I know about sex, let alone cheating? You definitely changed all of that, Mother. I was twelve-years-old, for heaven's sake."

Mother hadn't moved, hadn't shifted a muscle, and for one of the first times I could ever remember, was actually shutting up and letting me get out more than one sentence. I'm sure she didn't want to be shouted down again, so instead she was just glaring at me with venom in her eyes.

"It's not like you even pretended either, made any effort whatsoever to hide what you were doing. In fact, you went out of your way to tell me just how you were going to get revenge, show him how it felt. I couldn't count the times you made sure to tell me how bad Dad was, how much he had hurt you. How Dad didn't deserve you, how he had ruined your life. How much you had sacrificed to marry him and, even worse, to raise me. You hadn't wanted this life, and you decided it would be a smart thing to tell that to your twelve-year old daughter. And, oh yes, let's not forget that he wasn't going to get away with it that easy; you were going to make him go through what he'd made you go through, and together we would make him pay. Together, Mother?"

I was on a roll and couldn't stop. My mouth was dry and metallic, and I was breathing much faster than usual. The room felt like it was a hundred degrees.

"Did I like Roger or Jack more? Who was more handsome? Was Jack too young for you? Was it time to move on to a new man because you were bored, was my father getting angry yet? What the hell were you thinking? I was only a kid; it wasn't right."

Mother broke her ice-cold stare to look at her thin, diamond-studded watch with an expression of faked boredom. She exhaled loudly, punctuating the air with her impatience. She made every effort to convince me with that sigh that this was the most tedious conversation in the world and a complete waste of time. It was an obvious show of contempt, and her rejection of everything I was saying.

Ignoring her, I kept going. "Why in a million years would you put me through that, Mother? The only thing I knew during that time was that my mother and father hadn't spoken for almost a year, though they still lived in the same house with each other, and when you guys did speak, it was a screaming match in which you'd mainly threaten to leave and never come back. I hated being at home, dreaded when school ended every single day and did everything I could to avoid having to be in this house. Not that you noticed; you were so caught up in feeling sorry for yourself that nobody and nothing else mattered.

"Do you have any idea how miserable it was for me to have to come home every day? Other kids would come home from school to find their mothers either waiting for them, preparing dinner, running car pool, working, or doing other mother things, for heaven's sake.

"But no, not at our house; oh no, not you. I had to come home to your daily bouts of sobbing, you irreconcilable crying, and you lying in bed, still in your pajamas feeling sorry for yourself. I could have managed that one, actually felt sorry for you too, but not after what you put me through. You took things a screwed-up step farther and demanded that I sit with you and listen to you go on about how life had treated you so badly or how rotten Dad was. Forget about actually doing homework while you were still up, forget dinner, and heaven forbid I wanted to go visit Dad at work. That would have been an 'insult' to you, remember? I would be being 'disrespectful' for not letting you talk. Heaven forbid I wanted to have some semblance of normalcy.

"Why I didn't run away I'll never know, but I practically raised myself those years. Did you ever for one second think about me, how your behavior would affect your own child? I used to regret being an only child, but now I thank the stars every day that there wasn't another kid in the world who was exposed to what you did."

By some miracle Mother was actually still standing there, pretending to be bored, even after that last comment. I had never insulted my mother like that, at least not to her face.

"Did you really think I graduated high school early to get a head start in life, Mother? Did you really believe I begged to be able to go to sleepovers because I liked spending the night in a friend's guest bed? Not that you ever allowed me to anyway because of your crazy rules, but that at least would have made my time with you easier. No, Mother, I graduated early because that was my escape, my salvation, and the day I moved out was one of the happiest days of my life."

Mother stopped pretending to consult her watch and looked up at me with that last comment, but still she kept quiet.

"But not once did you ever take a moment to think of me. Hell, Dad was no angel, but at least he didn't drag me into the crap that was going on between you guys. He never sat me down like you did and insisted that I hear every last detail of his affair!"

Mother started shaking her head like she was going to object or deny it ever happened, but before she could attempt to open her mouth, I cut her off.

"You remember, Mother, you remember that day. It was right here, in this very spot. You know exactly what I'm talking about."

I stopped waiting for a response because Mother refused to acknowledge me. She arched her eyebrows, loudly exhaled again, and then looked back at her watch. It was as if she was timing me, counting the minutes of what she would think of as my breakdown. Knowing she wouldn't say anything, I went on. "Fine; let me remind you, because those words are burned into my memory, Mother."

In my best imitation of her, and making sure to emphasize the descriptors, I said, "'Now, Julia, your father has done a very, very disgusting, unforgivable, wretched thing, and I don't know what I'm going to do. He has hurt us, hurt this family, and I want to be the one to let you know . . .'

"And that you did, Mother. You actually told me how he had come to you to admit the affair. How he said he had had too much to drink that day, and he'd never meant to do it. How he swore to you that he would never do it again. Mother, did you really have to go into the details about it with me, did you really have to give me the play-by-play? Her name, how she looked, how young she was, where she worked, even which college she went to. You told me how you had followed her to her lecture and then to the bar where she worked.

"And if that wasn't enough, you even made me skip school so you could show her to me. Don't you remember? You thought it would be, as you put it, an 'educational experience' to see the 'home-wrecking floozy' in person, the 'woman Dad had chosen to ruin his marriage, your life, and our family with.'

"You dragged me into your crap, Mother, and worse, you used me. I get it; you were hurt, you were betrayed, but normal people move on with their lives. Normal people don't use their kids like their personal therapists. You weren't the only one living in the house, the only one who suffered. I'm your daughter, your child, and I should never have been your sounding board. You should have been taking care of me, not the other way around.

"You should have used someone else, a friend, a therapist,

anyone else. Oh, that's right, you didn't have any friends, but it still didn't give you the right to do what you did. How could you have done that to me?"

70

JULIA
MARCH 2008

"Julia, that's quite enough. I've just about had it up to here with this nonsense. I've listened to your emotional ranting for long enough and frankly, I'm bored with it. You're an unbalanced, unappreciative, spoiled little girl, and I've had quite enough of your whining . . ."

I was still fuming so there was no way I wasn't going to finish what I'd started. I had already entered the forbidden zone, so what sense was there in holding anything back now? I had quickly calculated that the damage had been done, so why stop there? I had only been speaking to her for what seemed like a couple of minutes and I had a lifetime to get out. Dad wasn't due back for another fifteen minutes, and as pissed off as Mother was being forced to listen to me, I just didn't care.

We were still in the living room, standing across from each other. I was leaning on the back of the white couch while she was standing with her arms folded in the middle of the room, halfway to the kitchen. Her face was bright red, her gray business suit was wrinkled, and she looked like a trapped animal getting ready to make its last stand.

Again I shouted over her. "Mother, I'm not finished. Be quiet!" As I've said before, I can be quite loud when I want to be.

She froze in midsentence and proceeded to fold her arms violently, like a spoiled toddler not getting her way.

I went on. "You'll listen to me whether you like it or not. This has been buried inside of me for way too long and I can't go on pretending it never happened. As screwed up as it was that you had multiple affairs during my childhood, what's even more unbelievable is that you directly involved me in them. You *insisted* that I know everything, be a part of your pain and experience the damage you said Dad had caused. Why, why would you ruin your only daughter's childhood? So I would know 'exactly what you were going through.'

"And to top it off, to make an already unimaginably dreadful situation even worse, you made me swear to secrecy to cover up your actions. 'Now, Julia, don't you dare tell your father about this. I'll be the one to tell him, but it has to be the right time, so promise me.' Or 'It will destroy your father, so let's keep this between ourselves, Julia. You wouldn't want to upset your father, would you, dear, no matter how much he hurt your poor, sweet mother? Promise me, Julia, promise me.' Or my favorite, the line you reserved when you saw I was on the verge of going to Dad, on the verge of collapsing from the guilt, 'Julia, if you don't respect my explicit wishes, child, then I'll leave both you and your father and never come back. Both of us know what that would do to your father, now don't we? You don't want to be responsible for that dear, do you?'"

I searched Mother's face for some change, a sign of shame, a hint of regret; hell, I'd even take just plain recall. I'd imagined saying what I had just said for years, rehearsed it over and over, and now it had come out. I had hoped, really, really hoped, that Mother would break down in tears and beg me to forgive her, admit how bad she had been and apologize for all she'd put me through. But no, not my mother; the woman could have been a world-class poker player. She just kept standing there with her arms folded, glaring at me with daggers in her eyes, her only movement the now steady, impatient tap of the toe of her dark brown heels.

Internally disappointed but unfazed, I continued. "How could you make me swear to that? How could you put that much guilt and responsibility on your own daughter? Why, Mother, why?"

I gave her no time to respond because I knew it was no use. "And you expected me to forgive you and play along? Pretend that nothing ever happened, that I wasn't part of the deceit? What kind of a woman does that? Do you have any idea how many years and thousands of dollars in therapy it's taken for me to finally stop blaming myself for what happened? To realize that I wasn't responsible for it, that I was just collateral damage? Tell me, Mother, exactly how long would it have gone on if Dad hadn't walked in on you that day? Another five years, another ten? When would it have been enough? When would Dad have been sufficiently punished, huh?"

Thanks to Mother, I knew everything about that day. It had been five long, drawn-out years of Mother getting even with Dad, and by that time I had turned seventeen. Thank goodness I'd been at school the day it happened because I didn't know if I could have handled being there. Mother had made sure to fill me in on all the details, though, smiling and laughing as she told me. That afternoon, when I grudgingly came home from high school, she'd insisted we go for tea, forcing me to miss my community-college calculus class so she could tell me the *wonderful* news.

Over a steaming cup of chamomile tea, she'd described in detail how Dad had come home early from his convention that day. How he'd found her in the bed in black lingerie, and Ted, the flavor of the year, was hiding stark naked in the bathroom. She gleefully went on to describe how she'd told Dad about all the different men she'd been seeing since his one-night affair, and how good they were, how far superior lovers they'd been compared to him.

Her tone had changed from giddy to serious then, and she'd made sure to tell me how Dad had broken down in tears and blamed himself for what she'd done. How he'd sworn again and again that he would have taken back what he did if he could. I could tell that she relished the part when he'd cried; in my whole life, I'd never known my dad to cry. She did this all with the calculated calm that a hit man would be proud of, insisting like usual that I know everything. In reality, it was her chance to boast, to share her *accomplishment* with someone who had no choice but to listen.

Now Mother's eyes narrowed, and she turned away and started walking to the kitchen. I felt my anger increase; she had no right to walk away from this, from me. I hurried around her and blocked her path, and she looked at me wide-eyed with disbelief. I could tell she was about to explode.

She raised her voice then, and said, "Julia, move out of my way this very instant, otherwise you are never, ever welcome in this house again."

I calmed myself enough not to shout back at her because if I did, all hope of getting out what I needed to say would be lost. Calmly, softly, rationally, I went on.

"How could you expect me to be close to you after that, Mother? Truly, how did you think that was going to affect me? Did you think about anyone but yourself? How can you demand *respect* from me? How can you possibly think I could feel anything but contempt for your actions? You know, to this day, Dad still doesn't know what you put me through, what you made me swear to. As much as he put up with you and your actions toward him, did you really think he would have tolerated what you did to me?"

I saw the flash of fear in her eyes, and I knew that at least that comment had struck home.

"Don't worry, Mother, as screwed up as it was, I never did and never will say a single word to him. I've kept my promise, Mother, for his sake."

I was too upset and angry to cry; I knew that would come later.

This catharsis was long overdue. The stress had built up over the last couple of months; my childhood and Dad's decision to stop therapy had led me to this place. A deep, dark, previously unacknowledged place between my mother and me. A place I had always been too scared to go, too afraid of the consequences of bringing up the past again. It came from a hurtful past, a past I had long tried to suppress. A past that had hindered a lot of new relationships and, according to my therapist, a past that I needed to come to terms with in order to fully move on.

I said, "What Dad did was inexcusable, but what you did was far worse, Mother. Dad at least made every effort to leave me out of it, tried to keep it between you and him. But you . . . you were too selfish for that, too narcissistic. It's beyond comprehension that you could be so self-absorbed that you would have brought me into that mess, robbed me of my parents and destroyed any semblance of my childhood. It was wrong, just plain wrong."

At that instant, I finally saw Mother's anger dissipate, either because she was tired or my last comment had somehow gotten through to her. She slowly walked back into the living room to the glass table, picked up her teacup and saucer, and slowly took a sip of her tea. She sat down in the white love seat. She suddenly looked ten years older, with her shoulders slumped and her head resting on her fingers.

Could this be our breakthrough? Could she have actually internalized what I'd said? Was she about to break down and admit to how wrong she had been?

As suddenly as she'd appeared worn and beaten, she transformed back into her usual defiant self. She sat up straight, re-crossed her legs, adjusted her jacket, and looked at me with a stone-cold expression that reflected her inner stubborn self. The woman had pride, and it was that pride that had kept her immune from everyone and everything else in the world.

In a firm but surprisingly soft voice, she said in almost a whisper, "It is obvious, Julia, that you have deep psychological issues, stemming from what, who can say? But like all children of your era, who think they're so hard done by, you're living up to the standard cliché. It seems the blame-the-mother school of thought has influenced you. With as much money as you wasted on your education, I would have thought you'd have been immune to such nonsense."

I wouldn't let her change the subject, try to brush this off, so I ignored her last comment and pushed on. I had given her a chance at a reprieve, but she'd obviously blown it.

"Mother, as much as you try to blame this on something else, the fact of the matter is that you were wrong. It was your own decision to stay with Dad after his affair; yours, not anyone else's. It was you who chose to *forgive* him, even though you did everything you could to punish him for it. It was also you who chose to involve me in your mess and, consequently, it was you who made my teenage years a living hell. Again, they were your decisions, your actions, not mine. You had no right to do to me what you did, Mother. Dad left me out of it, but you selfishly didn't."

It was at that point that Mother decided to acknowledge that we were even talking about Dad's affair, talking about my childhood, discussing a subject that placed blame directly on her. This whole time she'd done her best to distance herself from acknowledging anything attached to the affair, refusing to respond to any of my accusations, doing everything in her power to avoid broaching the subject. But finally, finally, she chose to engage. It must have been the your-choice-and-your-decision line that brought her in. She could never resist talking about herself.

Abruptly, her expression shifted again, and suddenly, she dropped the well-put-together, professional persona she'd tried so hard to portray. She transformed into the vindictive, hurt, scheming, self-absorbed woman of my teenage years. Her eyes narrowed to lizardlike slits, her lips pursed and eyebrows tensed, exposing wrinkles that no amount of chemical peels could hide.

She almost spat out the next sentence. "Julia, your father cheated on me with a twenty-year-old slut, for heaven's sake. Now that, child, that was inexcusable."

Realizing she had momentarily lost control, she ever so slightly shook her head to the left and then the right, as if she was snapping herself back into the now before putting on her standard holier-than-thou expression. But for a moment, I'd had a glimpse of the mother of my childhood.

Now, in a low, controlled, completely different voice from a moment before, she continued. "But dear, I didn't want my marriage to fail. I didn't want you to have the dreadful experience or agonizing embarrassment of having divorced parents, separate households. That would have made you feel like such a failure. It would have been awfully disconcerting for you, mark my words. And I can only imagine the trauma it would have inflicted. What would your friends have said? What would your uncles and aunts have thought? No, Julia, I would never have dreamed of putting you through that. I would never have done something as dreadful as that."

With pure disbelief, I listened as she went on. "So I put my feelings and my emotions aside, dear, for you, mainly, and to keep our wonderful family together. I'll admit we all weren't perfect, and there were some minor bumps in the road those first few years after the *incident*." She made sure to put air quotes and lower her voice when she said that last.

"But I forgave your father over time, and ever since we put that ugly occurrence behind us, we haven't spoken about it since. Julia, I stayed with your father for you, just as I told you I always would."

I shouldn't have been overly surprised at how incredibly psychotic the woman was, and how much denial she was in. Hell, it had taken working with a professional for me to get to this point. I had learned that my mother was so self-absorbed, so inherently narcissistic, that it probably truly had never occurred to her that she had done anything wrong. To the average person, it was as obvious as the sky being blue, the earth being round, but to Mother . . . well, as Kirsten continually said, she's a textbook narcissist.

Throughout this whole interchange, she still hadn't apologized for anything. She was insane, completely and utterly nuts. She didn't want to hire a babysitter back then because she'd thought she'd been protecting me; it was ludicrous. Should I have held her to a normal standard? Could she have helped the way she was?

I stopped myself before I started making more excuses for her. Before any guilt could try to creep its way into my psyche, I blurted out, "Any which way you spin it, it was still wrong of you, Mother. Taking me with you on dates was crazy, making me swear to secrecy was dysfunctional, and telling me in the manner in which you chose about Dad's affair—that was just screwed up. You know, I don't know if I said it before, but to this day, Dad has never, ever told me about the affair, never even hinted at it. He's kept me out of it, like any rational person would. I don't even think he's aware that I know about it, and if he is, he's never mentioned it—"

She interrupted me then, and this time she managed to shout me down. "Don't be naïve, Julia. Of course your father knows that you're aware of his affair. I told him that you knew about it, and just how incredibly hurt you were by it, the day after it happened. He will never bring it up with you because that's his personality, but rest assured, he does know."

I was feeling tired by this point, though I wanted to respond. I was suddenly too drained and, unfortunately, she went on with a confidence that demanded my silence.

"And before you start having another tantrum, I would appreciate it if you concentrated on your father for the next couple of months. Don't involve him in your emotional turmoil, and never, ever bring this up. Do you understand how much damage it would do to him right now? It would destroy him, just in case you're too emotionally disturbed to comprehend that. And besides, digging up the past isn't the best thing for my relationship with him either." She stared at me, and I could see the cold, injured pride reflected in her eyes.

It was at that moment that I truly came to terms with the fact that she would never apologize for what she'd done during my childhood. In fact, I would be surprised if anything I'd said had actually gotten through that thick head of hers. She had probably stopped paying attention to me as soon as I'd changed the subject from the one she'd so desired to talk about: death. What did it matter anyway? I had finally expunged my feelings about that terrible time in my life, met a goal my therapist had been trying to have me accomplish for years. Granted, it wasn't the ideal situation or presentation, but it had been done. According to Kirsten, life could go on now and, more importantly, *I* could go on.

I needed fresh air and had an overriding urge to get out of the house. Every nerve in my body screamed at me to leave; the room felt so small and I was practically choking, it was so stuffy. My sudden desire to go surpassed any I felt to see Dad. I had had enough drama for today. I didn't want to show any weakness in front of him, and I needed some time to process what had been said.

I got up swiftly and started heading to the door. She looked at me questioningly but didn't object when she realized my destination. I reached for the iron handle and felt its cool touch as my fingers wrapped around it. I made it halfway out before I turned back to her and, with a mixture of anger, frustration, and disappointment, said, "Don't worry, Mother, I would never do that to Dad. Tell him that something came up and I had to leave."

And with that, I closed the door behind me.

71

JULIA
MARCH 2008

We had been through this routine, Mother and I, and as maladjusted as it may seem to an outsider, it was standard operating procedure for us. We were both experts at the art of avoiding and ignoring someone you were forced to be around.

It had been more difficult when I was in high school and lived at home, but I had found ways. It had been a matter of never being at the house, always having a job or a friend's place to be at, or some reason to escape being by myself with her, or even Dad, for that matter. I had still been mad at him at the time, and it had been too close to the *event* for me to forgive them or be anywhere near him for long periods of time.

College had meant freedom, and when I got into a fight with Mother, at least I had had the option of going for months without ever having to be forced to speak to her. My relationship with Dad had never been the same afterward, but as time went on . . . well, at least we had grown a little closer and salvaged a little of what had been. And so, to phrase it more correctly, our relationship had grown less apart.

It's funny how life plays little tricks on us; as fate would have it, after I had married David and we had made tentative plans for him to be transferred out of state to one of his company's other branch locations, he had been offered the promotion of a lifetime. I had wanted to permanently escape my parents and San Diego, but of all the locations in the world, of course the job offer would have to have been none other than San Diego.

Yes, Mother and I were masters at this game of avoidance, and so despite Mother, I continued to spend time at the house with Dad every free moment I had, undaunted by my lack of conversation with her. Dad couldn't help but notice that there was a problem between us, and as much as we tried to pretend everything was normal between us, you could cut the tension with a knife. Frankly, there was nothing that could be done about it because she was still sulking, and I had no interest in speaking to her. I was still livid at her, mad at her complete self-absorption and upset at what had been said.

There was a small part of me that felt guilty, but not enough to change my general feelings of rage with her. I hated that this was happening now, and I couldn't have dreamed of a worse time for it to occur.

I could see that it was also affecting Dad, and it was that fact and that fact alone that led me to try to extend the olive branch to Mother about two weeks after our fight, and it was purely for Dad's sake. It was a dark and cloudy day; the afternoon clouds had not burned off, as they so often didn't do so close to beach. I went to the house at about three P.M., and I had resolved to at least try to speak to Mother. *What the hell*, I thought, *I'll try to be the mature one here.*

I heard Mother's heels on the hardwood floor as she approached the door, and as she opened it to let me in, with one fell swoop I tried to end our battle of wills. I broke our silence by casually saying, "Hi, Mom, how are you doing?" thinking that this gesture would be harmless enough.

She looked me up and down, abruptly turned around to put her back to me, and walked away with a "Hmmpff."

I shouldn't have been surprised. The woman was a master at sulking, and this fight had been a bad one. Obviously, I had hit home with what I had said, and it would be a long time before she got over it. The problem was that not only was she a narcissist but she was pigheaded and proud, which, I thought, was a deadly combination. Narcissism probably wasn't broken down into levels because once labeled a narcissist, you were pretty much pigheaded to start with, but I remember making a mental note to ask Kirsten if that was true.

Mother had never been one to forgive easily, so why would she start now? I had brought up the untouchable topic, after all, raised my voice to her, insulted her, and actually gone so far as to put it out on the table, and directly accusing her of being a bad mother.

Yes, this would take a while.

THE DOG DAYS OF THE PRESENT

72

BRANDON
MAY 2009

"Tom, like I said before, I worked real hard to get you this job, so don't screw it up and make me look like a punk."

Tom was a lanky, pimple-faced twenty-three-year-old kid who I had helped to get hired here. It was his first day, and I was showing him around, giving him the orientation, and praying that he wouldn't screw this up. If he did do something stupid, I was going to break Jake's legs. Jake is his brother and our band's singer, and he was the one who put me in such a difficult position. Besides, Thunder didn't need a singer who could walk anyway.

We headed toward the radiation room with Eddie following, wagging his tail. Like all retriever mixes, the dog was as friendly as a dog could be, and I kind of liked the little guy. Although I will say that I could definitely have done without all of the licking. His owner had been cool and had mostly held it together today, although it didn't take much to turn on the waterworks with that lady. At least today there was only a little bit of drama, nothing too serious.

I looked behind myself at Tom, who was following pretty close behind. Man, the kid was lanky; he looked like an Instant Noodle undulating instead of walking. I stopped right outside of the radiation-room door, turned around, and stared him straight in the eye with one of my you'd-better-pay-attention looks.

In a serious voice, I said, "Tom, we are about to go into the radiation vault, dude. That red sign we just walked under is basically a warning to be careful because we're going into a high-radiation zone. And you know what that means? It means no screwing around."

At the mention of the word *radiation*, I could see the pimples above Tom's lips start to quiver, a pretty normal reaction given all the crap on TV about anything with radioactivity. But before the guy could open his mouth, I said, "The answer is no, so don't even ask. You won't be radiated, unless, you act like a total dweeb and make me look like an idiot for recommending you for this job. With all the safety stuff in place, you would have to be a total moron to get zapped, but given you're Jake's brother and all . . . you'd better stay right behind me."

We walked into the room, and I waited for the usual reaction that people get when they first see the place. Tom was no different; I swear, at least four of his pimples exploded as his jaw hit the ground. Pretty much everyone gets blown away when they see this room, and Tom was no different.

"It's pretty high-tech; I mean you have the radiation machine console, which controls everything the machine in the next room does. It's got a ton of buttons and lights and looks pretty much like an airplane cockpit. You also have three computers scattered around on the tabletops all around the room, one of which is the radiation-planning computer. The other two computers are for records, but the radiation-planning computer, that's a beast unto itself. It's a thirty-two-inch computer screen that usually flashes the current radiation plan the doc is working on, complete with one special ergonomic keyboard and a mouse that looks like a joystick from the eighties. There's also one of the anesthesia stations."

I pointed to the wall opposite the machine console, where the anesthesia machine, the silver rolling gurney, and anesthesia-monitoring equipment are located.

"That's where we anesthetize the animals before they're rolled into the other room to be treated. There's another anesthesia machine in there; that way we can just switch out the animal that's been treated with the animal that's being rolled in. It's like an assembly line. Cool, huh?"

He didn't answer, just stared around, looking at the other three technicians in the room. I decided to introduce him to everyone before he made a total fool of himself. He didn't seem like the smoothest kid on the block, and since everybody knew he was one of my best friends' brothers, I decided to head off any social disaster before it happened.

"Tom, this is Caroline. She's the radiation therapist, and in all the time I've been here, I've never seen her wear anything but pink."

Caroline was standing right in front of the radiation console, entering the dose prescription for the current patient, and without missing a beat, she raised her hand and with one smooth motion managed to wave at Tom and then give me the finger. Still looking down, she said, "Nice to me you, Tom. We'll talk a little later. I'm just in the middle of a treatment. And oh, don't take anything Brandon says seriously; he's a real teddy bear."

Touché.

Smiling, I turned back to Tom. "Caroline operates the radiation machine. Speaking of which, big Bertha, as I like to call her, is a refurbished CLINAC 2100 linear accelerator. And that big Flash Gordon control panel that Caroline's standing behind, it's the machine console. It's the brains of the operation, and that's where she controls how much beam is delivered to each patient. The linear accelerator is in the other room; I'll show it to you in a couple of minutes. But since they're just finishing up on a dog—Fritz, I think—we can't go in. That is, if you still wanna have kids when you're older."

Tom still looked impressed, and he was nodding his head like he had a clue as to what I was saying. In reality, though, probably only about 10 percent was really sticking.

I went on anyway. "You see, when we radiate an animal, it's all about the positioning. The animals need to be in the exact same position every day, and that's another one of Caroline's jobs. She repeats what's done on the first day by the doc after he gets them exactly where he wants them. She takes pictures so she can repeat the setup, takes measurements, and does it the same way every day for the rest of the treatments."

Tom, who had barely said more than two-word sentences since he had gotten here, in a high, almost teenagerlike voice squeaked out, "Wow, that's cool!"

Then he hesitated for about three more seconds and stared at me, as if he was scared to ask the next question. "Um . . . I do have a question. Like, don't they move and all, but like, how do you keep them still so you can zap them every single day?"

"Whoa, dude, that's a great question, and you obviously like the word like, but welcome to the party anyway. It speaks! Seriously, though, each animal has his or her own positioning device. The most common one is a vacuum bag that's filled with tiny white polystyrene beads that mold to the animal once we suck the air out of the bag. Oh, by the way, that's what we make the new guys do. You are the official suckers."

Tom squinted his eyes and tilted his head ever so slightly. He started wrinkling his eyebrows, and a huge crease formed on his large, flat forehead. He gave me a questioning stare, but before one of the giant zits on his forehead exploded, I quickly said, "Just kidding, man. Learn how to take a joke."

"The way it really goes is that there's a machine that we plug into the bag that sucks out the air, and that makes a mold of the patient. Each patient gets his own positioning bag, and he keeps it for the entire course of therapy. So, basically, every day we put that animal under anesthesia and into his mold and voilà, he doesn't move and he's in the same position. You get it?"

He nodded really slowly, and I could tell he was trying to process everything.

I went on, "The doc says it's extremely accurate from day to day if we do it this way. And that's what it's all about: doing exactly the same thing every single day. We need to be radiating the same part over and over and be right every time, otherwise the treatment will be pretty much a waste.

"Dude, there are loads of other tricks and toys, but hey, it's your first day. Since your brother and you share the same parents, I don't want to overwhelm you with too much, but give it a week and I'm sure you'll get to see all of the magic."

Tom seemed genuinely stoked and was smiling from ear to ear. He was still nodding his head slowly, most likely completely unaware of what he was doing. Based on his kid-in-a-candy-store expression, I could tell he was genuinely interested in this stuff. The guy had definitely asked the right questions; annoying, yes, but at least he had been paying attention to what I said.

Tom was nothing like his brother. By now, Jake would have either had to leave for a cigarette break or would have found some excuse as to why he needed to get out of there. Tom, on the other hand, seemed like he actually wanted to be there.

I went on, "Tom, Eddie here is starting therapy today. After Fritz is finished, Eddie's up."

Tom stopped nodding and suddenly looked confused again. His head started to tilt to the side once more, and with an impatient sigh, I said, "Dude, Fritz, the dog that's currently being radiated, remember?"

Tom's stupid expression faded as recall kicked in.

"You're pretty lucky, because you actually get to see Eddie's setup from the start. We already did his CAT scan two days ago, so the doc has had enough time to do the computer plan off of that. So today, he'll line up Eddie for the first time so he matches the computer plan, and you get to see the whole process from the start."

73

EDDIE
MAY 2009

We entered a medium-size room, and I saw a short, pink-coated mom sitting on a chair behind a long gray table. The mom had short, straight brown hair and wore thick coverings that made her eyes look twice the size of normal. On the gray table was a long, square box with tons of flashing and blinking lights, which kept going on and off in no particular order. The pink-coated mom was scratching the lights, deep in concentration.

I looked around, taking in my surroundings, and instantly noticed that next to the pink-covering mom on the wall to her left was a square gray-and-silver hypno box. I wasn't too surprised by this, since every room I've ever gone to in this territory has had one of these hypno boxes, sometimes even two. I've seen them in all sorts of sizes–big, small, flat, round, noisy, or quiet—and usually when they were there, they tended to be the center of attention. All of the moms and dads I've ever known here just loved staring at the things.

This Crunchy Territory hypno box looked smaller than our territory hypno box, and it was obviously fast asleep, judging by its black, boring screen. There was no noise coming from it, and no flashing lights were lighting up its face. The pink- coated mom was staring at it, and as I looked to see what the shiny-headed dad and the puppy dad were doing, I saw that they were staring at the hypno box as well.

74

BRANDON
MAY 2009

"So when it's slow, do you guys get to watch TV?" Jake's brother said with a little too much excitement in his voice.

Strike one, and it had been going so well for the guy. Did he really just ask that? The kid did look like he'd spent most of his teenage years playing video games or Dungeons and Dragons, but that didn't mean I wanted to label him as a complete loser. In my experience in high school, kids like that spent most of their time at home, either too lazy to get a real job or too scared to get out in the real world. They just stayed home and mooched off of their parents until they got kicked out of the house, and then they usually ended up working in the local comic book store.

I really hoped Tom wasn't like that because over the last half an hour I had actually gotten to like him, Mount Vesuvius zits and all. We were still in the radiation room, and I looked over to where he was staring, hoping to give him the benefit of the doubt. I knew the geek-in-awe look, that hypnotic state geeks get when they see anything with a dragon or a science fiction creature on it. If he had had that look right then, all my respect would have gone out of the window, and I would have had to make fun of Jake for the next century for having such a dweeb of a brother. Luckily for him and for Jake, he was staring at me instead.

"First of all, it's never slow here; it's a freaking zoo, day in and day out. Second of all, the answer is a big, fat, sweaty mama no. Dude, that's the screen for the camera, you doof! No one can be in the room when the machine is on. Each treatment takes about five minutes or so, and we need a way to see what's going on with the animal that's under anesthesia. So we point one camera at the dog, cat, or whatever the heck we're treating, and the other camera at the anesthesia-monitoring machine, and that's how we make sure that he or she is alive."

Tom nodded his head, and I heard him exhaling the word "oooh." His facial expression changed from one of sound understanding to one of inquisitive confusion.

"So like, what happens if something goes wrong while no one's in the room? You guys have to have some way of shutting the machine off, right? You can't like just go in there while the machines on, right, or do they make you do that here?"

I stroked the top of my head, feeling the smooth skin. I had shaved it three days ago, and I loved the feel of the stubble against my fingertips. It was my natural reaction whenever I was impressed, bored, or looking for something, and somehow my scalp and my brain were connected. Right now, I was impressed because Tom had asked a good question; without thinking about it, I had reached for my head.

"No, you don't need to get radiated, although that's a very nice but very stupid gesture on your part. So the answer is no. You see those big red buttons on the machine console?" He followed my finger to where I was pointing. "Well, there are about four more in the actual radiation vault scattered around the room. As soon as you press one of those bottoms, the machine turns off, and there's no radiation coming out of it then. All it is, is a big X-ray machine, like the ones they use when you get X-rays at the dentist's office. But the difference, of course, is that this makes a lot stronger X-rays, and to answer your question, no, you can't go in when the machine is on. Before you ask the next question, because I can see where this is going, the animals aren't radioactive after they get their treatment. The only time there's radiation floating around is when the machine is on."

Tom went back to nodding his head, and I did my best not to stare at a big white head aching to pop just at the tip of his nose. Just then, behind Tom, I saw the door open, and in walked Susie, Shayna, and the little Jack Russell terrier, Fritz. Shayna was in her late forties, with mid-shoulder-length, dirty blond hair and a semipudgy body. She looked like a feminine version of the Pillsbury doughboy and always had a smile on her face. She had been working here for about eight years and was one of the most senior technicians in the place. In fact, she had trained me.

Suzie was Native American by birth and was about a head shorter then Shayna, with long black hair that reached down to the small of her back. She was a very skinny but muscular girl and had worked as a model for a woman's sports clothing catalogue before deciding to become a technician. She wasn't certified yet, but was going to night school to get her license. That's not to say that she wasn't the most talented technician in the place, so much so that if I ever needed to go under anesthesia, I would want her running it.

The girls hadn't noticed us, and before I could say anything, Suzie with one fluid movement hoisted the little Jack Russell terrier onto the silver anesthesia table. You could see her biceps flexing and couldn't help but admire her smooth brown skin. She put one arm around Fritz's head and with the other extended his elbow so his arm vein was nice and exposed.

"Hey, guys, this is Tom," I called out to them.

Both of them turned their heads toward us and said "hi" in sync. I could make out Shayna's lower baritone voice, as well as Suzie's high-pitched, tough-girl tone. They were complete opposites of each other, but that didn't stop them from being two of the most efficient girls in the practice. They had been working together so long that they pretty much read each other's minds and didn't need to communicate by words. But when they did, maybe out of force of habit or something, it was freaky, because they usually said the same thing, and at the same time, no less.

Tom managed to force out an answer that sounded like a mix between "hello" and "hi," and I watched as he turned bright red. "Dude, is that all it took?"

I shouldn't have been surprised, given what I knew of Tom already, but it was amazing to me that he was the complete opposite of his brother Jake. Jake was a real player; I don't think I can remember a time when he wasn't dating at least two girls at the same time. Sleazy, yes, but you couldn't deny that the guy had some crazy, mad talent. I wondered what the heck had happened to his brother, though. I guess he'd been taking a whiz on the bushes when those skills were handed out. Hell, you can't have two of those in one family; that would throw the earth off of its axis or something.

I put my hand on Tom's shoulder and felt him tense up underneath.

"Tom, pay attention to this, it's the best way to learn. You're going to see Fritz here get treated, and the lovely Shayna and Suzie will demonstrate how it's done. Since you don't have any anesthesia experience, I'll explain what's going on step-by-step. Shayna just gave Fritz a shot of something called Propofol; that's what's making him fall asleep so fast. That plastic tube she just reached for is going to be put in his mouth and throat so he can continue to breathe. Whenever they're under anesthesia, their throats don't work right and will close unless there's something there to keep it open. It's the same for us, man, like if you decided to take care of that nose of yours, which your bro's been saying you want to save up for, then you, too, will have a tube stuck down your throat."

Tom wiggled out from under my hand, his head jerking around as he stared at me with a look of utter shock and embarrassment.

In a semiwhisper, I said, "What, man, don't look so damn

surprised. He's the singer and I'm the guitarist; it's like we're husband and wife, without the whole sex or gay thing. Not that I have a problem with that or anything, and if that's how you roll, that's cool; people just got to be happy and not stress the small stuff. Point is, I know a lot about you, and that's why I put my neck out to put a good word in for you to get this job. So chill out and pay attention."

He opened his mouth to take a very shallow breath and then looked for a second like he was going to say something. But, instead, he slumped his shoulders and slowly turned back around and looked over to the table where the girls were working on Fritz.

"That thing is called an endotracheal tube, and those wires you see hooked up to him, they're called electrocardiogram leads or, as we like to say, ECG leads. Those are hooked up to the anesthesia-monitoring screen, which monitors a lot of things, including his ECG pattern. That's what that green line is over there; every time his heart beats, it makes that wave pattern. You see?"

I looked at him to make sure he wasn't completely confused. He had his shoulders rolled forward and was wrinkling his eyebrows like he was two seconds away from crying. I could tell that he hadn't gotten over the nose comment, and a little part of me felt guilty. Guess the guy was sensitive; definitely nothing like his brother.

I cleared my throat and went on in a softer voice. "We also measure other stuff, like the heart rate, blood pressure, and even the amount of oxygen in the blood. That's what's on the screen next to the ECG line. We also always watch them breathe, either by looking at their chest as it moves up and down or looking at that black balloon that keeps getting bigger and smaller. It's what collects the reservoir gas from the anesthesia machine, and it gets bigger and smaller whenever Fritz takes a breath."

I looked back over at Tom and saw that his face had gone from all hurt and sensitive to now looking overwhelmed. His eyes were opened so wide that I could see the entire rim of the colored part of his eyeballs. His head was tilted a little to the side and his mouth was hanging open. Information overload!

I put my hand back on his shoulder, and this time he didn't flinch. "Don't worry, man, I know it's a lot to take in, but you've got plenty of time. We'll go over this again and again until you don't have to think, you just do."

Just then, the door burst open and Dr. Lindy walked in, carrying three manila-colored charts in his left hand while he had his nose buried in the one in his right hand. He looked completely immersed in what he was doing, and I knew it wasn't a good time to introduce good old Tom to him. He was a nice-enough guy and would probably want to make Tom feel welcome and all, but I knew that would break his train of thought. I didn't want to do that to him now because I knew that look, and he was running behind.

"Tom, look sharp now, here comes the doc. You haven't met the guy yet, and since he looks like he's in a really big hurry, I'll have to introduce you to him another time. Now let's go look in the radiation vault."

75

EDDIE
MAY 2009

I looked over to where the dads had turned their heads; they were looking at two blue-coated moms standing around the table. One of the moms was a skinny brown color and had a long, flowing black mane, while the other was much more round-shaped and had a short, brownish-and-gray mane. The one with the long black mane was leaning on the waist-high silver table and hugging a furry friend.

The two moms hadn't even looked in my direction when they had walked into the room. They had seemed so busy with the small, muscular short-haired furry friend bouncing around their feet as they walked in that they hadn't even noticed me.

He hadn't noticed me either but he hadn't had enough time to give me a proper greeting after he was let into the room. One moment he was panting up a storm, making his way between the two moms with his chest out and his front paws pointing inward, and the next he was lifted onto the table by the black-maned mom.

I watched as the look of surprise overtook his face and his short, stubby legs suddenly left the floor. Now, the little guy's eyes were semibulging out to start with, but the moment his legs were lifted off the ground, his eyes opened so wide that I could see his entire eyeballs.

By the time his paws hit the table, a white-fluid–filled bee was already heading his way. It flew straight into the little guy's stubby arm. The roundish mom had tried to grab it—she actually had succeeded in slowing it down a little—but we all know that they are too strong to be held back. The little guy never had a chance against the bee, even with the two blue-coated moms there to protect him

And here's where things got kind of weird: Instead of letting out a high-pitched yelp, like any furry friend his size would do after going head-to-head with a bee that big, he just fell asleep. It was instant. There was no yawning, no stretching, no licking his paw pads to search for some compact food before a nap; instead, he went out cold like he had been chasing after bushy-tailed furry friends the entire light period.

I watched as the roundish mom grabbed a clear tubelike object and stuck it down his throat, while the black-maned mom cranked his mouth open. I tilted my head to the side and felt the tip of my ear scrape against the floor as I let out a short, questioning moan. What was going on?

I kept watching as they connected the end of the narrow crunchy tube treat to a long hose, which stretched back the length of the table and dived into the back of the wall behind the round blue-coated mom. I kept watching as the black-maned mom started connecting green, white, and black strings to the furry friend's legs. She connected the black one to his left elbow, the white one to his right elbow, and the red one to his left knee.

The only thing I could think of is that somehow, in some way, those strings were part of the reason why that little guy hadn't woken up yet. Those strings must have been doing something to keep him snoozing, like when Mom patted me between my eyes right in my secret spot.

I realized that I had been staring openmouthed at the sleeping furry friend for enough time that my left paw pad had started to grow tingly, and the sudden pinpricks as I shifted position made me snap out of my trance. That, and the fact that I felt my neck being dragged forward as the shiny-headed dad began to pull on my safety rope.

I had completely forgotten about the dads, and all this time they had been grunting together and checking out the sleepy furry friend. The shiny-headed dad moved with a strong walk, while the puppy dad followed closely with slouched steps. We all walked toward the door we had come in through, but at the last moment we made a right.

I couldn't believe that I had missed it when we first entered the room. In front of me was a huge, square doorway, with a red, rectangular flashing light above it. The doorway was as tall as it was wide and was opened halfway, and behind it was a dimly lit room.

As we walked into the room, I caught metal-smell that was coming from the large door, and I let out a short sneeze to clear my nose. It smelled terrible, like Dad's old paw coverings after he had gotten back from a run.

In the center of the room was another table very similar to the one the sleepy furry friend in the other room was on. Except this one wasn't bright shiny silver; it had more of an off-white color, like a bone once it's been dug up after a long time.

Lying on it in a deep sleep was another furry friend, only this one was a brown, medium-size furry friend with a hair coat very similar to mine. This furry friend was also out cold with a clear, tubelike treat sticking out of his mouth. He was lying on his side, snoozing away without a worry in the world. He too, had three multicolored strings attached to his legs.

This furry friend was being gently patted by a large, chocolate-colored dad who had the shiniest round, silver ear decoration I had ever seen. The dad was at least a full head taller than the shiny-headed dad and had a mane of short black fur. Both of his upper arms were huge, and each one was at least as wide as the size of my neck. The dad was enormous. I could sense the tremendous amount of strength in him, but looking at his face, I could also see that he was probably one of the gentlest dads in this place.

He smelled like spicy ginger cookies mixed with a little must, which in my world was one of the most settling and relaxing smells. It tickled my nostrils and opened a door to my puppy past. I don't have many memories of those early puppy days or my family before Mom and Dad; in fact, I don't remember how my original furry friend mother looked, but my only memory of her is of that smell.

I wanted to go up to the dad and introduce myself, try to take in as much of him as I could. Did he know my furry friend mom? Did I have any brothers or sisters?

The dad was deep in thought, all of his energy and attention focused on the brown, sleeping furry friend. It was obvious that this was neither the place nor the time for me to get his attention. Even all the noise the puppy dad was making with his high-pitched whining and grunting hadn't made him look up. He had just kept one paw on the brown furry friend while scratching a yellow piece of bark and a small, thin, blue scratching stick in the other.

76

BRANDON
MAY 2009

"It's pretty impressive, huh? Tom, this is the place where all the magic happens. This is the radiation vault, and it's the room where we do the treatments. Just look around, dude. Just in case you're not impressed by the massive lead door we just walked through, or even the machine itself, just realize that you're standing in a room that's made out of walls that are six feet wide and made of pure concrete. It's insane how much work went into this. Not to mention how much it must have cost to build this room alone. It's more than either of us will ever make in our lifetimes combined, no doubt."

I stared at Tom, who, to his credit, looked a little impressed. His nervous eyes were scanning the place with quick, jerky movements, trying to take it all in, and I could pick up on some awe in his face.

I pointed to the machine then, and said, "Tom, feast your eyes on the machine now. Okay, take a big, deep breath in . . . hold it."

Tom being Tom actually did gulp down a deep breath after a quick glance over at me to see if I was serious or not. Thinking that I was, or just playing along to satisfy my sick little game and avoiding me giving him an even harder time than I was doing, he stared intently at the machine. His lips ballooned out as he made a show of shutting them to keep the air in.

I said, "This, my dear man, is what we call the linear accelerator, in all of its glory. . . . Don't breathe out yet because I'm not finished. . . . It's one of the coolest pieces of hardware out there. Now, I'm going to try to explain this, so bear with me. I'll divide the machine into three main parts, just to keep it pretty easy and so you can keep up. First off, we'll start with the most obvious. The first part of the machine is the table, which is pretty obvious, man; I mean, just look at it. It's a frigging table, and if you can't figure out which part of the machine is the table, we've got problems."

I pointed to the waist-high, approximately eight foot by three foot, flat table, the part of the machine that all the patients were positioned on top of for treatment.

"Second off—" I pointed to the three-foot-wide vertical portion of the L-shaped segment of the machine. It had a brown casing that hid its numerous electrical wires and parts, like a hard-plastic exoskeleton. It reached up to the ceiling before doing a ninety-degree turn to extend another two feet or so parallel to the table. The short part of the L loomed over it, like an eagle about to pounce on its prey. The longer part of the L, the vertical part, was connected at its midpoint to the machine and, just like the arm of a compass, could rotate 360 degrees around the central point.

I traced the L with my finger and said to Tom, "That's what's called the gantry, dude. It's basically the arm of the machine and can spin all around the table. Lastly, now stay with me . . ."

I looked over at Tom and saw that that his face had begun turning red and his eyes were bulging out. The dweeb was actually still holding his breath. His head was shaking and his eyes were darting nervously from left to right. He looked like he was three quarters of the way across the swimming pool underwater and wasn't going to make it. I could see the guy was starting to panic from lack of oxygen.

In disbelief and feeling a little guilty, I said in a low voice, "Tom, take a breath, man."

Tom let out a large exhalation and then proceeded to take a couple of short, desperate breaths. I looked around just to make sure that no one else had seen what was going on, and luckily, Rick, the biggest, toughest-looking, and nicest guy you'd ever meet, hadn't noticed a thing.

Rick looked like your average black, six-foot-five linebacker who had dropped out of the NFL to be a veterinary technician. He could probably kill you with one finger and crush every bone in your body with the rest of his hand, but the funny thing was that he would probably be the last guy to ever do that. He was one of the gentlest giants I'd ever met. The guy wouldn't hurt a fly and, looks aside, was the most dedicated and caring technician in the whole hospital. I remember hearing that one of the radiation patients had run into the street and got hit by a car after getting loose from his owner on the way to therapy. When the owner arrived at the hospital to tell us what happened, rumor has it that the guy spent half an hour having to console Rick, who was absolutely devastated. What a scene that was!

Lucky for me, Rick hadn't seen Tom's performance because he had been working on Obie. I really respected Rick, and it would've sucked if he had found out I had been giving the new guy such a hard time.

Tom's sputtering leveled off, and he seemed to have regained his composure. He was staring at me wide-eyed and actually looked ashamed that he had had to breathe. He looked disappointed. Rather than lose my train of thought even more, I continued. "So, what was I saying again? Oh yes, I was about to tell you about the collimator."

I pointed to the roughly two-foot circular portion of the machine, which was connected to the end of the short part of the L, the horizontal part of the gantry. It was positioned directly over the patient, and that was where the beam itself came out.

"The collimator is that round part, and it's connected to the end of the gantry. Now, keep in mind, all three of those parts I just told you about can rotate around 360 degrees. So, dude, because of that, we can shoot a beam from any angle around the patient. Get it? The gantry rotates around the table, the collimator rotates around the gantry—oh, and I forgot to mention that the table also spins around. It can swing out 90 degrees in each direction. It's pretty high-tech, man; amazing stuff."

Looking at Tom, I could see that he was confused, and I knew that no amount of explaining was going to do it. It was definitely a lot to take in, and I remembered that it had taken me two days and watching about forty or so patients going through treatment to really get how the machine worked. He'd have to see it in action to really understand. Luckily for him, he was about to get to do just that.

I said, "Tom, that dog on the table; his name is Obie. We're treating a mast cell tumor on his leg and he's currently on his fifth dose of twenty. Don't worry about what a mast cell tumor is for now; I'll get into that later. My point is for you to pay attention to what's going to happen next. In about a second or two, Caroline is going to walk through that door and start setting good old Obie up for his first of two radiation beams. She's going to rotate the gantry to an angle of approximately 180 degrees so the collimator is directly above Obie's thigh, and then she'll line up the beam where it needs to be. After that, all of us will jam from the room and *bam*, she'll give the first beam of radiation. Next, she'll come back into the room and rotate the gantry to zero degrees, jam from the room, and give the second beam."

I continued as Tom stared at me like he had a clue as to what I meant. He obviously didn't. "Tom, during the time it takes to deliver the second beam—it's about two minutes or so—we'll get Eddie down under anesthesia, since he's up next. That way, when Obie's done, we can just switch him out for Eddie. It's like we're a fine- tuned radiation assembly line."

I could see Tom trying to digest what I had just said, and I knew it had gone through one ear and out the other. He had that confused look again, his eyebrows arched up, his head tilted at a slight angle, and his lower lip had started quivering again.

"Tom, just pay attention to what's going on. Don't sweat the details; we still have a lot to cover."

77

JULIA
MAY 2009

I couldn't leave. I just had to be there in case something went wrong. I was so damn nervous, I could feel the moisture soaking the back of my blouse. It felt like it had to be eighty degrees in there, but I knew it was just me.

I had already seen two dogs come out of the door that led to the back of the hospital, and each time the frosted glass door had swung open, I had expected to see Eddie.

Where was he? What was taking so long?

I didn't want to think about what could have gone wrong, but no matter how hard I tried, the thoughts just burst through. What if the doctor came out to tell me that Eddie's anesthesia had taken a bad turn, or that something hadn't gone according to plan? What if Eddie hadn't made it?

These thoughts weren't new to me, and I had gone through this process twice now, first with the surgery and then with the CAT scan. It was ridiculous. He had done great before, and he would be fine today. I just needed to hang in there a little longer.

The receptionist had been sweet and kind, like before, but behind her pink grandma glasses, I had sensed her staring at me. She had been looking a little too hard, with an intensity that bordered on the verge of being uncomfortable. I could feel that she had wanted to say something soothing. But I hadn't needed that; I had no desire for help. I wasn't that kind of girl, and despite her obviously good intentions, I hadn't been a fan of the stare.

So I had decided to perch in the far corner of the lobby, out of the direct line of sight of the receptionist. I had headed to one of the blue benches that were perpendicular to the glass entrance of the hospital, which allowed me a view of the spectacular landscaping outside. The lobby was pretty empty, although there was one guy sitting in the area with his head buried in a *GQ* magazine. He looked to be deeply involved in his magazine, so I thought I would be safe from all human contact if I sat there. I terribly misjudged.

The guy was in his fifties and had a receding hairline that hadn't stopped him from slicking back his residual stringy silver hair in a ponytail that reached past his shoulders. He had a black V-neck shirt that exposed way too much of his straggly, gray-haired, leathery chest, one that had obviously seen way too many years of tanning salons. He wore tight black slacks with a thick brown belt and a large, silver-squared buckle. His legs were crossed, and as his pants rode up, I could see he wasn't wearing any socks under his orange leather loafers.

He hadn't acknowledged my presence as I walked over to my seat, so I'd thought I'd be safe in a world of introversion, but as soon as I sat down, I knew I was in trouble. He had waited just long enough to lure me into a false sense of security and timed his introduction to coincide with the exact moment I made contact with the bench. Just as I was in the process of sitting down, he closed his magazine with a quick flick of the wrist and turned his head toward me.

"Well, hello there . . . I'm Matisse."

He had a thick Eastern European accent and a deep, throaty voice, and he made sure to accentuate the *s* as he pronounced his name.

I sighed inward because I really hadn't wanted to speak to anyone right then. I forced myself to turn toward him. I should've been thankful for what happened next, but I was so caught off guard that the only thing I could do was look at him and force a smile. I didn't have a chance to answer the guy, let alone give him my name because before I knew it, he had launched into the story of Fritz, his one and only "true companion." Without knowing who I was, or caring, for that matter, this perfectly creepy stranger was deeply engaged in a conversation with me, spilling out his life history.

He had adopted Fritz when he was just a puppy and swore that Fritz had been abused in just those short eight weeks of life. . . .

Fritz had been his only true love for the last fourteen years, after he had been dumped by his girlfriend of eight years and had sworn off relationships ever since. . . .

Fritz had rescued him from a deep episode of clinical depression....

Fritz had helped him kick his alcohol problem. . . .

The guy actually went on to tell me how he had also developed a serious drug problem, but before it went any further, I snapped out of my complete bewilderment and cut the rest of his conversation short.

In midsentence, I got up, apologized, and excused myself to go to the ladies' room. I had wanted to be by myself anyway, and having to talk to anyone, let alone a bitter, clinically depressed, alcoholic ex-drug addict was definitely something I didn't need right then.

When I exited the bathroom, I conveniently sat on the other side of the lobby, which also happened to be in line with the frosted door through which Eddie was meant to come. I didn't have the energy for anybody else's problems, especially not that guy's.

I absentmindedly grabbed the book I had put in my purse before I left the house and did my best to try to read. I needed to take my mind off things. I turned to the first page and must've read the same sentence about ten times without internalizing a single word. I couldn't concentrate. The door opened, and my heart skipped a beat.

No Eddie.

What made its way out of the door wasn't the doctor either, but rather a small, patchy ball of what looked to be fur surrounding something that was about the height of my knees. It had tufts of brownish-white hair scattered all over its black, scaly body, and I thought it had to be at least a hundred years old. It had one eye and a brown, rotting snaggletooth sticking out of the right corner of its mouth; this was one of the most decrepit and scary little dogs I had ever seen. My mouth almost hit the floor when I realized that its nails were painted pink and white. Not only were they painted, but the one-eyed Yoda had a French manicure as well.

I couldn't remember the last time I had had my nails done.

I couldn't help myself. Maybe it was the tension, the stress, the anxiety, or just the pure absurdity of the situation, but I began to giggle like a little schoolgirl.

Luckily, no one heard or had the opportunity to get offended; I was drowned out by the high-pitched squeal that came from none other than the weird guy across the lobby. This ancient, one-eyed anomaly of a creature with better nails than I had must be the infamous Fritz.

Postsqueal, the guy got down on one knee, and Fritz sprinted across the lobby and miraculously managed to launch himself into the guy's outstretched, leathery arms. Looks could be deceiving; it seemed the little lint ball had some life in him after all.

I noticed that Fritz had a shaved rectangle on the top of his head that was outlined with blue marker with a big X drawn in the center, and I remembered that the man had started to mention something about Fritz being treated for a brain tumor. I also remembered Dr. Lindy explaining that they had to shave the area they were going to radiate and mark it with a temporary tattoo. So

I guess that's where they were shooting the beam, and the *X* marked the spot. I wondered how big Eddie's square would be.

The snaggletoothed gremlin proceeded to lick the guy's face, and the man made no attempt to shy away. In fact, he opened his mouth to let the dog clean out his palate, while muttering something in some language I couldn't understand. This went on for a full twenty seconds before he grabbed what appeared to be an orange leather handbag and headed toward the sliding glass doors. The guy turned to me before he left and waved good-bye. I smiled back and nodded, doing my best to be polite and not launch into another giggling fit.

"See you tomorrow," he said as he pronounced, *see* with a *th* and left the building.

I really hoped not.

Another ten minutes passed, but it felt like an hour. I had attempted to read my book one more time but again made no progress. The door to the back of the hospital started to open and I held my breath. At about the halfway point, it stopped, and I could see a muscular hand sticking out through the crack. I heard the low murmur of conversation, as if whoever was behind the door had forgotten that they were on their way out.

Was Eddie safe? Was that the doctor, contemplating how he would break the bad news to me?

The hand disappeared, and I saw the door briefly start to close. It shut only about an inch before it exploded open and swung out, and there he was, prancing!

Yes, prancing. Eddie was practically skipping toward me with a huge smile on his face, his tongue sticking out and his leash flopping wildly on the floor, dragging behind him without a care in the world. I got a brief glimpse of his shaved shoulder, with a now large blue square and an *X* inside.

As he practically glided toward me, I couldn't help but laugh. If it weren't for the laughter, it would've been tears coming out, because I was an emotional mess, nervous as hell, worried to death about my dog, and there he was.

Prancing.

He was either the bravest dog in the world or completely oblivious to what was going on. Was David right after all? Maybe he didn't know what was happening, or did he? He must, right?

This wasn't what I'd been used to in a cancer ward.

The frosted door had started to close, but before it shut completely, it burst open for a second time, and I saw the bald technician, Brandon, semirunning toward us. Eddie bounded over and almost tackled me as he reared up on two legs to reach me. I grabbed him, ignoring the sharp pain in both of my shoulders where his nails dug in. I hugged tight.

I was so happy to see him that I didn't care about the scratches on my shoulders or that he had obviously escaped from Brandon. I should have been annoyed that he was loose, and seriously questioning their competence, but at this point, all I could think about was how happy I was to have Eddie with me.

I had so many emotions boiling inside of me and unfortunately, I turned into one of those people I had so desperately sworn I would never be. To my complete and utter horror, I started to cry.

Tears poured down my cheeks as I felt my body quivering. I was so embarrassed because come on: there was no rational reason for this.

I could feel my body being pulled left and right as Eddie shook his tail vigorously. He still had both legs on my shoulders and was now in the process of trying to lick me and my tears to death. I could feel his hot breath as I tried to avoid his tongue, and the effort was just enough to pull me back together. At least there had been no one around to see what had just happened.

I pushed Eddie backward, and as his paws hit the ground, he continued to pant heavily and wag his tail. I was in the middle of wiping both of my eyes with the tissue I had absentmindedly grabbed from my handbag when I realized that Brandon was standing right next to me. He hadn't said a word and had been waiting patiently while I tried to put myself back together. I looked up at him, shrugged, and blew my nose.

"It's fine, Mrs. Freed. He did great, no problems."

There was no concern or apology for Eddie being loose. Instead, he said in a very gentle voice, "Do you want me to give you a few?"

He was furrowing his thin eyebrows in a look of obvious worry and discomfort, and I could tell he didn't know exactly where he should be.

Oh, great, I was the crazy lady.

"No, no, don't worry, I'm fine. I'm just happy. You have something to go over?"

His eyebrows straightened, but he continued to look at me a second longer than normal, making sure that I was sane enough for him to continue.

"As I said before, he did great, and he even made a few friends back there. Today was the longest time; the rest of the days should only take about twenty minutes. As far as his radiation marks, please don't let them get wet; otherwise, we're going to have to repeat today."

He paused for a couple of seconds and then added, "Do you have any questions?"

I hesitated and then responded, "No . . . Thanks, though."

He nodded his bald head ever so slightly, cleared his throat, and said, "You're welcome; just make sure to schedule your appointment times with Kathleen. They should be around this time tomorrow and all the other days thereafter. You sure you're okay, Mrs. Freed?"

"I'm fine; thanks again."

Brandon broke eye contact, bent down, and gave Eddie a vigorous bear hug. Eddie continued to smile and pant, and Brandon broke his grip with an affectionate pat on Eddie's back. He let Eddie go but stuck out his hand palm up as he pulled away.

"Gimme five, brother!"

Eddie pawed at Brandon's hand, and in one fluid motion, Brandon reached into his pocket and tossed Eddie a small, brown Milk-bone.

Poor kid, he must think I'm crazy.

78

EDDIE
MAY 2009

I knew this game and I was good at it.

After I led the shiny-headed dad back to Mom—actually, I should rather say beating him in a race back to Mom—he decided to play the paw game with me. Granted, I got a little sidetracked right before he began the game because of the downpour of drool that had burst out of Mom's eyes, but as it turned out I didn't need to worry too much. Despite her eyes leaking worse than Dad after three cups of foul-smelling liquid, I didn't sense any sadness behind the eye water. It was drools of joy, happy eye slobbering, and luckily, it hadn't lasted long.

After some grunting on the shiny-headed dad's part, he turned his shoulders to me, bent down, and stuck out his fat paw.

Mom had been coming around by then, wiping her face with a soft piece of thin white bark, and had been clearing away the last bits of eye drool from her cheeks. She appeared to be seminormal at this point, and so I had focused on the shiny-headed dad's paw. As soon as he held it out like that to me, I hit it with mine, just like any other furry friend who knew how this game worked would do.

He snorted and tossed a small, brown crunchy treat my way. I was hungry so I pounced forward and grabbed it. This dad was trained well.

I wish I could have said the same thing about my dad, but training him had been hard. It'd taken him tons of practice to figure out that the treat came right after the paw tap, not before, not during, but after. No treat, no paw tap. Dad had finally caught on after many light period afternoons spent trying to train him. It had taken him forever and me putting on weight, but at least he had finally learned.

Before I had finished chewing, Mom gave a final raspy grunt to the shiny-headed dad and we headed back to the sniff box. With every step, though, her mood turned worse and worse. It was full-blown sadness by the time we reached the sniff box.

Mom stayed that way the entire ride home, and I'm happy to say the rest of the light period passed by uneventfully. The sun began to go down and the outside cooled while I continued to rack my brain, trying to figure out what I could do to change her mood. Unfortunately, she had been like this a lot, and no matter what I'd tried before, nothing had seemed to shake it. In fact, the more I had hung around her when she was like this, the worse she had gotten. So, instead of sticking around and making her even more sad, I decided to go outside and be with Paris.

By the time I heard Dad's sniff box pull up to our territory, I still hadn't come up with anything to explain it, although I did have three giant white snow balls of fur that I had yanked from Paris's tail in our game of contact tag.

I had hoped that when Dad came home he would think of something better. He did that sometimes, and as much as I thought I had been the champion in that department, Dad had a way with Mom that even I couldn't beat. Unfortunately, tonight, even his skills were useless.

In fact, after Paris and I made the mad dash from the outside territory into the front room to do our usual dark-period Dad greeting, we both saw a dad who didn't have a chance at cheering up Mom, or anything else, for that matter. The front territory door opened, and in walked Dad, shoulders slouched and black paw coverings semidragging on the floor. He was wearing his standard black leg coverings and had a blue button-down shirt covering on. His top button was undone and his white-and-blue-striped safety collar hung loosely around his neck.

He looked tired and if I hadn't known any better, he'd have appeared to be in the same sour and worn-out mood as Mom. His eyes weren't drooling, but I could feel a sense of dread and worry, like this was the last place he wanted to be.

I heard Mom's soft footsteps coming from the kitchen, followed by her soft grunt behind me.

79

JULIA
MAY 2009

"So, how did it go?" David asked.

His drawn expression and half-closed, bloodshot eyes meant that he had had a long day, but I also saw that he was forcing a smile in an attempt to keep from bringing his day home with him. He was good like that, and I couldn't remember the last time he had complained about work.

I had tried to call him from the car on the way home from Eddie's appointment, and although he had answered, he'd told me that he'd have to call me back later. He couldn't speak, which usually meant he was with clients, and I knew that he would either try me when he got a chance or just speak to me when he got home.

He hadn't phoned the rest of the day, and I found myself missing him, looking forward to when he would get back to me so I could finally tell someone about my day. I had spent the rest of the afternoon pacing around the house, pretending to rearrange the spice cabinet, watching the clock, and wishing time would move faster. I had been in the kitchen when I'd heard the dogs running to the front door in a hustle solely reserved for the times when David got home, and I did my best not to drop everything and join in. What a sight that would've been; I bet it would have scared the living heck out of him.

As soon as he saw me, he walked over and gave me a tiny peck on the forehead as a hello. His lips were soft but dry, and I instinctively took a deep breath in as they made contact. He smelled like sweat and copy paper, though there was a hint of that special David smell I loved so much. It was a mix of ocean water and soap, and it had always drawn me to him. He gently grabbed my hand and walked me over to the worn brown sofa, and we both sat down.

The dogs hadn't moved from the front door, where they had met David, and were now sitting motionless, staring at us. It felt as if they were being held back from getting any closer to us by some invisible force, seated next to each other with their eyes wide open and their ears standing up attentively. It was if they were waiting for something to happen.

It was unnerving; they kept looking from David to me and then back to David again. It was like they were trying to figure out which one of us would say something first. Strange.

We sunk into the couch, and a small cloud of dust blew into the air as the seat cushions compressed. David asked me how everything had gone.

I answered him with a little more excitement in my voice than I had planned. "He did great, fantastic, not a care in the world, completely and utterly the opposite of me. In fact, besides his new haircut and Sharpie marks, I would never have known he'd had anything done to him or that something was wrong."

My voice continued to be higher than usual. "It was me who was a freak. I was a complete nervous wreck. It took everything I had to actually drive up to that building, let alone force myself to walk inside, and it's a small miracle I didn't crash the car on the way. And then, when the bald guy, Brandon, came to take him back to me, I almost completely lost it. I sat in the waiting room for the next say, oh, thirty minutes or so with a book I had managed to grab right before I left the house. I just stared at the damn thing that whole time, and no matter how hard I tried to concentrate, I couldn't get past the first page.

"No, for all I know, I had the thing upside down. I was such a basket case that the secretary actually had to bring me some tea to calm me down. Can you believe it; a random lady thought I looked so horrible that I needed that much help? Oh, and there was this creepy Euro-trash guy with a Pekingese probably older than I am. . . . Never mind that, David; I was so nervous."

Wow. Had all that really just come out of my mouth? It'd just poured out; no hesitation, no filter, no barrier, and with no anger or regrets.

The silence that followed was deafening. David hadn't moved, shifted, or even blinked while I had been speaking. His expression suddenly changed now that I was done, and it seemed he had been more surprised by my verbal outburst than I had been. His red eyes opened wide and he arched his thick, black eyebrows. He opened his mouth ever so slightly, like he was about to say something, but before anything came out, his face suddenly shifted again. Instead of surprise, all I saw was confusion. His forehead wrinkled and his lips formed an *O*, as if he was about to speak. But before anything came out, I saw his look change yet again, and confusion was replaced with a look of caution as he visibly silenced himself by clearing his throat.

I knew then that as much as he had appreciated my confession, as much as he had been dying to say something, he had stopped purposely and forced himself to hold back. Like a kid who didn't want to get beat up after school for being the know it all, he just sat there with his arms folded and his mouth clamped shut.

I couldn't blame him; it was my fault he was reacting like this. Like I had seen him do over the last six months, he pulled back, afraid to speak his mind. At one time in our marriage, it would have been no problem at all for him to say what was on his mind— before my dad, that is—and it would have been natural for him to comment on what I'd just said. But no, his response, his retreat, his fear of speaking openly was a direct result of the last year. It was a consequence of how I had treated him, how I had chosen to struggle with my grief alone, not letting anyone close enough to me to share in that struggle. And heaven forbid they had tried; they would have had to face the miserable and grumpy consequences.

I knew I could have opened up more to everyone around me, especially to him, communicated better, let him know exactly how I felt and what I was going through, but it hadn't worked out that way.

Who was I kidding? I hadn't let it work out that way; in fact, I had gone out of my way to make sure of that.

So, after being treated like an emotional punching bag, he had inevitably backed away into his protective shell. It had started slowly, unconsciously, but as time went on and I continually closed up on him, attacked him, I had noticed it building upon itself. I saw him fighting to stay supportive, doing everything he could think of to be there for me, but I didn't need to be rescued and I had resented him for trying.

He had put so much effort into attempting to get me to open up and share even a small part of my burden, but I hadn't let him in. And each time he had tried, I had pushed him farther and farther away. It was my struggle, my grief, and, eventually, my loss, and I hadn't wanted to share it with anyone. Even him.

I didn't want help, I didn't need protection, I didn't need to be saved; I had my own way of dealing with things. Some part of me had convinced myself that if I caved, broke down my defenses, or hesitated even for a second, my dad would suffer. How could I have been that strong, positive person who needed to be there for him if I was weak? Hell, he had enough negativity with Mother around him all the time. I needed to be a beacon for him, even if it meant I'd had to go at it by myself.

As much as I have said I had completely closed myself off to David, that wouldn't be the truth. Even if he hadn't realized it, he'd ended up playing a large part in helping me deal with my grief, although definitely not in the way he had wanted. Poor man; I'd never meant for him to be my scapegoat, but that's how it had worked out. I'd ended up taking a large majority of the pain, the anger, and the frustration and, unfortunately, he had borne the brunt of it. There had been a lot of loud screaming on my part, and I knew that it hadn't been fair of me. That wasn't the way he had wanted to be there for me, but I hadn't been able to control myself.

So finally, instead of trying to force me to open up, he'd left me alone, left me to deal with my feelings my way, by myself, shut off from the world, behind my self-made emotional barrier. He'd stopped asking, and then he'd stopped trying, and now I hoped he hadn't stopped caring. But I couldn't tell him that, I couldn't tell him how I felt; things just needed to play out. I knew that if he truly loved me, no matter what I did, he would forgive me. From the depths of my heart, I hoped it would turn out that way, though I'd never expressed it. I'd needed him to understand and accept me because I didn't have the energy to worry about him as well; I'd to funnel everything to Dad.

I'll never forget the look on David's face the first time I exploded at him, focused my rage on him, and the utter disbelief and hurt in his eyes. That image will never leave me. It wasn't my best moment.

We were both sitting on this very brown couch, Eddie beneath my feet while Paris had situated herself at David's elbow as it dangled over the side. I was barefoot, my toes buried in Eddie's warm fur, taking advantage of a foot massage as his chest lifted up and down. It was just a month into Dad's chemotherapy, right after I had hung up with him on the phone. It hadn't been a pleasant conversation because I could tell that as much as Dad had tried to reassure me that he was handling it just fine, he wasn't doing well. There were way too many pauses in his sentences, and I could hear that he was making an exaggerated effort to keep his voice strong and even. It was clear he felt horrible, and I was helpless to do anything about it.

Suffice it to say, I wasn't in a good place when David tried to speak to me. Even though his intentions had been good, his timing had been terrible. Just about the last thing I needed then was for someone to tell me what to do or how to be.

"Jules, honey, it'll be all right. Are you sure you don't want to talk about it? It'll make it easier, honey . . . Julia, you can't just bottle it up like that."

Unfortunately for him, his voice had become a little too serious for my taste.

"Bottle up what?" I remember saying as some hidden compartment of suppressed rage burst.

Dad would be fine! What did David know about *fine*, and what did he think I needed to share? And for what purpose? Sure, Dad had been a little nauseated, but that would pass. We all knew it could happen; it was a pretty common reaction to chemotherapy. What was there to *talk about*?

My reaction to him had been harsh, loud, and entirely uncontrollable. He had initially started to gently rub my forearm while I had been speaking with Dad on the phone, and he had even continued massaging it while he was trying to make me *feel better*. The funny thing was that I knew he had been trying to be sweet and comforting; any rational person would've realized that he was attempting to be the perfect husband right then. What's worse was that he had probably genuinely thought he knew what was best for me.

But that didn't change my bubbling anger because, in reality, he had no idea how I felt. His words had grated like fingernails on a chalkboard, and I'd wanted to put my hands over my ears and yell at him to stop. Instead, I told him what he could do with his making-me-feel-better crap.

The moment I opened my mouth and started telling him what he could do with his psychobabble, I knew things would never be the same between us again. His hand had still been resting on mine when I started in on him, and I felt it tense up as I continued my attack. It was as if all of the emotion that had been building up over the last couple of months had been unleashed, and unfortunately for him, he'd been standing in its direct line of fire. My poor husband; he hadn't deserved that onslaught.

And the worst part about it had been his reaction, for it only cemented the guilt that I felt later. Instead of screaming back at me, getting offended, or even telling me that I was being a royal bitch, he'd just sat there and taken it. He hadn't said a single word for what had to have been at least five minutes of me being a complete banshee. And when I had finally almost wound down and was nearly out of breath, only then had he slowly pulled his cold hand away from me. His fingertips left ice trails on my arm, and his eyes, the deep-blue windows to his soul, looked empty except for the hurt that stared back at me.

As soon as I felt his hand start pulling away I stopped what I had been saying in midsentence. I think I had been finishing telling him how he should stop being so condescending toward me, or something like that, and between his look and his hand moving away, I had stopped talking. He had waited a couple of seconds to make sure I had nothing more to say. I hadn't; the truth of the matter was, I had just needed to shout at someone, and he had been right there for the picking.

I had needed to let off some steam and completely disregarded the fact that I was using someone I loved to do it. The look on his face and the long silence that followed was only made more uncomfortable when he'd apologized.

Yes, he actually apologized for being so pushy, even though I was the one who owed him the apology. Something in David had changed that day, and looking back, I believe it was the start of him admitting a personal defeat with me. I'm convinced that failure, in conjunction with my actions, had started to drive the wedge that had subsequently formed between us.

As Dad continued to get sicker and sicker, David and I had spoken less and less. I felt us drifting apart, but I didn't have the energy or the desire to do anything about it. I hoped he hadn't completely given up on me, despite the fact that I became extremely annoyed at him whenever I suspected even a hint of an attempt to get me to open up.

I couldn't count the number of times he'd bring up random things just to get me to speak to him. He never asked me how I was feeling, or made suggestions about how I should be dealing with my dad again, but I suspected he had ulterior motives with the small talk, and I had resented him for it. I found myself questioning why he was being so selfish, why he couldn't just leave me be, but looking back at it now, he probably had just wanted to have some interaction with me.

Eventually, after I'd made it clear to him that I knew what he had been doing and that it annoyed me to no end, he'd just hovered around me, waiting for any conversation or catharsis to come. I knew he was hoping to catch me if I fell, but I never did; never with him around, at least.

And here we were after Eddie's first day of radiation, and I had actually done the unthinkable. I did something that I hadn't been able to do through the last year; I had opened up. Even if it had only been a little, something barely noticeable, it had taken both of us by complete surprise.

I looked at David again, looked into those beautiful and loving ocean-blue eyes, expecting something, anything. The air around us felt charged, electric, like stepping outdoors during the first few minutes after a storm had passed.

Inevitably, I was the one to break the silence. "I couldn't believe it, David. I was speechless. I think he was more worried about getting something to eat than anything else."

David smiled, and it was a genuine smile, not forced or fake, and I could feel some of the sudden awkwardness between us melt. It had been an uncomfortable moment, and in a perfect world, a perfect marriage, this would never have been an issue. It would have been completely natural for me to tell him how my dog being treated for cancer had made me feel, but this exchange had disturbed our status quo.

So I went on like a sixteen-year-old on her first date, desperately trying to avoid a lull in the conversation, any chance for that uneasiness to return.

"And when he got home, he literally inhaled his food in about fifteen seconds flat. You know how he is."

I let out a nervous giggle, and suddenly the room was about five degrees warmer. I felt the need to keep speaking, keep the conversation going, anything not to have that quiet again.

"They said he did very well, that his anesthesia was uneventful and smooth. They said he had no problems whatsoever, except they did shave him crooked. I wasn't thrilled about that, or the blue marker they put on him; he looks ridiculous. If this was anyone else's dog, maybe it would be funny, but right now nothing about this whole mess is good."

I pointed to the blue marker outlines on his shoulder. "The tech said it's temporary. They should come off in a couple of weeks, and he made sure to warn me that Eddie can't go for any swims or baths until therapy is done. Actually, a couple of weeks after therapy, because the tech said he would probably still have side effects then."

I was out of breath, winded, and although I had had plenty to say a moment ago, I suddenly didn't want to keep speaking. It had been a big day for me, and this was turning out to be the icing on the cake. David had picked up on the pause in the conversation and reached over to squeeze both of my hands in his warm palms. He smiled and nodded lovingly, letting me know that it was all right to stop talking, that he didn't expect anything more. Then he took the opportunity to bend down and call the dogs over.

It was funny; instead of both Eddie and Paris bounding over to him and trying to knock him down, like they usually did, they just hung their heads and walked cautiously toward us. It was as if they had done something wrong or were afraid we were going to hurt them. What was with them?

Paris I could expect this weird reaction from, for no reason but the fact that she was Paris, my unpredictable one. But Eddie, my happy-go-lucky mutt, I had never seen him like this.

Eddie reached David first, and he started rubbing Eddie's back vigorously, like he always did when he was concerned or distracted. Paris stopped before stepping onto the dull brown Costco rug that lay sprawled under the sofa and the coffee table. She sat back down on the hardwood floor and just stared at us.

I looked back up at David then, really stared at him, examining the man that who had stuck with me through so much. He looked so sweet and cute as he rubbed Eddie's ears. He was such a good man; he was kind, sensitive, handsome, and he was my husband, mine. He had been unbelievably good to me, and what had I done in return? He had never stopped loving me, never stopped trying to be there for me, and what had I given him back?

I had been cruel to him, distant, a complete stranger living in the same house as him. I had yelled at him, fought him, ignored him, and expected him to take it, and forgive me for it. I had expected the world from him and took it completely for granted that he had given it to me freely, without complaint.

I'd always thought that someone could only be knocked out by love at first sight, swept off their feet like they were in a fairy tale by that magical and mystical initial feeling, but love in the real world was different. The overwhelming realization of how good he was despite what I had done to him hit me like a runaway train, and I felt so much for him.

I felt a knot starting to form in my throat.

Although he had been rubbing Eddie's ears, David hadn't taken his eyes off of me. And being the perceptive man he was, he took in what had to be a look of shock on my face, and his hands stopped moving.

I forced myself to recover and drove the choked-up ball of emotion deep inside. I couldn't have him worrying about this as well; I had done enough already. So I let out a sigh as I tried to concentrate on something else. I had been so stubborn; why?

As I found myself asking that question, I could still feel the aftereffects of the electricity lingering in the air. The hairs on my arms were standing up, and I was conscious of every pore in my body. Something had changed tonight; what had been out of place for too long was finally being put away correctly. This was one of those times; one of those moments when you knew a monumental change was taking place, like getting your first car, your first kiss, or going away to college. It was one of those times when it was clear that things could never go back to the way they'd been before; things would never be the same.

David finally broke eye contact and looked down, giving Eddie a tap on the head. He then halfheartedly said, "No bath for a month, huh? You're going to be one ripe little puppy."

"David . . ." I hesitated.

He looked up at me, and my voice was suddenly shaking. I couldn't hear myself clearly because I sounded distant, like my words were coming from somebody else's mouth.

"You . . . you know, being in the waiting room took me back to . . . well, you know."

I couldn't finish the sentence because the large lead-filled lump that had hoisted itself back up into my throat threatened to choke me.

He looked up from what he was doing and his eyes locked with mine, those deep, beautiful eyes, but the intensity of his gaze was too much. I couldn't stand it; it was completely overwhelming and I had to look away. I sensed that he was about to say something, so I forced myself to look back at his perfect lips.

He finished the sentence for me: "your dad."

He had actually said it out loud, taking the risk he had so successfully avoided of late, opening himself up once more. But he had that David look, that I'm-here-for-you stare that until last year had always left me a little breathless.

It all came back to that look. The way he furrowed his dark black eyebrows, straightened his lips so the corners of his mouth formed two sets of dimples on his cheeks, and stared with such concentration that you felt like the most special person on earth. It was a look that combined sympathy and love, and I found him completely irresistible. It was the same look he had given me the first time we met on the beach that night so long ago, and just like back then, it evoked a strong sense of comfort and belonging.

It was those eyes that I had fallen in love with, that familiar feeling I had gotten after being with him for only five minutes that first night. It was that sensation that we had known each other forever, a togetherness that I've only ever found with him, and an emotion that I pray will always draw me back to him, no matter what happens between us.

Throughout my dad's treatment, I had forgotten to look for those eyes. I had been blinded in more ways than one. Maybe enough time had passed by now, or maybe I had grown tired of being alone, but tonight his expression found me again. I felt the wall—my wall, my little barrier of protection—start shattering.

The lead lump in my throat released its firm grip and shakily, I found my voice. "Yes, my dad." There, I'd said it.

As if suddenly sensing defeat, the lump tightened its hold once more. I could feel my voice starting to go and had to fight to get the words out. I cleared my throat and managed to say, "For a moment there, I thought I was back in the waiting room in the hospital,

David . . . the waiting, that waiting, that agonizing time just sitting there and counting the seconds, hoping for the chemo session to be done. I was at therapy again today, waiting for Dad all over."

It had taken four weeks and numerous pleadings on my part to finally have Dad give in and let me come with him and Mother to his treatments. I had used the excuse that Mother hated driving on freeways, would probably have an accident because she was so worried, and I was the only viable option to take him. He needed a ride to the clinic, and I was able to do it.

"You know, when Dad finally did come out of the chemo room, he always tried to act like nothing was wrong. But he didn't fool me. I wouldn't admit it to anyone, especially myself back then, but I could see that he was suffering. He hated it, and it was so obvious that it was taking its toll. And no matter how much he tried to hide it, no matter what he said or did, I knew the mental as much as the physical was eating him from inside out."

For the first time in a while, no tears came, despite the fact that I was saying this out loud. By myself, when I knew no one else was around, I had cried oceans whenever I had thought back to what Dad had gone through. Knowing my reaction, I had conditioned myself not to reminisce when anyone was around, especially David. I hadn't wanted him to see me like that.

But now there were no filters, nothing was stopping me, and the words had a life of their own. The lump in my throat was a memory, and once again words poured out. I found myself able to speak about it without breaking down, which was a monumental first for me. David was still staring at me, frozen, his eyes beckoning me to go on.

"It was so important to him that we viewed him as strong, tough, the man he had always been. But as much as I denied it back then, I could see that mind of his was working against him. I tried to stay positive; you know that better than anyone alive. Hell, I wouldn't hear anything about him losing the battle. I refused."

I spoke faster because I didn't want him to respond. "I thought I was doing it for him, but David, I've finally accepted that it was all an act; it wasn't real." I paused for only enough time to take a deep breath because part of me was desperately trying to get loose and I didn't want to be interrupted.

In the brief second it took me to inhale, I remember thinking to myself, *Who is this person? Am I really saying all of this?* I didn't have enough time to answer because my mouth was uncontrollable; it seemed to have a mind of its own. "You know the hardest thing, the thing that keeps me up at night? It's that deep down, part of me was scared that he'd seen right through me. He always knew me better than I knew myself, and I was scared to death that he could see that it was all an act. He could always tell with me.

"I know he was scared for us, for Mother and me, about how we would get along when he was gone. His mind just couldn't, wouldn't make peace with it, and David, even until the very end, when he told me there was nothing more they could do for him, when the pain was so intense that half of his time was spent in that awful drug-induced semicoma, all he cared about was how Mother and I would be after it was all over."

I couldn't stop myself now even if I'd wanted to. It was the first time I had dared say this, and what a time I had picked. Eddie was still lying there with his chest barely moving, as if he was doing his best to stay still, and David was resting his hand on his head. Paris was situated a couple of feet away from them in the same spot past the rug with a blank expression plastered to her face. They were all frozen statues staring at me.

It had been a year since Dad had passed away, and never once during that time had I felt the way I felt now. I had never wanted to talk about it, but now I found myself scrambling to get out the rest of what I needed to say. I couldn't get it out fast enough.

My sentences were on the verge of frantic, like I was reaching the finish line in a 500-meter sprint. "I also knew he was scared. He was scared of dying, and I know that's something he would never admit. He hated the chemotherapy, and even though they gave him things for the nausea, he still hated it. He hated the whole process of it, being made to do something he dreaded; he hated everything about it. I knew it made him feel weak, something my dad had never been before. That mind of his was so damn strong that nothing we said could help him because he had already convinced himself. He smiled, he nodded, he listened to everything Mother and I told him to make us feel better, but it didn't change anything."

David finally moved, slowly nodding his head and blinking. I looked back because I wanted to go on, but I was searching for more to say, though I found I was out of words again. I had done it, though. I had finally done it. I hadn't meant to do it, especially tonight of all times, it had just happened.

He waited and kept looking at me, but for now I was done. He stayed there unmoving, frozen, making sure the silence was continuing, and finally, when enough time had gone by and both of us were sure I had nothing more to say, he slowly began to move.

First he took his hand off of Eddie, who raised his neck in a silent protest. Then he readjusted his position and closed the distance between us. It was deliberate and measured at the same time, like approaching a wild animal, scared that it would run if he moved too fast. But he was wrong on that one; the moment I saw him move toward me, I wanted to be near him. He cautiously put his arms around me, drawing me to his chest, and that David smell, his essence, enfolded me in its pleasant embrace.

He was so warm, soft, so comfortable, and I felt safe. The rough cotton of his starched dress shirt scratched my cheek, but I didn't care. I was so content, nothing could ruin it.

We stayed like that for I don't know how long because in his arms I lost track of time. David finally did speak, and he couldn't have picked something better to say. "I love you, honey. I always will."

I choked back the tears that had finally welled up. "I know David, and I love you, too."

Just then, we both turned toward an extremely loud sigh that came from Eddie, who had proceeded to put his head on the ground and use both of his paws to cover his eyes. It was as if he was too embarrassed to watch us like this any longer.

It was an incredibly cute gesture, and both David and I started giggling simultaneously. I looked up at him, and there was something lighter between us; a weight in our relationship had shifted. That charged feeling, that electric air that had been surrounding us earlier had faded, and I could feel things were starting to get back to normal.

Leave it to Eddie to make us laugh, to find a way to bring smiles to our faces. It was Eddie; all of this was thanks to him. It was because of him that this had happened with David. It was because of him that I had spent the last ten minutes pouring my heart out, opening myself up, letting out my deepest and darkest secrets.

A part of me was proud, but another part couldn't help but feel a little embarrassed, revealing so much and after so long a time.

I looked up at David, and all of a sudden I felt an overriding urge to justify myself, to explain the reason why I had told him everything I had just shared with him. I stopped squeezing him and leaned back into the sofa.

He looked at me expectantly, ready for anything more I had to say. "All of this with Eddie is bringing back so much, David. What I can't get over, though, is that it's basically the same thing as Dad's stuff, but it's also so different. Yes, it's the same conversations, the same processes, the same tests, but Eddie acts like he doesn't even know he's sick. Yes . . . sure . . . he's a dog. I know what you're thinking, but just for a second forget about the fact that he's not human; he's still going through the same things people do, and it's still me, David, who has to take him there.

"It's different from Dad. It's so unbelievably different. With Dad, there had been such a buildup, such preparation for his first treatment, that by the time it finally came, he was so damn exhausted from worrying about it and dreading it. When he did finally walk out of the chemo room that first day, Mother told me that he looked worse off than after he had been going through it for months. Like I said, it was the buildup, the dread of what he thought it was going to be like, that wore him out, just as much as the chemo did.

"Even with those couple of times when it didn't make him sick, it didn't matter. Just the thought of going back there and having to have it pumped into his body all over again . . . well, it beat him down. The mental part of it was horrible. Every treatment was like that for him."

I tightened my grip on David's hand. "With Eddie today, David, when he came out of that room, he didn't have a care in the world."

THE DOG DAYS OF THE PAST

80

DAVID
SEPTEMBER 2008

It really hadn't taken much thought after what happened yesterday; my mind was made up. Allyson had to go.

Was this my fault? Had I caused this? Had I been too friendly with her and given her the wrong impression? I knew I shouldn't have been so open with her about my life; I knew I should've kept it more professional, but it had been a rough year and she had been so gosh darn easy to talk to, so empathetic. I had found myself just babbling on and on with her. It must've been those green eyes, or how she would just sit there staring at me, sucking the words out of my mouth, nodding her beautiful head and pursing those full red lips.

Either way, she had to go.

I was a married man, after all, and even if my relationship wasn't great right now, there was still no excuse. I could never do that to Julia; I could never look myself in the mirror after that.

She'd already had a written warning before, so it wouldn't be coming from out of nowhere. I had made sure to document the time she had misplaced the Gonzálezs' loan docs. Sure, I had been nice and understanding, but I had written her up. If there's one thing I've learned over the years, it's that everything needs to be down on paper because you never know. So this would be kosher with HR, and since she had also just screwed up the Silvers' loan documents three days ago, the timing would be perfect.

I couldn't believe what she'd said; I mean, no beating around the bush, just a flat-out open invitation, in broad daylight, and in my own office, no less. From the moment she had walked into the office yesterday morning, I had sensed that there was something different about her, something playful, something very unprofessional. but I hadn't been able to put my finger on it. She had come to work dressed in a red-and-black-striped miniskirt, black fishnet stockings, and a red blouse with both top buttons open to expose a little more cleavage than usual. I did my best not to stare, and I even made it until after lunch, but I am a guy, after all, and unfortunately, my eyes did wander once.

As Murphy's Law dictated, it *would* be the time that she looked up, and I'm ashamed to say that she caught me red-handed, staring like a teenager looking at his first porn magazine. I quickly looked down, but not before she flashed a cute little smile my way. I'll admit it wasn't my finest professional moment, but it still was no excuse for taking it where she did.

Toward the end of the day, she strolled into my office, closed the door, and sat down in the brown leather chair across from my desk. In one smooth motion, she crossed her legs and leaned forward, letting gravity do its magic, and started that extremely awkward conversation. And that's the reason why I was letting her go today.

Now, I know that I'm a little slow on the uptake with these things, not to mention that I hadn't been on the dating scene for the last seventeen years, but even as dense as I am, I knew enough to realize what she was getting at.

Like I said before, it was a flat-out invitation, what else could wanting me to meet her at her apartment for drinks later that night and getting to know each other better mean?

She had said more after that, but I was too surprised to remember anything specific. What I do recall, though, is that at that moment, that ill-intentioned moment, she had absentmindedly reached forward and started playing with my 1998 Padres World Series baseball, the same one Julia had given me for our fifth anniversary. I had still been in shock at what she had just said and its implications, enough so that I hadn't formed a coherent sentence, but as soon as she touched that ball, something snapped inside of me.

What the hell was she thinking? What kind of a person would even think such a thing, knowing full well that I was married and the crap I was going through? It just wasn't right, and it would never happen.

Never!

Suffice it to say, I went home that night and hugged my wife. And the next morning, the first thing I did was to stop by HR to tell them what I was about to do, and then I wrote Allyson a final check from the company. As soon as she arrived, I explained to her that it wasn't working out, and that today would be her last day working here.

THE DOG DAYS OF THE PRESENT

81

EDDIE
MAY 2009

Mom and Dad had been in each other's paws for a long time, and it appeared as if they were stuck together. When they finally decided to unstick themselves, Dad walked over to me and started scratching my shoulders. I had my head resting on my paws and I rolled over onto my side to give him a better angle. With my right paw up, I reached into the air and waved a couple of times before Dad's nails began rubbing my chest. Like always, his nails felt great, and I enjoyed his touch. What made it even better was that it cheered him up and made him happier as well.

It had always been like that. The more he scratched me, the happier he usually grew, and no matter what his mood or how many times he did it, once he started he got happier. His claws continued to work while Mom grunted, but already I could sense Dad's mood changing for the good.

It had gone on and on until I had finally sensed that Dad was almost back to his normal happy self, and I knew that in a couple of more minutes, he'd be all fixed.

Paris still had no idea what with going and was still lying on the floor just past the fur floor covering. Just like me, she had come into the room to greet Dad when he came home, but she also had sensed that it hadn't been the best time to be near him. Mom needed to grunt with him first.

Everything in Mom had screamed that she had wanted to have private time with Dad, and both of us hadn't been brave enough to interrupt that. It's hard to tell how we knew; the closest thing I can say is that the air around her smelled like fire. Whenever we smelled anything resembling that, that burny, singe-you-if-you-get-too-close smell, we knew well enough to keep away.

When they first started grunting, it had been intense, but the smell had gradually faded by the time Dad had started scratching my chest. It was then that a different smell had wafted my way. It was the smell of a ticked-off, jealous poodle, a mixture of overlicked, saliva-caked fur and jasmine, and it grew stronger and stronger with every scratching circle Dad made.

Never one to accept not being the center of attention, Paris simmered for about as long as she could take it before she took action. Her elbow bones clicked as she got up, and I heard her distinct give-me-attention pant as she walked up to Dad and offered her side to him for a greeting.

Unfortunately for her, Dad was so caught up with Mom that he didn't even notice. It was just by pure luck and my having been in the right place at the right time that my chest was being rubbed, and I didn't think Dad had known what he'd been doing. But Paris being Paris, and being the frizz ball she was, wouldn't accept anything less than being noticed, especially if I was getting attention. And so, with a very loud slurp of a grunt, she wedged her muzzle beneath the arm that was doing circles on my chest and flicked it away from me and toward her back.

The grunting suddenly stopped, and when I looked up to see where Dad's arm had gone, the sudden quiet was replaced with happy snorting. Dad turned toward Paris and with his free paw, he started rubbing her back while he put the other one back on me. The snorting died down and Paris rolled over beside me so we were both on our backs getting rubs. Dad grunted a couple of times back to Mom and then wedged himself in between Paris and me. Out of the corner of my eye, I saw Mom was smiling as she turned and walked into the feeding room.

82

EDDIE
MAY 2009

The next early gray period proved to be the same as the previous one, and I realized it was the start of a new schedule. Mom and Dad battled with the white tree, put on their body coverings, and fed themselves a meal that smelled a whole lot better than anything we ever got. Mom, like the light period before, only prepared one food bowl.

By the time I remembered that when this had happened yesterday I had gone hungry, Mom had already hooked my safety rope onto my necklace and was in the process of putting down the full bowl of food in front of Paris.

Mom and I left our territory and went to the large black sniff box. She seemed a whole lot more relaxed today, and I hoped that whatever had been eating at her and causing her to be such a stress case was finally over, and for good this time. She was giving off a peaceful smell, a mixture of flowers and freshly cut ground covering, and I couldn't remember the last time she had smelled this good.

I was excited to be going to the Crunchy Territory, not just because of all the amazing gossipy smells but also, more importantly, because this was an opportunity to get some much-missed food in my belly. I had scored big the couple of times before, and I hoped for more.

When we arrived, we were greeted by the eye-covering mom behind the semicircular desk. Her cheeks were an unnatural shade of red today, the same color any amount of overlicking an itchy body part can cause. She had on a pink covering and thick circles of blue, glittery dirt painted around her eyes, and her claws were gently tapping on a paw exerciser as we walked to her desk. Her ear-to-ear smile remained plastered onto her face and there was only the smallest of pauses in the tapping as she nodded a greeting to Mom. I didn't think her smile could get any bigger, but her mouth looked like it swallowed her ears when she looked down at me. The paw tapping came to a full stop.

I realized that now was my chance because I had her full attention. It was my opportunity to snag some food, and even though it would be a late breakfast, I would take better late than never. I hoped that she would reach down into that desk of hers and throw over a crunchy treat, just like she had the other times I'd been here, so I put on my best give-me-some-food-now face.

It had an effect, all right, just not the one I was going for. Instead of the eye-covering mom giving out her crunchy treats, she squealed like a pink cloven-hoofed friend in heat. Her neck rolls of fat jiggled with each snort, while her eye coverings looked like they were going to drop to the floor with each chest heave. Still squealing, but not paying up with the crunchy good stuff, the desk miraculously held her entire weight while she stretched over and managed to get in a big, wet kiss on my forehead.

It wasn't exactly what I'd had in mind, even a measly little kibble chunk would have been better, so I shook my head to straighten my ears and sat down next to Mom while she started grunting. I guess I would just have to settle for no food and itchy ears for now, and I was amazed at how the loose skin on her shoulders and chest continued to wobble even after she had settled back into her seat and returned to paw tapping.

83

KATHLEEN
MAY 2009

Well, bless her heart, she looked tons better. She actually had some color in her cheeks today.

"Good morning, Mrs. Freed, you look gorgeous today. I wish I still had the hips to fit into those pants."

She blushed, adding more red to her flushed face. "Good morning . . . Kathleen." I had obviously caught her off guard, and she hesitated before continuing timidly, "Thank you. I wanted to check Eddie in."

She wanted to be anyplace besides in front of me, but I knew that was a charming person, and it would only be a matter of time before my southern love worked its magic on her. I handed her the white clipboard with the questionnaire about how her pet had done overnight.

Had there been any vomiting? Was there any diarrhea? Did she need to speak to the doctor? She would get used to this routine; they all did.

She was signing in with her cute little bundle of love sitting patiently right next to her, and like all my little babies, I made sure he got the royal Kathleen good-morning kiss. Why in the world would anyone work in a veterinary clinic and not take advantage of all the perks?

With those long ears and those adorable puppy love eyes, it took every iota of my mommy control to resist feeding him and giving him one of our brand-new, all-natural, preservative-free chew sticks they all loved so much. I knew the routine, though, and that they needed to be fasted. Heaven knows that had been drilled into me that first day, after I got into all that trouble for giving those two dogs the tinciest-winciest bit of food. Then they had to wait the whole day before they could treat those poor, hungry creatures, and it had all been because of me.

It hadn't been my best first day, not by a mile. I learned the radiation mantra, though, and committed it to my sometimes senior-moment memory. It had been three wonderful, blessed years of working in this place, and I could say it in my sleep: "No food for eight hours before treatment, and no water for two hours before," no matter how cute any of the little babies were, or how hungry they looked.

"Well, sugar, aren't you the friendly little cherub? Are you taking care of your mama?"

Mrs. Freed turned a shade even darker than red, and the woman's hands finished signing in faster than a dog could lick his backside. She handed me back the sign-in sheet and made her way to the benches to sit down. Well, a little color is better than none at all, and the woman would grow to love me.

I paged Brandon to come take Eddie back.

84

JULIA
MAY 2009

Well, he was here again, and in full form today. By the looks of it, those were some very expensive, not to mention very tight shiny black slacks, and there was a pink button-down shirt to go with it. The two top buttons were open, revealing a very large gold chain and a clean-shaven, tanned to overdone chest. He was sitting by the window in the same seat as yesterday, with his legs crossed and his loafers, showing no socks.

I didn't have a chance.

"Hello, Eddie's owner, how are you doing today?" he said, emphasizing the *s* and drawing out the *you*.

"A little better than yesterday, I hope, because not to be rude or presumptuous, I could tell it wasn't the best time for you. By the way, I didn't catch your name."

I started to answer but only got out the *Ju*. Before the *lia* left my lips, the guy had already interrupted me and started speaking again.

"My first day was the hardest, too. I was convinced that little Fritzie wasn't going to wake up, or some other dreadful thing would happen. Imagine that! I'll tell you, though, it has taken a long time, but I finally have started to relax while he is here, and without any Valium."

He smiled, waiting for my approval or for me to acknowledge what I think was meant to be a joke; however, I wasn't quite sure if this strange man was serious or not. I hadn't even put down my purse, let alone managed to get two words out, and this quirky man was talking to me like I was his best friend.

I managed to put my bag on the seat between us, settled into my own seat, and then smiled uncomfortably, which, unfortunately, he took as an invitation for him to continue.

"This is the first vet I ever actually liked, and the people here are grade A. There is excellent service, and they all have their hearts in the right place. Not to mention the coffee; baby, you have to try the coffee. I've traveled the world, spent most summers in Milan, and I had to come all the way to a cancer center in America to have a decent cup of coffee."

He slapped his knee with his alligator-skinned hand and let out a raspy smoker's laugh. His thick, gold bracelet slipped up his wrist and lodged on his forearm, threatening to cut off all circulation. I looked left and right to see if anyone else was taking in this scene, but as it turned out, we were the only ones in the lobby. Without any reinforcements, I acknowledged his joke with another uncomfortable smile.

"This is Fritzie's second-to-last treatment."

The guy actually stopped talking, and there was a brief lull in the conversation. Amazingly, I think he was waiting for me to respond. It took a moment for me to internalize the fact that it was my turn to speak, and after a brief pause and feeling more talkative than yesterday, I decided to answer. So far, the guy had seemed harmless enough, though his outfit was very unique, he spoke a million miles an hour, and he'd appeared to be perfectly content with a one-sided conversation.

I thought, *what the heck?* I didn't feel like reading and had twenty minutes to kill.

"Hi . . ."

"Carl," he snapped before I had time to think.

There, again, was a brief moment of silence, and I seized my chance to continue small talk. "So, your dog has a brain t—"

He interrupted me before I could finish the word. Excitedly, and in a voice one octave higher, he said, "Oh yes, a brain tumor, and it's Fritz to people who have only just met him. Once he gets to know you, you can call him Fritzie, or Poo Bear, whatever he's in the mood for."

He slapped his Wonder Woman–braceleted wrist on his thigh and giggled. "I'll make an exception this time for you, snookums, because you seem like a nice girl. You can call him Fritzie if you like."

I didn't bother answering; it would have been useless.

"Let me tell you, I thought it was the end. One minute he's was with me in his doggy pouch"—he held up what looked like a purple-and-gold handbag—"having a perfectly delicious croissant at this quaint little coffee shop downtown, and the next his doggy pouch was vibrating like an oversize cell phone. It was one of the scariest things ever."

He paused for breath and then went on. "I didn't know what to do, but luckily, my friend Burgett, who has four of her own little Pekingese, was there to handle the situation, because, sweetie, I was nothing less than a mess. One of her dogs, Cherokee—who has a little bit of an attitude, by the way—coincidentally was also being treated here, so she insisted that I take Fritzie in ASAP."

I held back a guilty smile as I imagined the scene of this man reacting to his little dog having what sounded like a seizure in public.

"I rushed straight to Dr. Lindy and demanded an appointment without even bothering to call my veterinarian. She obviously had missed the problem the month before, when I had taken poor little Fritzie in for his one-year checkup."

The guy had two things working for him with me today. Number one, I was bored. Number two: for the first time I could remember, I actually felt social; instead of getting up and bolting for the door to get away from this eccentric man, I decided to listen to the rest of the story.

He sat upright and turned very serious, lowering his voice to the tone he had used when I'd first met him. "They were amazing. It was like the show *ER*. They took little Fritzie to the back to get examined, and I could swear I could hear the music in the background."

After singing the theme song of *ER*, punctuated by head, neck, and hand movements, he went on speaking, while I almost drew blood biting my lip to keep from laughing outright at the scene in my mind. It was a performance that deserved an Emmy.

He went on to tell me how Fritzie was diagnosed and treated, and then moved on to other topics, such as religion and politics. Just like his drug-abuse conversation yesterday, the novelty of the man quickly faded, especially when he launched into a monologue about how America should be more like Europe in its immigration policy.

If I was looking for a way out of the conversation, my salvation came in the form of Fritzie himself. It took one look and a high-pitched, ear-splitting squeal and Carl forgot all about me. I should have been prepared for it, given yesterday's performance, but the sheer volume of the noise still scared me half to death. Without as much as a good-bye or an acknowledgment of my continued existence, Carl headed out of the door.

During our conversation, a few other people had come into the waiting room. An old man in his midseventies with a long, scraggly gray beard was reading a magazine a couple of feet away from me, while a lady with long, flowing black hair and a business suit was seated near the desk, talking on her cell phone. I wondered what was wrong with their dogs.

85

EDDIE
JUNE 2009

It's amazing how one's routine can change, and it's even more amazing what takes the place of what we think is normal. Before the Crunchy Territory, I hardly ever left my territory. Sure, there were the brief trips around our block to do some territory claiming, not to mention the occasional outing to the place of sandy water, but mainly I had stayed at home.

Now, though, my idea of normal was completely . . . well, abnormal. For the last ten light periods, Mom had forgotten to feed me in the early light period. She had forced me to stay home while she took Paris to run around our territory block, making sure to shoot me a look like my leg was broken or something.

And then there were our daily trips to the Crunchy Territory. At least they had formed some kind of a routine, which in case you haven't guessed, I really liked. We furry friends aren't fans of change, and too much makes us nervous.

My Crunchy Territory trips went like this. I was first greeted by the eye-covering mom, who, by the way, appeared to be stuck to her chair because she never moved. I had never seen her stand up and would have been surprised if she even had hind paws. Next, I was greeted by the shiny-headed dad with a good rubdown before he took me into the hypno box room. I was then greeted by the white-coated dad, with his standard white-coated greeting, followed by the red-and-black-maned mom's rubs of attention. After a couple of hugs, it was the bee's turn, and *boom*, a bee sting.

Once the bee got me in the arm, the whole world would fade to black. Poof, one minute I'm cursing the day that all bees were born, and the next minute . . . lights out. And the thing that I kept coming back to was, how had I fallen asleep again?

It's not like I didn't get enough sleep to start with. In fact, being a typical furry friend, some of my days were spent doing exactly that: catching up with sleep when needed. Not to the extent of Paris, of course; oh no, no, never that bad. For the amount of beauty sleep she had, she should have been the prettiest furry friend in the world by now. So why I kept passing out was something I still didn't understand.

For all ten light periods, as soon as I woke up in the hypno box room, the shiny-headed dad had been right next to me with three juicy, mouth-drooling crunchy treats ready in paw. Of course, it took a little bit of time once I felt myself coming to stop the room from spinning, but that hadn't stopped my muzzle from sniffing out treat paradise.

I was then given meaty, mouthwatering, put-your-nose-into-overdrive treats. Granted, the first two treats were always inhaled through clouds of clearing haziness, but by the time the third came, I was myself. Then it was back to Mom in the big room and off to our territory for the day's activities with Paris.

It was a good routine, especially the crunchy treats part, but just when I had settled into that new schedule, yet another change occurred. As you can imagine, I wasn't all that happy about it. I even knew of a couple of furry friends who were so sensitive to any sort of change that the moment something different happened—and I'm talking about even changing the time they ate breakfast–it turned their world completely upside down.

I wasn't that delicate, but I did get to see the aftereffects of their shell-shocked sensitivities, and the wet puddles of semisolid black gossip smelled like something that no one wanted to fully investigate. There ain't no information that's worth sniffing that.

So, like always, my new change in schedule didn't totally stress me out, but it definitely made me uneasy. It occurred on exactly the seventeenth gray period after I had started my trips to the Crunchy Territory, right after the dark period that I had the dream.

It hadn't been your run-of-the-mill dream . . . well, maybe at first, when it started with the crunchy treat about the size of Dad. It then changed and in entered the poodle. I dreamed that Paris thought my shoulder was tastier than a licking treat, and I was helpless to move while she slurped away with her wet tongue. No matter what I did, no matter how much I tried to pull away, it had been useless. None of my paws had worked.

It was a very strange dream that must have kept me tossing and turning because the next light period, I was tired, like I had been chasing bushy-tailed friends the entire dark period.

As Dad's loud ringing box howled its wake-up call, I found myself actually too tired to get up. It was the first time in my entire life that I could remember that I didn't just bounce awake. My mind was fine and, like usual, was ready to attack the light period ahead of me, but like I said, my muscles were a different story.

After trying to get my legs into action, I remember thinking maybe, just maybe for this light period I would be like Paris and join her in her usual light-period sleeping schedule. Sure, I had made fun of it my whole life and thought the poodle was lazier than any clawed friends I knew, but had that really been fair?

So, deciding on to having a mellow day and with the fading memory of the dream still present, I focused on relaxing and drifting back into sleep land. But as I lay there, I became aware of a cold, wet feeling on my right shoulder. Had it been a dream after all?

No, there had definitely been something going on with my shoulder. It wasn't quite the same tingly feeling I'd felt pre-Crunchy Territory time, but it still felt quite odd. It was cold, wet, and felt like a furry friend had slobbered on it and was now panting on it. Like I had tripped over my ears on the way to my water bowl, fallen shoulder-first into it, and now was waiting for it to air dry. It didn't exactly hurt or feel painful; it just felt cold.

So, I did what every self-respecting furry friend would do faced with a new and different feeling. I turned my head around and took a giant lick.

86

DAVID
JUNE 2009

Things had been going so well; Eddie had been acting like a champ throughout treatment and nothing had gone wrong. There had been no surprises, no pain or suffering, no unforeseen side effects; in fact, no side effects at all. At least with Eddie, that is. As far as Julia was concerned, it was a different story altogether.

Julia was the one the treatment was directly affecting and, surprisingly, I couldn't have asked for a better result. Every new day brought out more and more of the Julia of old, sparks of the warm, beautiful woman I had first met and fallen in love with. As each day of Eddie's radiation treatment went by, I felt Julia opening up little by little, slowly letting me back into that part of her life that she had worked so hard to shut everybody out of.

It had been amazing. *She* was amazing, and unlike the denial that had drowned our lives during her father's battle, she had come to terms with the fact that Eddie had cancer and was dealing with his treatment in a realistic way. It was so much different from the last time around. As selfish as I felt for even thinking it, I couldn't remember being this happy in a long while.

We were finally talking, actually speaking about real things, not stupid, irrelevant small talk designed to fill a void, an emptiness that had replaced the conversations that should have been, that used to flow as naturally as the sun coming up. It felt so good to be close to her again.

Things couldn't have been going better. That's at least what I had thought, but being somewhat cynical, I was dreading the moment when it would all change. I knew the time the doctor had warned us about would come, the moment Eddie would start to show some side effects from the radiation. I prayed he wouldn't get them, that he would defy the odds and cut me a break. I hoped for Julia's sake, for my sake, and, especially, for our marriage's sake, but I might as well have been asking to win the lottery; things don't usually work out that way.

I was getting ready for work and had just finished straightening my blue-and-black-striped tie, the one Julia had bought me for

Father's Day. As I stepped out of the bathroom, I caught Eddie licking his radiation site, smearing the corner of the blue box they had marked on his shoulder. Since the treatment had been going so well, and it was still only 5:30 in the morning, it took me a second to realize the significance of his messing with the site.

Despite not having coffee in my system, I faintly recalled the doctor saying we should be extra aware of the Eddie about halfway through the treatment, looking out for him starting to lick. That was a sure sign of side effects, and we should tell them as soon as it started. The vet had said a lot that day, and I had been focusing mainly on Julia, only hearing about half of what he said, but I did read about it later that night in the handout they had sent home with us.

I had hoped for Julia's and my sake that it wouldn't happen, but life hadn't been kind to us these last two years. So I thought I'd better let her know before she discovered it for herself and cushion the blow. She was due to get up in five minutes anyway, so I went to her side of the bed, stepping over Eddie in the process, and, as gently as I could, touched her shoulder to wake her up. She didn't move at first; it took a full twenty seconds for her to respond.

"Jules, Jules . . .wake up; wake up, hon," I whispered in the most softest voice I could.

Just as she started to stir, I bent down and kissed her forehead in an attempt to make her transition into consciousness a peaceful one. Nobody liked to be woken up, and if it had to happen, at least I could make it as kind as possible. She took a deliberate deep, conscious breath while opening her eyes, and I could still feel the heat of her on my lips as I straightened up. She blinked a couple of times before focusing on me and smiled. She looked so warm and peaceful; I knew breaking this news wasn't going to be easy.

With my hand still resting on her shoulder, I said, "Sorry to wake you up, honey, but I wanted to tell you something before I went to work today. I caught Eddie licking his shoulder, and he smudged his marks. Will you ask them about it when you go in today?"

Her eyes opened a little wider and followed that with an exaggerated blink, and I dreaded what I thought was going to come next. But instead of panic, her jumping out of bed and leaping toward Eddie to examine his radiation site in pure, unadulterated terror, her reaction was one of unexpected calm.

"Huh, oh . . . well, let's put the cone on him again. We still have it in the garage."

She yawned, and then continued in that raspy, still-not-quite-awake voice, "The doctor said as soon as he starts to lick, put the cone on."

I sat on the bed, wondering if she had really heard me, if she had truly registered what I had just said. That hadn't been the reaction I'd expected, and I kept staring at her, waiting for her internal panic button to go off. But instead of histrionics, instead of turmoil, she sat up and looked at me with a smile. She appeared to be amused.

My hand had slipped off of her shoulder when she had straightened up, and I gently put it on her right forearm. I had to ask the question I knew could pop this unreal and unexpected bubble of calm. I did everything in my power to project the most unalarming and unprovoking tone possible because, as much as I appreciated this unforeseen reaction, I had to make sure what I had said had registered.

"Jules, you seem awfully calm about this. I know it's early, but you heard what I said, right?"

The bed frame creaked as she shifted her weight to sandwich her left hand over the hand that I'd put on her forearm and reassuringly said, "Sweetie, I'm fine."

She smiled lovingly, and as the remnants of sleep vanished from her voice, she continued. "Don't be such a worrywart. I've been waiting for something like this ever since the consult, mentally preparing myself for it to happen."

I waited for her to finish her yawn before she added, "Baby, this is no surprise, and it's going to be different this time. I'm not in denial, I knew it would happen, and now I'm going to deal with it. So stop stressing out; I'm fine."

She started chuckling then, because the expression on my face obviously gave away my utter astonishment. She playfully said, "Don't be so surprised. I'm not that much of a stress case. It'll be all right."

I just nodded, more in disbelief than in acknowledgment, and put on my best poker face so as not to provoke her playful bantering into something more serious. Was this the same woman? This reaction seemed so hard to believe, and a small part of me thought she must still be half-asleep, but the other part of me begged for this to be real. Whatever the case, I wasn't going to mess with it.

I let go of her forearm, and the wood floor creaked as my weight shifted off of the bed. I bent down next to Eddie to get a closer look at his radiation site. Besides having some smudged blue marker lines, the part of his shoulder in the outlined radiation box was a bright shade of angry red, like someone had slapped him with a paddle. It looked irritated, and I could feel the heat emanating from it before I touched it to confirm my suspicion.

Ironically, it was me who was starting to get worried, and without thinking, without taking into consideration what would happen, I opened my stupid mouth and screwed things up.

Maybe because it was early, or maybe because I had had a late night and wasn't thinking straight, or maybe because some sick part of me didn't truly believe Julia had internalized what I had said; regardless of the reason, what came out next was probably the most stupid, ill-timed thing that could ever have come out of my mouth. It pushed its way out, though, and with that sentence I inadvertently surpassed the boundaries of Julia's being-prepared speech.

"Honey, are you a hundred percent sure that's all we need to do, because this, this looks pretty bad."

I paused while finishing the word *bad* as what had just come out of my mouth registered. I took in a sharp breath in a vain attempt to suck back out what I had just said. But it was too late; there was no taking it back now.

I heard the rustling of the duvet as she kicked it off, and the familiar creak of the floor as she got out of bed to kneel beside both Eddie and me. I desperately tried to make eye contact with her as she moved toward me. She was looking down, so I didn't have a good angle to see her expression, but I finally had the opportunity to look right at her as she gently pushed Eddie's head away as he tried to lick her good morning.

I watched her face intently, waiting for the change.

87

EDDIE
JUNE 2009

After being awake for what couldn't have been more than a couple of moments, and after just a couple of good licks to my wet shoulder, I started to sense that old sensation of unease. There was that unsettled smell, the same biting feeling in Mom and Dad that had gnawed at me for this last part of my life.

It had been going on for what seemed to be ages now, and had shifted their smells from their usual happy smell to a tickle-your-nose-to-get-it-out-before-it-burned-your throat stink. It had gone from sweet to sour, from happy to sad, and then, finally, finally, after I didn't know how many unsuccessful tries on both myself and Paris's part, these last couple of weeks had seen their smells start to return to a normal, calm, less burned and relaxed flavor.

At least, that's what I had thought, but suddenly this early light period, without even the slightest bit of warning, like Paris passing gas, that stressed-out, sour smell was back in full force. What had taken many light periods to finally and thankfully fade away was stuck all over them again.

And wow, did it stink.

I tend to be a pretty light sleeper, but even if I weren't, the smell would have woken me. I had to do something to fix the situation, and so, without thinking, I gave a halfhearted lick to Mom's paw, the paw that had been scratching my head while I had tried desperately to think of a better fix for what was going on. She didn't even notice the lick; with her other paw resting on my back behind the wet spot, she continued to look closely at my wet shoulder. She was on her knees beside me, and being in that position and with her muzzle so close to my face, I couldn't help but think that a potential solution was staring right at me.

Given that gentle paw lick had been about as effective as marking on a rainy day, I decided to step up my attempts and went for the most obvious target. Timing was everything with these things, and obviously, the dream plus the sleepless dark period threw mine off. My tongue hit the air as Mom pulled back her head and turned toward Dad.

She had been grunting with Dad, who had been sitting next to her the whole time. Although the majority of my attention had been focused on Mom, I picked up on Dad's odor which had a different scent to it, earthier and grainier, but it was still about as obvious as water being wet.

I had smelled worry from the moment he had given me the first good-morning rub. It had been a dry, salty scent, not too strong, but not too weak either. And after he had woken up Mom and grunted with her a little, his smell had changed into something way worse. It had gone to a burn-your-throat stress smell and after hearing Mom whine, his stress had changed into frustration and sadness all in the blink of an eye. He was worried about Mom.

I put Mom's spiciness on the back burner because Dad's new smell worried me even more. I didn't get to think about it too much, though, because after a short, stressful grunt from Mom, Dad suddenly got up and headed for the door. The floor creaked as he stomped out of the room, and he snapped his claws and grunted my name on his way out. I broke off Mom's patting and ran after him.

I caught up with him, or at least a part of him, as he opened the sniff box resting room door, and I had just enough time to see the back of his leg and his furry paw pad covering as he went inside.

A short time later, the white sniff-box resting room door swung open again, and I felt a mist of air pass over my wet shoulder. Dad's furry paw coverings came into view, but that wasn't what caught my eye.

Instead, the semicircular, blur-all-peripheral-vision, drown-out-all-surrounding-sound, round, clear necklace made its way in all its smell-like-a-new-food-bowl glory.

I backed away a total of two steps, trying to avoid the necklace and almost managed to turn around completely. But Dad had a head start on me, and with two large steps he caught up, slipped his large, muscular paw under my necklace and got a good hold. Without any hesitation, I felt my ears being pulled back as the necklace slid over my head and found its home, resting at the base of my shoulders.

Once the thing was on, I just stood there, not moving a single muscle in my body, as if my staying still would cause it to fall off. And without even a twitch of my head, I managed to shift my eyes to where Dad was standing and saw that he was doing everything he could to avoid doing the same.

He finally gave in, and with a mild tilt of the head and a whine, he looked at me with sorry eyes. They looked to be on the verge of watering, something so out of the norm for Dad that despite my collar, I jerked my head up and tilted it in surprise. For Mom to whine and make buckets of eye drool was something that wasn't that shocking these days, but to see Dad do the same thing would be like watching Paris roll around in mud on purpose. It just didn't happen, and I didn't think I could handle it if it did, given the already obvious change in routine that had just happened.

So I decided to do what I do best: avoid any form of sadness and put my cheer-up skills to good use. What are we furry friends good for if we can't do something as easy as changing the mood of our moms and dads?

So, hoping that he wouldn't be as hard to cheer up as Mom had been over the last couple of months, I gave one loud cheer-up bark, unfroze the rest of my body, and closed the space between us in one big jump. As soon as I landed, I let out another bark and used my momentum to do two circles around him, making sure to avoid clipping either of his paws with the necklace and also being sure to rub my side onto the back of his shins when I got behind him.

It only took two circles, mixed with a couple of barks and leg rubs, before I smelled the sweet, happy, nose-tickling scent of a furry friend evasive cheer-up maneuver well done.

I felt good despite the hollow drone that surrounded my head and my inability to see things clearly, and at least I knew that I had fixed whatever had been broken with Dad. I felt pretty happy and with Dad smiling and buzzing around, and with Mom upstairs, doing battle with the white stubby tree from the muffled but obvious sounds of it, there was only one thing left to do.

It was time to reintroduce Paris to my clear friend.

88

JULIA
JUNE 2009

"It's the start of the radiation side effects we spoke about, Mrs. Freed. Unfortunately, that redness is probably going to get worse and turn more moist. My question to you is whether Eddie is comfortable at home at this point in time," Dr. Lindy said.

He had shaved his beard and replaced it with a thin layer of black scruff. His long, white lab coat was perfectly pressed, and he was close enough for me to see that his brown eyes had flecks of green in them today. He was sitting next to me with Eddie's manila file cradled in one arm while using the other to lean ever so slightly toward me on one of the bright blue plastic benches in the lobby.. His soothing voice had already put some of my concerns to rest.

"Is he uncomfortable?" I repeated, thinking back on whether Eddie had seemed any different recently. "No, he seems to be doing okay so far, but this morning I had to put the cone back on, and I just know he's depressed about it."

At least being proactive with the cone had made me feel a little less helpless.

With his musical voice, Dr. Lindy answered, "Good. Just keep in mind, the side effects are reversible, but most dogs' natural inclination is to lick the radiation site. If something feels strange, they usually lick the spot to investigate it. So it's very important that you keep his E collar on at all times. Self-trauma can be irreversible."

He paused for a couple of seconds to emphasize the point before he continued. "I'm going to start Eddie back on anti-inflammatories for now, the same ones he had after his surgery because we know he tolerated them well. I'm also going to send home the same painkiller he was on before, just so you have it in case he needs it. I realize that his pain level is practically nonexistent right now, but these things have a habit of creeping up over the weekend, when it's difficult to get hold of a doctor, and I would rather you have it on hand. If he shows any evidence of pain, go ahead and give him the pills. And we can always add more pain medications if he needs them."

He said pain. How could I tell that? Eddie couldn't tell me, so how was I meant to know? I was too embarrassed to ask because I probably should have known. Eddie was my dog, after all; what kind of person didn't know when her own dog was in pain?

I swallowed hard and resigned myself to thinking that Eddie would just tell me in his own way if he were hurting. I wasn't satisfied with this conversation, though; I needed something else from Dr. Lindy. Something was missing and incomplete, and I knew that if I left without it, it would eat me up inside and out.

"You know, I really hoped that he would be the exception, one of the dogs that didn't get them. He's done so well so far; why did this have to happen to him?"

Dr. Lindy put down Eddie's file and clasped his hands together in front of him as he leaned in closer to me. In a slow, drawn-out voice that made me feel like I was sitting in front of a fireplace with a hot chocolate and a blanket, he said, "I'm sorry; I know it's difficult to see and it's the hardest thing about this process, but . . ." He turned his head ever so slightly, and the green flecks in his eyes shone like emeralds, "It will get better."

Dr. Lindy had a gift, one that had worked its magic with me during the initial consultation, when he'd miraculously made something as dreadful as cancer, surgery, and radiation seem tolerable. Listening to him then, it had all felt doable, something we could all get through together. I couldn't pinpoint what it was about the man, but he had a way of making everything seem fine, and now, as in all of our conversations, his soft voice did the trick. Surprisingly, I felt satisfied, and that unanswered question, that feeling that something was missing, had slipped away.

He kept staring at me, waiting to see if I had more to say, but I couldn't think of anything. So with that, he smiled and nodded, picked up Eddie's file, and made his way toward the back of the hospital.

It was nice that he had been so available, and it definitely had made this process more bearable. When I had arrived earlier, I had requested to speak to him, and shortly after they had taken Eddie back, he had come out to speak to me. If only it had worked that way in human hospitals.

But no, I probably would have needed to make another appointment or battled the nursing staff to drag the doctor away from whatever he deemed more important than having to deal with a patient's family and actually speak to me. Or maybe it was the same when people had radiation and I had been jaded because of what my dad and I went through when we had questions about his chemotherapy.

The routine at this place had become pretty straightforward, and after doing it for two weeks now, both Eddie and I had gotten used to it. I was an old pro, so being here was no longer an intimidating, traumatic experience that I couldn't wait to get away from. I didn't feel the need to be left alone anymore, or even the desire to isolate myself in a corner and hope that nobody bothered me. In fact, I now found that I actually wanted to socialize during the forty-minute wait. I would never have pictured myself feeling that way a couple of months back, but something had changed.

I realized that speaking to people actually helped pass the time. Forty minutes can seem like a lifetime if you had to just sit and stare at a wall, and it was about as exciting as watching paint dry. The seconds slowed down even more if you were waiting for a loved one undergoing cancer treatment. All sorts of bad thoughts found their way into your mind, and after I ran out of fingernails to chew, I figured I'd better change something before I moved onto skin and bone. I decided to be social during the wait, and what followed was something that I never could've predicted.

At first it had been an exercise in taking my mind off of where I was and what was going on, but it evolved into something more. I could only describe it as one giant nervous-tension release valve, an annoyingly clichéd reality that confirmed what everybody around me had been so insistent on me doing during Dad's fight, especially David.

"Just talk about it; it will make it easier, Jules," he had dared to say before he'd known better.

But as infuriating, aggravating, and obnoxious as all those people who at the time I thought were just being holier than thou had been, maybe there had been something to what they had said after all. The more I spoke to other people in the lobby who were having their own dogs treated, the more at peace with the whole process I became. The funny thing was that the waiting time for Eddie seemed to melt away.

I would never admit it out loud, especially not to David; too many fights and harsh words had gone by for that, and besides, it would probably do more harm than good. Why bring up the stormy past? He had been right, though.

I turned to the bench to my right, and Debbie was staring intently at me, waiting for me to pow-wow about what Dr. Lindy had just said. She was a mousy-looking woman in her early thirties; small, petite, with shoulder-length black hair and fading freckles on her cheeks. Debbie was one of my newfound lobby-support-group friends, someone I had met about a week into Eddie's therapy.

"I knew they were coming, I prepared for them, convinced myself that when they finally showed up I would be all right with them, but I'll be honest with you, deep down inside I thought they would skip him. I know I'm being stupid, but there was a part of me that thought and hoped that we wouldn't have to deal with this. He's been through so much already."

Debbie had heard the whole conversation, so there was no need to repeat anything Dr. Lindy had said. That would normally have been part of our little support group protocol.

When I had first met Debbie, she'd the same expression I must have had on my face Eddie's first day. She looked like a wreck and scared out of her wits, and just seeing her like that left me no choice but to break out of my shell and approach her. It was horrible to see that look on somebody else; besides being a little bored myself, I felt sorry for her.

I had started the conversation, and as it turned out, I was like a seasoned veteran when it came to talking about the therapy by then. Her cat, Napoleon, was being treated for a vaccine-associated sarcoma that had been in between his shoulder blades, and as it turned out, he would be scheduled to be treated right after Eddie from that day forward.

We spoke every day, and unlike me, this lady was a natural when it came to nervous conversations. We mainly talked about our families. She had been married for thirteen years and had three kids, two girls and a baby boy. She told me about Napoleon, a snow-white cat she had adopted while she was in college. He had originally belonged to the fraternity house next to her apartment complex, but he had found his way to her door.

Fortunately for her, the frat boys hadn't missed him that much, and when she'd finally gone over to see if he belonged there, they had told her to keep the cat and seized the opportunity to hit on her. Go figure; it had actually worked out for one of the boys, which was how she had met her husband, Alan. Napoleon, she had said, still to this day remained her "main man."

He was also getting radiation therapy but, unlike Eddie, was going to have the surgery to remove his mass after the radiation, not before. In theory, if they got all of it at surgery, he would have at least over three years or so of his tumor not coming back.

Debbie wasn't the only person I saw on a regular basis. In fact, I continued to meet people in the waiting room, the majority of them with pets going through treatment. Fritzie, the ancient fur ball with the Eurotrash owner, had long ago finished, and truth be told, I hadn't been all that upset. I hadn't felt an overwhelming need to ever see his owner again, and thank goodness my experience with him hadn't jaded me enough to make me crawl back into my introverted grief-dealing shell.

There was Shirley, a gorgeous, tall and slender, blonde-haired and blue-eyed, single twenty-five-year-old who had a 105-pound black-and-tan Doberman. Tiny had a mast cell tumor on his right knee, and Shirley had to pick up extra shifts bartending in order to cover the cost of his treatment. Tiny's prognosis was great, and the chance of his tumor coming back in five years was less than 10 percent.

And there were also Roy and Jennie, with their twelve-year-old, shorthaired brown-and-white mutt, Buddy, who was a mix between a boxer and a pit bull and was being treated for a thyroid tumor. Roy and Jennie were a retired couple who must have been in their late seventies and were the perfect example of what all married folks aspire to be when they grow old. They were always holding hands and whispering in each other's ears.

Buddy had already had surgery; the radiation therapy was to get the cells that were left over in the surgical site. This was very similar to Eddie's situation, but Buddy's average survival with treatment was between two and four years.

There were others as well, but they were either arriving while I was leaving or leaving while I was coming, so we never got an opportunity to speak. A simple hello or head nod had been the extent of our relationship, but there was a warm understanding, a sort of unspoken depth to the greeting, an acknowledgment of empathy and support.

I got to know Roy, Jennie, Shirley, and Debbie really well, though. We were strangers thrown into a hard situation, and all packed into the waiting room at the same time. Whether we would've ever spoken if we hadn't been forced into a situation like this was unclear, but we liked one another's company and took comfort in one another's support. Before we knew it, we'd formed an unofficial mini therapy group. Whenever the doctor had said something to anyone of us, we all had to hear about it, pick it apart, and read way too much into it. There was always a group huddle after the doctor left after speaking with any one of us.

We were like a bunch of teenage girls who'd just gotten their own phone line, picking apart the minutia of every interaction with Dr. Lindy and overanalyzing anything he said. When Shirley's Doberman Tiny went on antibiotics, we all needed to know why. When Debbie's Napoleon was put on diarrhea medication, we all wondered whether our pets would also get diarrhea, and whether they would have to be put on the same thing. Whatever happened to someone else's dog or cat could potentially happen to ours, and we had to be prepared.

It was so different from Dad's chemotherapy waiting room; *I* was so different. Back then, I had made a point of ignoring everyone there, hadn't wanted anything to do with anything other than keeping to myself. I couldn't remember how many people were in the lobby or what they had done every day, whether they spoke or whether they didn't, or even if it had been the same group of people showing up at the same time because I had spent most of the time looking at a book or a magazine. I hadn't been interested in their lives or their problems, and the last thing I had wanted to do was to be forced into talking.

Speaking to total strangers this time around had somehow made Eddie's treatment more tolerable. Making the decision to open up to David also had done wonders for my mood and, more importantly, our relationship. As I've said before, maybe there was something to not holding everything in, not bottling it up inside. It had sounded so cliché, so PC, so sickening, yet it didn't feel that way this time.

Debbie was still looking at me, waiting to see if I had anything else to add, but I was all out of confessions. Jennie and Roy had already left with Buddy about fifteen minutes earlier and I hadn't gotten a chance to speak to them, and Shirley wasn't due in for Tiny's appointment for at least another ten minutes. I would have loved to have included them in this recent conversation with Dr. Lindy and gotten their feedback. I actually craved their opinions and words of encouragement. I needed them to know what had happened to Eddie.

I knew that Buddy had broken out with a large, red, weepy spot on the bottom of his neck last week, and that Roy and Jennie had been instructed to put a special radiation burn cream on it once a day. He was also on a pain medication, an anti-inflammatory, and an antibiotic, and as far as the radiation schedule was concerned, he was exactly a week ahead of Eddie. Of all my newly acquired support friends' pets, he was the canary in the mine, because the things that happened to him could also happen to Eddie a week later.

At that moment, I would have loved to have heard them tell me that the burn on his neck hadn't bothered Buddy, that it was easy to deal with, and that I shouldn't worry because Eddie would also probably not even notice it. I made a mental note to arrive early tomorrow so I could catch them.

Just then, my thoughts were interrupted by a loud and high-pitched commotion coming from the front desk. I looked up and saw a little brown, round-headed Chihuahua with an oversized black-and-silver-spiked collar trying to attack an overweight Rottweiler about ten times his size. The owner of the Chihuahua was a potbellied, middle-aged, biker-looking guy who had on a black Harley T-shirt and whose beard was hanging to midchest, tied with a red rubber band around the tip. He bent down and scooped up the little dog before it accomplished its goal of committing suicide.

"Spike no, bad dog, bad dog!" he said, cradling the still barking dog. He grabbed Spike's mouth, and the barking suddenly stopped, to be replaced by high-pitched growling. The guy turned to the Rottweiler's owner, a short, thirtysomething Asian lady who was about the same size as her dog and looked to be checking in for the day.

"I'm sorry. Spike's just like his daddy, all bark and no bite. He just doesn't get it that the world around him is a lot bigger than he is. He thinks he's my own personal bodyguard."

The lady started to say something, but Spike launched into a new tirade of barking, while the Rottweiler angled its head in confusion and eyeballed the little thing.

With my disappointment temporarily forgotten, I smiled to myself and thought that Spike was one lucky little mutt to still be alive.

As the biker got a firm grip on Spike's muzzle and the barking was finally muffled enough for me to hear what was being said, the Asian lady responded through her giggling, "It's okay. Petunia is the biggest wimp you'll ever meet. She would never hurt a fly, and I'm surprised she wasn't halfway out the door already."

89

EDDIE
JUNE 2009

As far as my shoulder was concerned . . . well, the cold and wet feeling continued to grow worse. As the light periods passed one by one, it became the center of my world. Crunchy treats didn't seem that important, exploring the neighborhood territory and dreaming about claiming every square inch of it lost its appeal; just about every thought I had was about to my weird, tingling shoulder.

It changed as the light periods went by, growing slimier and more wet. It got so bad that I could even feel cold air brushing over it when I was passed out on my sleeping cushion and was perfectly still. So, I did the obvious thing and didn't move that much, avoiding any chance of extra cold-air contact or any excuse for it to feel wetter than it already was.

This was also about the same time that I started to feel really tired and worn out, and the tiredness was insane given my inactivity. It got to a point that I felt more tired than after I had after running around our neighborhood territory with Dad as he huffed and puffed, panting like an overweight bulldog.

All I wanted to do was pass out next to Paris and sleep, although Paris wouldn't get anywhere near me with my clear necklace. I also didn't think it was a coincidence that it started happening right about the time Mom started giving me the bitter treats again.

It began around the time that my shoulder was tingling so bad that I hadn't been able to put my paw down properly without feeling like I had just hit my not so funny bone. As soon as Mom had come downstairs into the feeding room that morning and saw my semi-three-legged balancing act, she had let out a loud pity whine. She had then reached into one of the white feeding-room wall doors and grabbed a small, orange semi–see-through cylindrical tube full of bitter-smelling, pea-size treats.

Then Mom took out one of my brown, slimy reward treats, and stuffed one of the pea-size bitter treats right into the center of the slimy treat.

And then it happened—not right away, but when enough time had gone by to get rid of the cinammony aftertaste of the reward treat. It was as if something had come out of nowhere and sucked all of the energy out of me.

I felt like every bone in my body weighed twice as much as it really did, and that everything was moving in slow motion. All I had wanted to do was either lay on my sleeping cushion upstairs or pass out in the back territory. I only wanted to stare at the sky or, even better, sleep, and for the first time in my life, I actually wanted to be left alone. It was surprising how utterly drained I felt, and just when that feeling started to wear off, there was Mom with another reward treat with a crunchy, bitter-stuffed center.

Even though the last thing I wanted to do was have to get up and walk anywhere, the good news was that in that state I could have walked if I'd wanted to. Unfortunately though, it took every bit of concentration I had to take the next step without taking a face plant

Overall, it hadn't been the best time in my life because feeling like that wasn't enjoyable. Being tired, down, and lazy beyond the realm of even Paris wasn't fun. And what made it even worse was how much things changed with Mom and Dad; with their moods, their schedules, and even with their behavior. What I remember was the shift from both of their states of unsettled calmness into a change of outright rip-your-fur-out worry. And no matter how hard I tried, I couldn't change their moods.

Mom was much worse than Dad, and that salty, bitter smell got so bad that it made my nose burn again. It stank. I made every effort to be around Mom, when I wasn't unconscious, that is, but I was unconscious a lot!

And Mom, well, she didn't make my life any easier. It was at about that time that she decided to change her usual schedule of going out at least two or three times a light period to now solely being an indoor Mom. She chose to be in our territory all hours of the light and dark period.

Dad was another story altogether; although his salty, bitter smell was more directed at Mom than me, his way of dealing with being depressed was far more enjoyable. Instead of locking himself in our territory, his natural way of trying to make himself feel better was to load me up with claw-sized, brownish and yellow crunchy treats whenever Mom wasn't looking.

Dad however, also stopped wrestling with me and instead treated me like I was made out of leaves. I missed getting a rough hug or a deep, massaging rubdown good-bye, but whenever he touched me back then, he did it with soft, gentle pats, the kind you gave a small puppy or something you were worried about breaking. I hated every moment of that.

I felt like a failure. I had one self-appointed job in this world, and that had been to make Mom and Dad happy at all times, but during this period no matter what I did, no matter how much I tried, I couldn't get them to cheer up. Nothing worked; no amount of licking, barking, or cute head tilting had any effect at all. Me being near them had exactly the opposite effect; they became more sad when I was around.

Mom would just lay there on the brown sitting cushion, staring at me, letting the drool trickle down her muzzle while I tried to think of what I could do to change the situation. At least Dad's eyes hadn't drooled, but even a blind and deaf furry friend could sense the sad change in his mood whenever he'd been around me.

It proved to be the low point in my life.

90

JULIA
JUNE 2009

I was upset and sad. I was also scared because the radiation site had been changing every day. I was in the waiting room with Debbie, the only one left from our mini support group. Shirley's Doberman Tiny had finished four days ago, while Roy and Jennie's dog Buddy had been done two days after that. Debbie had been trying to help, but her cat had absolutely no side effects as of yet, so she hadn't been able to offer much. It had been explained to her, and thus to our support group by her afterward, that cats usually didn't get skin side effects, so good old Napoleon would never see pain or burns from radiation. She was lucky.

Tiny, however, had developed radiation burns, and had been put on the same pain medication as Eddie. He'd looked a lot worse off than Eddie, though; he had angry, red, moist, irritated skin that encircled his right knee, completely confined within the blue oval radiation marks that delineated where his field was. He had also stopped eating as much, and Shirley had resorted to feeding him soft canned food instead of his kibble. If Eddie's appetite ever changed like that, I would know that something was really wrong with him, like he was dead or close to it.

The good thing about Tiny had been that despite his leg looking like he had just fallen off of a motorcycle, at least his pain had been well controlled. He hadn't even limped on his last day of radiation; in fact, he had bounded to Shirley after his treatment, scaring the new folks who were just checking in. Hell, there's no better cup of coffee than a hundred pound Doberman with ears pointed straight up running toward you off leash.

And Shirley . . . well, that woman had been a rock through and through. Every word out of her mouth had been positive, and the fact that her dog's leg looked like it was mincemeat hadn't outwardly bothered her one bit. She reasoned that if it didn't bother him, it shouldn't stress her out either.

Me, on the other hand . . . I was not Shirley. It had taken my last shred of sanity not to break down and completely lose it. This whole thing might have been different if I hadn't just had to deal with my dad's death. It probably would have been easier; at least that's what David thought. He was convinced that I had linked the experiences in my mind, and that's why it was so hard on me. Maybe he was right; it seemed to be the obvious answer, but maybe not.

Even if I had connected the two events and there was something to David's theory, it didn't take away my feelings about Eddie. I tried to explain to David that this whole thing would have affected me the same way no matter what. Ever since the day when the gynecologist had confirmed that I couldn't have children, that same day David, Dad, and I had rescued Eddie from that homeless guy for fifty dollars, I had thought of Eddie as family, and . . . well, he became my child. David just nodded and told me he understood, but I don't think he really got it. He was a man, after all, and probably just couldn't believe it.

The worse the radiation side effects became and the site looked, the more the same questions haunted me. I doubted myself and questioned my decision to put him through it. And as the side effects continued to intensify, I kept asking myself if I had done the right thing. Had I tortured him for my benefit?

It was so hard to see him like that, so tired and lethargic, definitely not the same Eddie I knew. He was sad all the time, and I couldn't bear him staring at me like he did. With his big, droopy eyes and his long ears pasted against his head, I could just imagine him wondering why the hell I had done this to him. If he could talk . . . well, I feared what he would say. But he couldn't talk, and I had made the decision to put him through all of this for him. For what? For me? Had I been fair?

It was tearing me apart, and I now craved constant reassurance. David was great, telling me that I had made the right decision, but I didn't think he truly believed it. It got so bad that I needed more than David could offer, so toward the end of the therapy course, when I didn't think I could take the guilt anymore, I finally decided to speak to Dr. Lindy again. I was fully aware of what he was going to say, but I wanted to hear it anyway.

"I know it's hard, but hang in there. His side effects are right where they should be at this stage, Mrs. Freed. As hard as it is to believe he's actually doing well, keep in mind that I'm making him lethargic on purpose with the medications, and what you see at the house is mostly due to what I gave him. We want him to be lethargic and not to feel that much. It's also completely normal for you to question yourself and whether you did the right thing."

His white lab coat had a small wrinkle on the left side of his collar that day, and I hadn't been able to take my eyes off of it while he and I had been speaking. I had nodded methodically because he had taken the words right out of my mouth, verbalizing what I'd been agonizing over for the last week.

"Mrs. Freed, the last week of therapy is always the most challenging time, and it's normal to question your decision. I'll tell you, though, that this will heal, despite what we do, and in three to four weeks he'll be back to his normal self again. He's got three more days of radiation and needs you to remain positive because I truly do believe these animals can pick up on our feelings. In the meantime, I'm going to start him on an antibiotic, given how his site's looking today."

My face must have changed because he quickly continued before I could fully form the question. He raised both of his well-manicured hands up in the air and clasped them together in front of his chest, which caused the wrinkle in his collar to almost fold in on itself. With a very calming gesture, he said, "This is standard for this stage of therapy. I expected it, and frankly, I'm surprised it took so long to manifest. I don't want a secondary infection, Mrs. Freed, that's why I'm giving him the antibiotic. He'll be fine, though. He's an amazing dog who loves you very much, and he's very strong. Just keep reminding yourself that he's almost done and the prognosis is in his favor. We'll speak again in three days, at his discharge appointment, but feel free to call us or speak to me again before that."

He had waited for me to say something, but I never did. I had nothing more to ask, so I just nodded. I did feel better, though; reassured, but not by much.

91

EDDIE
JUNE 2009

Things had changed, and not in a good way. No longer was Mom just a little upset like she had been when we had first started going on the Crunchy Territory trips; oh no, she had taken a turn for the worse. It had gone from a semi-sad daily excursion, where Mom and the other moms and dads had spent time grunting and snorting together, and had changed into a daily eye drooling and whining fest that no amount of licking, nudging, or even head tilting on my part could fix.

The more I had tried, the worse she had got, and I hadn't thought it possible for her to get any sadder through my efforts. I was a failure, and since I had still been in the hazy, tired reward treat state of being, I'm sure things had been even worse than I remembered them.

Mom had grunted with either the white-coated dad or the shiny-headed dad almost every time we had gone to the Crunchy Territory, and her grunting usually turned into half-panicked whines. It took a whole lot of smooth, relaxed grunting on their part to calm her, and I could tell even their efforts were starting to not work as well.

But despite Mom being wound up tighter than a clawed, meowing furry friend in a roomful of Rottweilers, time flew by, and before I knew it, Mom and I were led into the rectangular, red-stoned room again. It was the same room, where Mom, Dad, the white-coated dad, and I had all met when the Crunchy Territory experience first began.

By this point, my shoulder had changed into a wet, cold, slimy blob. It tingled but didn't outright hurt; however, given my state of drowsiness, I wouldn't have thought that getting hit by a sniff box would have hurt either.

The lack of pain was good, but there was one thing that was worse than the crazy urge to sleep. It was the strong craving to have just one satisfying lick of my shoulder. It wouldn't have taken much; just one long, fantasy-fulfilling, slime-removing, slurp. Not that I didn't try.

I had rolled, kicked, flexed, somersaulted and backflipped, just to get to it, but no matter what fancy move I did, I had no luck. Our territory still has the marks of my efforts, with scratches on the walls and smudge marks that never had come off of the wood floors.

The meeting with the white-coated dad happened right after I woke up from yet another inescapable blackout. After three wake-up chewy treats, instead of going to the front of the territory, where they usually brought me, I was led into the rectangular room where Mom and the white-coated dad were already sitting across from each other and grunting away. The grunting stopped as soon as they saw me walk in.

92

KATHLEEN
JUNE 2009

She had come so far, the precious little hon, and I'll admit that I'd miss seeing her sweet sunshine of a face every day. It had taken a while, but she had warmed up like a spring day in April, and now she was as friendly as I knew she would be. I just loved it when they blossomed like she had, and it was one of life's little perks, working in this blessed job. I just loved seeing people shed their burden and find peace within themselves with the help of the other people around them, and I thanked the Lord that I was privy to witnessing such a miracle on a daily basis. That made it a pleasure to come to work every day, that and the cute little love muffins, of course!

Mrs. Freed had adjusted well enough and fallen into the cycle of the radiation routine. There was the initial visit and the fear of the place, and she had been quivering like a leaf that first day when she checked her Eddie in. She had been about as nervous as a long-tailed cat in a room full of rocking chairs, but she had come around.

She had settled like an old comfortable shoe, and after a couple of nail-biting days, she had found her rhythm. Mrs. Freed, like just about every client who walked in here and whose little sugar muffin went through treatment, had also found her inner circle of friends. For those cynics out there who believed that the world was a bad place and there was no love left between men, I truly believed they should spend just one week behind my desk to witness the good there is.

Like almost all of the little support circles, Mrs. Freed's had been there for her when her little angel's treatment had gotten rough and his shoulder had looked redder than a monkey's backside, bless their hearts.

They all did that, and it was the darndest thing. All the clients formed their cliques, every time and in every fresh cycle. It was like watching magnets in an empty cereal bowl, they all just stuck together. And for the occasional soul who decided to go it alone . . . well, let's just say that Dr. Lindy worked overtime for them.

I would miss Mrs. Freed and Eddie; it was always sad to see them go, but such is the circle of life in a veterinary radiation facility. She had reminded me of myself twenty years earlier and fifty pounds lighter, and it was hard to miss the strength in that woman. She radiated independence and femininity all packed into one tight bundle, and even though this last week had been a tab bit rough on her, I knew she would endure the next couple of weeks just fine.

I called out her name because it was about that time, and led her into room eight, where Dr. Lindy was waiting with Eddie's file in hand.

THE DOG DAYS OF THE PAST

93

JULIA
MARCH 2008

My father was a stoic man. He was tough, confident, and never complained to anyone. He was also a quiet man, never offering an opinion unless he was asked for it. His silence could be intimidating, unless, of course, you knew him like I did. To me, he was soft-spoken and warm, and one of the greatest things about him was that he was not overbearing. He had always supported my decisions, most of my relationships, and generally anything I had undertaken throughout the years. He had always given me the emotional support I had needed, and my relationship with him was probably only second to my relationship with David. He was the much-needed balance to the other half of the parental duo, Mother.

Mother's first reaction to any major life event or personal news was almost always negative. It was as predictable as the sun rising in the morning and the sky being blue, and it usually went something like this: The first step was denial, doubt, or, my favorite of all, criticism. The second was how that life event would directly influence her. How would she manage? What would people think? What would she say?

That part of the process might have gone on for a minute or a month. But finally, after exhausting every aspect of how something would influence her and change her life, she might actually have something constructive to say. Unfortunately, by that time it was usually too late.

I remember right after David proposed to me and I had called my parents to share the good news. I had been ecstatic, on cloud nine and, up until then, it had been the happiest day of my life. But by the time I hung up with her, I had wanted to cry. First Dad had gotten on the phone and, like any sane person—or father, for that matter—he hadn't stopped congratulating me. He knew how happy I was, knew how much I loved David, and I truly felt the sincerity in his voice. To hear me that joyful, he said, was the greatest gift in the world. Then he had handed the phone to Mother.

Her voice had been cold and piercing, and I shouldn't have expected anything else from her. The first thing that had come out of her mouth was, "He did . . . well, dear, don't you think you're a little young for this? Don't you think you could do better? I would hate for you to settle. This David seems like a nice enough man, but Julia, when I was your age, I looked for someone who had greater ambition."

I had been stunned. All I could do was stand there in shock with my brand-new ring wedged against the phone. David had been watching with a big smile on his face as I had relayed the good news, but his grin faded when he saw my expression.

My mother had taken my silence as a sign to proceed to "educate" me about how she had waited a sufficient, preapproved-by-Grandmother time before she got married. Her parents had insisted that it was the right thing to do, and being a respectful daughter . . .

I hung up in midsentence and we didn't speak for two months, when she called me, acting like nothing had ever happened.

I remember getting my admission letter to UCLA, the school I had dreamed of going to ever since eighth grade. My room had been decorated with posters, ribbons, giant football hands, and just about every piece of UCLA memorabilia I could get hold of. So after I received and read the golden ticket, the UCLA admission letter, that senior year of high school, I thought it only obvious that my parents would be happy and congratulate me on my acceptance.

I had made the mistake of telling Mother the news first. Her reaction . . . well, she'd told me it wasn't the right school for me, and that if she could do it over again, she would only have applied to Ivy League schools.

Like they were going to pay for my tuition to start with. Dad, at least, had been honest with me from the start, telling me that, unfortunately, they couldn't afford to send me to an out-of-state school, let alone a private one. But my mother had insisted on the smoke and mirrors; heaven forbid she should have to admit the harsh reality of their financial situation to her daughter.

Instead, she had gone out of her way to justify their lack of funds by telling me that they couldn't afford to waste money on educating a daughter. Rather I should find a nice, rich husband to take care of me. She had gone on to say that if I did insist on wasting my time with a worthless education, I should at least go someplace that better "catered to your abilities." Whether that had been a compliment or an insult, to this day I still didn't know.

And then there had been the time when I had just completed

my master's in English and had held a party to celebrate the event; Mother couldn't resist voicing her unsolicited opinion. All my closest friends had been there, and David had rented out the back room of Carvers, my favorite steak house of all time. I had gone back and forth as to whether to invite my parents, knowing I ran the risk of Mother being Mother, but I couldn't leave out Dad. I had been so happy, so proud of my accomplishment, and everyone in the room had been having such a good time. Everyone but Mother, that is, who had been sulking because she wasn't the center of attention. And so, being the narcissist that she was, she had decided to change that.

From across the table and in a voice that was purposefully loud enough to be heard by everyone in the room, she had made her opinion known.

"Julia, dear," she had raised her voice and her wineglass with a haughty, accusatory air, "I still don't know why you didn't pursue a degree in something more useful for the amount of time you put into school. Really, dear, what are you going to do with this degree anyway? If I had just done three extra years of school, taken out loans for countless amounts of money on academia, I would have at least done something more useful with my time."

The shock and sheer audacity of what she had said silenced the entire room, and if it hadn't been for Dad giving her the stare of death, she probably would have gone on. As she had mouthed "What?" to my father and sat back, sipping her glass of Merlot, David had broke the silence by laughing at the top of his lungs and playing it off as a joke. "Oh, Cybil, you always were the joker."

Suffice it to say, my mood had not been what it should have been after such an achievement.

And, finally, let's not forget that oh-so-memorable time, the decisive moment in my life when I had painfully decided to stop trying to have a child. After my third miscarriage, the one right before David and I had been told kids were not in our future, being the masochist I was, I had actually called her for support.

Instead of the loving, nurturing, and caring woman who should have been at the other end of the line, her first comment had been, "Why didn't you take care of yourself like I did when I was pregnant with you?"

Just as she had started to tell me how not ever being a grandmother was going to be so embarrassing to her, I hung up on her, imagine that. We didn't speak for a full six months after that, until her birthday, which in my family had always forced a phone call.

After the most recent fight I had had with her, I wouldn't have been surprised if we never spoke again. No birthday could undo the damage that had been done that day. So when Dad called me to ask—no, insist—that I meet with Mother to apologize and sort the whole thing out, it had taken every ounce of my strength not to argue back. The fight had still been fresh; it had only been a month.

His voice had been stern but soft, and in a typical Dad tone, he'd said, "Jules, I don't have the energy to see or deal with your mother and you like this."

Then, in a very untypical fashion, he had continued, "It's wearing me out, Jules. Honey, I'm not as energetic as I used to be, and to tell you the truth, seeing my family like this is even harder than anything I've been through. The chemotherapy was a walk in the park compared to this. Jules, I can't see you and your mother like this; I just can't do it."

Dad had never spoken like that, about feelings, about weaknesses; he had always been impenetrable in that department. His voice had faltered and nearly cracked, and hearing him like that had made me want to crawl under a rock.

"I don't know what you fought about, and frankly, I don't want to know. I don't have the strength. All I know is this: Julia, you have an amazing ability to forgive people, even when they won't forgive themselves."

I had started to say something, but he'd stifled my response. His voice changed, and with a finality only my dad could muster, he had said, "So let me make this loud and clear, Jules. Your mother and you will—I repeat, *will*—make up or come to some sort of an understanding."

He'd paused, and I'd heard his voice truly crack this time. "If not for anything else, for me."

I hadn't dared to say a word as the lump in my throat had threatened to burst out and bounce onto the floor. But I wouldn't break the silence on the phone; I knew he had more to say.

His voice had softened, and suddenly he'd changed back into the soft-spoken Dad I was used to.

"And just so you don't think I'm picking on you, or blaming you for this, just know that I'll be having this same conversation with your mother tonight. You're to meet her on Sunday at 11 A.M. at the Coffee Shop. Understood?"

Like the little girl he had just made me feel like, I responded with the only thing that could have been said. "Yes, Dad."

94

JULIA
APRIL 2008

It had to happen. I had to swallow my pride for Dad's sake.

Dad had actually pulled it off. Surprisingly, he had called me to confirm that Mom would meet me for coffee. Dad had arranged the place and the time, and obviously he had forced her to come as well. I could just imagine the fight that had ensued to get her to be here, and I hoped she hadn't worn him out too much.

He needed to conserve his energy to battle this thing, this parasite that had started in his pancreas and was now invading other parts of his body. I knew that if Dad hadn't been sick, he would never have been able to guilt her into doing this; on no account would she be here meeting me after what had happened. We'd never had a fight like that before because I had never daringly and purposefully ventured into the forbidden place, the *unspoken topic* with her. But as much as I resented her and as much baggage as we had, she did love Dad, after all, and, like me, that was the only thing that had brought her to the Coffee Shop.

I saw her the moment she rounded the corner of the block. It was a street dominated by family-owned stores, small storefronts that hadn't changed in years. They were all one-story buildings, and the general theme had been to make them as cute and small town as possible. Given the fact that the beach was just two blocks west, between the town and the boardwalk, it was quite the tourist trap.

She had just passed Delicate Tess, hands down one of the best sandwich shops on the West Coast, and I took the opportunity to ready myself for the upcoming chore. Her steps were rigid and stiff, and she looked like she was marching toward battle. She was wearing a maroon dress with a matching jacket, had a small purse slung over her shoulder like the strap of a rifle, matching closed-toe heels, stockings, and a buttoned-up white blouse. The two top buttons were open, and I caught the sparkle of her diamond necklace as it reflected the sun. She also had on her diamond earrings, the ones Dad had given her for their twentieth wedding anniversary. They were the same ones she had nonchalantly told him were "okay looking, but Richard, two carats would have been better."

Despite the snotty comment, I knew she loved those earrings, and she only wore them on special occasions. She also put them on when she was trying to impress someone.

This was definitely not a special occasion, and seeing her dressed like that, like she was going to a formal dinner or running for senate, annoyed me to no end. It was seventy-nine degrees outside, everyone was in shorts, and hell, some people were even in bikini tops. What was she thinking? Why couldn't she have come in casual clothes? It wasn't like I didn't know how she usually dressed. Was she trying to intimidate me? Overwhelm me? What was her motive?

It was just so typical of her, treating this like it was a meeting between two strangers. On second thought, though, maybe that wasn't too far from the truth.

Once inside the Coffee Shop, she scanned the square, rustic wood tables and spotted me in the far corner. She walked briskly over, her heels echoing on the hard, adobe-tiled floor, each step like a bullet being loaded into a magazine clip. I had picked this table for privacy, and it was the one farthest from the door. That way, it would make it harder for either of us to get up and stomp out. I knew this meeting had to go well; we had to come to some sort of an understanding, and even it killed me, we were going to leave here on speaking terms.

It was a quaint shop, a wannabe Starbucks that had jumped on the coffee-shop bandwagon back in the nineties and buried itself into the cottage feel of this beach community. It was mostly decorated in a Mexican rustic theme, with wooden chairs, simple tables, and desert paintings on the wall. It had your standard rebellious, early twenties barista behind the counter, complete with a nose ring, an assortment of earrings mishmashed along the vertical length of both her ears, a lip ring, and, of course, an eyebrow ring above her left eye. There was soft jazz playing, and the air conditioning made it a pleasant seventy-two degrees.

I had gotten there twenty minutes early and had already bought her favorite tea for her, figuring the gesture might help break the tension. I had gotten her caffeine-free Earl Grey that was still steaming as she marched over.

With a voice that would make the North Pole seem like the tropics, she said, "Hello Julia."

Did I expect any more from her? Did I really think she was going to hug me, give me a kiss on the cheek, and say, "All is forgiven sweetie?"

Of course not; this was my mother, after all, and even if we hadn't fought two weeks ago, that would be as likely as her admitting fault in anything she had ever done. She greeted me formally, coldly, and looked me up and down. I knew she was giving me the once-over; judging my outfit, looking to see if I had makeup on, analyzing if I had put on weight, and looking for something, anything to use as ammunition. At one point in time, I bet she had consciously made an effort to do it whenever she met anyone new, but now it was so engrained in her psyche that it was as natural to her as blinking.

She was furrowing her eyebrows, tensing the corners of her lips, and even through her thickly applied makeup, I could see the tension lines under her eyes. I could say she had laugh lines, but that would mean that she would have had to have laughed and smiled her whole life, a far cry from reality. She was still standing next to the table with her arms folded, and judging by her expression, she was still in a deep sulk. Saying that she was still angry with me would have been an understatement, but I had promised myself that I would make peace with her despite whatever she said. More importantly, I had promised Dad, and I would not renege.

I took a big breath and said, "Hello, Mother, please take a seat," because unlike the rest of society, my mother actually required a formal invitation to sit down with her own daughter.

The chairs were a heavy, solid wood, and as Mother pulled out the one across from me, it scraped on the rustic tile like chalk on a blackboard. She sat down and quickly looked up with eyes that bore right into me.

I pressed on. "I got you some tea, Mother, Earl Grey, and there's honey in it instead of sugar, just the way you like it."

She looked down at the tall, black mug and the tail of the tea-bag string sticking out, and I saw a brief break in her exterior. Without touching the tea, she sat back, crossed her legs, and folded her arms. She hadn't let go of her purse and was gripping it like she would be leaving at any second. She half-looked at me, keeping her head turned ever so slightly to the side. Her eyes darted from me to the surrounding tables, pretending to be more interested in what was going on at the table next to us, making a point of letting me know she was being forced to be here. She was only gracing me with her presence because she had to, and she was doing everything in her power to let me know it.

I decided to start, because if I waited for any sign of warmth from her, I would be waiting until hell froze over. About the only positive thing about her current mood was that whenever she was like this, which seldom happened, it was one of the few times anyone could actually get a word in without her interrupting. So I decided to use it to my advantage, and to say what I needed to say.

"Mother, our last conversation was terrible, and I wanted to start out by apologizing."

She turned her head to face me and I knew I had her full attention. It was good that I had started with a concession; I had obviously planned it well. This was going to be extremely difficult, but there was no way around it.

"If I hurt your feelings or upset you, I'm sorry for that. It definitively got out of control, and I wish what I had said had come out in a more constructive manner. But it didn't."

Mother reached over to her teacup and placed her hand around it. I could see she had just gotten her nails done, and the red nail polish matched her outfit perfectly.

I controlled my voice, and in as calm a tone as I could manage, I continued. "Mother, those were some pretty deep-seated feelings that had been bottled up in me for thirty years, and as much as I wish they could have come out differently, they didn't. So I apologize if I hurt your feelings by the manner in which I chose to express them."

I had conceded by actually saying I was sorry, but she realized that it was only an apology of methodology and not of content.

She still was in her silent mode, and her hand pulled away from her tea and her back suddenly stiffened. Obviously, my apology wasn't satisfactory to her, but before she had the opportunity to get offended or to get up to go, I continued.

"Mother, I don't want to fight with you anymore, and I don't want you to be mad at me. I don't want us to hurt each other; I'm sick of it. More importantly, this thing between us has to be in the background or buried for now; it can't be the center of all of our lives with what Dad's going through. We can't be doing this; it's not good for you, it's not good for me, but mainly, it's terrible for Dad. I know you can see how much of a toll it's taking on him, Mother, and for his sake, we need to resolve this. We need to end this, no matter what happens, for Dad."

I knew that mentioning and repeating Dad was the only thing capable of breaking through her sulking exoskeleton, and as expected, her expression finally softened. Her shoulders relaxed, and she put both of her elbows on the table. To my utter amazement, she put her left hand to her forehead and started massaging her temples with her index finger and thumb.

She looked very old to me then, and I just sat there, waiting for her to respond. I wondered if that had been enough for her, contemplated whether she wanted to hear me grovel, or if what I had said had gotten through. Was this all it was going to take?

She stopped massaging her forehead and looked up at me with the defiant expression only toddlers and their mothers could pull off. She didn't look old anymore, and suddenly I felt my stomach drop. This was going to be rough. I needed to shut up and let her talk; no matter what she said, I needed to be quiet.

Her voice was artificially calm, measured, and I had the feeling that she had rehearsed this speech.

"Julia, let me start out by reminding you that you are my daughter, my own flesh and blood, the girl I went through labor with for ten excruciating, nonmedicated hours, and despite how vindictive or rude you are, I will always love you."

After that opening, I sat back in my chair, took a deep breath, and readied myself for the next barrage. Besides the F word, *wow* was the only other thing that came to my mind.

"I've been doing a lot of thinking since your tantrum, and I've reached some conclusions. The main thing your little outburst showed me is that after you moved away to college, you obviously developed a variety of emotional issues and psychological problems. As to the causes or reasons why you are the way you are, that I cannot fathom or even begin to understand, and I definitely won't attempt to justify them. I know that your father and I, especially me, did everything for you as a child; provided you with a great education, taught you nothing but the best values, and gave you an upbringing that can only be described as one step away from perfection. Therefore, I have concluded that this anger, this emotional instability, this weakness, can only be attributed to the outside influences of your confounding generation. The only other option, dear, is that you have something inherently wrong with your personality, because as a mother, I have given you nothing but the best."

I felt the anger burning, searing, and I thought I would spontaneously combust. I did everything I could to control myself; mentally timed every breath while the poison-tipped sentences flew by. I had to let her finish; I had to fight the urge to yell back at her. The woman was in utter denial.

She leaned over again and reached for her tea, like a hawk zeroing in on its prey. Picking up the cup with four fingers, because she insisted on extending her pinky like the Queen of England, she swirled it three times around, releasing a wisp of steam before she went on.

"This generation is a very troubled one. It makes me so angry that everyone feels the need to put the blame on someone else for his or her own problems. You know, in my day, we were stronger, more responsible, and we would never need a therapist to solve anything. We took responsibility for our own issues; we resolved them with a strength that is utterly lacking in your contemporaries. If we needed advice, then naturally we would turn to our parents. If we needed help with a problem, again, we would turn to our parents. That's how it was done, Julia; that's what they were there for, to guide, to teach, and to offer advice. But Julia, you always thought you knew better."

I was literally biting my lip to keep quiet; the woman was certifiably crazy, but I wouldn't give in to the demons begging me to interrupt and yell at her at the top of my lungs.

She paused to take a small sip of her tea, and a thought suddenly occurred to me. Maybe she was just being spiteful, knowing that I would just sit here and take it, fully aware that I would do anything for Dad. Was this her way of getting in the last word from our fight?

She was right about one thing, though; I would sit here no matter what she threw at me and take it. I wouldn't give her the satisfaction of drawing me in, give her an excuse to go back to Dad and play the saint who went out of her way to make peace with her ungrateful, horrible daughter who only wanted to fight and disrespect her even more. Woe is me, woe is me!

No, I wouldn't let it go that way; I wouldn't do that to Dad. So I just sat there, face expressionless, waiting for her to be done.

After realizing I had nothing to say, she continued. "Julia, I won't begin to tell you how much heartbreak you caused me that day. To hear you raise your voice like that, show me that much disrespect, my own daughter no less; it was like a knife in my back being twisted around and around. Young lady, I would never have spoken to my mother like that; never. And never would I have upset her by thinking I could converse with her as if she were my equal. It was not appropriate, Julia, definitely not appropriate."

Her ice-cold eyes stared at me, daring me to answer, but I wouldn't be drawn in.

She paused again, seeing whether I had taken the bait, but I still didn't respond. She seemed more satisfied now, and her demeanor had softened, pacified by her presumed victory. She was taking advantage of this apology, all right, but I had made a promise.

"Julia, I won't beat a dead horse, but I have to say that I don't pretend to like it or accept it."

She took another sip of her tea, and as much as I hoped that she was done or would choke on it going down, I could see she wasn't finished talking yet. At least her sulking seemed to be over, though, and with every sip of tea, she became bolder.

Mother readjusted her chair, attempting to move it closer to the table. The chairs at this place were too tall to fit under the solid tables, and as the arms of her chair made contact, the table rocked. I was purposefully staying as still as humanly possible because I feared that if I moved, I might actually become violent.

And so she went on, now with a casual tone to her voice, like we were discussing the weather or some other harmless topic. It was usually that tone that cut the deepest, and I braced myself for what was to come.

Like a practiced assassin, she continued. "I won't deny how troubled I was to find out that you are seeing a psychologist. In my day, that was something we kept very private. It was never brought up, especially not in public. You don't know how much harm that could do to a family's reputation. Oh, of course you don't, dear. How could you; it's beyond you."

She put down her tea and leaned forward, then quickly glanced to the left and right, as if she was concerned about someone hearing what she was going to say next. With her elbows resting on the hard table, she said in a low and feeble attempt at a compassionate tone, "You know, you could have come to me for help."

I did everything in my power not to choke down laughter then, but the rage that was flowing within me allowed me to keep a straight face.

"I am always here for you, dear, like any good mother would be."

She straightened up, and her voice returned to her normal, grating tone, "That is my role, after all. But if you insist on keeping to your stubborn ways, I will take some consolation in the fact that this person, this psychologist, is helping you to correct your problems. But Julia, I should have been the person to whom you turned."

I couldn't believe it. I was flabbergasted, floored, and completely stunned, although I knew I shouldn't have been. My lip was a millimeter away from bleeding, my teeth were biting down so hard, and I had lost feeling in both of my hands from clenching my fists so tight. My face betrayed no emotion, though; at least there I had won. I had succeeded in keeping quiet through her barrage of insults and denials, and at least she was talking to me. That was headway.

Didn't she get it, though? Had she not heard a single thing that day? She was the cause of my problems, her, Mrs. Come-to-me-for-help-because-I'm-the-perfect-mother. She was the entire reason I was in therapy. And the worst part about it was that in no way whatsoever had she acknowledged her role in all of this, her responsibility. Hell, she was so incredibly self-absorbed that the thought of her having done anything wrong was beyond her. I was upset, mad, frustrated, and my only consolation was that I was doing this for Dad.

I remembered my conversation with Kirsten after that last battle with my mother. I had called her right after, and being the professional she was, she had fit me right in for an emergency appointment.

I had sat on the clichéd black therapy couch across from her and sunk into its warming embrace. It was a couch that had absorbed years of personal trauma and supported many a person who had been trying to reassemble the pieces of life's shattered moments. Kirsten had sat across from me on her blue La-Z-Boy, a woman in her late fifties weathered with the wisdom of a master.

After I had unleashed my frustration at the events earlier that day, and before chiming in with sage advice, Kirsten had given me a paper cup of water. She'd waited for me to finish and held out the small plastic wastebasket for me to throw in the white, triangular cup.

"Julia, let's start by saying that, by the sound of it, it was a very rough day for you. But there was definitely a positive side to it. I'm glad you finally got to say what you said, albeit probably not in the best venue in which to communicate with her. What I want to add is that it's a very challenging time for you with your Dad, and that was probably what pushed this to the surface.

"Julia, you mother is a narcissist. You know that, and we have discussed in detail exactly what that means. In our sessions so far, I also have, hopefully, given you some tools to deal with in your relationship with her. The positive—and I always look for the positive—is that as hard as it may seem, this was a breakthrough for you. With your mother the way she is, she will never acknowledge fault in this or practically anything else, because frankly, she can't admit that she did anything wrong. It's beyond her; the ego dominates with her. She ignores that nagging voice we find in ourselves that forces us to claim responsibility for our actions. In fact, I wouldn't be surprised if she found some way to blame this fight on some exterior factor, such as your father, your mood, or any event she can think of to which to shift responsibility away from her."

As always, she had my complete and entire attention. A moment earlier, I had glanced past her to the wall clock directly above and behind her head, and the black roman numerals faded into the background of a large yellow rooster. It had been 2:28 P.M., and I was amazed that I had been speaking to her for twenty-eight minutes. It was like that whenever I had an appointment; time just flew by. Her office was small, about fifteen by fifteen feet, and the only furniture was Kirsten's La-Z-Boy, the black couch, and a desk. The only decorations were two black-framed prints of Paris on the light-blue walls: the Arc de Triomph on one side and the Eiffel Tower on the other. It wasn't a brightly lit room; there was more of a soft, dim light that was very soothing. It was easy to open up in this room, to divulge things you would never tell anyone else.

Kirsten went on. "But Julia, what I want you to remember is that you didn't have the conversation for her sake; it was for your sake. And now, now, you can finally move on. Even if your mother didn't internalize a single thing you said, even if she didn't comprehend one iota of what you put out there, at least you spoke your peace. You were strong and you stood up for yourself. You can put your fear of being helpless against her behind you now and be assured that you're not the weak person you have labeled yourself to be. This fight will be a positive thing in the long run, and what I want you to be proud of is that you succeeded in having the 'difficult conversation.'"

I stared blankly at my mother as Kirsten's words replayed in my head and felt myself starting to relax. She had prepared me for this meeting; she'd made sure to tell me what she thought might happen.

"Julia, don't expect an apology, and don't be surprised if this turns into something about her. She won't admit playing a part in your emotional past because that would mean that she actually had made mistakes. That would mean admitting she wasn't the perfect mother, and it would deflate her self-perception. Don't be surprised if she insults you, because by the sound of your last conversation you left her with her ego bruised. I bet she tries repairing that ego, and unfortunately, I would expect her method to involve insulting you. She's like a little child; you insulted her, so she needs to insult you back worse. Just be prepared, Julia. I hope I'm wrong and it doesn't happen that way."

She was right, of course, and this conversation came as no surprise to me. So rather than continue to be angry with her, and let her get the better of me by inciting me, I decided to let it go and move on. Anger transformed into amusement as I pictured my mother as a crazy four-year-old, waving her hands and screaming, "You hit me first." I managed to keep a straight face, though.

Mom paused again, searching for a response, an acknowledgment, a validation of her feelings. All I did was nod my head once, leaving it up to her to take it any way she wanted to.

Her voice softened, and this time I sensed a genuine change in her. This was the mother who, after hours of frustration, would actually say something semimotherly. Usually by this time, though, she had screwed it up so much that it fell on deaf ears. But finally, after I had endured ten minutes of her insults, she said something intelligent. "Julia, I don't want to fight with you either. I'm your mother; why would I ever want to fight with you? You're my daughter, my family."

If she had stopped there, it would have been more than I could ever have asked for, but being my mother, she had to talk about herself even more. She just couldn't help it.

"Julia, I never fought with my mother, bless her soul, and I always listened to her. Even if she had said that the earth was flat, I would never have contradicted her because I loved her. I love you, dear, more than you will ever know. You're my daughter and I only want the best for you. It hurts me to see you so upset. You know, dear, you're more right than you know."

Wait; could I believe my ears, was she actually going to admit fault? A *huh* escaped my lips.

"I also can't bear to see your father like he is. It's tearing me apart. It's so difficult for me."

Nope. I didn't think so.

She went on. "My world is unraveling at the seams. I feel like I'm being torn in two, and I wonder how I'm ever going to go on. It's so hard to see him have bad days and Julia, they're becoming more common than the good. He won't admit it to you, but I see how he is. He's in pain, and the last thing I need is for him to worry about this, something as minor as this tiff between us."

As crazy as it sounds, as much as my mother had just directly insulted me, delegitimizing my feelings with that last sentence, negating the gravity of our conversation and minimizing my deep-seated issues toward her, I actually felt a small pang of pity for the nutcase. It was minor, but it was there nonetheless.

This was her husband, after all, and no matter what had transpired between them all those years ago, they had forgiven each other and had reconnected their relationship. It was obvious that they loved each other, and as much as she would deny it, she really depended on Dad. As hard as it was for me to see him like this, I couldn't imagine what my mother was going through.

She picked up her tea again and took another sip. The rest of the meeting was uneventful. We talked about Dad and his medications for the next fifteen minutes. Actually, she talked, and I mainly spent the time listening, back to the status quo. It seemed that everything had been put aside for now, and I think that was the closest to an apology I'll ever get from her.

95

JULIA
APRIL 2008

Over the last ten years, I had spoken to my mother at most about once a month, not to mention birthdays and holidays. I've usually limited it to small talk and never delved into anything more serious than what I was making for dinner. And even that subject I approached with kid gloves. I avoided talking about myself because I didn't want to give her the opportunity for any further criticism, and frankly, she had always done most of the talking anyway. Conversations usually went on for hours, and to this day, I haven't found an effective way to limit them, much to the chagrin of my therapist.

"The best way to deal with a diagnosed narcissist is to limit your time with them if they aren't good for you. Luckily, your mother isn't an extreme case, but to avoid arguments, I agree with your current communication patterns. Your situation could be a lot worse; at least there are no kids thrown into the mix. You know that in some cases, for the sake of the children, we sometimes advise that the kids have little-to-no contact with the narcissist, especially if the exposure to that person is going to be damaging to them.

"The thing to remember, though, is that to truly get past this, to have a relationship that works for you, there have to be limits and boundaries. It ultimately means that at some point—when you're ready, of course—you're going to have to disallow certain behaviors that are an impediment to your relationship with her.

"Now I don't need to tell you this, but she won't take it well. In fact, anything that challenges her behavior or limits her actions will be viewed as a personal insult to her, an affront to her own image of her self-perfection. But that's where you need to be strong, and, hopefully, the transition will be smooth. Don't be surprised, though, if it leads to a disagreement, and from what you've told me about your mother, she'll probably sulk and not speak to you for a prolonged period of time. It may take a while for her to get over it, and I'm confident it won't be a one-time thing either. Be prepared to set rules for different situations with her, and make sure to verbalize what is acceptable and nonacceptable behavior for you. That's what it's going to take to build a new foundation with her. That is, only if you truly want your relationship to change.

"Julia, throughout our sessions together, you've told me that you do want to continue to have a relationship with your mother, but it's not healthy for you to have it on these terms. I don't recommend it."

Well, I hadn't got to the setting-boundaries-and-limitations part with Mother yet, but after the apology, at least I was on speaking terms with her again. There was now a peaceful understanding between us.

I had long ago given up on the dream of a mother who was more like a best friend than an authority figure. Mother, unfortunately, had not completely given up on the fantasy of a daughter who blindly obeyed her, unconditionally respected her, and took her word as law. We were very different people, and our relationship in the past had been strained, to say the least. It had taken years to come to a mutual understanding as to how not to fight. Those were hard lessons to learn, peppered with years of bickering and, at times, not speaking for months on end.

After our most recent brawl and my subsequent apology however, things had finally shifted between my mother and me. As Dad had started to become weaker and his condition deteriorated, both Mother and I found ourselves in a situation in which we were forced to reach out to each other. Dad hadn't shown any signs of the cancer spread and I was under the impression he never would. For the first time in over thirty years and with my feelings about the past out in the open, I found myself speaking to Mother nearly every day.

It developed into a symbiotic relationship. I desperately needed to know how Dad was doing, and she longed for the support of family. Both of our needs increased as he continued to decline. At least I had David, but given that I was an only child and lived less than twenty minutes away from my parents, I was her only natural choice. She did have a sister and a brother, but they were far away.

It's a good thing she had siblings, because I couldn't handle her alone. The ironic thing is that she had made it abundantly clear in one of her many rants and calls for attention last year, that if anything were to happen to him, she would move in with her sister. Aunt Jilly lived in Florida and had lost her husband five years earlier. She lived alone in a three-bedroom house right across the street from a golf course, which she visited on a regular basis.

Mother had said in one of her long, drawn-out diatribes, "I wouldn't want to be a burden, Julia. I know how irritable you get. You never did keep a friendly countenance, you always look angry, and personally, I don't think I could be around that all the time. You know, dear, that's probably why you're wrinkling so early in life. But on a more important note, I wouldn't want to be a strain on you or David. If your father passed and I was left alone, I know exactly what I'd do. I would sell everything: all my memories, all of my belongings, everything that is dear to me. The furniture . . ."

I had blanked out but still managed to bite my tongue over the wrinkle comment, and after she had listed pretty much everything but the kitchen sink, she finished with the coup de gráce: "I would do that, because I know that she would be happy to have me live with her."

It was meant to elicit guilt, a response, and a plea for me to beg her to please live with me instead, if that hypothetical situation ever happened. But little did she know how much truth there was to her words. I chose to ignore the comment that day, not wanting to give in to her cry for attention, and had curtly told her that nothing was going to happen to Dad, but the conversation was burned into my memory.

Our relationship now, though, had finally changed for the better after my "apology." It had a lot to do with the situation in which we found ourselves. Mother and I were meeting each other's needs in part because she was making an extra effort to be on her best behavior with me, and I, in turn, had continued in my role of providing the strength necessary for her to get through this.

Sure, our conversations felt extremely artificial, but it was the closest to a good relationship with her that I had had in years. I kept positive in our conversations, always speaking in terms of Dad getting better. I never cried, never gave up hope, and never talked of anything but recovery. I was so blinded by my confidence and so convinced that Dad would beat this that Mom couldn't help but gain strength from me.

My therapist had been right, after all, and with the traumatic events of my childhood finally out in the open, I felt a sense of closure. I could move on, I could deal with Mother without the deep, dark guilt that had haunted me all these years. Our new relationship wasn't perfect—I knew it never would be—but at least it was semifunctional.

96

JULIA
APRIL 2008

David and I continued our routine of visiting Dad every Sunday, and it was six weeks after he finished chemotherapy and four weeks after learning it had failed and spread to his lungs and spine that things took a turn for the worse. We were seated around the dark brown mahogany dining-room table, which was polished to a shine, as expected. Not like we would actually get to enjoy the view, since Mom had put a large, maroon tablecloth over it; heaven forbid the table should be exposed to a potential scratch. She had even put the table pad underneath, like the dice were really going to leave an indentation. Right before we sat down, she had insisted on reminding us to be careful, and that she would let us play here just this once. She made sure to point out that this room was usually reserved for "special guests," but she would "make an exception" for us this time.

We were in the middle of a game of Monopoly, and I had gotten lucky and landed on a yet unpurchased Park Place. I had the cash and bought it immediately, and it seemed I was moving up in the world. I had just finished paying Dad, who was always the bank, and he suddenly winced in pain as he leaned back into his chair. The curved Queen Anne hardwood-backed seats with the cream-colored cushions still looked beautiful, which wasn't surprising, since Mom never let anyone use them, but they were as uncomfortable as hell to sit on. They offered little-to-no back support, which must have taken a toll on Dad.

He had been grumpy and quiet ever since we started the game thirty minutes earlier, and I had thought he was getting upset at not rolling good numbers, but it all made sense now. He was gritting his teeth by the time he stood up. He winced again as he rose and steadied himself by driving a fist into his lower back.

All conversation had stopped, and we were staring at Dad. The room was quiet, and the silence was deafening, infused with an unspoken concern that threatened the tenuous reprieve of Dad not showing signs of his disease. The cancer had loomed in the background these last couple of weeks, and although never mentioned outright, it had hidden in the shadows, just waiting to leap out.

David broke the silence, asking Dad if he was okay. It wasn't a question but more of a statement of concern, and it at least broke the tension in the room.

Realizing all eyes were on him, he steadied his expression, put on his best face, and waved David off by saying, "I'm just a little stiff, you guys, nothing serious. I am old, you know."

He was trying to hide his pain, but it was written all over his face. He had an ever-so-slight tremble in his lower eyelid and his mouth was pulled closed so tight, it was amazing he had been able to pry it open to speak. His voice had been higher than usual, and it was obvious he was doing his best to sound happy, which only made it sound even more serious.

He continued, "Come to think of it, I'm a little tired all of a sudden. Do you guys mind if I sit this one out? I think I'll rest a bit, try to take a nap. Go ahead and finish without me."

And with that, I knew that something was terribly wrong. My concern had to do with what he had just said because it was so out of character for Dad. I would never have thought it possible for him to mouth that sentence. His Monopoly stamina was a long-standing joke in our family, and he was basically still undefeated; nobody counted that one time David had beaten him eight years ago. Dad had been five whiskeys to the wind and had still managed to give David a run for his money.

I had been unconsciously clutching the maroon tablecloth and suddenly became aware of the overstarched cotton pressed between my fingers. I looked down and realized that my fingers were white from squeezing the fabric so hard. I turned to Mom, because the lady had extra human senses for picking up things that involve dirt, laundry, or damaging furniture, and I knew that I would get a mouthful for putting wrinkles in the fabric if she saw it being handled the wrong way. But Mom hadn't noticed the tablecloth; she was following Dad with her eyes as he rounded the corner into the hallway. Her face was pale under her layers of makeup, her lips were slightly open to mouth an inaudible groan, and she was breathing hard. She looked both concerned and terrified at the same time.

David again broke the silence and got up to get a drink, asking Mom if she wanted something from the kitchen while he was there. She absently shook her head and turned to me, jerking her eyes down at the newly wrinkled finger marks on the tablecloth and then looked up. Instead of the judgmental, annoyed, and condescending tone that usually was sure to follow after I had committed so heinous a crime, her expression remain unchanged. She didn't say a thing, which unnerved me even more. She quickly turned to look back at the hallway, her eyes reaching out to be in the same room as Dad.

I knew she wanted to check on him, but she was so stuck up about appearances that she would never say a word. She would never drop an unrealistic, self-imposed façade, even to me, her own daughter, her flesh and blood, and it bugged me to no end. It had always bothered me.

Her expression, though, the purity of her features, which screamed with concern, that had gotten to me, and I genuinely felt for her. She actually managed to pierce through the apathy that had built up over so many years, and stirred something in me that I thought had been long dead. So I gave her an out. As much as I also wanted to go check on Dad, I knew he would despise being the center of attention.

"Mom, I think we're going to go a little early today. I forgot that I have a bunch of things to do still. I hope you don't mind."

When I checked in with Mom the next day, she didn't have her usual arrogant, sharp tone, but rather sounded tired. Her voice was hoarse and worn, as if gravel had gotten caught in her throat. After telling me just how tired she was, that she hadn't had a minute of sleep, how she wasn't as energetic as she used to be, and that someone like me could never have the stamina to deal with what she was going through, she finally gave me the update on Dad.

I bit my tongue because I just wanted to hear how he was doing and I didn't feel like any more drama. She told me that Dad had been tossing and turning all night, that he hadn't been able to get comfortable. Even though he had objected, insisted that it would pass, she planned on dragging him to the doctor today.

Good for you, Mom, I thought to myself; at least her personality would come in handy for something.

Then, true to Mom style, she said something only that woman could manage.

"Julia, as I told you, dear, I am not as young as I used to be, although Angie—you know, my friend from book club—told me that both you and I look close enough in age these days that we could be twins."

I knew who Angie was, her old crony who had had more work done to her than should be legal.

"Anyway, I need your father to sleep because frankly, I need at least seven hours of straight sleep at night. I'm going to insist that they give him something, anything, to keep him knocked out. I can't do another night like last night."

97

JULIA
MAY 2008

Nothing had worked, and here I was. The Percocet, the Neurontin, the Fentanyl patch; none of it had lasted very long. Sure, he would have a day or two in which he could steal a couple of hours of sleep, but the pain ultimately broke through. He was in so much agony, so much so that despite his best efforts, he couldn't hide it. He didn't want us to see him this way, but he had no choice.

Mother needed the help, and besides, I wanted to be there for him and, surprisingly, for her too. I wanted to spend as much time as I could with him and had been over to their house every day that week while he had attempted to take it easy in bed. He hadn't been able to get comfortable, and I had made daily trips to the pharmacy for new types of drugs to help with the pain.

The house was the messiest I had ever seen it, with a stack of unopened mail left on the dining-room table and mail-order catalogs, house keys and untouched newspapers scattered on the floor. There were unwashed dishes in the sink, and the trash had been allowed to fill over halfway. In all my life, I had never seen anything out of place in my parents' house, and any form of dirt was never tolerated. In fact, if plastic furniture covers weren't "tacky," according to Mother, there wouldn't have been a single inch of exposed material to be seen. She kept a house that was clean to a fault; everything had its place and, according to her, her outrageous standards were normal, while everyone else on earth "lived in dirt."

It had spread. There were multiple bones involved now, and his lungs had numerous nodules. The cancer's sinister and ravenous appetite was impossible to satisfy. It needed new victims, new organs, and its hunger was never ending.

I have learned to hate calls that come after 10 P.M. at night because they're never good. It's either one of three things: a wrong number, a drunken prank caller, or bad news. Unfortunately, when Mother called me that night, or should I say that morning, it was with bad news.

"Julia, this is your mother."

My mother; no kidding, as if I hadn't been able to see the caller ID on the phone once it had started ringing. As if I couldn't pick out her grating voice in a crowded room, let alone a one-on-one phone call. As if I hadn't been listening to that same calculating voice for the last thirty-five years. Of course it was my mother; why the heck did she always have to treat me like a perfect stranger? It was so annoying!

She started out by stuttering, "I . . . I . . . I'm so sorry to wake you up, but I don't know what to do. Your father's in so much agony . . ."

She was interrupted by a wail in the background, a high-pitched sound that, to my horror, I suspected was probably coming from Dad. My loathing of her instantly forgotten, I jerked awake. I hoped that I had misheard the sound and it had really been coming from their TV, but in the next moment it happened again. This time I knew for sure it was Dad; he had yelled, no, screamed out her name.

"I'm so sorry, but Julia, I need help . . ."

She didn't finish the sentence because the tears took over. My mother, of all the people in the world, was completely losing it cn the phone with me, and it shook me to the core. Here I was, in bed, at one in the morning, half asleep, with Mother having a real-life breakdown and, worse yet, my father screaming in pain.

It was dark in my bedroom and David was still fast asleep. The dull red glow of the LED screen on the phone was the only light available, and my reflection in the dresser mirror was horrific. I looked like a skeleton, with dark silhouetted eye sockets accentuated by the long shadows of my cheekbones.

I couldn't freak out. I had to stay calm, and it took every ounce of control for me to say what came out of my mouth next without breaking down myself.

"Mother, just try to calm down, we'll be there in twenty minutes. Just hang tight."

I hung up the phone and violently shook David's shoulder to wake him up.

98

JULIA
JUNE 2008

Why is it that every hospital I've ever been in has chosen to make their wall colors either pink, baby blue, or a pastel cream white in some misguided attempt to pretend the place is *soothing*? And why are the bedsheets always light colors, especially given what lands on them? I can understand the economics of attempting to maximize the use of bleach, but trying to pretend that hospitals are anything but a place for sick or hurt people is just plain obnoxious.

And why do they all smell the same? It's that stale disinfectant smell, deceptively meant to make the place clean, but in reality, it really just chokes the senses and gives you an overriding feeling of claustrophobia. It's always confused the living hell out of me, and I'm convinced that all the hospital CEOs got together one day and decided to use the same lunatic designer, who had the erroneous impression that pastel colors were meant to evoke a feeling of serenity for the masses. Well, I'm not the stereotypical person, and oh, how I hate pink walls!

Mother couldn't stop crying, and David was taking care of her while I took charge of Dad's care. She was a mess. I had finally officially met Dad's oncologist for the first time that day. Circumstances had not afforded him a good impression, and I loathed him for what he had said. It had been a long night.

We had been in the emergency room for four hours before being transferred to a box of an excuse of a room. It was a Saturday night, and thank goodness we had avoided being stuffed in the waiting room too long. It had been packed, and for the ten minutes they forced us to wait while we filled out Dad's paperwork, I had felt like a cow being corralled. I counted at least five different people who were coughing, there was a baby crying, and there was a drunk woman, holding a half-filled Styrofoam cup of coffee, pacing back and forth. And that was just on our side of the lobby. It was surreal, and it was the last thing we needed right then.

The receptionist took one look at Dad and bumped us to the front of the line. After we got to the room, we managed to get Dad to lie down on a cold, plastic hospital bed that had only one lonely thin sheet on it. I found two blankets on the ledge above his bed, but Dad threw them off as a wave of pain hit. The emergency-room doctor had appeared shortly thereafter. She looked to be fresh out of medical school, a woman barely in her thirties, and had spoken a million miles an hour. She was short, a little fat, and moved unnervingly fast for her size. She spent a total of ten hurried minutes with us, and as she tried to leave, I insisted she call Dad's oncologist for advice. I didn't care what time of the morning it was. She was offended, but I didn't give a damn, and I hadn't seen her since. Whether she made the call or not I never did find out, but at least Dad was admitted, scarecrow-thin cream-colored sheets, pink walls, and all.

Dad's oncologist was a short man in his fifties with glasses and a receding hairline. His white laboratory coat was wrinkled, and there were blue lines above his left front pocket, where he had obviously forgotten to recap his pen. He had finally seen us toward twelve in the afternoon. The young ER doctor had at least done something right and had ordered them to have Dad hooked up to an IV drip. The drugs they were giving him had worked, thank goodness, and he was mostly unconscious. He would wake up about every forty-five minutes in a haze, murmuring incoherently before passing out again. Unfortunately, not before he gave out a moan of agony.

"Mrs. Freed, I'm so sorry, but there's nothing more we can do. You have a couple of choices at this point. We can keep him here, hooked up to his current drugs, or the other option is one I've discussed at length with your dad. In fact, it was his preference, and he had already set up the arrangements. That was to spend his remaining time at home in hospice care."

I couldn't help it; at that moment the only thing I wanted to do was to hit the man.

"I am so sorry, Mrs. Freed. I wish there was something more we could do."

So it was official. I had been hoping for some kind of miracle, and I had convinced myself that I wasn't in denial, that everyone around me just didn't know Dad, or what he was capable of. He was strong, he was a fighter, and he was meant to get through this. Even up until this very moment, some part of me had believed that this was just a minor setback, that at any moment he would snap out of it and the pain would go away. I had refused to listen to anyone around me who would say different. I know now that it was ludicrous to think that way, but it made perfect sense to me at the time.

I spent a long time just staring at the pink wall while my mind was being forced to internalize the situation. I had refused to do it before, dismissing it as being negative and a waste of time.

Mom had accepted it, David had accepted it, and Dad had long ago accepted it. I, however, as crazy as it sounds, I still had not come to terms with the reality of the situation.

But now I forced myself to do so, even if I didn't entirely believe it. I had to do what Dad wanted. It was then and for the first time that I actually said it, whispered it, forced it to finally be verbalized. In a soft voice, I said it out loud.

"Dad won't get better."

I told myself that my father was going to die and there was absolutely nothing I could do about it. I could hear myself; I knew what I was thinking, but why was there such a disconnect? I should be crying like my mother, unable to think straight.

But I wasn't.

I was still in reaction mode, and without any emotion, I turned to Mother, who was curled up on a dark gray plastic chair next to Dad's bed, squeezing his hand. I had to find out the name of the hospice company I needed to call.

THE DOG DAYS OF THE PRESENT

99

JULIA
JUNE 2009

This day couldn't come soon enough because I had been at my wit's end with how things had been going of late. Eddie had been a zombie from all of the drugs and had basically spent the last couple of days sleeping the whole time, and his shoulder . . . well, it looked like someone had taken a blowtorch to it. It was red and shiny and to say it appeared irritated would be like describing my mother as mildly unpleasant. As much as Dr. Lindy had tried to describe how bad it would look, it turned out to be worse.

David had been on edge as well, and as much as I would like to think that it was because of what was going on with Eddie, I knew it was because of me. He had kept giving me that are-you-stable-or-are-you-going-to-have-a-nervous-breakdown look, and as sweet and caring as his concern for me was, it had grown to be annoying. It seemed that little Paris had been the only happy one in our household.

Dr. Lindy and I were meeting in the same exam room as our first appointment about a month earlier. It seemed like so much time had passed since the last time I had been seated on the same plastic chair, waiting for him to start speaking. So much had happened since that first day, and I felt like an entirely different person from that angry and unstable woman I had been just a short while ago. Although I hated seeing Eddie like this and had been worried sick about the radiation side effects, overall I think I was a lot more at peace. I felt calm, happy, and the ghosts that had haunted me after my father's death had finally been put to rest. Debbie, Roy, Jennie, Shirley, and especially David had played a large part in helping me achieve that, and I couldn't imagine how I would've made it this far without their help.

Today was Eddie's official discharge appointment, at which Dr. Lindy was meant to go over some final things about Eddie and what to expect from here on out. I didn't know what else he could possibly tell me, though, because I had been picking his brain nearly every day for the last week. I thought I had heard just about everything there was to do with radiation side effects and how they were going to get better ad nauseam.

Dr. Lindy was sitting on the chair directly across from me, close enough for me to see some gray specs starting to appear on his well-groomed face. His lab coat was a bright, shiny, and wrinkle-free, and, like always, it looked like it had just come back from the dry cleaner.

"Well, it's finally graduation day for Eddie. You must be so relieved," he said in his slow, melodic cadence.

I couldn't help but smile and nod because he had hit the nail on the head. I didn't have time to answer before he continued. "I think Eddie has done very well throughout therapy, and as you have heard me say all this last week, he obviously has developed acute radiation side effects to the site. The good news is that they're no worse than I expected. I know it will be hard to believe what I'm going to say next, but since you've trusted me over the last month with your boy, I hope you'll internalize this."

Dr. Lindy had my full attention now.

"Although his shoulder is red and inflamed, it will get better, Mrs. Freed. In about two and a half weeks' time, it should be completely healed. Now, my main question for you is whether his pain was still well controlled yesterday. Did he sleep through last night?"

Eddie's pain level had been tolerable because he had slept like a log, snoring loud enough that David had wanted to move him out of our room. I had forced David to put in a pair of wax earplugs instead because there was no way in hell I was going to have Eddie sleep in the hall. David also knew me well enough to realize that if he had asked again, he would have been downstairs on the couch faster than the time it would have taken to form the sentence.

"Yes, he seems to be more comfortable; in fact, I think he's a little too comfortable right now. It's very disconcerting to see him like this because all he does is lie around all day and sleep; it's very unlike him. It's not my Eddie, and like I told you two days ago, I'm worried that he won't ever get back to his normal self."

Dr. Lindy nodded understandingly and stroked his chin before he answered. "His grogginess and drowsiness are a positive thing in my book, Mrs. Freed. In fact, it's the exact level of sedation I was aiming for. I'd rather he be sleepy and not feeling much than vice versa. Please take my word for it that he'll be back to his normal self as soon as I discontinue his current drug regimen. Now, let's talk about what to expect over the next week. The thing to keep in mind is that the radiation side effects may get worse before they start to get better. . . ."

He had said that before, but hearing it out loud again made my stomach turn.

He saw my reaction and quickly continued, "It's not always the case, but I don't want you to have any surprises."

I nodded and did my best to keep a straight face, desperately attempting to hide the wave of panic that had just engulfed me. I knew it was irrational because I had heard this countless times from Roy, Jennie, and Shirley as their animals had finished up, and Dr. Lindy had repeated it on numerous occasions. I couldn't help my feelings, though.

In all the time I'd interacted with Dr. Lindy, despite his hypnotic and calming voice, he had always told me the worst-case scenarios, and as professional as he had been and despite his reassurances, I wondered if he could have been just a little more positive. I knew the answer had to be no; it had been his job to prepare me for the worst, but a small part of me had hoped that I would hear that Eddie would be fine and heal completely over the next couple of days with no problems or complications.

Dr. Lindy stopped stroking his chin and sat back in his chair before continuing. "Usually, by the end of the first week, the radiation side effects will have reached a plateau and will have stabilized. Then we'll see them make a turn for the better. That's when we see the skin start to heal noticeably. In the meantime, though, there are three main things we have to address."

He raised his right hand and extended his index finger and said, "Inflammation." He raised his middle finger: "Infection." Then he raised his ring finger and, holding all three fingers up, added, "And, most importantly, pain.

"I know you've said that he's comfortable at home, so I'm not going to change his medication doses, but call me if his pain gets worse. What you're looking for is restlessness, panting, and, as hard as it is to believe with Eddie, a decreased appetite. These are common signs of pain, but I have hopes that what we've given him already should suffice and you won't be faced with that scenario. I also want you to continue the anti-inflammatory and antibiotics I've given him because they're controlling any chance of a secondary infection, in addition to the inflammation the radiation has caused. I suggest giving the medications with food to decrease any chance of nausea, and don't worry about giving them all together because they don't cross-react.

"I'm also going to give him something new today," he went on without missing a breath. "It's a combination of two topical medications to be applied to the irritated part of the radiation site. The first is an antiseptic, to sterilize the spot, while the second is a cream that should sooth it. Neither of these medications have proven to speed up healing or radiation side effects, in case you look them up on the Internet, but in my experience they do help to make the dogs feel better. Both of them should be applied every twelve to twenty-four hours, and only put them on the moist spots. Don't be afraid to be liberal when applying these things; you can't overdose with the topicals."

I had heard what he had just said, listening attentively, nodding my head for effect, but internally I had grown completely overwhelmed the moment he said he was adding something. I now had more stuff to give! Eddie had been taking so much already, he'd become a living pharmacy, and for someone like me, who hated to give any sort of medication or anything unnatural, this whole giving-drugs thing had been really challenging.

I mentally went over what he had just said to make sure I had it straight: one for pain, one for inflammation, one for infection, and now two more things to pile onto that. Five things to keep track of, and I'd really hoped they would give me a printout summarizing everything. As good as it was to have labels on each bottle, it would be very easy to screw this up, and I thought maybe I'd print out an Excel sheet for David and me as soon as I got home, just in case.

Dr. Lindy raised his well-manicured hand and started stroking his chin again. "Lastly, and the most important thing of all to keep in mind, Mrs. Freed, is that despite what we do, despite how everything looks today and the pharmacopeia of drugs that are prescribed for him, remember and keep telling yourself that the radiation side effects will get better."

I let out a deep sigh and slouched about an inch into my chair as I felt some of my back and shoulder tension ebb away. He had finally given me some good news, something besides the doom and gloom.

"The side effects are going to look significantly better in a week," he said, "and they should appear to be completely healed within two to three weeks. Oh, and I forgot to mention, my staff will give you a printed sheet summarizing all the medications and everything I just went over. Do you have any questions?"

Did I have any questions? I straightened up in the chair, feeling the hard plastic pressing up against my right thigh, the one that had been supporting the weight of my crossed legs.

Yes, I have questions, I thought to myself, and I could feel a semipanicked pressure tingling mercilessly up and down my spine. Was Eddie going to live? Was the tumor going to come back? Is he really going to heal, or was this caring, compassionate man with the perfectly pressed white lab coat a charlatan just telling me what I want to hear to make me feel better? I was full of questions, but none of them could truly be answered, and I knew that if I opened my mouth something irrational would pour out. Besides, it would have been my nerves doing all the talking, and he had already been over these things before.

I took a deep breath and did my best to sound calm and rational. "No, Dr. Lindy. I've spent more time speaking to both you and your staff this last week, as well as my husband, and I think I've asked everything that's important. You guys have been great. Unless you think I'm missing something?"

He put down his hand, shook his head, and arched his eyebrows.

As I stared at him, expecting him to leave shortly, one more thing suddenly popped into my mind. "This may be a stupid question, but I know David would want to know the answer. When can Eddie take a bath? I love my dog, but he could really use a wash."

"Unfortunately not for at least two more weeks, but it really depends on how the radiation site looks and how fast it heals. Don't let him get wet in the meantime, and try to keep him out of situations where either he or the site will get dirty. Don't take him hiking or to the beach or anywhere that will expose him to excessive dirt. As far as cleaning him, though, I advise using baby wipes to give him a good wipe down."

I cringed at the mention of baby wipes; I didn't need to revisit that issue now. Eddie was my baby.

As he was getting up to leave, the doctor said, "I always remind my clients at the end of the discharge consult not to rub the site as it heals and, as tempting as it may be to take off some of the crusts that will form over the wet spots, they should be left alone. On that note, Mrs. Freed, I can't stress how important it is to keep his E collar on at all times, no matter how much either you or your husband may think he'll be the exception that doesn't bother his radiation site. I say that respectfully; it's a well-intentioned gesture, an attempt to make their companion feel better. But in all the years I've been doing this, I've never encountered a dog that didn't attempt to lick a radiation site when given the chance. Just remember that although radiation side effects will heal, self-trauma from him licking the area may not get better completely."

Dr Lindy had a very warm smile on his face. Looking into his blue eyes, I couldn't help but feel reassured. He slowly extended his hand, and I shook it in a semihaze, feeling the warmth of his palm as it touched mine.

"It's been a pleasure treating Eddie, and I look forward to seeing both of you next week at the recheck appointment."

Just as he turned to head out of the door, Eddie came into view. He was being led by Brandon, who had a piece of paper that must be the instructions in one hand and Eddie's leash in the other. Eddie was clumsily pulling Brandon toward me and his tail was wagging. His eyes were glazed over, but he was smiling from ear to ear, with his tongue hanging out to the side.

Oh, how I loved that dog!

100

EDDIE
JUNE 2009

It happened again, unfortunately; yet another change in routine. Just as I had been getting comfortable with the new Crunchy Territory schedule, life took another changing bite.

Don't get me wrong; as much as a routine change could throw one off, this change hadn't been as bad as the other ones. It might have had something to do with the crazy amount of hazy tiredness I felt, and not having to get up and go anywhere hadn't been the worst thing in the world. Sure, I'd been tired and completely out of it, but overall, not having to get up and go out from light period to light period hadn't been that bad.

My memory was a little cloudy about this period , but what I do remember is Mom giving me a ton of slimy reward treats with crunchy, bitter-stuffed centers. I also remember that during most of those first seven light periods, my time was spent on my sleeping cushion wondering how to get to my shoulder and give it one large, satisfying lick. I also tried to come up with an answer to a question that every furry friend throughout time wants to know: how could I get the clear necklace off?

I never did get to solve that question, but at least Mom had done one of the next best things to give me some relief. She started putting these small white squares drenched in a minty-smelling, blue-colored drool and forced me to just lay there while they soaked my shoulder. It hadn't been that hard of a feat, given my tired state.

What a good couple of moments those were. The cold square somewhat scratched the drive-you-up-a-wall-crazy itchiness that had overtaken my shoulder, at least for a short period of time, anyway.

I hadn't been the biggest fan of what came after that, but since a little relief from blue drool had come before it, I hadn't freaked out much about it. As soon as she lifted off the drool-soaked square, she spread a thick, slimy goo all over it, caking it in what she probably thought was a layer of protection against my tongue. Not that I could have gotten to it anyway, with the necklace in the way.

I spent a lot of time with Mom during those light periods and, unfortunately, her mood stayed sad. She spent most of the time on the floor by my sleeping cushion, lying on her back and turning each individual page of her square, bound paper stack from one side of the stack to the other. She would stare at it for hours on end, only taking the occasional break to give me a rubdown or lick the top of my head. I liked the massage part, but I could've done without the eye drool and whining, especially when she put her paws on me. I had mostly given up on my cheer-up tactics with her because I was totally spent, and it only made her eyes drool more anyway.

We did this for a total of seven light periods, and Mom went through at least three separate bound paper stacks. The eighth light period proved to be different. Instead of her plonking down on the floor next to my sleeping pillow, she decided to change things up a bit and left our territory in the sniff box with Dad.

The thing I remember about that light period was that Mom had been at her worst as far as her mood was concerned. It started the moment she woke up, and the stale, sour smell was probably about as strong as any smell could be. It had been thick and so intense.

I knew that to try to cheer her up would've run the risk of just making her worse, so I forced myself to let her do her thing and get ready to leave with Dad without my getting involved.

Dad had been giving off a stale, worried smell, but it had been different from Mom's. It hadn't been as strong, but it had been enough to get my attention.

He kept staring at Mom, waiting for something to happen. For a moment I thought that her smell might had been strong enough for even him, a dad no less, to pick up on it, but I knew that couldn't be the case. It's common furry-friend knowledge that moms and dads don't have a sense of smell, and so despite the strength of the stink, he probably hadn't smelled a thing.

Either way, he looked and smelled worried, and I knew that something was upsetting him. He couldn't take his eyes off of her.

101

JULIA
JUNE 2009

I would like to add to the old saying that time flies when you're having fun because it's obviously lacking in complexity and detail. In fact, I'll go further and say it's a load of simplified bullshit as it stands and shouldn't be confined to times of fun. Unfortunately, when you are in mourning, time doesn't fly, it sprints, but only when you're meditating on it in retrospect. During the fact, it's one of the slowest and most painful things anyone will ever endure.

Today was the one-year anniversary of my dad's passing, and I almost missed it because I was so preoccupied with Eddie and what was going on with his radiation side effects. If it hadn't been for Mother's phone call, I would have outright forgotten about it. Me, the one who was supposed to have been the closest to my father, had to be reminded by of all people in the world, my mother. But, surprisingly, instead of an obnoxious and passive-aggressive attack about how surprised she was that I hadn't remembered the date of Dad's passing, she actually had been quite pleasant and noncombative.

Our relationship had taken a strange, positive turn this past year and, astonishingly, had been transformed into a semifunctional bond. It was a cautious and hands-off bond, but it had been an improvement compared to the days of old. Let's just say there had only been room for an upgrade because of the way it had stood before. It may have had something to do with the fact that Mother and I spoke a lot less than we had when Dad had been around, so there was a significantly lower chance for her to say something offensive. In the beginning, right after Dad passed, I had spent a lot of time over at the house with her, and I had made it a point to check in on her, talking to her nearly every day. She'd mainly done the speaking, and I the listening.

As much of a narcissist as she was, as egocentric as the woman appeared to be, what had surprised me was how completely devastated she had been those first couple of months. The strong, self-absorbed warhorse of a woman became a meek, helpless, shell; suffice it to say, David and I had taken care of everything. The funeral arrangements, carrying out the will, selling the house, the moving company; we had handled it all.

Dad's passing had been extremely difficult for Mother because Dad, I realized, hadn't just been her lifelong companion; he had been much more than that. Sure, he had been her husband, her significant other, but he had also been the center of her life, her strength, her foundation, and one of few people who could bear to be around her for long increments of time. She didn't have any friends, I could barely tolerate being with her, and her only surviving sister lived out of state. Losing him hadn't just been about losing her lifelong partner; it had been about losing her whole way of life. Without him, she didn't have anything.

Seeing her like that those first couple of months really had me doubting she would ever fully recover, but Mother being Mother, that grieving state of pure helplessness hadn't lasted long. That same stubborn strength and aggravating self-centered vigor that had led us to butt heads so often actually helped her cope. It had been a slow process at first, but by month six, she had almost returned to her old self.

David had made the offer to have her come live with us, but she had graciously refused. As it turned out, she hadn't completely relied on me after all, and she and her sister had already decided they would move in together after Dad passed. So, with the majority of her things sold and only enough furniture to fit in a small trailer, we drove her to Florida six months later.

David had flown back to San Diego the same day we arrived, but I stayed on to help settle her in. After just three days, my aunt had assured me that she had everything under control and gently insisted that I go back home to David. I had been worried about my mother, but after she had started asking why I had chosen to do an English degree if I knew I was going to be a housewife, I knew she was returning to her old self and probably would be just fine. I took my aunt's advice and had visited Mother twice since then; she appeared to be getting along well.

After Mother's call yesterday, I had spent the rest of that afternoon thinking of just how to make the day meaningful. There was a lot going on with Eddie, and I had been concentrating on nothing else but him for the last month and a half, but I needed to take a break from that, especially on a day like today. I wanted some time to be immersed again in Dad and nothing else. I needed to concentrate on my father, and as hesitant as I had been to leave Eddie by himself, I had to get out. This was important, and besides, Eddie would probably sleep just for the time I was gone anyway.

My first thought yesterday had been to spend the time by myself with Dad at the cemetery. It was beautiful there, a green, well-manicured graveyard on a hill that overlooked the ocean, a resting place fit for a king. But as I had contemplated being there, something hadn't felt right about that plan. I had imagined myself staring at Dad's gravestone alone, as I had done countless times before, with the hot sun beating down on my back, surrounded by the smells of the ocean, and it had felt wrong. It wasn't where I was meant to be on this day, and I didn't want to be alone. As strange as it sounds, I actually craved company.

I knew it had been the right decision not to go to the cemetery. Sure, that was where Dad's body was, but that was just it: it was only his body. I needed a different and better place; somewhere that captured the essence of him and our relationship. I needed a place with life, with vigor, a place that celebrated all the good memories we shared and a spot that both of us had found special. The cemetery hadn't been what I'd been looking for on this particular day.

I reminisced about my favorite times with Dad, and the one location that had stood out in my mind, a common denominator for a consistent positive experience, had been the Duck Pond. As soon as the thought of it entered my mind, it had overwhelmed me with a profound sense of relief; at peace, I knew that's where I needed to be.

I remembered that last afternoon we spent together there, when Dad could still walk semicomfortably, without the pain of the cancer overtaking him. We had discussed everything but the cancer that day as we had done laps around the dull green pond before we'd settled down for a nice picnic on Mother's extra-large red blanket. It had been heaven to have those conversations with him; frankly, I couldn't remember what we'd spoken about, but what had mattered was being together, soaking up each other's company and cherishing every second of this time alone. It had just been Dad and me and a much-needed break from the pain, sickness, and negativity of the beast he was battling, a moment of escape. It had been the last time I had truly seen him happy and at ease, one of the best days of my life. The Duck Pond had been our place, and that's where I wanted to go.

I told David that night and asked if he would come with me, apologizing for the last-minute request. By this time he was getting used to the new me, the Julia who actually communicated and reached out to him. He looked deep into my eyes, giving me his full attention as I stammered through my request, and without giving it a second thought hugged me and told me he would do anything for me. He took the morning off from work to be with me, canceling three new clients in the process. I tried not to cry, listening to him call his secretary afterhours to make sure she would get there early in the morning to make the calls, but I couldn't help it. It was just so unbelievably sweet and just one of the reasons why I loved him so much.

The day was perfect. The sky was blue, it was sunny, and there was a gentle breeze to keep it comfortable. There must have been at least fifteen ducks there that day, and about as many people. Thank goodness tourist season hadn't kicked into full swing. I was quiet and introspective on the car ride, lost in my own thoughts and memories, overtaken with a deep sense of calm and tranquility. David respected my silence. He knew he didn't have to say anything, and even though the drive was spent wordlessly as I stared out of the car window as the Spanish-style houses flew by, I loved and appreciated that he was there with me.

When we reached the park, I found myself bypassing the thick crabgrass that grew, undaunted by the years and multitudes of picnic blankets it had supported, and gravitated to the white picket fence that lined the path surrounding the dark, peaceful water. As always, the worn concrete path had been swept clean in the morning, our tax dollars being put to good use supporting the Parks and Recreation staff. A melodious exchange between a couple of blue jays and another unidentified bird served as the perfect background noise, and the gruff quack of the ducks added the harmonious bass to their song. It was late enough in the morning that we'd missed the joggers and exercise warriors, and the empty path was a welcome invitation to journey uninterrupted down memory lane. This was Dad's and my place, our special world, and as David and I set out, slowly walking hand in hand, an overwhelming feeling of warmth and tranquility overtook me.

I started the conversation then, and was amazed at how easily the words flowed. I told David how special this place was for me, how Dad and I had come here that day, over a year ago. I spoke about how close my dad and I had been, and how in all the years I was with him he had never truly raised his voice to me. I shared with him that everyone always thought of Dad as such a tough, intimidating guy, but I knew he had truly been such a teddy bear.

I spoke about the times before the cancer, skipping over the Mother drama, concentrating mainly on attempting to put into words the deep, subliminal relationship, most of it unspoken, that had existed between my father and me. Inevitably, though, the conversation evolved to follow the passage of time and steered toward Dad's cancer diagnosis, the ups and downs of his treatment, and, unavoidably, his final days.

I'm not entirely sure how it happened, but the conversation shifted from being about my dad to focusing more on me. I found myself sharing how I had felt during that long, drawn-out process, how each individual breakthrough had made me think we had conquered the enemy and were on top of the world, safe from an adversary so sinister as to take away loved ones in the dead of night. And how despite everything medicine had to offer, the best treatments and the most powerful drugs, the cancer had gained yet another foothold, and there had been yet another challenge to overcome.

I replayed my thoughts and feelings through each one of those events, suddenly and desperately overcome by the need to have David understand the joy of the victories and the personal hell of the defeats I had endured each step of the way. The words flowed effortlessly and without pause, and like bubbles rising from the depths of the ocean, unimpeded by any obstacles in their attempts to break to the surface, I found myself replaying those last six months day by day, tear by tear.

I had fought Dad's cancer battle by myself, attacking anyone who attempted to help me through the process. I had thought I could handle it alone, believed that it was strength that allowed me to go at it by myself, but in retrospect, it was a false sense of bravado masking a very scared and fragile girl afraid of losing one of the people she had loved most. I had chosen a lonely path inundated with denial that had prevented true emotional closure.

It was an easy way out, and although I had thought the strong person was the one who never cried, never complained, and definitely didn't lose it in front of others, I had been wrong. In reality, it's the strong person who has the confidence to let her feelings show, not caring about what the world thinks, coming to terms with the pain and hurt that wells up inside and festers like an infected wound if left untreated. It's the strong person who reaches out and shares her pain, and that was a road I had chosen to avoid, to bypass, at least until now. I couldn't help but wonder if I had only opened up more, would the last year have been different? Would I have been different?

But life is always like that, and if you spent all of your time wondering how things would've turned out if you had just done something else, you would drive yourself crazy. I had enough to worry about, so rather than beat myself up over something that couldn't be altered, a past I might have handled wrong, I made peace with my decisions because there had to have been a bigger plan and reality at play. Call it cosmic karma, religion, or any higher power so many people grab onto, but I have always believed there's a reason that events happen the way they do.

And this was obviously the right time and the right place now for me.

David didn't stop me. He was smart enough to realize that this breakthrough was long overdue, the catharsis he had been hoping for, my long-delayed chance to finally let it all go and make peace with my loss. It was on my terms, though, not forced, not faked, not preemptively or emptily given, and definitely not rushed. I was finally ready to let go, and it had taken my dog going through cancer to unlock the parts of me that had been so long sealed.

It was because of Eddie that it was all happening now. My poor, beautiful little dog, my floppy-eared gentle soul suffering through his own fight; he had been the key. It was because of him that a past that had been so forcefully buried and locked away had finally broken loose and unearthed itself, precipitated by a process that afforded me the opportunity to relive my father's battle in a different context, a more controlled and realistic process devoid of the denial that had kept me from coming to terms with the reality of my father's battle. Eddie had given me the strength to come to terms with my feelings now and my experiences back then.

My dad's death had done more than just put a tear in my heart; it had put a rift in my relationship with David and with just about everyone I knew. Eddie hadn't meant to, but he had managed to start the process of repairing that rift. He brought out all the memories I thought I had so successfully suppressed. They needed to come out. They had been putrefying; rotting away and polluting me and everything that I loved. That gorgeous dog was the impetus to improve, to heal, and to fix what had been ignored for so long.

Sure, I was saddened by Eddie's cancer and what he was going through, but it was because of him that I had come to be more at peace about my dad. Was I selfish? Was I that insane that it took another one of my loved ones to get cancer to face Dad's ordeal?

No, it had just forced me to face my demons, to face life, and, more importantly, to face death. I could move on now. That's what true strength was: facing the pain, dealing with it, and moving on. That's what Dad would have wanted for me: to be happy and to move forward.

I looked at the dark green pond then, as the sunlight bounced off the serene water. At that moment there was not a ripple to be seen, and it resembled a marble ice rink. In the far corner of the water, I noticed a large, beautiful white duck holding his neck perfectly straight, an icon of confidence, pride, and beauty undaunted. He was bigger than the other ducks and had an air of self-confidence that commanded respect. He was swimming effortlessly toward the other, smaller ducks, and as he approached, they noiselessly separated, making a path for him. He must've sensed my eyes on him because he slowly turned his head and fixed his glance straight at me. No duck challenged him as he changed direction and swam toward me, his black and sunlight-yellow eyes never leaving me as he made his way smoothly across the water. He stopped about five feet from shore and floated in place, statuesque and proud, with not a ripple around him. I stopped walking then, lightly grabbing David's hand to signal him to halt, and we both turned around to face him.

After he was sure he had our full attention, his eyes finally left me as he slowly and deliberately raised his head toward the peaceful blue sky and extended his neck in a perfectly straight line. As his bright yellow bill opened, he let out a long and surprisingly soulful song before lowering his head and resting his bill on his majestic white neck. He looked at me out of the corner of his eye and gave one big, long wink before gently turning to make his way back into the center of the pond. I thought of Dad then, and knew he was right there with me.

102

EDDIE
JULY 2009

The cold, tingly feeling in my shoulder finally stopped six long dark periods after the last visit to the Crunchy Territory. Unfortunately, what took its place it made me wish that it had never gone away because the new feeling was worse. It was such an itchiness that even I would not wish on my worst, territory-competing enemy.

It got so bad that I found myself wishing back the cold, tingly feeling that had so suddenly left instead of this new craziness. Of course, I did everything in an attempt to scratch it, but just like before, I had absolutely no luck and almost knocked myself out in the process. What I did succeed in, though, was further scaring Paris. With my necklace launching in every direction with my attempts at scratching, Paris refused to be around me.

There was no more just keeping her distance at the other side of the room anymore; the poodle took it to the next level, deciding that she didn't even want to be in the same territory as me. To make a long story short, absolutely nothing soothed my insanely itchy shoulder but time, fourteen light and dark periods of helpless, wishing-you-were-dead, gnawing moments of time. But like all things, it did pass.

And when it had pretty much gone, we paid another visit to the white-coated dad at the Crunchy Territory. It didn't prove to be the standard   be-greeted-by-the-shiny-headed-dad-and-whisked-off-into-the-back-of-the-territory-to-pass-out-and-wake-up-to   a chewy-treat kind of visit; instead, Mom and I found ourselves in the red rectangular room with the paw exerciser waiting for a grunting session. The furry-friend smells were there as usual, and I took some time to catch up on the latest gossip before the white-coated dad came into the room. After a couple of warm grunts toward Mom, he offered me his standard greeting, ear extenders, body massage, and all.

He settled into a blue plastic chair to grunt with Mom. Mom's mood had been somewhat happy on the sniff-box ride over, but hidden in the semihappy smells of flowers and chocolate perfume was the underlying burning odor of stress. It was the same smell that had overtaken our territory for the last month or so.

It was nothing more than amazing; as soon as the white-coated dad started grunting, the smell started to fade. Of course, before that happened, Mom had put in a solid two minutes of the eye drooling.

I had watched her the whole time he was grunting, and although her eyes had begun to drool, which was no surprise as of late, she had also begun to make the happy snorts of genuine joy. I knew then that the eye drool wasn't a bad thing this time around.

It was interesting because with every grunt out of the white-coated dad's muzzle and with every passing moment, her smell got better, and I hoped it would be permanent this time. I kept looking at Mom and then at the white-coated dad and back to Mom again, and as the grunting continued, I saw that Mom's eye drooling was replaced with a smile that extended from ear to ear. All it had taken was a couple of grunts from the white-coated dad, and just like that, her chocolate and flowery smell returned to the days of old; it was utterly amazing. I wished the white-coated dad could have kept on grunting forever.

103

JULIA
JULY 2009

Dr. Lindy hadn't been overexaggerating; right after the treatment ended, the radiation site had gone from bad to worse in the looks department. The first week had definitely been the most extreme, and if it hadn't been for the in-depth preparation by Dr. Lindy and his staff, the pain medications, the antibiotics, and the anti-inflammatories, I'm convinced it would have been a completely different experience. Eddie probably would have spent every waking moment yelping in pain and I would've been a complete nut case, with a guilt trip that I would never have gotten over for the rest of my life.

But as it turned out, and as much as I hated to admit it, Eddie appeared to lack the one thing that I had found to be an even worse adversary than any side effects of cancer treatment: the ability to understand what you were going through and your comprehension of what it truly meant, both to you and the people around you.

Either Eddie had been an expert at suppressing his fears or he had lacked the mental capacity to internalize exactly what was going on. He also felt no pressure to make everyone around him think he was doing just fine even if he knew he wasn't.

He had no anxiety about the pain or sense of abandonment he would cause to those people when he left. He was immune to the trauma of knowing that those same people who had always viewed him as the strong, indestructible patriarch, had to witness his body shrink away and his mental state decline.

Thank goodness for modern medicine and the inability to comprehend, because I didn't think I could've gone through it again, and so close to Dad's passing. I couldn't have handled seeing Eddie like that, especially with the radiation site looking like a piece of raw meat. It had become red, shiny, weepy, similar to the worst case of carpet burn I'd ever seen. At least it had started to dry out and form scabs, and it now looked a hundred times better than before.

That first week had been rough, and Eddie mainly had slept all day and night, and I figured that was due to either the medications or depression. He just hadn't been the same dog I was used to, spending way too many hours in his dog bed or lying outside, staring into space. I kept reminding myself that he hadn't truly lost his spark, and that his mood was due to the medications and their side effects. I kept repeating what Dr. Lindy had told me: that the side effects would get better and that we were making him drowsy and a vegetable on purpose. It hadn't stopped me from feeling awful for him, though, and I made sure to spend a couple of days lying next to him, reading or catching up on e-mails.

David and I had one fight during that first week, which had consisted of an argument as to whether Eddie was depressed or stoned. David had insisted that it was just the effects of the drugs, but I was convinced I knew my dog better than anyone in the world, and I took a firm stance that it was due to depression. I even went as far as to shout at him about the way he always thought he knew better than me, but rather than let the fight morph into some hydra-headed monster, he had told me he was going to turn in early and went to bed.

Now that I think back on it, it was silly because we were probably both right; Eddie most likely had been both depressed and stoned. But we'll never know.

As challenging as the entire Eddie cancer experience had been, I felt like a different person this time around. Unlike Dad's journey, I had taken a completely different path in dealing with the complicated and unpredictable roller-coaster ride of emotions surrounding the cancer process. I had reached out this time, timidly at first but aggressively as time went on and I grasped for support from those around me. I couldn't have been happier with my decision.

I couldn't imagine how lonely and scared it would have been without my radiation friends and David. Shirley had given me strength, Roy and Jennie had given me warmth, and Debbie had given me company through some pretty trying moments. And David . . . well, David had been the husband he always was: sweet, compassionate, understanding, and forever within reach.

The most enjoyable thing I heard throughout the whole process had been at Eddie's two-week recheck, when I had been sitting in one of the uncomfortable plastic chairs in the red exam room, facing Dr. Lindy with Eddie at my side: "He looks great and will be completely healed within the week."

The relief and joy at that one comment had been close to surpassed by my emotions at his three-week recheck, and I could have hugged Dr. Lindy when he said, "Mrs. Freed, no need for his E collar anymore. His radiation side effects have been completely resolved."

No more E collar, no more drugs, and finally, finally the ripe little beast could have a bath. I loved Eddie, but it had gotten to a point that even I'd had a hard time being in the same room as him, he had smelled so bad. A mother's love only extends so far, and in his case, it needed to be at least one arm's length away.

Dr. Lindy advised me that Eddie should be rechecked once every three months for the next two years, and at those appointments he would need to have X-rays of his lungs to check for any potential disease spread. He'd also said the chances of spread were very low, less than 5 to 15 percent, but in order to be thorough and for him to keep track of the radiation site, it would be a good idea to bring Eddie in. If the disease was going to spread anywhere, Dr. Lindy had said the lungs were the most likely place.

Surprisingly I hadn't worried too much at that because I was too happy about Eddie being free of his E collar. I was the most content I'd been in about a year; for the first time since Dad had been diagnosed with cancer, I actually felt at peace.

I cried when Dr. Lindy removed the E collar.

THE DOG DAYS OF THE PRESENT

EDDIE
JULY 2009

It was a beautiful, sunny, hot light period, and I could feel the warmth of the sun beating down on my fur. The smell of sand and water filled my nostrils, drowning all other scents with its powerful, salty feel. It was so strong and wonderful that I could actually taste the smell in the back of my throat, which just moments earlier had had the joy of having a chewy, meaty treat. I couldn't have imagined any other place in the world that I would rather be than here at the place of sandy water.

Life was good; my clear necklace had come off and nonregretfully destroyed at the first possibility that it was left unguarded. Silly Mom, thinking she could store it in the sniff box room without someone chewing it to shreds at the first chance he got. Thankfully, my shoulder also felt completely normal.

Paris and I were in a tug-of-war with a piece of salty rope we had found on the sand. She seemed to have forgotten about the whole necklace thing. The moment she'd seen me come back to our territory without the necklace, she had run up to me and given me the warmest greeting sniff known to white, fluffy poodle kind. Basically, she had given a sniff to the muzzle and then a sniff to the behind and off she had gone to catch up with her beauty sleep in the back territory.

I know it doesn't sound like much to you, but for the poodle to give an unforced warm greeting sniff to both ends . . . well, it was pretty darn generous for her. As it turned out, the poodle had missed me, but not enough to have gotten around her fear of the necklace.

Life had pretty much returned to normal starting the light period that my necklace had come off. Paris, after the earth-shattering greeting, had gone back to being her lazy self, I had finally gotten back my energy and kicked the cloud of sleepiness that made me feel like I had been living underwater, and, thank goodness, Mom and Dad were almost back to being the Mom and Dad of old. I say *almost* because as much as they seemed the same, there was something different about them.

Mom was finally happy; not just pretending to be happy for Dad, but truly content. She was giving off her chocolate-spiced scent. She smiled, she snorted a lot, and there wasn't a whiff of the sadness and stress I had once thought had taken her over. Whatever poisoned her had been driven out, hopefully for good.

Dad had regained something that I hadn't sensed in him for ages, something that nobody, including myself even realized disappeared. It hadn't been that obvious because I think it had slipped away little by little, light period after light period, so slowly that I forgot it had been present to start with.

Dad used to be an extremely playful and fun dad to be around, continually wrestling, always inventing games to play with Paris and me, and making Mom snort every chance he got. And now that Mom changed back to the Mom of old, carefree and stress free, Dad also changed back to his old playful self. Mom brought out the best of Dad, and with both of them seeming genuinely happy, I could finally relax, without having to worry about having to cheer them up. Dad got back what he had lost and we were all the better for it.

Mom and Dad were standing paw in paw, quietly watching us in our battle of tug-of-war when suddenly the salty rope snapped in half and Paris did a full-on backward somersault to the sand. Mom and Dad snorted loudly, but before Paris could pretend to be embarrassed and go sulk by the water's edge, Dad let go of Mom's paw. He bent down and reached into the blue-and-white-striped bag he lugged across the sand and brought out one of the shiniest and furriest yellow rocks I had ever seen.

As Dad wound his arm back to chuck the rock with his claws shining in the sunlight, every nerve in my body woke up and became alive. I loved life, my family, and my trip to the place of sandy water, and as the yellow rock whizzed overhead and sailed over the water, I took off in a sprint, bounding past Paris toward my prize. This was true happiness.

ABOUT THE AUTHOR

Dr. Jarred Lyons has passionately dedicated a majority of his life to the betterment of animal comfort and care. Becoming a cutting-edge veterinarian is the fulfillment of one of his earliest childhood dreams.

Dr. Lyons received his Bachelor of Science degree in Psychobiology from UCLA in 1998, was awarded a doctorate in veterinary medicine from UC Davis in 2003, completed an internship in veterinary surgery and medicine in 2004, and was board certified in radiation oncology after completion of an oncology residency at NC State University in 2006.

He currently practices veterinary oncology in Los Angeles, California, and is one of the few veterinarians worldwide who treats animals with stereotactic radiosurgery. Dr. Lyons is also a consultant and is actively involved in numerous veterinary clinical oncology studies. He has published articles in several scientific journals and magazines, and frequently gives lectures around Southern California.

He spends his free time with his wife, children, and standard poodle, Alice.

For further information, Dr. Lyons can be reached through his website at dogdaysofcancer.com